Switch
A Novel

ALLEN KENT

To my creative and imaginative granddaughters:
Andrea, Belle, Megan, Avrie, Ally, Sophia, and Rhea.

ACKNOWLEDGMENTS

Grateful thanks to my team of readers: my wife Holly, Diane Andris, Marilyn Jenson, Alison Koralewski, Anne Clement, Elin Roberts, and Judy Day. You all made this a much better book. And special thanks to Uvi Poznansky for her wonderful cover!

Ally

So, try to get your brain around this! Suppose, without any warning, you found yourself in another place and time? *Zap*. Just that fast! And even worse, in someone else's body. Then, a month later, *zap*. You're back where you were before, as yourself, trying to explain to people what had happened to you. But no one believes you because during that month, people didn't think you'd been gone at all. Just that you'd been acting *really* weird. Because someone else had been there in *your* body, someone who claimed she was another person. Everyone would think you were completely nuts. Right? I can promise you they would. Because that's just what happened to me.

My name is Ally. Well, actually Alyssa. And people think I'm crazy. If you asked my mom, she'd say it's because of something that happened when I was a kid. Some trauma. Probably because of my dad. When she says, "when you were a kid," I guess she means maybe six or seven years ago because I'm, like, only sixteen now. Seventeen next April. And as for blaming Dad, she blames him for everything, so you've got to take that for what it's worth. Which is about nothing. As a single mom, she's fiercely independent, but as over-protective as a mother bear. As the daughter of a single mom, I'm fiercely independent and hate being over-protected. Kind of a volatile combination most of the time. Though she says she "loves him to death," Mom makes my boyfriend, Julian, so nervous he'll hardly come in the house, which doesn't exactly reduce the tension.

Dad's got nothing to do with these personality changes, though I haven't been able to convince Mom or Dr. Westover of that. And when I say *people* think I'm crazy, I mean practically everyone. Mom. Lots of my friends—or at least the kids who used to say they were my friends. My dad, when something doesn't come up that keeps him from picking me up for his weekends. Just about everyone.

Dr. Westover doesn't say crazy. He calls it Dissociative Identity Disorder. I think that's what they used to call having multiple personalities. You know. Like, schizophrenia. For me, it means that every twenty-eight days, pretty much to the minute, I become someone else. And I don't mean, like, I begin to *act* like I'm someone else, though that's what everybody thinks. What I mean is, I show up in another body in another place and time. And twenty-eight days later, I come back. That's when they tell me all about "my other personality." Her name is Emmeline. But they really don't need to tell me about Emme. I know way more about her than they do. I've been living her life for the last month.

When it happens, in most ways I'm the lucky one. *Zap*! So fast you can't even say a second passes, I'm there. In Emmeline's body. In Emmeline's house. In another country and *way* in the past. The first time, Emme must have been asleep, cuz I found myself in bed. The switch woke me up and I was lying there, feeling these lumps in the mattress and hearing the *baaing* of sheep outside through an open window. There was a breeze coming through the curtains that smelled like salt and wet grass. I know now that what I smelled was the ocean, though it's about eight miles away. I'd never seen the ocean until I switched, but now I can describe it to Dr. Westover like I'm still looking at it. It freaks my mother out. The doctor says it's because I've watched *Hawaii Five-0* or videos—like *Planet Earth* or something. I mean, really? *Planet Earth*? I don't think I've *ever* watched *Planet Earth*. But I've seen the ocean now and walked on the beach and picked up shells and starfish and stuff, and it's a whole lot different than *Five-0*, I can tell you that!

When it first happened, I was in chemistry class. Mr. Payne was

4

explaining valence and how it's a measure of how one atom bonds with another. Kind of a weird coincidence when you think about it. Then, *blink*! I was lying on that lumpy mattress in pitch black and thinking "what the f---?" But I stopped myself because that's something I don't say. But it just shows how completely blown away I was. I just lay there for a long time and thought *Did I just pass out in class, and this is some kind of hallucination or something?* Cuz that's exactly what they told me happened to Emme when she switched. That's what I call it. Switching. She jumped right into the middle of Payne's lecture about valences and must have still been asleep. Mom told me later that the principal said I just fell out of my chair. When they tried to help me up, I started screaming and pulled away from everyone. It wasn't me, but they didn't know that. I guess what she saw when she opened her eyes must have scared the crap out of her.

And, I mean, I can relate! I switched back two hundred years to a little village where people speak English like in Jane Austen movies. I say I was the lucky one because I had time to just lie there and try to figure out what had happened.

The funny thing is, it's still my mind. I still know who I am and think the way I always do. And know what I've always known. When I found myself in that bed it was like I was waking up in my room in Texarkana. But I could feel that bad mattress and tell that my body was different. I'm pretty tall. Five-eleven. And thin. Thinner than I like to be. Not exactly flat-chested but wishing when we dress out for soccer that I had a little more to show for sixteen years. When I woke up in Emmeline's room, I was wearing this white nightgown thing instead of the shorts and top I always sleep in. The first thing I felt was that I had more boobs. You might not think that would be the first thing you'd feel about being in a new body, but it was for me. So I felt my chest and, I mean, it was like another "what the ----?" moment. Emme's not huge. Just bigger. And when I finally pulled the covers off and stepped onto the floor—just plain wood instead of carpet like I have in my bedroom—I could tell I was shorter. Emme really has a pretty nice figure. About five-six and not heavy. But I decided right then that I'd rather be tall and skinny.

The second big surprise was that I was having my period. A total bummer because I'd just finished two weeks ago. It kind of struck me funny that when I could feel it, instead of thinking *Something really weird is happening here*, I thought, *If I'm hallucinating, why did I pick this?* It didn't feel heavy. Like it was my third or fourth day. But I could feel some kind of pad and could tell it was tied around my waist. Bigger boobs, a period, and some kind of strapped-on pad. Definitely a *bad* dream!

I was still thinking I'd got a whiff of something in chem class and passed out. But it all felt so *real* that I wasn't about to open the door of the room and see what was outside. If this was some kind of nightmare, opening doors seemed like a bad idea. So I felt my way over to the wall and groped around for the light switch. The wall was rougher than I expected and scraped at my hand as I fumbled around beside the door. No switch.

There was a little light coming through the curtains that covered the window, so I felt my way over and pushed them aside. The windows were the kind that swing out like double doors and had been pushed wide open. The first thing I noticed was that there were no lights outside and no noise, other than the sheep. I mean, *no* lights. No street lights. No porch lights. No glow in the sky that showed the city was still alive out there somewhere. There were stars. A sky full of stars. And just this *baa* every now and then. There was enough moon that I could see the shadowy silhouette of trees across an open field. And I could smell animals other than sheep. Horses or cattle. The place smelled green. Not East Texas dry. Dark, and quiet as death, and green.

I climbed back onto the bed and sat with knees tucked up under my chin, my back against a high wooden headboard that was nothing like anything I'd pick for my room. Carved scrolls across the back and posts with knobs on top. Something like they have in the old historic houses over on State Line Avenue. I noticed then that the nightgown, or whatever I had on, smelled like it hadn't been washed in a couple of weeks. Stale and kind of sweaty. In fact, *I* smelled stale and sweaty.

The sky was beginning to lighten beyond the window and I could make out a dresser and chest of drawers that were just as great-grandmother as the bed. The dresser had a mirror, but with the dim light and what I knew wasn't going to be my own face, I wasn't about to have a look.

So, what do you think about when you're sitting in the dark in a stale nightgown wondering what just happened to you? Well, I can tell you. You think *This is weirding me out, and I don't like it. What do I need to do to wake myself up?* And then you think, *But it feels so real. More real than any dream I've ever had.* I mean, you know how dreams are and how sometimes you sort of experience things like you're in your body and sometimes like you're seeing yourself from outside? But this was different. Real smells. Real feeling of my feet on the wood floor. The real dampness and cramping of the period and the strangeness of this new body. And then I heard footsteps coming up stairs somewhere beyond the door.

Emme

I have been bewitched! The old Xhosa headman, Noluvo's grandfather, has cursed me for leaving the house while I am still showing blood. Noluvo warned me of this. She said that when she has her time, she must stay in a hut on the edge of the village. The elders believe that if a woman walks through a field or is close to cattle while bleeding, the crops will wither, and cattle will not be able to calve. I asked her if that would be true of an English girl who had been forced to come to Africa by no choice of her own, or just of Xhosa women. She was certain that my being English would make no difference whatsoever. A curse is a curse, no matter what my color or land of birth.

Mother tells me this is nonsense. Bleeding, she insists, is a natural part of becoming a woman and releases humors that might otherwise lead to hysteria. She has shown me how to use a thick cotton cravat, tied about my waist with a ribbon. But Noluvo helps me dress and knows when the bleeding comes. She told me the old men would curse me if I left the house before I was clean again. I did leave, and now I have been cursed.

I opened my eyes to see a circle of legs about me. Some bare. Some in men's trousers. I was on a floor that was as hard and smooth as polished stone. I looked up to see people staring down at me. Young men in coarse blue trousers and plaid shirts. Women of my own age who were bare to above the knees, some with hair as short as the men's. A girl with large round spectacles bent over me and said, "Ally, are you okay?" One of the young men knelt and began to lift me up. It was then I saw that my own legs were covered with the same blue trousers, but with tears that showed my knees and legs. On my top I had only a tight thin chemise with writing on the front. And I could feel and see that this was not my body at all. I started to scream.

Two of them lifted me and I fought to be free of them. But the men held me by the arms and pulled me through this room full of black-topped tables with silver basins and silver tubes and handles sticking from their tops. The walls were covered with charts of evil design and the air stank with the sulfur stench of hell. Above me, the ceiling glowed like the mid-day sun, and the room hummed as if swarming with insects. My arms—the arms the men were dragging me by—were thin, and firm, and as dark as a Dutch sailor's. Not mine at all. But I could feel the men's strong fingers pressed into my own flesh and feared I was being taken to be cast into hell to stand before the devil himself.

Beyond the room was a long hallway. Longer than any I had ever seen, with doors on each side and the same light streaming from above. Though my own flesh appeared darkened by sun, two arms that held me were darker still. I looked up into the black eyes of a young man I recognized to be Colored, the name the English gave the offspring of one of the native African women and a Boer farmer or sailor. He stared at me with eyes full of worry. The other man, white and older, led me to a chair along one wall: smooth, curved, hard as the stone floor. The colored boy knelt beside me, and I pulled instinctively away.

"Are you okay, Ally?" he asked again.

I looked from one to the other, confused and frightened beyond any ability to speak.

"I'll call your mother," the Colored said. His words were English, but spoken with an unfamiliar hardness. While I watched in horror, he drew a thin black and gold case of strange material from a pocket and poked at its dark surface. It turned instantly a light blue, and he jabbed at it with a *click, click, click*. Then he held it beside his face, waited quietly for a moment, then said to the box, "Mrs. Wallis? This is Julian. Ally's taken a fall at school and is pretty disoriented. If you can, I think you might want to come take her over to Wadley to get checked." He waited another moment, then said, "Okay. We'll be in the nurse's room. She seems pretty confused. Okay. Bye." Then he put the case back into his pocket.

The older man crouched at my other side and said, "Ally, do you know who I am?"

I struggled to choke out a reply. "I am not Ally. I am Emmeline. Please—what has become of me?" My legs, much longer than they rightly should be, stretched in front of me like cloth-wrapped poles. Instead of my normal slippers, my feet were covered with gray shoes with thick, white bottoms, yellow canvas ties, and white stripes along the sides. I wiggled my toes. Much more room than in my slippers, but still tight about my feet. My heart was beginning to calm, and I no longer feared it would burst from my breast. I looked over at the white man who was now only an arm's length from me. He wore a collared blue shirt with a long strip of yellow, blue-spotted cloth hanging about his neck. He did not look angry nor hateful, but his brow was furrowed with worry.

"You think your name is Emmeline?"

"It *is* Emmeline. Emmeline Caywood."

"And where do you think you are, Emmeline?"

I glanced about. Other than the colored boy, who now stood with hands deep in his pockets and a look that I understood to be more one of fear than worry, there were no others in the bright hallway.

"I am certain I do not know. A moment ago, I was in my own bed in Bathurst." The colored boy again drew the thin box from his pocket, tapped on its surface, lifted it in front of his face, and spoke to it. "Where is Bathurst?"

My heart nearly leapt from my body when a woman spoke to him from the tiny case. "I find two Bathursts. One in New South Wales, Australia. One in South Africa."

What sort of dark magic could this be? But I needed to assure these men, whoever they were, that my family had *not* been banished to some prison colony in Australia!

"Certainly not Australia." I said forcefully. "I live in Bathurst in the new Cape Colonies, very near to Port Kowie."

The Colored tapped at his box and grunted, "There is such a place. But it shows it near a Port Alfred, not Kowie."

"We'd better get her to the nurse's station. Can you go with her?" the white man asked. "I need to get back to class. I take it her mother's coming."

The Colored nodded. "Be about twenty minutes."

"Make sure she stays awake," the older man said, and left me with the colored boy. He again took my arm, this time more gently, and helped me to my feet. "Let's go to Mrs. Davis's room. Your mom will be here in a few minutes. You might want to lie down."

I looked in both directions along the bright, empty hallway. He pulled me toward the closer of two branches. As I walked beside him, the thick-bottomed shoes felt good against the hard floor. I looked down at my legs, feeling that they must be mine, but knowing at the same time that they could not be.

"Do you know who I am?" the Colored asked, looking ahead as he spoke.

"I most certainly do not. You are not Xhosa. Are you a Colored from the Port?"

The boy stopped for a moment, looked at me curiously, and slowly shook his head. "I'm Julian. You know. We go together."

I hesitated beside him. "Go together? And what, pray tell, do you mean by that?"

He looked at me directly—more directly than any Colored had ever dared. "Well, I mean we go out together."

I pulled away. "We most certainly do *not*. I have no colored friends. Mother would be mortified."

He shook his head again and sniffed. "I don't know what this is all about, Al. The funny talk and this colored stuff. And pretending you don't know me. Where did you learn about this Bathurst anyway?"

I returned his gaze just as directly. "We moved here from Suffolk some eight months past. Father is administrator for the village, brought down by Sir Donkin himself."

"Come on, Ally," the boy said with a most dismissive smile. "*Sir Donkin?*"

"It *was* Sir Donkin. Sir Rufane Donkin. He serves as governor of the Cape Colony and invited Father to establish our village." I wondered fleetingly if this colored boy might know the true reason we had fled England.

"Bathurst?" he repeated.

"Yes. Sir Donkin wished to name it after Sir Henry Bathurst who is His Majesty's secretary to the Cape Colonies."

The boy again pulled the small case from his pocket and asked, "Who was Sir Rufane Donkin?" In less than a moment, the woman in the case replied, "*Sir Rufane Shaw Donkin was a British army officer of the Napoleonic era and member of Parliament. From 1820 to 1821 he administered the Cape Colony in South Africa. He named the rising seaport of Algoa Bay Port Elizabeth in memory of his wife.*"

His brow furrowed more deeply. "Is this part of some paper you're writing for Bayless's class, Al? What's with the accent and the roleplay?"

"I am *not* Al," I said emphatically, stamping one thick-soled shoe. "I am Emmeline Caywood, and I would be most grateful if you would lead me out of this place."

He again took my arm and, with a slight shake of his head, eased me forward down the bright hallway. "Whatever you say, Emmeline."

Ally

From beyond the closed door, someone called "Emme, are you awake?" in a soft, feminine voice. "If you wish to go into Port Kowie with me, you should be dressing."

I held my breath. The door opened. And there was Jane Eyre. She smiled at me, then I could tell she saw something was wrong. Her forehead kind of wrinkled and she said, "Aren't you feeling well?" I didn't know what to say.

She walked over and sat on the foot of the bed, put a hand on my arm, and looked at me with that "I can tell something's wrong," look. She was a pretty lady. About Mom's age. She had on this Jane Eyre dress: long, with a high collar, gathered waist, and sleeves that puffed about her shoulders. There were ringlets around her face, with the rest of her light hair piled on the back of her head. Though she was wearing some kind of flowery perfume, she smelled musty too. Like she hadn't washed very recently either.

"Emme, is something wrong?" she asked.

I decided right then that I needed to tell her I'd lost my memory. If I said I'd just dropped in from chem class, dream or no dream, things were going to get even more complicated. I needed time to figure this out.

"I can't remember anything," I said, then swallowed back the strange voice. It was higher than mine and sounded more like Kimberly Jacobson who sits next to me in lit class.

She leaned toward me with that same puzzled look.

"You can't remember anything?"

"No. I don't know who I am or where I am. I can't remember anything."

The concern in the woman's eyes turned to fear. "You do not remember that you are Emmeline Caywood and live in Bathurst?"

I shook my head.

"Your speech has changed," she murmured. "Stay in bed. I am going to get your father." She moved quickly to the door, turned and looked at me with that same troubled frown, then hurried down the stairs.

Right move, I thought. I'll just say I don't remember anything and play along until I wake up or regain consciousness, or whatever. I decided they'd probably taken me to the hospital and were trying to resuscitate me. I could almost feel those electric paddles on my chest and half-expected a blast of electric shock to kick me back into reality. Or maybe I was just feeling these bigger boobs.

With the growing light, I could see more of the room. The dark wood dresser and chest of drawers, and a tall wardrobe I hadn't noticed earlier. A table beside the bed with a big bowl and pitcher that looked like they were made of porcelain and a covered pot beneath the table. A lamp, that old kind with a glass chimney like in western movies, sat beside the bowl. But there were no other lights.

I heard them coming up the stairs and tucked my chin back against my knees. The woman came in first, followed by a man dressed in work pants and a plain, long-sleeved shirt. His hair was as light as the woman's, medium length, but with long sideburns that stretched into a close-trimmed beard and mustache. His gray eyes showed the same worry, and he came and sat where the woman had on the bed. He smelled just as sweaty, but with no perfume to cover it up.

"Emme, your mother says you can't remember who you are."

I nodded into my knees.

"Do you know who I am?"

I shook my head.

"Are you feeling well otherwise? Do you feel ill?"

A quick headshake.

"Your mother is taking the wagon into Port Kowie to get provisions. Get dressed and go along. She can take you to see Dr. Begley."

I nodded. He reached up and gave my arm a light squeeze. He stood, kissed me on the forehead, and left the room, giving the woman's arm a concerned touch as he passed. I glanced around at the chest and wardrobe, then said to the woman before she could leave, "Can you put clothes out for me?"

She hesitated, her frown deepening, then went to the wardrobe and took out a yellow dress with a light check that looked a lot like the one she was wearing. Ankle length with a high waist and gathered sleeves. In the second drawer of the dresser she found a pair of long white stockings and from the top drawer, some knee-length bloomer-looking things and a top that looked like a nightgown with the bottom cut off.

"I don't think you'll want a corset if we are seeing Dr. Begley," she said. "Just wear the chemise."

"Shoes?" I asked.

She looked over at me with even greater alarm. "In the wardrobe, where you always keep them. Come down when you have dressed, and have some breakfast."

When alone again in the room, I slipped out of bed, closed the door, and cautiously eased in front of the mirror. *Oh, my God*! The face that looked back at me was a younger version of the woman who had just put out the clothes: a mop of wavy strawberry-blonde hair over a round face. Blue eyes, a nose that was shorter and slightly wider than mine, but okay. And full lips. Lips I'd love to have. Not a plain face, but not super-pretty. I felt at my nose and lips with fingers that belonged to the girl in the mirror. But I could feel the touch. Boys would probably think this Emme was prettier than I am. As far as new faces go, this one was alright. I stood there a minute, turning to both sides to get a better look. I can't think of any way to describe what it feels like to look in a mirror, knowing that you're inside the head that's looking back, but it isn't yours. It freaked me out—but at the same time, there was kind of a weird fascination. And she *did* have better boobs.

I pulled the nightgown up over my head and had a look at the whole new me. About what I expected. Softer, fuller, and rounder, but not heavy. Pale and pink as a new baby. Even my new arms! Didn't this Emme ever get out in the sun? I mean, I try to be careful about catching too many rays, but just playing soccer has tanned my face and arms. None of that on this body.

Light hair covered my legs, and I raised an arm. There too. So gross! When I got to town, I needed to get a razor and get this all cleaned up. And talk about gross! This pad was tied about my waist like some Sumo wrestler. Mental note. Get razor and tampons.

I wanted so badly to wash, but there was no side door that indicated a bathroom. The pitcher on the bedside table was half-full of water, but there was no soap and no washcloth. Just a small cotton towel. The bathroom must be down the hall.

Back at the bed, I sorted through the clothing. No panties. That's what the bloomers must be for. I pulled them on and cinched them about my waist with the drawstring. Not exactly soft! No bra either. But the chemise-like thing must go under the dress. I usually wear a pretty soft sports bra, and the top was even scratchier than the bloomers. I pulled it on anyway.

The bloomers had tie ribbons at the bottom and I rolled on the stockings, tied them beneath the frilled lace, and slipped the dress over my head. It hung pretty loose until tied in the back with a wide ribbon that drew it snug beneath the chest. The ribbon was just high enough I couldn't get my hands up to it—and low enough my arms wouldn't stretch that far from the top. Just like a dream! There's always that one thing that really frustrates you. I reached and stretched and turned every which way, then left it untied, wondering if this was one of those dreams like where I get to school and can't remember my locker combination—or have a test

I didn't remember.

There were four pairs of shoes in the wardrobe: all flat, pointed cloth slippers with leather soles. White, tan, brown. and black. I chose the brown pair and took another look in the mirror. Jane Eyre all over, with messy blonde hair. I tried to lift the curls back into place, ran a brush from the dresser through hair that fell to my midway to my shoulders, and thought how weird it was that my mind was directing this body that wasn't me at all. With a deep breath, I headed to the stairs.

They descended into a hallway with what I guessed to be the outside door straight ahead at the bottom. Voices came from a room to my left. I walked into a plain dining room with a bare wooden table and six chairs, two narrow side tables along the walls, a window to my right. Another door on the left must go back into a kitchen. The couple sat opposite each other at one end of the table. Both stood as I came in, the woman's face wrinkling again into a concerned frown.

A girl of about my age with chocolate-brown skin stood beside the kitchen door. She was barefoot but wore a black dress and white apron and had white beads threaded through her short-cropped black hair.

"I tried to wash before coming down," I said. "But I couldn't find the bathroom. And I need help tying this dress in back. This must be a two-person job." The woman seemed even more distressed and looked frantically across at the man.

"Noluvo, please help Emme with her dress," she said. "And help her put her hair up." Then to me, "Why didn't you call for Noluvo's help? She was waiting to come up."

I looked at the girl who stared back at me with dark, curious eyes "I didn't know about Noluvo," I said. Pleading amnesia was turning out to be easier than I'd expected. Everything around me was strange, including this barefoot servant girl. The couple again exchanged troubled looks, and the maid hurried up behind me and deftly tied the back of the dress.

"Please—sit," the woman said. "Noluvo will bring your breakfast," I took the seat at the end of the table away from them. The girl returned seconds later with a plate heaped with eggs, sausage, sliced ham, and a dark purple-black mass spotted with flecks of what looked like fat. It was more breakfast than I ate in a week.

"I'd be fine with a bowl of cheerios and orange juice," I said. "I'm a pretty light breakfast eater."

The man looked at me for a long, silent moment, then said, "Eat what you wish," and turned back to his own plate. My mind told me I shouldn't be hungry. We'd had lunch just before chem class: a couple of pieces of pizza and chocolate milk. But I felt starved. The eggs and sausage smelled wonderful and tasted even better— so good that it really began to worry me. I didn't remember ever tasting things that distinctly in any dream or having the feeling that the tea they gave me was so hot I had to let it sit for a few minutes. I could see the steam rising off it and feel the warmth of the cup against my hands. This was no dream. Was I tripping out on something someone had slipped into my drink at lunch as some kind of joke? Had some chemical leaked into the classroom from the lab? Too weird!

The woman glanced up from her plate. "You need to spend your hour on the piano when we return. And I would like an hour of reading this afternoon. Write a brief accounting of what you read for us to discuss. But Jama has the wagon ready. As soon as you like, we can go into Port Kowic."

I looked up at her. Practice the piano? *That* should be interesting. I wondered if in this new body, I'd be able to play. And being in this house was one thing. But going outside, quite another. I had a gnawing fear that if I stepped through that outside door, Ally Wallis may never be coming back.

Emme

The colored boy directed me into another bright, empty hallway. Near its end, we entered a small room with another beside it, separated by a long window. A woman in white sat at a desk of gray metal and looked up as we entered.

"Julian. Ally. What brings you here?"

"Ally took a fall in chem class and is acting like she thinks she's someone else."

The woman stood, gently took my arm, and led me into the room beyond the window where there was a low cot draped in white. Beside it were two of the strange smooth chairs and a white cabinet. She sat me on the cot, seating herself on a chair in front of me.

"Let's check you over." Her accent was hard and abrupt like the men's, though she spoke with a kindness that told me I was not in some circle of hell. She drew a short metal rod from a breast pocket and pushed her thumb against its back. I shrieked and threw an arm up across my face as a beam of light burst from its end. I had indeed been transported to a realm of sorcery where ceilings glowed white and beams of light streamed from silver wands!

She waited until I lowered my arm. "It's okay," she said kindly. "This won't hurt you. Look straight ahead and try not to blink." She shined the light directly into my eyes. I pulled away, staring at the rod. She followed with the beam.

"Your pupils aren't dilated. Let me have a listen to your heart." From a drawer in the cabinet she drew an object with a small disk, attached to two tubes I judged to be of fine rubber. She placed the ends of the tubes in her ears and pressed the disk against my breast.

"Just breathe normally."

I realized that I had not been breathing normally since I first awoke on the floor of the room with tables. I struggled to slow my breath, believing it would be wise to do as I was told. She lifted one of my arms, placed two fingers against my wrist, and closed her eyes.

"Your pulse is a little rapid, but if you're having temporary amnesia, that's to be expected. What aren't you able to remember?"

"Before I awoke on the floor, I remember everything quite clearly," I assured her. "Yesterday, I spent an hour at the piano, as I do each morning, and read much of what remained of the Scott novel Mother recommended. During the afternoon hours, I walked with Noluvo to the river and painted. We then watched men sheer sheep in the yard behind the new mill and the Xhosa women preparing it for the looms." I could clearly recall the vats for soaking the new wool, the drying racks propped against the outer walls of the shed beside the shell of the mill, and the rattle and clatter of looms against the plank weaving floor. "I returned to the house quite exhausted. Mother suggested that I retire after supper, and so I did."

The woman in white studied me with thoughtful eyes. "What Scott novel have you been reading?"

"The Bride of Lammermoor,"

"I don't know that I've heard of it," she said. The colored boy had been standing in the doorway and again drew out his speaking box, tapping at its top.

"It is most recently published," I said. "Mother acquired it the month before we left for the Cape." The boy looked at his box, shook his head in disbelief, then nodded at the woman. She patted my arm.

"Lie on the bed here until your mother comes. I'd like her to take you to the ER, just to be safe. You just rest, but stay awake. I'll be right next door." She left me seated on the cot and returned to the other room where I heard the colored boy ask, "What do you think?"—a most unusual question in a most frightening circumstance!

The woman returned to the door and closed it tightly. I heard their murmurings through the large window but could make nothing of what was being said. I laid myself down on the cot, thinking that, despite her warning, if I could only sleep this horror might leave me. But the sense of this new, long body and images of bright hallways with mysterious rows of doors haunted every thought. At last I must have dozed, opening my eyes at a touch against my shoulder. A woman with a spare face, narrow nose, and troubled light-brown eyes sat beside the cot, leaning forward with a hand on my shoulder. She wore a man's shirt and tight men's trousers of the same blue cloth. Though I knew her to be a white woman, her skin was also sun-darkened and toughened by being in the open without cover.

"Ally?" she said. "Are you feeling any better?"

I twisted to sit up and drew away, feeling again the strangeness of my body and clothing. "I am Emmeline," I said. "And I do not know what has become of me."

The woman turned to the one who had led me to the cot and now stood in the doorway. "I'll take her over to Wadley and have her checked," she said. She stood and took my hand, lifting me from the bed. We walked through the room beyond the window and back again into the corridor of light. At its end, it opened into a wide room with glass cases filling one wall that displayed rows of small golden statues. Opposite the cases, the wall was made entirely of doors of glass, and beyond the doors . . . !

Oh, what magic was this? Closed carriages of all colors moved along a broad avenue, completely without horses! An enormous red coach drew behind it a wheeled box the size of a house. Beyond the avenue, buildings crowded side-by-side with fronts of glass and bright metal. The sights were more than my dazed mind could fathom and I felt my legs fold beneath me. Then there was darkness.

Ally

The only explanation I could come up with was *coma*. I just couldn't wake up from this dream! Do you dream when you're in a coma? Dream as if you're really living somewhere else as someone else? Like, in an Amish village? I had forced myself to walk through that front door into the open air. Everything was just as real and just as OMG as it had been inside.

The outside of the house was pretty much what I'd expected: two stories made of rust-colored stone. The front was covered with the same rough white plaster I'd felt on the bedroom wall. It stood at the edge of a small village that climbed a gradual hill—really, a *tiny* village of about thirty houses. The others were all single story except for a miniature stone church that stood at the hill's crest. The church was no more than one of the houses with a steeple straddling the ridgeline and the door at the end, rather than in the side.

Within sight of the village, maybe a quarter mile down a dirt path, I could see round mud huts with roofs made of grass or something that made them look like Chinese coolie hats. They were too far away to see very clearly, but it looked like there were little kids running around between the huts. All black and all naked.

A black man stood beside an old-fashioned wagon in front of the house, the kind of wagon with a board seat in the front and, like, an open bed at the back. My first thought was an *African American man*. But then, I didn't think my dream had me in America. Not with the Jane Eyre accents and the mud huts at the end of the village.

"Good morning, Jama" the woman said, leading me toward the wagon.

"Good morning, Miz Caywood." He also spoke with an accent I

didn't recognize. It was like the Jane Eyre accent, but spoken by someone whose normal language was something else. I turned away and walked to the side of the house to see what was behind. Only what I could see from the window upstairs. Hedge-lined pasture stretching to a row of trees and beyond, low wooded hills. Lots of sheep, and two horses. Nice looking horses. A roan stallion and a dun gelding.

The woman called after me, her voice edged with frustration. "Please, Emmeline. We must be getting you into Port Kowie to see Dr. Begley."

"I just wanted to see what was behind the house," I said, turning back to the wagon. She looked nervously at the man she called Jama who didn't seem at all surprised that I'd be looking around. Noluvo came out of the house and climbed into the back, while the woman got up on the seat. Jama pulled himself stiffly up beside her. I grabbed the side of the box and gave myself a push-jump up into the bed. I barely made it and ended up rolling on my stomach over the sideboard. These arms weren't nearly as strong as my old ones and didn't seem used to doing anything physical. The woman turned back with a look of complete shock.

"Emme! What in the name of God . . .? And your dress! Please come up here and sit beside me."

I brushed off the front of the dress and checked for tears. "I'm good here. And the dress is fine. I'll sit with Noluvo."

The brow wrinkled. The eyes became more alarmed, but she didn't say more. The man came out of the house, walked to the wagon, and pulled the woman toward him until he could hold her face in both hands and give her a tender kiss. "Please try not to worry," he said, and looked back at me with a reassuring smile. She touched his cheek with a tenderness I hadn't seen in a long time and nodded uncertainly.

A black mare was harnessed to the wagon and Jama flicked the reins over its back. The wagon jerked forward and I leaned back against the side of the bed, arms stretched along the rough wooden edge. Noluvo's forehead knitted into a worried frown.

"You do not know who you are, Emme?" she asked with an accent like Jama's.

I shook my head.

"And you do not know *where* you are?"

Another shake.

"And you do not know that I am Noluvo, who helps you each day?"

"Something happened during the night," I said. "I don't remember anything."

"You remember how to speak. But you do not speak like Emmeline."

I sniffed. "I don't speak like myself. My voice has changed." The girl's frown deepened, and she leaned forward across the wagon bed.

"It has happened," she whispered, glancing up at the back of the woman on the wagon seat. "Grandfather said that you must stay in the house when you are showing blood. You have been cursed."

"Showing blood?"

Noluvo's forehead wrinkled more deeply, and she stared knowingly at my hips.

"Ohhh," I said, shaking my head again. This wasn't my body, but I knew I was through with the period. "No blood now."

"But yesterday. And the day before. You walked into the village and among the cattle."

"I don't remember yesterday—at least, not here."

Noluvo looked at me darkly. "You *have* been cursed," she whispered.

I've been something, I thought, *and I wish it would end. I can't keep up this amnesia thing forever.*

The wagon track followed a river, about fifty yards from the bank. I was sitting with the sun at my back, casting a long shadow across Noluvo. By habit, I reached for the phone that was as much a part of my front pocket as the stitching. No pocket. No phone. No way to tell the time.

"You *do* have phones here?" I asked Noluvo.

"Phone? I do not understand. Tell me. What is a phone?"

I looked around at the hills surrounding the valley. No sign of a tower in any direction. "You know. A cell. I-phone. Android. Whatever. Can't you get service here?"

Noluvo seemed confused to the point of silence. She just shook her head.

"How do you know what time it is?"

"There is a timepiece at the house. And one in your chamber."

"And when you're not in the house?"

She shrugged. "I do not need to know the time when I am not in the house."

The road looped away from the river around another collection of mud, China-hat huts. Noluvo pointed over my shoulder. "This is my village."

I turned to look at the elongated circle of huts. "Your village? What is it called?"

She stared at me nervously. "What is it called? I am Xhosa." She pronounced the word *Khosa*, her tongue making a sharp *click* on the K.

"Xhosa? That's your family?"

She nodded slowly, then swept an arm in a broad arc. "All of the people are Xhosa."

This seemed like a good time to see what else I could learn before we reached this Port Kowie. "And what state is this?" I asked.

"State?"

"Yes. Like Texas? Arkansas? Louisiana?"

Noluvo was silent for a moment, then said, "This place? It is called by the English *Africa*."

"Africa?" I chuckled nervously. Weird had just become *so much* weirder. "You mean like the continent? Like the Congo, and Senegal, and Botswana?"

"Botswana?" she said as if surprised to hear the word come from me. "The English call this place Africa."

"Africa? And what month is it?"

Noluvo's confusion only grew. She called to the woman on the seat. "Ma'am. What do you call the month?"

Mrs. Caywood turned and looked back cautiously at the two of us. "The month? I have been teaching them to you, Noluvo. This is September."

Well, at least that was right! But while I had the woman's attention, I asked, "And the year? What year is this?"

"Emme, you know the year. It is 1820."

Another nervous chuckle. "Not 2020?"

"Don't be absurd, Emmeline. You know it is 1820."

My heart began to pound furiously inside my chest. If this was some elaborate joke, something Julian and his friends had cooked up, how did they get me to this place—with all the mud huts and the horse cart?

The mare was just topping a low hill that climbed beside the river. In front of us the countryside sloped away to a very sad collection of houses like those in the Caywood's village, but even fewer in number, some rough stone and some plastered with the same white mud. Ten or twelve buildings crowded along our side of the river, and about the same number on the other. One very large house was perched up the slope on the opposite hillside. Beyond the divided village stretched a beach of white sand and then nothing but water, all the way to a gray horizon. Near the mouth of the river, a ship like *Pirates of the Caribbean* floated like it was painted on the glassy surface, with rolled sails and rope netting hanging from its double masts. I realized, with a sudden, gut-wrenching twist in my stomach, that this was not a joke!

Emme

The room was light green, the color of spring grass. Through the window I saw only treetops. In the distance, there was a constant rumbling, as if there were an approaching storm or a herd of cape buffalo thundering across the veldt. I was in a bed with thin pipe railings along its sides. It was a very soft bed. Softer than any I remembered. I wore a green smock and wondered how my other clothing had been removed. A small clamp squeezed one of my fingers, with a green thread or wire that extended from it to a box beside the bed. On the side of the box, a red line magically beeped and bounced into small peaks. My heart thumped wildly within my breast and I feared I would again swoon. I drew a deep breath and was able to keep what senses I had.

A pull against my flesh caused me to lift the top of the smock. I saw again that this body was not my own—leaner, firmer, with the sun-browned skin extending down to a line above smaller breasts. Just above my heart, a round disk was pressed against this darker skin, its own thread running down my side and beneath the coverings. The ceiling above again burst into bright light. I squeezed my eyes tightly shut, then felt a hand against my forehead. When I opened my eyes, a woman in a blue tunic and blue men's trousers stood beside me. She wrapped a wide band about my arm. Without warning, it began to squeeze until it hurt, then slowly released. The woman grasped my wrist and gazed at another small disk, then removed the band.

"How are you feeling?" she asked in the same hard, rapid English.

I shook my head dizzily. "Where am I?"

"You were brought to the hospital when you fainted at school.

Your mother and doctor are keeping you here for observation."

"Have I been bewitched?" I asked the woman.

She smiled. "You've had a blow to the head. There's still some confusion." An older man entered the room, stood at the foot of the bed while the woman lifted the top of a thin case she held in her hands and tapped with her fingers at its inside.

"Pressure and pulse are slightly elevated," she said. "And she's still disoriented." She left, and the man moved a chair to the side of the bed and sat. His hair was very white, and he wore dark-rimmed spectacles. His face was long and brown, not brown like Noluvo or the Colored's, but like the face of Boer shepherds and cattlemen who spend their days in the sun. He wore a white jacket, buttoned up the front over a white-collared shirt and what appeared to be the knot of a cravat.

"I'm Dr. Westover," he said in a kindly voice. "I'm the resident psychiatrist and want to visit with you for a few minutes about your fall. Do you feel up to talking?"

"I am most frightened," I confessed. "I fear that I have been cursed by Noluvo's grandfather. Are you an apparition? A part of this witchcraft?"

He sat silently for a moment, studying my face with great solemnity. Then he said, "No. I am not an apparition. You may touch my arm if you wish to see that I am real."

"I know that this all *seems* very real," I acknowledged. "But I am in a place I have never been, and surrounded by *such* wonders . . ." I waved my tethered hand toward the box beside the bed. "I have never seen such things."

"Hmmm," he said, continuing his examination of my face. "Can you tell me your name?"

"Why, I am Emmeline Caywood, of course."

He nodded. "Would you like to sit up?"

I began to pull myself upward. He grasped a white box beside my arm and pushed a small square with his thumb. The bed behind me whirred and began to rise! I threw off the covers and lurched away from the doctor toward the railing, but he grasped my arm.

"It's okay, Emmeline," he said softly, drawing me back onto the bed and stopping the whirring. I found myself partially uncovered and hurriedly pulled the drape back over my hips. There was no back to the green gown. He turned away and waited until I could again fully cover myself, calm my heart, and breathe more normally.

"Tell me about Noluvo, Emmeline. This person who said you were cursed."

"She is our maid servant. She is Xhosa."

"Xhosa? I am not familiar with Xhosa."

"Her tribe. Noluvo is of the Xhosa."

Dr. Westover drew a pad of paper and a small tube from a side pocket of his white jacket. I expected it to again burst with light, but he pushed the end with his thumb and instead scratched with it at the pad. I leaned forward to see his scratching. Writing, as with ink, came from the tip of the tube! I pointed at the paper with the clamped finger.

"This!" I said. "This is the magic I am speaking of. You write with no quill or ink!"

He lifted the tube toward me, but I refused to touch the thing. "Keep it away!" I sputtered, pushing myself against the far railing. He withdrew the object.

"You think Noluvo's grandfather has cursed you." It was not a question, but a statement of what I had just said.

"She told me he would if I ventured outside."

"For what reason?"

I felt the blood rush to my face and heat follow.

"It is not something I can speak of. Not with a gentleman—and particularly one I do not know."

The doctor *hmmmed* again. "But for whatever reason, he placed a curse on you?"

"I am most certain of it. I was asleep in my bed. I awoke on the floor in this strange place, surrounded by strange people and even stranger objects that are beyond my imagination. I could not be dreaming of such a place."

"You speak with an English accent, Emmeline. And you have a different manner of speech. Are you British?"

"Why, of course I am British."

"And where do you live with Noluvo and her grandfather?"

"In the village of Bathurst."

"I am not familiar with Bathurst. Can you tell me where it is?"

"Here in the Cape Colonies. It is a new village—but not so very new. We have been here the better part of a year."

"Here in the Cape Colonies?"

"Yes. My family was given passage to Africa by Sir Donkin. Father administers the village." I guessed them to have taken me to Port Elizabeth and again wondered if this man might know of my father's escape—if he might be an agent of the Crown.

"I see," Dr. Westover said. "Tell me, Emmeline. What year did you come to the Cape Colonies?"

"Why, the early spring of this year. 1820."

This time the doctor was silent for a very long time. Finally, he said, "And some of the things in this room are very strange to you?" He held up the writing tube. "My pen? This heart monitor? The bed that moves?"

"To me, they are things bewitched."

He nodded slowly. "I am going to show you one other thing. It may startle you, so be prepared and remain calm. It is nothing that can harm you. Are you ready?"

"I cannot say that I am. But if you give me your assurance I will not be harmed . . ."

"I promise," he said. "See the black rectangle up on the wall across the room?"

I nodded, having become aware of it earlier when the woman in the blue tunic was with me.

He lifted another small object from a table beside my bed, raised it toward the black square, and squeezed. A green dot appeared at the bottom edge, then to my complete horror, the entire space was filled with people, talking and moving about as if a painting had come to life! I threw the covers up over my face and curled beneath them.

"*Stop this, please!*" I begged. "Have I gone completely mad? Tell me what has happened to me, or I am certain I will lose my mind!"

Ally

What Dr. Begley called his "surgery" was no more than a back room in a white plastered cottage that faced the river just before it emptied into the bay. Jama tied the mare to a hitching post in front. During the ride in, Mrs. Caywood had asked him to get a couple of what she called carding combs from one of the shops. As soon as we had climbed from the wagon, he and Noluvo headed toward one of the rough stone buildings along the river that seemed to serve as both shop and home. Mrs. Caywood led me to the doctor's door, guiding me by the arm like she thought I might escape or get lost walking the twenty steps. She maintained her grip until I stood staring into the face of a big brass lion-head knocker.

The black woman who answered smiled a big toothy smile like she'd been waiting all morning just to greet us. She waved us in and led us into a side room in the front. It smelled musty and the stuffed chair she led me to was damp to the touch. I'd barely taken a seat before a round, ruddy-faced man tottered into the room, took Mrs. Caywood's hand, and gave a little bow.

"A very good morning to you, Rebecca. I trust you are well and not here seeking some remedy." His head had a halo of curly gray just above his ears, and he had the same long sideburns I'd seen on Mr. Caywood. I could smell his breath from ten feet away. That, and his red nose, as gnarled and lumpy as an old oak burl, told me he started his day with a good shot of something stronger than coffee and kept at it all day.

Mrs. Caywood returned the little bow. "Not for myself, Edward, but for Emmeline. I fear she is suffering from some malady that causes forgetfulness. She does not seem to remember anything before this morning. We hoped you might know of such a condition and be able to offer assistance." She talked like I wasn't in the room at all.

"Step with me into the surgery," he said to Mrs. Caywood, again as if no one else was with her. He led her through a door to my left and closed it behind them. I don't know what the inside walls were made of, but I could hear them talking like they were still standing right beside me.

"Forgetfulness, you say? And what, pray, does she not remember?"

"Not a thing. Had we not called her by name, I fear she would not have known it. She looks at us as if we are strangers. And she did not know Noluvo."

"Can she speak?"

"She can, but strangely."

"Strangely? In what way?"

"Both in speech and in the words she chooses. It is English, but of a most unusual sort."

"Are there other signs of hysteria?"

"None. She seems otherwise to be very well."

"And not a danger to herself or others?"

"Not at all."

"Ahhh. Then you see no need to confine her?"

"No. Though her actions have been unusual this morning. She chose to take her breakfast at the far end of the table and asked for 'orange juice' and something I had no knowledge of."

"And what might that have been, if I may ask?"

"Quite honestly, I do not recall the word. Something cheery. And she seemed not to know how to dress. Coming into the port, she chose to ride with Noluvo in the back of the carriage."

"With the servant girl? Most curious," the doctor murmured. "Will she understand me if I speak to her?"

"Oh, I am quite certain she will."

"Do you fear that she might speak unwittingly about your past? Divulge that you are not Caywoods?"

"At the moment, she appears to remember nothing. So I have no reason to fear she will bring up our past. When she is herself, she is fully aware that it must remain secret—among the family, Sir Donkin, you, and the reverend."

"I shall visit with her," he said, and the door opened.

I'd heard enough to know I'd better stick with the lost memory story. What were they talking about? "Will she reveal that we are not Caywoods? Does she need to be confined?" I mean, like, locked away? Were these people fugitives of some kind? And if I tell them I feel like I came from another place—and possibly another time—who knows what they'll do. I'm sticking with amnesia.

Dr. Begley dragged a straight-backed wooden chair over beside me and plopped onto it, sitting up very straight with his hands on his knees. He had the look of a man who, if he relaxed for a second, might topple onto the floor. The booze wasn't the worst of it. The man smelled like he hadn't showered in a month.

"Do you know who I am, Miss Caywood?"

"Yes. You're Dr. Begley."

His puffy face rolled into a smile. "Then you *do* remember some things."

"No. I knew that's who I was coming to see."

"Then you do not recall having been here before?"

"No, sir. I don't."

"If you would be so kind, please tell me what you do remember."

"Only what I've been told. That my name is Emmeline Caywood. I live in Bathurst. And I was told on the way here that this is Africa."

"And where did you think you were before being told you are in Africa, Miss Caywood?"

"I really had no idea. I'm trying to figure this all out."

He cocked his head to one side and stared at me over his lumpy nose. "And how did you acquire your new manner of speech?"

I shrugged. "This is how I've always talked, as far as I know."

He thought about that for a moment, then said, "And what sorts of pleasures do you have, Miss Caywood? How do you like to spend your days?"

"You mean, what do I like to do?" I paused, wondering how much it would be smart to tell the man. Maybe I should throw out a thing or two to see how he reacted.

"I like soccer. And horses. I like riding horses."

"Soccer?" Dr. Begley said, leaning back and steepling his fingers beneath his fleshy chin. "And what, Miss Caywood, is soccer?"

"You know . . . " I wondered if I'd already screwed this up. "The game. Two teams. Each tries to kick the ball into the other's goal."

"This sounds like some sort of public football," he said, turning to look at Mrs. Caywood. "But among young ladies?" He turned back to me. "And where do you play this game?"

"On a team. After school."

Dr. Begley looked again at Mrs. Caywood. "Have you been able to start a school with such a small settlement?"

The woman gave him a nervous shake of the head. "Nothing quite so formal, Doctor. The younger children do meet at one of the homes in the morning for instruction in their numbers. But all else is provided at home. And there is most certainly no public football involving the young women!"

"What school might you be referring to, Miss Emmeline?" the doctor asked.

"It's all pretty fuzzy," I said.

"Fuzzy?"

"Yeah. I mean, like, not at all clear."

"But you *do* remember enjoying the riding of horses."

"Since I was little. We have three at our place. Mine and two of Mom's. Sometimes I help her give lessons. And Dad's a vet. I ride when I stay with him." It all tumbled out without my really wanting it to.

"Your mother has two horses of her own?" The doctor's bushy eyebrows lifting as he glanced again at Mrs. Caywood. "And you say Mr. Caywood is a *vet*?"

"A veterinarian," I explained. "Not Mr. Caywood, but my father." I knew immediately from his drooping face that I'd crossed the line that might lead to being locked away. Better get vague again, or I'd be headed for some local loony bin. "It's all confused," I said hurriedly. "Who and where I am. Who my parents are . . ."

"And do you know *why* you have chosen this unusual manner of speech?" he asked again.

"*Mmmm*—no. It's just what's natural to me."

The rolls in Dr. Begley's forehead folded more completely into themselves. "Most puzzling. I have read of such transformations but have never encountered one. Are you feeling quite well otherwise?"

"Yes. Very well."

He turned to Mrs. Caywood. "I fear this is beyond both my training and experience. I see no reason to believe these delusions should be harmful to either Miss Caywood or to others. I suggest we give her time and keep a watchful eye. If there are seizures or other debilitating problems, or if she begins to talk of some imaginary past, please bring her back immediately. I shall find some means of calming her." He pushed heavily up out of the chair, signaling that he was through with his examination. Mrs. Caywood didn't move toward the door.

"Emmeline, would you please wait for me by the carriage. I will join you shortly."

I made my way back through the house and stood beside the hitching post, stroking the mare's neck. She was a beautiful black with a white blaze on her forehead and seemed to take to me. Beyond the sand of the beach, the gray sea had begun to roll gently and stretched as far as I could see. I wondered if this was what the ocean would actually look like if I were seeing it in my regular, conscious life? What was at the other side? Anything, really? Or just what I imagined to be there? I remembered reading once that dreams seem to last longer than they really do and wondered how long I'd been unconscious. It seemed like a couple of days now. Had it really been? Or had my dream mind packed all this into just a few hours? Had Dad been called and come to be with me? Mom must be out of her mind, not knowing what had happened to me. In fact, this whole thing was turning out to be a bigger mess than I thought possible when I first woke up in that bedroom. The mare nuzzled her head against my shoulder. It felt and smelled so much like a horse. I heard the door to Dr. Begley's house open behind me but continued to stroke her satin neck and look at the endless expanse of ocean.

"I see that you have decided to be more comfortable around Maisy," Mrs. Caywood said. "Perhaps some good will come of this, if we can find a way to restore your memory." She paused on the step, then led me along the row of riverfront houses to a stone building with a wooden upper floor. A shop filled the bottom level with an open-sided forge beside it. A hand-painted sign hanging from the front of the forge identified its owner as Jacob Pickering, Blacksmith and Tinsmith.

The inside of the shop looked like it had come right out of *Little House on the Prairie*. Wooden crates of tin cups and plates. Barrels of square nails and iron fittings. A counter with a display of brass bells, pewter mugs, hand tools, and smaller boxes of what looked like foot-long pieces of wire. Along one wall, stacks of silver and gray metal ingots took the place of legs under a long bench. Noluvo sat at one end, holding two wide brush-looking things on her lap. Jama talked to a tall, rugged-featured man who bent over the counter, his huge arms scarred by his work at the forge. He looked up as we entered, smiling through a row of brown, broken teeth.

"Mornin' to ya, Rebecca. And Mizz Emmeline. I've just been

tellin' your man here that we're likely to be havin' another ship in this month with new colonists. At least, that was the word from the captain of the frigate in the bay, headed to India."

"Will they be settling on the coast or coming inland?" Rebecca wanted to know.

Mr. Pickering shrugged his thick shoulders. "That's all I know. He just said his Mighty Highness, the Regent, is turnin' more people into poppers, and more's leavin' to come."

"I'll tell Robert," she said. "He will want to be prepared if more come to Bathurst."

I had been wandering around the shop, examining the tools and trying to figure out what some of the fittings were used for. I pointed at four of the shiny ingots under the bench where Noluvo sat. "Are those silver?"

The blacksmith laughed a deep, rusty laugh. "I could only wish as much, Mizz Emme. They's zinc. Come from the mines of India. I talk the sea captains out of a block or two every now and then. If I want to make an iron piece that will n'a rust, I can dip it in molten zinc."

I mumbled something about that being interesting and lifted a heavy horseshoe from a box beside the bench. "Someone's got some big horses."

The blacksmith's smile turned quizzical. "Those are for Angus's Shires. Have you taken a new interest in horses, then, Emme?"

I dropped the shoe back onto the box. "Yes. An interest," I could tell from Rebecca's worried look that it was time to keep quiet.

Mrs. Caywood came over and gently took me by the elbow, leading me toward the shop door like I was a kindergartener acting up in class. "Noluvo, you have the cards," she said. "And Jama, I see you have the nails we need. I believe we should be making our way back. Emmeline needs to be getting to her piano."

Emme

Dr. Westover and the woman he presented as my mother determined that I could best be treated by assuming that I knew nothing at all and should be reintroduced to each person and object as if they were completely new to me—which was, in truth, how I found them. I was taken from the building to one of the closed carriages that moved of its own accord and placed on a rear seat that appeared to be of polished leather, but not as warm and supple. The new mother sat in front, pushed a button, and the carriage began to rumble with the sound I had heard from the green room. I threw my arms up over my head and hunched down between the seats. The rumbling stopped. I heard her get out of the carriage and open the door beside me. She put a hand on my back, took my arm, and encouraged me back up onto the seat where she wrapped me tightly in her arms.

"You're safe here, Ally," she said softly. "I won't let anything hurt you."

I managed to remain sitting upright as she drove the carriage with a wheel, touching images on a surface in front of her as she went.

"You don't remember cars, then?" she asked, watching my eyes in a small mirror above the front window as they widened as the carriage gained speed.

"I do not," I managed to stammer through my fear. "What is a car?"

"This thing we are in. The way we get around from place to place."

"It is something I have never seen—and is quite frightening."

The slight shake of her head showed her distress. "And what do you see outside that is new to you?"

I looked beyond the window glass, so clear I had to touch it to know it was there. "Everything is new. Everything."

We rode along a roadway that was hard and black as tar in winter, with other carriages passing with such speed I could hear the *whoosh*. Homes of all shapes and of every description lined the broad avenue. As quickly as one new wonder came into view, another of equal curiosity replaced it until my mind was spinning. We were moving at such speed! More rapidly than I had ever dreamed men could travel.

While I still struggled with the mix of homes, all surrounded by carefully-trimmed gardens, we left them suddenly and were in the countryside, with only a scattering of dwellings. Each had the speedy carriages, many with a boxed back like a wagon, sitting beside them. Tall poles, the height of fully-grown trees, lined the roadway, tied together with black cord. Below, shorter poles of green or rusty orange held rows of wire that I realized must serve as fences or hedges. Beyond them, the largest cattle I had ever seen roamed across open pastures.

The carriage turned from the roadway onto a narrow lane, hard and gray as smooth stone. At its end, a building of red brick, a single story in height but as long as three of our homes in Bathurst, filled much of a wide garden. Large windows, the largest I had seen in a home, filled much of the building's front. As we approached, the new mother squeezed a small box on a flap above her head. To my amazement, a white square of wall began to rise, displaying behind it a large, open room with another white carriage, the sort with the wagon back, filling one side. She drove into the room and stopped beside it.

"Here we are, Ally. Does this look familiar now?

"I fear there is nothing familiar here at all," I stammered. "But one display of magic after another. What am I to think?"

"Let's take you to your room. Maybe that will look more familiar." She guided me around the second carriage and through a door into a small room with shelves on one side and two large white boxes against the opposite wall. The room smelled of soap and washed clothing. Through another door, we entered a room of even greater mystery. Cupboards with doors of rippled glass lined the walls, set above large white boxes, one with a glass window and top that shined like polished ebony. Another, as tall as myself, displayed twin doors with shiny silver handles. Still another hung beneath the cupboards, also with a glass door and numbered black squares on its front. A shelf of mottled gray stone stretched along two walls, with more glass-fronted doors beneath. I stopped to touch the stone, finding it cool and smooth as the marble tabletops in my family's Suffolk manor before we left for the Cape. I looked up to see the new mother watching me with worried curiosity.

"Does this jog your memory?"

"Do you mean, 'Am I familiar with this room?' I fear that I am not."

"Can you lead me to your room?"

"I have never been in this home before. All is new to me, and I must say that I have never seen such a room as this."

"Come with me." I followed her anxiously into a wide hallway past a much larger door that appeared to open out upon the front garden, then down a corridor into a spacious bedchamber. The bedcover was the color of fresh cream, a rich yellow gold, and was piled high with pillows of the same hue. A window looked out onto a rear garden. Beside it was a writing table of polished wood. Side tables of the same design stood on either side of the bed. Two doors in the wall opposite the bed were closed, a matching dressing table with mirror standing between them. The new mother pointed to one of the doors, then the other.

"Your closet and bathroom," she said.

It had been some time since I had used the privy and I was feeling the need to relieve myself. But looking about the room, I saw no chamber pot and no washstand with basin.

"Please," I said with some embarrassment. "I have need to visit the privy. I see no chamber pot. Is there a necessary room in the rear garden?"

She placed a hand on top of her head and looked at me as if she might weep. "Oh, dear God, what has happened to you, Ally? Do you need to go to the bathroom?"

I felt the color rise in my face. "I do not need a bathing room. But a privy."

She opened one of the two doors. "The toilet is here. Come in and have a look."

I walked tentatively into the room. It had a smaller chamber within it with two sides made entirely of glass. A wash basin had been lowered into a washstand and had a curved silver pipe not unlike those I had seen in the room where I awoke. Beside the stand, sitting on the floor, was another basin of unusual shape with a white porcelain box perched behind it and a ring of what appeared to be painted wood circling its top.

"Do you know what this is, Ally?" Her voice was becoming desperate.

I had decided there was nothing to be gained by insisting I was not Ally. "No," I said. "I truly do not."

"This is the privy. You sit on it. When you have finished . . ." She reached over and turned a paper roll that hung beside the basin. "Wipe with this, put the paper in the bowl, and flush." She pushed a handle on the side of the porcelain tank and water rushed into the basin, then disappeared in a swirl. "See? It's gone."

I stared into the basin in wonder. "And where does it go?"

She threw her hands up, bewildered. "Into the sewer. Gone. You don't have to worry about it ever again. And look here . . ." She moved to the small, glass-sided room, reached in and twisted another handle. Water burst from a round disk attached to a pipe that extended from one wall.

"Each morning—or evening, if you choose—you remove your clothes and step in here." She drew what I recognized as a bar of green soap from a small tray attached to one wall. "Close the door, and wash yourself under this water. Is that all new to you?"

"To wash every day? I fear that I would be taken ill!"

"It *keeps* you from becoming ill," she said, her voice rising. "Now, I will step out and you use the . . . the privy. Push the handle when you finish. Wash your hands here." She twisted a silver handle beside the wash basin and water poured from the pipe. She pointed from left to right. "Hot on this side. Cold on this side."

I raised my hands to my eyes. "Oh, how can I possibly learn all of this? I have never seen such things!"

"When you're through, come out and I'll give you some lessons," the new mother said and retreated to the bedchamber.

I did as she said, pushed the handle, and watched the water rush through the basin. I turned to the wash bowl, then immediately backed away, startled by the face that peered back at me from a large, clear glass that sat above it. It was the first opportunity I had been given to truly study this new face and body. I lifted a hand to my face as I studied the girl's features, tracing each curve and hollow with my fingers as if I were the village blindman. The nose was narrower and longer than my own, the eyes colored with rays of brown, green, and yellow. Quite lovely eyes. The face was more oval, but very pleasant, with brown hair pulled back tightly to form what looked like a tail sprouting from the back of my head. My body appeared even leaner when seen in the glass, the arms and shoulders sinewy like those of a laborer. I could feel the difference in strength, as if there was not an ounce of softness on me anywhere.

I continued to study this strange new face while I twisted the lever on the left side of what the new mother had called the sink, holding my hands beneath it. The water was immediately warm, heating rapidly until I was forced to draw my hands quickly away. Twisting the handle back, I pulled open the door of the cupboard beneath, expecting to find a small stove of burning coals. But there was nothing.

In the bedchamber, the new mother stood beside the writing

table. As I approached, she lifted the top of a thin black case that sat on its top.

"And this, Ally? Do you know what it is?"

I shook my head dumbly. The lower inside of the case was covered with small squares, some showing letters, others numbers, and still others strange symbols. A small black object, either of stone or wood, sat beside it on another flat, black square.

"Watch what I do carefully," she said. She pushed a round dot above the upper row of symbols and instantly, the inside of the top began to glow. A circle spun magically at its center. I drew back, again shielding my eyes.

"Now, you can't be afraid. This tablet can teach you what you want to know about things you can't remember or find strange." As she spoke, a painting appeared on the glowing top—a painting of the person I had become, standing beside the colored boy who had helped me when I awoke. The two looked directly back at me, smiling broadly.

The new mother gave me a moment to puzzle at the picture, then grasped the black object beside the case and moved it on the dark pad. A small arrow flitted across the painting as if magically tied to her movements.

"Now look."

I leaned forward, unable to resist seeing what might appear next. "When I move this . . ." She pushed the black object about on the pad. ". . . this cursor follows." She swept the object in a circle, following the arrow on the picture with a finger of her other hand, then lowered the arrow onto a black strip.

"Put the arrow onto this symbol here . . . then push your finger onto the top left side of the mouse . . ." She pushed the top of the small object and it "clicked." In an instant, the painting disappeared, replaced by a white space with a small, much ruder drawing at its center. Above the picture, in brightly colored letters, was the word "GOOGLE."

"The mouse?" I asked.

She held up the black object. "We call this a mouse. Why? I have no idea. Now, see this box here in the center with the line that blinks? Using these keys . . ." she pointed at the letters on the squares, ". . . you type in a question you would like an answer to." She paused and looked at me quite soberly. "You *can* write, can't you Ally?"

"Of course," I said indignantly.

"What would you like to know?"

"Where I am."

She slumped back in her chair. "Please, Ally. Surely we don't need to start at the very beginning."

"I *am* sorry," I whispered apologetically. "But I remember nothing about this place."

For the hour that followed, the new mother helped me learn how to put words into this marvel she called a computer and find descriptions of every object that was new to me. I led her back through the house, pointing at all that was unfamiliar as she wrote the names on a sheet of paper taken from the bedchamber's desk. We practiced until I was able to find *Texas*, *refrigerator*, *microwave*, and *television* without assistance. Then, she gave my shoulder a gentle squeeze, kissed the top of my head, and left me to my task. With each explanation, I found new words that meant nothing to me and my list grew much more quickly than I was able to reduce it. I had become trapped in a world whose mysteries expanded around me more rapidly than I could comprehend them. As I slumped over my labor in confused despair, the soft whisper of weeping drifted from elsewhere in the house.

I rose from the desk and crept quietly into the hallway. It was now dark beyond the broad expanse of glass and most of the rooms languished in shadow. In a small sitting room, lighted only by the pale green glow of a shaded lamp, the new mother hunched forward on a leather-upholstered settee, sobbing quietly into her hands. I hesitated, then made my way quietly across the deep carpet and sat beside her. She looked up with a start, sniffling away her tears.

"You shouldn't see me like this," she murmured.

"I am sorry that my being here has brought you such sorrow," I said.

She wiped at her nose with the back of her hand and smiled sadly. "Oh, Ally. Although I know you won't believe it, you are all that really matters to me in the world. And I don't know what to do about what's happened to you. This is all so . . . so unbelievable! How do I tell your father about this? I just don't know how I'm going to cope with it on my own."

I looked cautiously about the dimly lit room. "Where is your husband?"

The sadness slipped from her face, replaced by a puzzled anguish. "You truly don't remember?"

"I remember nothing of this life."

"Your father and I have been divorced since you were ten."

I felt her sadness flow into this new, unfamiliar body as if some dam had broken that had been holding it at bay for those many years. It was a sadness as profound as the fear created by my new surroundings. "Is this a place," I whispered, "where we are surrounded by marvels beyond imagination, but each of us has been cursed?"

She wrapped me in her arms and pressed her cheek against my hair. "Sometimes it seems that way," she said.

Ally

"Would you like to help with the sewing?" Mrs. Caywood asked the day after our trip to see Dr. Begley. We were seated in what she called the sitting room while she stitched at a sleeve of one of Mr. Caywood's shirts. I sat across the room from her in one of Emmeline's high-waisted dresses, trying to think of something that might help me figure out what had happened. I had insisted before coming down to breakfast that the servant girl, Noluvo, bring me a full pitcher of water, a soft cloth, and a bar of what turned out to be strong brown soap. Before putting on any of the same clothing that had been there for me the day before, I scrubbed what I could reach of this smelly new body, using the big porcelain bowl as a wash basin. With the last few cups, I rinsed my hair, knowing that the soap would split and dry these new blonde curls like a bad color job.

At breakfast, both of the Caywoods had stared without saying a word at my wet, limp mop, then instructed Noluvo to "do something with her hair before she leaves the house." Mr. Caywood had asked that I please call them Mother and Father, but it just didn't feel right. I told them I'd be okay with Robert and Rebecca, which didn't seem to please them. But they agreed.

"I don't sew," I said when she asked if I would help her, trying not to sound rude. I knew she was pretty desperate to find a way to keep me occupied. "I don't think I could even sew on a button."

"You sew beautifully," she objected. "The dress you have on is as well-stitched as any I have done."

I glanced over at one of the gathered sleeves. "I guess it's one of the things I forgot."

"One does not forget how to sew."

"I have. I wouldn't know where to start."

47

She put down the shirt. "And you say you no longer remember how to paint or play the piano. What will you do to fill your days, Emme? You mustn't sit in your room all day."

"I'd like to go to the Xhosa village with Noluvo."

I could see the color drain from her face. "You know your father would never allow that."

"Oh? Why not?"

She dropped her hands heavily onto the shirt. "We are here to pacify the Xhosa. Give them work and teach them about our Lord, but not to be among them. We bring some into our homes, but we do not go into theirs. And after your brother's death, we could not bear it if you became ill. There is so much disease in those villages."

This was the first I'd heard about a brother. I hadn't seen any evidence of one anywhere in the house. How much did I dare ask? But if I was pretending to remember nothing, what harm was there in playing dumb?

"I'm really sorry, but I don't remember a brother. Tell me what happened to him."

Rebecca's mouth tightened into a narrow line and her lips trembled. "You do not even remember your brother, Emmeline?"

"No," I said contritely. "I don't remember anything about my past here."

She again picked up the shirt, her fingers fumbling and eyes downcast to hide sudden tears.

"The year before we left Suffolk your brother James became afflicted with the white plague. He was eleven. It was our reason for moving him from Ipswich to Stowmarket where he could take in the country air."

"The white plague?"

"Consumption. He died of consumption."

"Stowmarket?"

She looked up again with visible confusion and distress. "The village where my sister, Emily, lives. I accompanied him, and you stayed with Father to maintain the hall and continue your painting studies with Mr. Constable."

"The hall?"

She again dropped her sewing into her lap and gazed at me with a mixture of wonder and irritation. "Do you not remember Grenfell Hall and anything about why we left England?"

"Nothing," I said very honestly. She hesitated, seeming to wonder if it was wise to confide again in a daughter who couldn't remember who she was.

"And James died the year before we left?" I prompted.

Her head again drooped and her voice faded to a whisper. "I could not save him. His death so angered your father, who was already a radical, that he wrote and sent those tracts to his brother in Preston—the tracts that aided in inciting the Peterloo riots and massacre." She looked up again, her face reflecting new resolve. "Your uncle was taken into custody by the Crown and your father charged with violating one of the new laws passed at the bidding of that imbecile king of ours. You both came to Stowmarket for a time. Then Sir Donkin convinced your father and several of the other outspoken radicals to flee to the colonies."

"Dr. Begley among them," I guessed.

"You do remember that, then."

"No. I overheard you talking about being worried that I might say too much if I started to remember."

She nodded and thrust her needle aggressively into the cuff of the sleeve. "Dr. Begley and Reverend Sutherland. You must be most careful not to reveal anything about this."

"I only know what you've just told me. And I don't have any reason to tell anyone."

"Not even Noluvo."

"Not even her. But I would like to visit a Xhosa village. They seem like very good people. I doubt there's consumption here anyway." I wasn't sure I even knew what consumption was.

Her face clouded with the old worry. "They are good people,

but completely uncivilized. You have seen the women walking beside the road with nothing to cover their tops. And their village is rife with disease."

"What kind of disease?"

"Serious diseases of the bowel. And all manner of worms and sores of the skin."

"Noluvo and Jama seem pretty healthy."

"They are now. We do not allow them here when they are ill."

"Okay," I muttered. "So, no Xhosa village. But I think I'd like to ride."

"To ride?"

"Yes. The horses."

"You are terrified of horses."

"I love horses."

Her brow lifted in surprise, then slumped with resignation. She lifted the shirt sleeve to her mouth and bit through the thread. "When your father returns from shearing, you may talk to him about riding."

SWITCH

Emme

Julian, the colored boy, comes to visit almost every afternoon. I have found that the people here do not choose to call the dark people Coloreds or Blacks. The students at the school seem not to notice. I have wondered if this is because the cursing came from Noluvo's grandfather.

Most of the young men remain after school to practice for a contest held each Friday they call football, though it is not at all like the village free-for-all that was football in Ipswich. In this match, the men dress in tight breeches and wear helmets and hard plating on their shoulders. They crash against one another with such force it is a wonder they do not crack their heads wide open or break every bone. The object of this game, Julian tells me, is to run or throw an odd-shaped ball to one end of the pitch, while the other team strives to prevent it. I was taken to one of the matches but asked not to go again. Those who came to watch became a frightening mob, shouting, blowing loud horns, and stomping their feet. Some seemed to quite lose themselves in the frenzy of the contest. There is enough noise and confusion about me without seeking more.

Julian does not participate in football. He tells me he is too light and worries about what all the crashing together might do to his brain. After he realized I knew nothing about where I was or who the people around me were, he told me that we had started to "go together" because neither of us truly fit in.

"I don't play football, and you don't like sitting in the cafeteria with the girls who only want to talk about clothes, guys, and who's going with whom. In fact, that's how we first started talking. I was

51

sitting by myself. You came over and asked if you could sit with me and get some help with a trig problem." His familiarity with me makes me most uncomfortable. He believes me to be his friend Ally and treats me as if I have simply lost my senses.

Some of the other students call Julian "Brainiac." That is a character in a graphic novel. I learned from the computer that graphic novels present stories in both word and picture, something I believe I might enjoy. By nature, Julian is a very gentle and patient young man and most attentive, but approaches me as if we are somehow equals. I strive not to be rude with him, but when I am near him, I hear Mother's voice, speaking as she did when we first arrived in the colonies. "We do not socialize with the Coloreds or the Blacks. It is our station to instruct, not to befriend them."

Julian comes to the house to help with my studies and, despite my efforts to treat him as I might Noluvo, he responds with a kindness unlike any I saw among any of the boorish men in Bathurst. They are farmers and sheep men, and the sons of farmers and sheep men. They speak to me as if I know nothing at all and, as a wife, would have no use to them beyond bearing them sons who would grow to be sheep men. Father hopes to send me back to England when I reach eighteen to live with an aunt in Cambridge, hoping I will catch the eye of a gentleman and marry well. Mother is afraid that if I return, the Royalists might arrest me and force me to tell what has become of Father. She would have me marry one of the few eligible Bathurst men, or possibly some better-born man from Port Elizabeth. None of the girls my age here at the school seem at all interested in marrying.

Julian says little about my condition, yet I know he is most concerned. At our first meetings, he wished to sit with our arms linked or legs lapped across each other while we studied. But after I pulled away and showed discomfort, he has not attempted it since.

"Whatever makes you feel safe," he says.

I do not object to his help as a tutor, though I know it must appear most unusual that *he* should be helping *me*. He is the only person in this city of Texarkana who knows about the cursing: that I was sent into this magical world because I broke one of the taboos of the Xhosa. He asked that I tell no one but Dr. Westover with whom I meet weekly to talk about my memories. Julian tells me that I should say simply that I am having memory problems because of my fall. He is right, of course. But when I explain to him that I remember my past very vividly, and I tell him about the Xhosa and Bathurst and sailing to Port Kowie from England, he taps at what he calls his tablet, reads a story that appears, and looks at me with such troubled eyes.

"I don't understand how you know all this, Al," he says to me. So I know that he, too, does not believe me.

Each day I am taken to school. I have never attended a school before but was taught by a tutor before leaving Ipswich and by Mother since fleeing to the Cape. The school is the large building where I first entered this world. Two of my cousins in Ipswich attended school. They were boys, of course. They allowed me to play school with them when we were young. We read stories, wrote on our slates about what we read, and practiced making our letters as perfectly as we possibly could. I wrote more beautifully than either of them. Before the cursing, mother had me write about what I read each day and judged my penmanship as well as what I wrote. At this school, there is none of that.

The new mother kept me in her home for two days to see if my memory would return before taking me to the school. When I did attend, all of the subjects but two were completely confusing and terrified me. Other students look at me as if they know me, but find me to be different—as if I have some strange illness or deformity. I see them whisper and shake their heads and try to avoid being close.

The first day, I forced myself to remember that the new mother and I were both sent here to endure, and that I must be strong to protect myself, and to spare her further distress. Yet I became as frightened as the day I awoke in what I now know to be the chemistry laboratory, and she was summoned to come for me. She gave me a pill from her handbag that relieved some of the anxiety, and took me to a woman she called a counselor.

"I believe we need to move you into resource sessions during most of the day," the counselor advised. "You can receive special instruction there until you feel ready to return to the regular classroom." I chose not to tell her I had been cursed, and that I feared I may never return to my former self.

In the resource sessions, I have my own tutor as I did in Ipswich. Her name is Mrs. Wilkins and she attempts to teach me what is being discussed in the classes I am not allowed to join. She is very patient, but is surprised that I know so little. It quite embarrasses me. I am asked to write about what I learn, but not with quill and ink. Mrs. Wilkins wishes for the writing to be done using the computer. Julian and my new mother, whose name is Jennifer, have shown me how to type and print my writing. I could write much more quickly with quill and ink. I am working diligently to speak more like the people here do, but Mother would be most troubled by the change. The people here run many of their words together, as in saying "we're" rather than "we are." And their pronunciation grates against my ears, though I am careful not to appear judgmental.

I have chosen to call Jennifer "Mother" since that appears to be my plight in this bewitched world and she is much less distressed when I do. In fact, she asked that I use Mom, saying that Mother makes her feel old and distant. She takes me to the school because I have heard her say that she is afraid to let me drive, by which she means she fears allowing me to take one of the automobiles on my own. I have no desire to attempt it! They move at such speed, and I am just learning to find my way about the city. Mom has given me one of the small tablets she calls a cell and taught me to push the numbers needed to bring her voice to me. I am to use it if I ever "find that I can't cope." She comes to the school each afternoon and takes me back to the house or to see Dr. Westover. When at home, I read what I can and wait for Julian.

Two of the subjects are complete mysteries to me. I have learned my numbers well and can figure sums in my head as well as Father. But the maths at this school are as puzzling as this accursed world. Some letters become numbers, and numbers become letters. Julian tells me that I "learned the basics" in earlier years and have forgotten them. "You may just have to wait until this all comes back to you," he says. "I don't think I can catch you up."

In the subject called Chemistry, taught by Mr. Payne, the man who first helped me from the room when I arrived, I am taught about a world that I find completely baffling. Julian read the beginning of the book with me to help me "get back up to speed" in this subject. Mrs. Wilkins goes through each chapter as many times as are necessary to help me understand. There are, the book tells me, tiny, tiny particles called atoms, far too small for the eye to see, that are the "building blocks of matter." Every object about us is made from these particles that cling together to form all things, including ourselves.

"Different atoms make up different substances," Julian tells me when we review in the evening. "That's all you really need to know. All the rest is just figuring out which atoms link up with which others, and what the new compound creates. That's what Mr. Payne is teaching us now in class." I can connect the particles, as the book and Mrs. Wilkins describe, but remain doubtful that we are nothing more than masses of tiny atoms. What would make us grow? How would we think?

The subjects I do understand and am most grateful for are Chorale and Literature. I return to the classroom with other students in the afternoon for these subjects. The schoolmistress in Literature, Mrs. Bayless, is instructing us in the reading of Miss Austen's novel, *Pride and Prejudice*. It was in her class that I first began to understand what this enchantment has done to me—cast me two hundred years into a make-believe future.

"Why do you think *Pride and Prejudice* remains so popular after two hundred years?" Mrs. Bayless asked. Yet I know Mother purchased her copy of Miss Austen's work very shortly before we left Stowmarket. And the book had only recently been published.

"What is the year?" I asked Julian as soon as we were dismissed from the class.

"You mean, 'what year is it?' Like 2020?"

"No. I mean, we are in the month of September. But in what year?"

"Twenty-twenty," he repeated, just as Mrs. Bayless had suggested.

"That cannot be. It would mean I have moved forward two hundred years!"

He said nothing, but his countenance fell, and he shook his head as he always did when unsure what to do or say.

In her class the following day, Mrs. Bayless asked if any of the students knew who might have influenced Miss Austen's writing. I liked the manner of her teaching, asking questions and allowing all who wished to express their views. Each student lifted a hand if he wished to comment and waited for her to call his name. When no one else responded, I swallowed my fear and timidly lifted my hand.

"I read Miss Fanny Birney's novel, *Cecelia*, with Mother," I said. "Mother pointed out to me that in this work Miss Birney no longer uses an exchange of personal letters to tell her story, as authors before her had done. She relates it as if she is observing it as a person who is not mentioned in the story at all. Miss Austen chose this as her way to tell her tales, perhaps because of Fanny Birney."

"Very good, Ally," Mrs. Bayless said and I felt my heart swell. I dared not look about me at the other students.

Mrs. Bayless addressed me directly. "Have you or your mother read other earlier women writers who preceded Austen?"

"We have both read Mary Wollstonecraft," I said. "I quite enjoyed her *Original Stories from Real Life*."

"Ah. Mary Wollstonecraft. Do you know who her daughter was?"

"I know that Mrs. Wollstonecraft died giving birth to a daughter. And I know that the daughter also writes. But I do not know the woman's name."

"Mary Shelly." Mrs. Bayless said. "She wrote *Frankenstein*."

"I am not familiar with *Frankenstein*," I said. Some of the students about me laughed.

Ally

The only saddles in the shed beside the paddock that served as a tack room were English. I'd tried one a year ago at a show over in Lewisville, Arkansas, and didn't like it. There's something reassuring about having a heavy saddle horn in front of you, room to stretch your legs into solid stirrups, and a higher cantle to cradle your hips. The girl who let me try hers was into dressage and said that with your knees higher, it is easier to keep a straighter back—something the judges look for in show riding.

Robert was pretty excited that I wanted to ride. Maisy, the black mare, and the roan stallion in the paddock are saddle-broke. He calls the stallion Prince George, his way of slamming the king who'd tried to get him arrested.

"It explains the horse's disposition," he said with a laugh, "and gives me extra pleasure when I ride the beast. Be cautious around him. He is very spirited. And the gelding? I purchased him off a ship returning from India. He has never been ridden, so please stay away from him until I can have Angus break him in. But I am so pleased to see you have lost your fright. Would you like me to teach you to ride?"

"No need for that," I said. "But it would help if I could have a pair of your old pants—and one of your shirts. I don't want to try the stallion with an English saddle and this dress." Robert was an inch taller and probably eight or ten inches bigger around the waist. But I figured I could find some way to cinch up a pair of his pants.

"I fear we haven't a proper woman's saddle," he said as he showed me the two that straddled a sawhorse in the tack shed.

"I don't want a woman's saddle. And I'd like to ride in pants and a shirt."

"Oh, I fear that would never do." He glanced cautiously toward the door to see if Rebecca had overheard. "A few of the women here in Bathurst ride, but they dress quite fashionably with dresses, gloves, and fine hats."

"That doesn't sound like riding to me," I said. "More like a parade. Can I have a pair of your old pants? And a shirt?"

He cocked his head to the side and looked at me for a long moment. I could almost hear the wheels grinding away. He was thinking, *What am I to do with this crazy girl? If I tell her no, will it make her worse? Or should I just humor her?*

"If you wish," he said finally. "But as you learn, please ride away from the village. There are no secrets in Bathurst, and I fear word of your condition has spread. We mustn't give the neighbors greater reason for gossip."

"There must be *some* secrets," I said, watching him closely.

His expression didn't change. "I am referring to the life of the village."

I spent the evenings in my room reading from a pile of books Emme kept on her bedside table. A part of each day included being quizzed by Rebecca about what I'd read. It was like she'd memorized everything in the stack and remembered every detail. Mrs. Bayless would love this woman. I was reading a lot more carefully than I ever did at home, just to please her. That night I was really getting into a book by Sir Walter Scott called *The Heart of Midlothian*, one I think Emme had already started. I heard Robert and Rebecca talking in the kitchen below, heard him say something about taking in some trousers, and crept to the door.

"I do not think it wise that we support her uncivilized behavior," I heard Rebecca say. "She will surely injure herself if she tries to ride Prince George and will be an embarrassment to us all if she goes out in men's clothing. We certainly do not wish to draw unwanted attention to the family."

Robert stood his ground. "My only wish is for her to be well. You must agree that she has never seemed so self-assured. If we deny her the few pleasures she wishes to pursue, we may lose her completely. Let us humor her in this one wish and see what comes of it."

"She has also become much less refined and has abandoned her former interests. She refuses to play the piano, which once brought her great pleasure. She no longer paints, and she claims not to know how to sew."

"But she now thinks she likes horses. If we support her in what she says she does enjoy, perhaps she will return to those you believe will make her a woman of refinement."

Rebecca's voice cooled. "You wish her to marry well as much as I do. Though our living circumstances have greatly been reduced by our exile, when we send her back to England I wager the eligible gentlemen will value her abilities at the piano much more than her skill at riding in men's clothing."

"Perhaps the men she finds most interesting will admire her riding ability and will wish for a wife who can do more than simply entertain guests."

Rebecca huffed. "As you wish. I will alter a shirt and a pair of your old trousers. I pray that she does not kill herself and leave us childless." Silence followed, and I knew Robert had pulled her to him. He was alright, this Mr. Caywood.

The pants and shirt were on my bed late the following afternoon. Both Caywoods looked up with surprise when I wore them into the sitting room. Rebecca's face slumped into the distressed frown that now seemed to have taken up permanent residence. His expression masked a satisfied smile.

Robert watched from the paddock fence with curious amazement as I threw a saddle over the back of the black mare and cinched the girth strap under her belly.

"You have been paying much closer attention than I would have guessed, Emme," he said nervously. "But being observant does not teach one to ride. Are you quite certain you wish to make this attempt without assistance?"

Without a horn, I couldn't swing myself up into the saddle but thought that with my hands on the pommel and cantle, I could still hop-jump and push myself onto Maisy's back. Other than my attempt to get into the wagon, it was the first time I'd really tested the strength of this new body. The arms and legs failed me miserably. I made it halfway up the mare's side and slid back to the ground.

"Maybe you could give me a leg up," I said.

"A leg up?"

"Yes. I'll lift my left leg and you grab my ankle. As I push up, you lift at the same time."

He ducked through the rails and grasped my raised ankle. "Okay. *Up*," I said, and he hoisted me onto the mare's back.

I clucked and prodded Maisy gently with my heels. She took a few reluctant steps forward. I could feel the hesitation. She'd been used as a harness horse to the point that she instinctively moved with caution. I wondered if she would be willing to gallop at all.

We circled the paddock, and I eased her into a cautious trot. "I think I'd like Prince George better," I called. "Maisy's been trained to control her gait. It may be best to keep her that way."

"He is too temperamental," Robert objected. "I have difficulty keeping a rein on him myself. I have thought we should sell him."

"He's a beautiful horse. I may need a day or two with him before we ride. But I think we can get to like each other." I reined Maisy in beside Robert and before he could offer to help me from the saddle, swung back to the ground.

He looked at me as if seeing me for the first time. "You astonish me, Emme. Has Jama been teaching you in secret?"

"I've been riding since I was old enough to sit a horse," I said, knowing that I was only adding to his confusion. But I'd been playing at the amnesia game long enough. If I was going to live in this coma world, it was time to begin to shape it as I liked.

I dressed the next morning in my new outfit and, after breakfast, put a bridle on Prince George. He had never been thoroughly broken in the way a horse needs to be broke, learning to trust his rider and feel like he's a partner instead of just some pack animal. We spent two hours walking about the paddock. Every ten minutes, I stopped to stroke his neck and sides and talk to him, watching the frightened caution slip from his eyes and the quiver in his muscled shoulders and flanks slowly dissolve away.

"You're a beautiful boy, Prince," I whispered, stroking his cheek. Instead of pulling away, he nuzzled his nose against my shoulder. "I don't believe anyone has ever given you much attention, have they." He lifted his head as if he knew exactly what I was saying.

In the early afternoon, he let me lift each foot and check his shoes. They were well fitted and expertly nailed.

Robert had returned for lunch from shearing and stood along the rail fence watching me work the horse.

"Good farrier job," I called over to him. "Who does the shoeing?"

He cocked his head and stared at me quizzically. "Mr. Pickering in Fort Kowie." Then he added, as if beginning to realize I truly didn't know much about people or places, "He came here to farm, but hardly lasted a month. Returned to being a smithy and moved back to the coast. And yes, he does a right nice job of it."

"Time to give him a go," I said. "Can you help me up again?"

He hoisted me onto the roan's back, this time with more confidence and what I felt to be a curious interest in how this would all work out.

Prince stood rigid for a moment, the quiver returning again to his shoulders. I leaned forward across his withers, stroking his neck. "It's just me," I whispered. "We'll stand here until you feel like moving." He pranced a few steps to his left, stopped again, and I felt him relax beneath the saddle.

I turned to Robert. "I think we're ready to go. Could you open the gate?"

"Don't you want to take him for a few turns about the paddock?"

"No. He needs to know I don't need the practice."

Robert hesitated, then opened the gate. I urged Prince forward with my knees. He took three tentative steps, broke into a trot, then bolted into a full gallop toward the road that ran from the village to the coast.

"Hang on, Emme!" Robert shouted after me, but I was leaning low over the stallion's back, urging him to run. In a mile, he would learn who had the most stamina. And it wouldn't be his lordship.

He ran for what I guessed to be nearly two miles, then slowed to an exhausted canter before easing into a trot. I waited until his head began to droop, then gently reined him around and walked him back along the road. Halfway to the house, Robert approached on the mare.

"You are unharmed, then?" he asked as Prince stopped beside Maisy.

"He's worn out. I need to get him watered and brushed down. But we had a good ride."

"Where . . .?" Robert began to ask again. But the words faded into a shake of his head. "I don't know what to think."

"That's two of us," I said, and urged Prince back into a trot.

For the next three weeks, I spent part of each morning breaking the gelding and the early hours of each afternoon exploring the countryside on Prince. Robert insisted I stay out of the low, heavy trees that covered the slopes surrounding the valley. "You will see lions," he cautioned. "Just give them space and they will leave you alone. But there are leopards. They are night hunters and stay in the bush. If they have not made a kill, they hunt at any time. You do not wish to tempt them." During our second trip into Port Kowie, he pointed out a good-sized deer with stripes down its back, what he called a kudu, hanging twenty feet up in the fork of a red-barked tree.

"Leopard," he said. "They hang their kill where nothing else can reach it." That was all I needed to stay out of the bush.

But the veldt, the name the Dutch settlers around Bathurst gave the open grassland that separated big expanses of forest, was a perfect place to let Prince run. He loved to chase the smaller duiker antelope and warthogs that were favorites of the Xhosa hunters.

Early one morning, one of my favorite times to ride because baboons, giraffes, and small herds of elephants came to drink at a pool about a mile from the village, I sat on Prince beneath a tree on a low hill above the river. Four Xhosa hunters moved silently along the bank to my right, forming a pocket as they crept forward, hoping to force a wild pig or duiker into the river where, once in the water, they became easier targets for their long bows. The men wore only short skirts of animal skin and a leather pouch about their waists that held their knives, pipes, and tobacco. They moved with the same silent care as the animals they stalked, closing slowly on a family of warthogs that drank nervously fifty yards from the hunters.

A male raised its ugly head, tested the air with upturned snout, and issued a piercing squeal that startled every animal at the pool. The men sprinted forward, arrows drawn. I kneed Prince into a gallop down the hill, cutting off the hogs' retreat and turning two back toward the river. Prince wheeled as if he had been trained as a cutting horse, seeming to know instinctively that I wanted to force the animals into the water. As the larger of the tusked hogs tried to escape the closing trap, the horse cut him off until he thrashed, shoulder-deep, into the stream. Two arrows struck him instantly. The four hunters were in the water, finishing the kill with their knives and hauling the heavy carcass to shore.

Once out of the river, two of the men danced toward me, thrusting their bows up and down and chattering like blue jays. I reined Prince back, watching nervously. Had I broken another taboo? A woman helping men with the hunt?

The two danced up beside me and patted at my legs, smiling up broadly through tobacco-stained teeth. The other two had lashed the boar's feet over a long pole and hoisted it onto their shoulders.

The hunters at my sides beckoned for me to follow and started back along the river bank. I hesitated, unsure what they wanted and remembering Rebecca's warning to avoid the Xhosa villages. The men halted, waved insistently, and didn't move. I knew that if I turned and kicked Prince into a gallop, I'd be away before they could do anything to stop me. I knew also that one of Robert's jobs was to keep peace with the surrounding villagers. And I was curious.

I urged Prince forward and walked beside the men as they carried their kill for nearly a mile along the bank. We forded the river at a wide shallow and walked what must have been another half-mile to a cluster of the round mud huts. As they approached, the hunters began a high clicking song. People poured from the huts: old men with gray hair; women in brightly patterned, hand-woven skirts; girls no older than me, naked except for the skin wrap the hunters wore, bare babies propped on their hips.

The men's chanting excited them and they swarmed about me, touching my legs and patting at Prince's shoulders and flanks. Their language was full of the clicking sounds and, with all chattering at once, the air vibrated like the grove behind the house in Texas when the cicadas hatched.

In the center of the village, one of the hunters began to pantomime the hunt, pulling the other three in beside him to show how they had crept toward the pigs. The four men clicked back and forth, holding their bows in front of them and reforming the pocket that had closed in on the wild hogs. Then the animals were in flight and the hunters threw up their hands in resignation. But what was that? Ahead of them from beyond the huts came a rider—he pointed the tip of his bow at me—and the pigs turned! They drew their arrows and made the kill, smiling and chattering again at the rider who had forced their quarry back into the trap.

The villagers pulled at my pants, urging me down from the

horse. I shook my head, pointing back across the river toward Bathurst. But they were insistent and I could see they meant no harm. Somehow, they wanted to show their thanks. I put a hand on the pommel to swing down. In the next instant, I was sitting in the dark looking at a wall-sized screen, and knew I was in a movie theater.

Emme

In the Chorale class, we do nothing but sing. And I *do* like to sing. The choirmaster is a Mr. Lee who so enjoys music that one can hardly keep from enjoying it with him. We stand during the entire class on steps on one side of the classroom while Mr. Lee conducts from the front. The room has the largest piano I have seen, large enough to fill our sitting room, with keys in seven octaves rather than six. When I first went into the room, I wished so badly to play it but knew that I should not without permission. Jennifer has a piano in her home but cannot play. She shows great amazement that I am able. I truly miss my hour each morning with Bach and Mozart and Haydn and try to play them by memory. Though this body is agile and my fingers longer and stronger, when I first tried to play, they were clumsy and did not respond as my mind commanded. But they are beginning to obey. Jennifer, though she remains astonished, enjoys telling others that I now play the piano. In Mr. Lee's class, one of the other students plays while we sing, and this appears to be her role.

We are preparing a concert of what Mr. Lee calls "show tunes" for a performance we will present entitled "A Night on Broadway." I do like this music! Some selections, such as "I Dreamed a Dream" are beautiful ballads, while others, like "Oklahoma" have an energy like nothing I have heard before. It is all so new to me that it causes me to wonder if I am in something other than a dream. Could I have conjured up such exciting and unimaginable music?

One morning when Mom was unable to drive me to school, Julian came for me. As we started into the city, he drew a round disc from a case beside his seat and slipped it into a slot in front of us. The car immediately filled with the sound of a violin as I had never heard one played and some strummed instrument that was new to me. A man soon joined them, singing in a rolling voice that slid smoothly from one note to the next with a brightness that passed right through to my toes, leaving them tapping against the floor.

Julian's hand bounced against the wheel, head nodding and his own voice singing, "So rock me mama like a wagon wheel; Rock me mama anyway you feel."

"What is this music?" I exclaimed with an involuntary laugh. "I have never heard such a thing."

"This is one of our favorites," he grinned. "Darius Rucker and 'Wagon Wheel.' Want'a pull over and do some boot scootin'?"

I had no idea what he meant, but the music tempted me to agree.

"When we are not hurrying to school," I suggested, and he looked over at me with the first hope I had seen in his eyes since he lifted me from the chemistry room floor.

During my second week at the school, the girl who plays the piano was not in class. "Down with the flu," Mr. Lee said. The girl next to me on the second row said, "She's too afraid of needles to get a shot." Everyone laughed.

Mr. Lee raised his baton. "A lesson to all of you. Get your shots, and stay home if you aren't well. We can't afford to have half of you out with the flu." He looked at all of us with a broad smile. "I want to take a break from show tunes this morning and sing something different. Are any of you pianists comfortable enough with sight reading that you'd be willing to try a little Beethoven?"

Without giving it thought, I lifted my hand. I wanted so badly to play this beautiful piano! And I have been playing Beethoven every day since turning thirteen.

"Ally! You've been keeping something from us! I didn't know you played."

"It is one of my greatest pleasures," I said. "And I can play Beethoven."

"Are you familiar with "Ode to Joy?"

"I do not believe that I am," I admitted. "But I am confident I can play it." It was not at all like me to be so bold, but I did *so* wish to play that piano—and I wished to show these other students that I have talents of my own.

"The accompaniment isn't too challenging," Mr. Lee said. "But there is a piano prelude that is a bit more complicated. If you play Beethoven, you probably know that this is the final movement of his Ninth Symphony."

"I do not know it," I confessed. "Perhaps he has written it since we left England."

Some of the students laughed aloud. I looked about with embarrassment. Others were whispering to each other or turning away to hide knowing grins. Julian was not in the class but Lena, a girl who sits beside me in Literature and whose English is also accented, loudly shouted "Hey!" and the others became quiet.

"I believe I can play it," I said less confidently.

Mr. Lee waved a hand toward the beautiful piano. "Give it a try,"

"May I play something I know for a moment—to become familiar with this piano?"

"Please do. But just briefly. We need to get into our program."

I chose my favorite piece, Mozart's Piano Sonata Number 14, and played through what I remembered to be the first sheets of music. As I began, my fingers were still not entirely responsive to my thoughts, but the piano had a touch and richness of tone that were unlike any I had heard or felt. This new body warmed to it quickly. I wanted to play and play. But there was a program waiting. When I stopped, the room was as quiet as the veldt before nightfall. I feared all had slipped away while I played. I turned on the bench to find everyone silently staring. Lena was wiping a tear from her cheek.

"I think you can handle this," Mr. Lee said and handed me the music. It was not a difficult arrangement. After we practiced for half an hour, we returned to the show tunes. By then, my fingers and thoughts were working perfectly together. I had never found such joy in playing! As students walked past me when the class ended, they touched my shoulder and said "Very cool, Ally" and "You rocked me, girl." I wished so badly to say, "This is who I am. I am Emmeline."

The third week of the enchantment, Lena stopped me in the lighted hallway and asked if I thought I was ready to play again. By "play," Lena was referring to the game they called soccer. Julian had told me I was part of the team, but had cautioned Lena that my fall was affecting my balance, and that I should not play until better.

"We need you, Al," she said. Both she and Julian often chose to call me Al. "Coach has moved Kaylee to center midfielder, but that takes her off the left wing. We're not scoring like we used to. If we're going to get to regionals, we need you." She told me that she was the striker. "We work together so well. *I* need you back."

When she came to me again and asked if I was ready, I felt that, other than Julian, Lena might understand what had happened to me.

"I know you will find this hard to understand, but I quite honestly cannot play," I confessed. "I am not Ally. My name is Emmeline and for some unexplainable reason, I find myself in Ally's body. It moves differently than I am accustomed. I feel that I am more agile. When I have had to run, I do so more easily and with greater speed. It responds well when I play the piano, but somehow my mind still does not know how to tell my body what it should do in every case. I watch you play at your game—so swift, and moving the ball so easily with your feet—and I know I could never do that."

Lena directed me to the side of the corridor. "I can understand you forgetting things, Al. Like how to do math, or who the first man was to walk on the moon. But the muscle memory stuff? I can't see how knocking yourself out would change all that."

I looked about to insure no one was near. "Have you decided how a blow to my head taught me to play the piano, Lena? Or to speak with this accent that you say is 'so weird?' I've only told Julian about this, and I have no understanding of how it happened. But Ally Wallis is not in here. I am Emmeline Caywood. My home is in Bathurst in the British Cape Colony of South Africa in the year of 1820. And Emmeline Caywood does not know how to play your soccer game."

Lena leaned forward and peered into my eyes as if she might be able to see who was truly looking out at her. "You *do* seem like someone else," she admitted. "Not just like Ally who's forgotten everything. But *two hundred years*?" She shook her head with a dismissive frown. "I don't see how that's possible."

"I know even less about it than you do, Lena. Before I arrived here, I knew nothing of Texas, or chemistry, or cars, or cellphones, or your soccer. I had heard of America. It was a vast continent, largely unsettled, and populated by rebellious Englishmen and savage red men." I pulled a pad from the pocket of my jeans and gave it to her to examine. "Each day, I use a pen that three weeks ago I knew nothing about, to write lists of things that are new to me. When I return to Jennifer's home, I use a computer— something I still find completely magical—to learn about the objects or people I have seen or heard about during the day. There are times when even the explanation is not understandable to me. There is too much I do not know. And the computer does not know about the students at school. I enter a name, and there are hundreds of choices."

"Are you still on Twitter and Instagram?"

"There! I do not even know about these things."

"Then I'm not sure I should tell you," Lena said with a wry smile. "Sometimes I wish I could disappear from them." She returned my list and stood silently, looking me over from top to bottom. "There must be some way to find out what's happened to you. Let me think about it awhile. And by the way, do you remember going to a movie? Ryan's taking me to see the newest Marvel movie next Wednesday night. You and Julian should come along."

"I have not been to a movie. But I have heard of them, and it is on my list. It is like a large television . . .."

"*Right* . . ." she said. "And come to think of it, a Marvel movie may not be the best way to start. Those movies take 'unreal' to a whole new level. It might screw with your head even worse."

"I would like to go. Julian will come to Jennifer's tonight after his Tech Club. I shall ask. And I will ask Jennifer. She must agree if I am to come." It surprised me that I had agreed so quickly to go to a public place with Julian. But this was not Bathurst. And I *did* want to see a movie.

Julian wished to go and Jennifer agreed. "I think this will be good for you," she said.

I learned when we arrived that movies are not at all like TV. They are in a building all of their own with a small shop within the building to purchase a delicious buttered treat called popcorn. The seats are so luxurious that I knew I would surely fall asleep. Then suddenly the entire wall of the room appeared to come to life, with sound coming from every direction. The picture was of people as tall as the ceiling talking about a place called Technicon where one could learn about goggles to wear to see even more amazing and indescribable wonders! As I gaped at the monstrous picture, Julian took my hand and squeezed it softly. Though I knew he wished to, he had never touched me and it frightened and thrilled me. But I could not allow this colored boy—or any boy, for that matter—to become so familiar. This was not a part of being in this future that I thought to be good. I felt his squeeze as one of comfort and friendship, but I withdrew my hand and he pulled his quickly away.

Lena leaned over to me. "I've been thinking," she said. "What about if we . . ." And it was suddenly daylight and I was seated astride father's most frightening horse, surrounded by Xhosa tribesmen who were reaching up as if wanting me to come down among them.

Ally

Julian was seated beside me, leaning away as if I smelled like my early Bathurst self. Lena Morales, a friend from lit class and one of my soccer mates, was on the other side, shoveling a handful of popcorn into her mouth.

"Oh, my God!," I said, way too loud for a theater. Everyone in the whole place turned, and Julian sort of jumped like I'd punched him in the gut.

"I'm sorry," he said. "I thought maybe you wouldn't mind."

"No!" I said, again too loudly. "It's me!" I pushed up out of the seat and hauled him past Lena and her boyfriend, Ryan, out into the hallway without even noticing he was with her. I let go of Julian's hand and collapsed onto my knees on the carpet, planting a kiss on the flowered print next to a smashed-in gummy bear.

"Ah! Popcorn!" I shouted and twisted over with my back against a wall, soaking in the feeling of again having my own legs and arms and chest. When I looked up, Lena was crouched beside Julian with Ryan standing behind her.

"Are you okay?" she asked.

"I'm terrific." I grabbed Julian and pulled him down beside me, cupping his jaw with one hand and giving him a wet kiss. "Oh, you smell so good! How would you like to go get me a large Diet Dr. Pepper and a bag of caramel M&Ms? I'm really craving some junk food."

He pulled back, grinning at me quizzically. "So—does this mean Emme's gone?"

I glanced at the other two. "You know about Emme?"

Lena nodded at Julian. "Tell her," she said.

One of the theater people, a girl I know from school named

Sydney, came down the hall. "Is everything okay here?"

Lena waved dismissively. "Personal thing. She just got some bad news. We've got it, though."

"Can I help?"

"No. We just need a couple of minutes."

Sydney turned and walked back toward the lobby, looking over her shoulder every couple of steps to make sure I didn't have a seizure on her gummy-stained carpet.

"You've been telling everyone your name's really Emmeline and you come from some place in Africa," Julian said. "Don't you remember that?"

"Have I been in a coma or something?"

"No. You've been doing what you always do, but saying you can't remember anything about your life here—just some life you think you've been living in South Africa."

The euphoria cooled into a knot in my chest. *Oh, God,* I thought, shaking my head. *Can I be that screwed up? Have I been imagining this life in Bathurst while I've been walking around here like some zombie, playing the amnesia game here too and telling people I'm Emme?*

Lena took my hand to pull me to my feet. "I think we'd better get someplace else. Let's go over to the Icehouse and see if we can get a booth. I want to hear all about this."

Julian stood, grabbed my other hand, and the two pulled me to my feet. I bounced gingerly from one foot to the other. Yup. The same old body—but maybe a few pounds heavier.

"Do you feel like talking about this, Al?" Julian asked. "Are you really feeling like you're back to your old self?"

I looked down at my legs and torn jeans, shook myself like a wet dog, and took a deep breath of the popcorn-scented air. "Yeah. I feel great! A little out of shape."

Lena chuckled. "You haven't worked out at all. Said you couldn't play soccer."

"Yeah. I'm not surprised. You wouldn't believe what's been

going on in my head. How long have I been acting weird?"

"Maybe a month."

I nodded. "That would be about right."

Julian helped me up and steered me toward the outside door. "You'd better call your mom. She's been pretty worried."

I reached for my pocket and was surprised to find a phone. "I've had my cell all this time?"

Julian took a quick look over at Lena. "We had to teach you what it is . . . and how to use it."

I pulled it out. It was a new model. I tapped in my security code. The phone buzzed and returned to blanks. "What happened to my old phone?"

"Your mom couldn't get into it. She bought a new one for you and created a new code. You don't know what it is?"

Before thinking about what it implied, I said, "Emme would know. I think I'll wait to call Mom until after we talk. I'm not sure what to tell her. The Icehouse sounds good. And then, I really want a long, hot shower."

Ryan was driving. He's what Lena calls a boyfriend, to the degree she has one. None of us approve. He's a gamer of the worst kind. Spends every minute he can with a controller in his hands and his nose in some game. When he's not playing one, he's talking about whatever his latest obsession is. Lena seems to be the only person alive who can entice him away from *BattleBots* or whatever he's into. But the way he treats her, we can't see why she puts up with him. But that's Lena's business. All she says is, "He gets me."

During the fifteen minutes it took to drive across town, nobody spoke. Everyone seemed to want to puzzle this all through in their heads before we got serious about it. On a week night, Hopkins Icehouse isn't too busy. We found a back booth with no one close around.

"You want to eat something?" Julian asked.

"I'd love a burger with fries. I haven't had anything but eggs, sausage, lamb, and potatoes for weeks." They glanced at each other, like maybe I'd zoned out on them again, but didn't say anything. Samantha Howard, our team's goalie, works evenings at the Icehouse. We waved her over and ordered burgers all around. She's about two inches taller than I am, just as thin, and has the kind of face you'd see in a cosmetics ad. Perfect skin. Hollywood kind of face. If we had to pick a girl from our team who could make it in New York and walk down the runway in that model strut kind of way, Sam would be the one. But she slouches so much I want to scream, "Stand up straight and be proud of what you've got, girl!" But that's not Sam's way, and she's got plenty of other stuff on her mind.

As she hunched over to the table, she gave me an "I'm not sure I should say anything" look but decided to anyway. She slid onto a chair at the end of the booth, glancing around to make sure the boss didn't see her sitting, then asked, "How you feeling, Ally?"

"I'm good. Feeling like my old self. How's your mom?"

Sam's mom has some kind of serious blood disease and spends about half her time in the hospital. The rest in bed at home.

"She's home right now. My little sister's looking after her. Are you feeling like you can play again?"

"I think so. You mean, I haven't been playing *at all*?"

"You've said you didn't know how."

"Well, I'm feeling pretty good. A little out of shape. Guess I'll find out tomorrow at practice."

"I hope so. We really need you." She glanced around again, stood quickly, said, "I'll have your drinks here in a minute," and hurried back toward the kitchen.

"How *is* her mom?" I asked.

Lena shook her head. "Not good from what I hear. She needs a bone marrow transplant and is supposed to be taking this drug every day, but they can't afford for her to take it that often. So she's on it every other day. Sam works her butt off to try to pay for even that. They've had a drive through her church, but I think they're just getting by." We all sat without saying much, distracted by thoughts of sick moms, until she brought our drinks.

For the next hour I nibbled on fries and told Lena, Julian, and Ryan about waking up as Emmeline Caywood, about Bathurst, Noluvo, and Prince George. And about seeing the ocean. Ryan is a cynical bastard and couldn't let anything pass without testing me on it.

"This Port Kowie," he challenged. "I just checked out a map of the coast of South Africa on my phone. There's no Port Kowie near Bathurst. A Kowie River, but no port."

"Google it," Julian said, showing the same disgust for Ryan. "It's now Port Alfred. I checked it when Emme told me about it." He paused, screwed his face into a thoughtful frown, then asked, "How do you think Ally knew they'd changed the name back in eighteen-whatever?"

"Like you say," Ryan sniffed. "It's all there. You just have to look it up, ask the right questions, and throw some half-assed story together. Like, how could anyone really go back in time? The minute when we came in here an hour ago doesn't exist anymore. It's gone. *Kapoowie!*" He burst his fingers apart like a little explosion.

"Not completely gone," Julian held up his phone. "Like *you* said. Look it up. It's all here."

"Yeah. Like she got sucked into the damn internet," Ryan scoffed.

"And whoever came out to take her place could play the piano like nobody's business," Lena retorted. "How do you explain that?"

Ryan issued a muffled snort. "You're really buying all this shit?" He folded his arms and pushed back into a corner of the booth with a scowl. "Leave me out of it!"

I'd hardly had time to get to my burger and it was calling up to me. "So, tell me about Emme," I said, taking a small enough bite that I could still talk. "Or do you want me to tell you about her, and you tell me if I'm right."

"Like you haven't been acting her out for the last month," Ryan groused. "I'd guess you'd know all about her."

"I thought you were out of this," Lena snapped over at him, giving me one of the first signs I'd seen that she was seeing through this shithead. "And how do *you* explain the piano thing?"

"I just heard you say she could play. I didn't really hear her do it."

Lena brightened. "You were *so* good. I mean, like, better than our accompanist."

Ryan hunched farther into his corner.

"And when she said she was Emme, she couldn't do any of the normal things," Julian added. "Couldn't drive. Couldn't play soccer. Was scared of her horse. Wouldn't help her mom with riding lessons. And it was like she'd never been to school. She could write. Real fancy cursive-type writing. But in every one of our classes, it was like she'd never been taught all the stuff that comes before. And Ally's always been a whiz at science."

"Except Emme was great in lit," Lena interrupted. "She blew Bayless's mind with what she knew about old English writers."

They were talking about Emme like she was some completely different person and I wasn't there at all. I jumped to her defense. "She reads that stuff all the time. I got into one of her books while I was there. It was actually pretty good."

"What's it called?" Julian asked.

"The Heart of Midlothian."

He arched an eyebrow. "I've been with you almost every evening. I haven't seen you reading anything but our texts. Tell us what it's about."

"Well, it's kind of long—a couple of books long—and I only got partway into it. Rebecca—that's what I've started calling Emme's mother—said everyone knew it was written by Sir Walter Scott, but the book says it's written by a Jedediah Somebody—a long last name I just skipped over—who was supposed to be a schoolmaster. It's written in this Scottish-type language and sometimes I had to go over it a few times. But Rebecca made me write about what I'd read every day, so I remember it pretty well."

Ryan pushed back to the table and pulled out his cell. "Hang on a minute. Let me check this out. How do you spell the last word in the name?"

"Midlothian." I spelled it out.

"Okay. Let's hear it." He scanned over whatever had come up on his screen.

"Well, it starts with a riot at this prison called Tolbooth that's in the middle of Edinburgh. Rebecca says '*Edinbura*.' Anyway, this prison is in the center of the town, which is in the middle of a Scottish county called Midlothian. That's why the book's named that. Heart of Midlothian. These three men get arrested for stealing and are sent to prison. One gets away, but the other two get hanged. And since a lot of the people around don't believe they did it, there's this riot. The captain of the guards, a man no one really likes much, orders his men to shoot into the crowd, and some innocent people get killed. So that makes things worse. The captain gets arrested and they hang him too."

Ryan's face was screwing into a pissed-off knot.

"But in the prison, there's this woman named Effie who's been charged with killing her baby but isn't really guilty. During this riot, they try to break her out, but she won't go. She's from a real religious family named Deans. A lot of the book is about doing what's right and being true to what you believe. That's about all I got read."

Everyone turned toward Ryan. He shrugged sourly and held up his phone. "Could have learned that anywhere."

Lena took the last of my fries and swabbed them in catsup. "Yeah. She just went out and looked all that up so she could tell us about it tonight." She bit off the catsup end of the fries. "We've gotta figure out what's happening to you, Al. I was just about to tell you—well, maybe it was Emme—about this idea when you popped back in. Wanna hear it?"

"I'm ready for anything," I said.

"Do you know Emme's birthday?"

"No. It didn't ever come up."

"But Emme was sixteen?"

I nodded.

"And this was supposed to be 1820. So she'd have been born in 1804." She paused, then said, "And you said they had just come from England? Do you know where?"

"A place called Ipswich. In Suffolk. But they'd gone to a village called Stowmarket just before they left. I think her dad was in trouble of some kind."

"Parents' names?"

"Rebecca and Robert."

"Okay, perfect. So we have names and a birth year, and a place to start looking. They've got these family search sites that go way back. My *abuelita* loves this stuff, and this is from England where they kept really good records. All we need to do is find an Emmeline Caywood, daughter of Robert and Rebecca Caywood, born in Ipswich, Suffolk, England in 1804." She turned to Ryan. "If she's there, do you think you could convince your cynical brain that there might be something to this?"

He nodded pointedly in my direction "If *you* can find it, *she* could find it. Maybe you should check to see if someone else from Texarkana looked it up earlier."

Lena turned away and rolled her eyes. "Sometimes," she growled, "you make me wanna barf up my burger."

Emme

This time I was looking *down* on the circle of people standing around me. Rather than bare legs, there were black heads and bare arms and shoulders. The same urge to scream almost overwhelmed me, but I had learned from my time away that I must not react too quickly to something new or unexpected. Taking a moment to think and observe always seemed to improve a situation. And besides, I knew I had returned home.

I twisted from the back of the horse, saw that it was Prince, and instinctively pulled away. He snorted and drew away at the same moment as if surprised to find me on his back. The Xhosa around me were chattering and wanting me to follow them. I shook my head and looked desperately about to try to determine where I was. This was not a village I recognized. As I turned, I felt the pull of a tight shirt and looked down to see that I was dressed in men's clothing. I felt at myself, fearing that I had returned with the tall, lean body of Ally Wallis. But I was again softer and fuller, though firmer than I remembered being before the cursing.

"Noluvo," I said. "Where is Noluvo?"

The villagers looked at me as if they were also surprised to find me there. A girl of my own age, naked but for flaps of brown skin, tugged at the arm of one of the elders and pointed across the river. I heard 'Noluvo' in what she said. The old man shouted at one of the boys and waved a long rod in the same direction. The boy started toward the river, running as fast as his thin legs and bare, calloused feet would carry him. The old man led me to the largest of the round huts and motioned for me to sit on a coarse woven blanket. He and four other men sat in a half-circle in front of me. One of the women brought a shallow wooden bowl with strips of dry, roasted meat and held it out to me. I shook my head as politely as I could. All of the men took some and sat chewing in silence, staring at me as if I were some new animal, suddenly discovered on the veldt.

I must have been sitting for the better part of an hour, wondering how I had arrived here on Prince and why I was dressed in what I now recognized as Father's clothes, when I heard the wagon. The old man rose first, then the others. He signaled for me to follow him out into the center of the huts, then pointed toward the river. Jama sat on the wagon seat, guiding Maisy down into the water, with Noluvo beside him. The Xhosa boy sat in the back, looking very pleased to be riding. I wanted to rush to them but knew that it would seem that I was not grateful for the help the villagers were offering. Father would never approve of that.

When the wagon reached us, Noluvo and Jama sat quietly for a moment, looking first at me, then at the villagers.

"I thought you must be injured," Noluvo said after a moment.

"No. I am quite well," I said.

"And the horse? Is the horse injured?"

"No. I believe he is also well."

"The boy said we must come for you. Could you not ride the horse home?"

"You know I do not ride," I said testily. "And I was not at all certain how I came to be here."

Novulo leaned toward me on the wagon seat. "Is that you, Emmeline? Are you no longer cursed?"

"I am quite myself again," I said. "And I would very much like to go home."

Noluvo spoke to the villagers who nodded and smiled, then related some tale with wild, excited gestures while looking at me gratefully. Jama tied Prince George to the back of the wagon. I nodded my thanks and climbed up onto the seat, feeling again the tightness of Father's clothing, then twisted back over the seat and dropped into the wagon bed.

"Sit with me," I said to Noluvo. "There is so much I need to ask you."

As Jama led the mare into the river, I asked, "Noluvo, when you are cursed are you sent to a different place?"

Her look was one of surprise. For a moment she chose not to answer.

"I do not understand. A different place?" she asked finally.

"To some other land. To another time?"

She thought again, then said, "I cannot say. I have not been cursed."

"Do you know of any who have?"

She nodded solemnly. "Yes. I know of two."

"And what happened to them?"

"They died."

I had not expected anything so . . . so final. "What did they do?"

She tilted her head back, remembering. "One was a man. He took another man's cattle and sold them as his own. When Grandfather learned of this, he put a curse on him and he died."

"Did the people kill him?"

"No. One morning, he did not come out of his house. When the people went in, he was dead."

I shuddered against the hard side of the wagon but could not resist asking, "And the other?"

"She was an evil woman with a crooked back. The children dug in her garden and chased her chickens into the bush. She tried to curse the children, but Grandfather turned the curse back on her. While trying to find her chickens, a leopard took her. One of the men saw the leopard carry her into the forest."

"It sounds to me as if the children were evil," I said. "They should have left the poor woman alone."

Noluvo shrugged. "They were children."

We rode in silence until I could see the steeple of the Bathurst church beyond a low hill.

"Did the cursing take your spirit to another place?" Noluvo

asked.

I answered truthfully. "I cannot say. I seemed to be in another body—and in a time many years in the future. Was I not here?"

"You were here," she said. "But you had a new spirit. You had forgotten all you know but were able to do what you have not wished to do before."

"And that would be . . .?"

"You have been riding every day." She nodded back at the horse that trotted behind us. "And you have chosen to ride Prince George. You told your father Maisy has no spirit."

"And I wished to have these clothes?"

"You wished to ride like a man. You said your dresses made it difficult to ride."

Ally! I thought. *Ally has been in my body.* "Did I say I had other pleasures?" I asked.

Noluvo smiled broadly "You said you liked soccer. No one knew anything of soccer."

"Would it be possible," I asked, speaking mainly to myself, "for two people to be cursed at once, and for their spirits to change bodies?"

Noluvo's dark face furrowed. "I have not heard of such a thing. I will ask Grandfather. But look!" she said, pointing ahead as we crested the hill. "Your mother and father are waiting. They will be so happy that your spirit has come home."

Ally

I'd never met this Dr. Westover, but he talked to me like we were BFFs. There was something a little scary about the man. He sat in a black, rolling office chair that he'd pulled out from behind his desk. One knee was crossed over the other and he had a little pad in his lap that he never looked at and didn't write anything on. I was in a bigger easy chair with rolled arms and a high back. It made me feel very small. The doctor looked at me with sort of a half-smile pasted on his face.

"So, you feel that you actually were taken back in time and visited this other place as Emmeline Caywood."

"Well, not really *as* Emmeline. But as me in Emmeline's body—and in South Africa."

"As you know from everyone you have spoken to this week, you were here all the time but thought you were Emmeline Caywood. Do you think it possible that you were having a very vivid hallucination that created this place in your mind, and you were unable to distinguish the real from the imagined?"

"Possible, I guess. But from what everyone's been telling me, Emme was trying very hard to adapt to things here while I was there. I don't remember ever trying to manage both lives at once. It seems like that would be a hard thing for a brain to figure out."

"The brain is an amazing and baffling creation," Dr. Westover mused. "I am constantly surprised at what it is able to do. When we spoke last, you said you believed you had been cursed by someone you called Noluvo's grandfather. How are you feeling about that now?"

"I don't remember meeting with you before."

"I have our sessions on tape. Would you like to hear some of that discussion?"

"Yeah. I really would." I wondered what Emme would sound like if she were speaking as me. Dr. Westover reached over to his desk and hit the button on a digital recorder. He'd been expecting my reaction to his questions and had it cued to Emme talking about being cursed. Her voice sounded just like mine, but with the accent of the people of Bathurst—a very *good* accent that I couldn't have faked if I'd wanted to. "The only reasonable explanation I can come up with is that I have been cursed by Noluvo's grandfather, as she said I might be," the voice said.

"Sounds like me talking like Emme," I said. "Just like I talked like me when I was there, but with Emme's voice. And Noluvo *did* believe in the cursing thing. I never did. So why would I be saying that to you here?"

"Hmmm," Dr. Westover murmured, like you'd expect a psychiatrist to do. "Why indeed? I thought you might be able to help me understand that."

I shook my head. "The only thing I can figure out—as crazy as it sounds—is that we switched places. Our bodies didn't switch. Just our minds, or spirits, or whatever. Me there, and her here."

"And why and how do you think that happened?"

"I've no idea. Seems impossible to me too. But I'm as certain as I'm sitting here now that I was in Bathurst."

"And when you were there, you looked like this Emmeline— and felt that you were in her body." It was one of those therapy statements that's supposed to mirror back what you just said. I pulled the sketch pad I'd found in my room out of my backpack.

"Emme had Mom get her some painting and drawing stuff while I was gone. She said she loved to paint—something I do about as well as my five-year-old niece. She didn't get any painting done, but she did a lot of drawing." I flipped to one of the pages and held it up. "This is her. And a really good picture."

Dr. Westover's brow arched in surprise, then furrowed as he uncrossed his legs, leaned forward to take the pad from me, then studied the sketch intently.

"This is quite remarkable. Very professional. Quite a pretty girl, though she doesn't look at all like you, Ally."

"Yeah. Thanks," I said.

"No. I didn't mean it in that way at all. You are both lovely girls, but she is quite your opposite. Round face. Softer features. Light hair. And I would guess from the sketch that her eyes are light."

"Yeah. Blue."

"Have you wondered since seeing this picture if this might be someone you have wished you were like?"

Okay. Here comes the shrink stuff. I could hear Mr. Davidson in the psych class I had last year saying something about my ego wanting to emerge as Emme.

"I haven't had to think about it," I said. "I've been living as the girl for the last month and I prefer being me. *Much* prefer!"

"May I look at these other sketches?"

"Sure. There's one of the village with the church on the hill. One that's sort of a landscape that shows what the country looks like around Bathurst."

"Sketched memories or a fantasy world?" Dr. Westover murmured. "Though you say you wouldn't like to be this Emme, were there aspects of her life that you think you would prefer?"

Another shrink question and one I had to think about. "She lives near the sea," I said after a moment. "I liked that. And her mom and dad get along real well. I liked that. In fact, her dad is a really cool guy. Listens to her and cares what she thinks."

"*Ah,*" Dr. Westover finally scratched some notes. "Her father openly displayed his affection for her."

"Yeah. And toward her mother."

"Do you miss that in your parents?"

"Sometimes. But I don't miss the arguments and the, like, living in a war zone. They're better off apart."

"And were you better off when you again felt that you were

living with two parents who were loving and caring?"

"I'd much rather be here."

"Are you feeling completely your old self now?"

I couldn't resist a glance down at my body. "I'm completely out of shape. I don't think Emme did anything to work out. I tried to practice this week and ran like a toad in mud. We've got a match Friday. I'm not sure coach will trust me to play."

"Well, I am delighted you are largely feeling better," the doctor said. "How is your relationship with your mother?"

"She seems glad to have me back. And she wants to talk to me more than before. I guess she and Emme spent a lot of time talking."

"Has that been good? This better communication?"

"Yeah. I think so. But I worry that she just liked having someone who needed to be taken care of."

"Or, she may just wish the two of you spoke more often."

"Well, this has definitely given us something to talk about."

Dr. Westover *hmmmed* again. "Let's schedule another visit for a week from today and see how things are then." He stood, the same half smile rising with him. I got up and headed for the door, then stopped. "How about these drawings—and my being able to play the piano? How do you explain that?"

The smile didn't change. "We'll visit about that next week. But have you ever had a dream in which you composed a song you knew was pretty amazing, but had never heard? Or played some instrument as if you had always known how? The brain, as I said, is an amazing, but mysterious, creation."

Lena's *abuelita* is about as English as Jennifer Lopez. In fact, we joke that she looks like Lopez will when she gets to be sixty. Her name is Louise, so since she's Lena's grandmother, we call her G-Lo. But even though she's not English, she knows all about this genealogy stuff. Spends hours online tracking down her ancestors in Guatemala. Lena's name is Morales and her mother was a Benitez. She's trying to trace both families back as far as she can and always jokes that it's like trying to trace Smith and Jones if your ancestors are British.

She was sitting at the kitchen table sorting through photos of church records from a city called Villa Nueva when we went to Lena's house. G-Lo lives with them and has her own bedroom and bathroom in the back. Her English is okay, but Lena, who calls her *Lita*, talks to her in Spanish. G-Lo doesn't like to have to stop and think about some of the English words. Every time we go there, she wants to grill us on what Lena's doing in school, how the soccer season's going, and what's up with Ryan before she'll talk about anything else. She doesn't like Ryan any more than I do, which is not at all, and is a lot more willing to let Lena know. While she interrogated me about Lena and chem class, she led us over to the kitchen counter where she pulled the top off a covered plate.

"She made some *rellenitos de platano* this morning," Lena said, rolling her eyes when G-Lo's back was turned. "She says she'll help us, but we have to eat some of her *platanos* first." Which was okay with me. These cookie-looking things are made out of boiled and pureed plantain with a kind of black bean filling that you'd think would be pretty gross. But the way G-Lo sweetens and flavors them with sugar and spices, they're really good. Lena got a couple of cokes from the fridge while her lita put three of the *platano* things on two plates and carried them back to the table. She dropped back into her chair, beckoned for us to pull one up on each side, and said "eat."

I obeyed but remained standing, leaning over G-Lo's shoulder while I sampled the *plantano*. They were as good as I remembered. Lena unfolded the piece of paper with *Emmeline Caywood* and her parents' names, *1804*, and *Stowmarket, Suffolk* written on it. Her grandmother pushed a pair of black-rimmed glasses farther up her nose. She peered at the information and, like she was Julian, ran the cursor around while she minimized the records screen, opened a new query, and typed the data into empty boxes. She'd hit "search' before I could even follow what she was doing. A circle swirled in the center of the screen for a few seconds, then "No record found" appeared in a box against the shadowy backdrop of a family tree.

"*Mierda*," Lena muttered. G-Lo's hand shot out and swiped her on the arm.

"Sorry," Lena said. "Lita doesn't like me to say that. But I was sure we'd find something."

Her grandmother spoke briefly in Spanish, then tabbed back to the query box. "She thinks we need to be less specific. Just try *Emmeline Caywood, Suffolk*, and her parent's names. She may not have been born in Stowmarket. You can put in 'circa 1804' and it will look on either side of that date for a few years for people with that name."

"She wasn't born in Stowmarket," I corrected. "They were there just before they left for Africa."

G-Lo hit "enter." A single line of information populated a row in the center of the screen.

Marriage record, St. Botolph's Parish Church, Cambridge, East Anglia, UK

My heart bounced like I was about to have a heart attack and I dropped into the chair. I really hadn't expected there to be an Emmeline Caywood. After a few days back, it all seemed so unreal that I'd begun to believe like everyone else, way back in my head, that she was a creation of some kind of trauma-induced hallucination. I figured this little experiment would remove any doubt.

"There she is," G-Lo said with a satisfied smile and in very plain English, sitting back with her hands in her lap. "Shall we see?"

For the briefest moment, I didn't want to look. If there really *had* been an Emme—*my* Emme—what did that mean? Sure, I could have come across some information somewhere about English migrants to South Africa and about a town called Bathurst, then forgotten about it. And maybe the fall in chem lab could have jarred it out of my subconscious. But there was no way in the world I could have known about this one particular girl, where she had come from, and the names of her parents. Unless. . ..

G-Lo and Lena were staring at me, not saying a word. They must have been thinking the same thing. "Oh, my God!," I said, staring at the boxes. "What if she's real?"

Lena studied me for another few seconds, then leaned over her grandmother's shoulder and clicked on the record. The screen showed the whirling circle for a few seconds, then was filled by a photo of a page from an old church registry. Lines of script ran down the page, written in a beautiful, flowing hand by a William Thompson who had left his signature after each entry. The photocopy showed two marriage entries for Saint Botolph's parish in the city of Cambridge, County of East Anglia, for October 1st of 1823. The top entry was for *Emmeline Caywood and Charles Pearce, full age, bachelor and spinster.* Charles' profession was recorded as *schoolmaster.*

"It could be some other Emmeline Caywood," I suggested.

Lena pointed at the next box on the record. *Father - Robert Caywood, Farmer, Bathurst, Cape Colony.*

"She's real," Lena murmured under her breath. "I *knew* it! She had to be real after all you knew about her."

"I didn't believe it," I said. "I thought I'd made her up."

Lena laughed. "You married at nineteen, Al. Hardly a spinster! And to a schoolmaster. Is that a teacher, or principal, or what?"

"Teacher, I think. And in Cambridge. Emme must have gone to live with her uncle and aunt, like her dad wanted."

"See? How could you know that?" Lena paused. "I wish there were pictures. I'd like to see this Charles. If you looked like that drawing, I'll bet you found someone pretty hot. I wonder why you didn't show up in the birth records?"

I was thinking of something I'd heard Dr. Begley say to Rebecca when they'd been whispering in the other room of the doctor's surgery. *"Do you fear that she might speak unwittingly about your past? Divulge that you are not Caywoods?"* I should have thought of this earlier. Emmeline may not have been born a Caywood. But I didn't have any idea what name to try, and this was more than Lena needed to know right now. She was bending over her grandmother and the computer.

"Let's see if we can find Emmeline Pearce and see if she had kids."

"Can't today," I said. "Dad's picking me up for the weekend and will be here for the game tonight. We're leaving right after. I've gotta pull some things together. Maybe when I get back." The truth was, at that moment I really didn't want to know.

It was *not* one of my best matches. I still didn't feel a hundred percent—kind of sluggish and out of breath before the half ended. We lost 3-1. In the second half, Coach pulled me after about five minutes and gave me one of his butt-chewings about not staying in shape. I'm center midfielder, and Coach sort of counts on me to manage what's going on across the field. I can usually pick up a goal or two from outside the box and I follow Lena in scoring. Before my time as Emme, I'd have been pretty pissed to be pulled. But I knew he was right this time. I was really dragging.

Dad wasn't impressed. As soon as I came out of the gym after changing, he gave me his usual quick kiss on the cheek and grabbed my bag.

"We'll stop over in Jacksonville this evening," he said. "That's about three hours. We'll drive on into College Station tomorrow."

"We could stay here tonight. Some of the players are getting together at Madison's."

"I don't want that long a drive tomorrow."

"I saw you and Mom didn't sit together."

He frowned over at me. "No sense risking a row in the stands."

"You wouldn't need to talk."

"How likely is that? She always has something to say."

"You *both* always have something to say. Probably good you stayed apart."

Then he was silent for the next thirty minutes, so I knew what was coming.

"You had a couple of good shots," he said finally. Before he could say anything else, I added ". . . *but!* . . .." There was always a 'but.'

He cast me an irritated glance. "Well, there *are* some 'buts.' For one thing, what was the problem with your goalie? That Samantha? Where was her head tonight?"

"Sam has all kinds of family issues you don't know anything about. You need to give her a break."

"Then Gillion should have put someone else in goal."

"She stopped four shots nobody else would have been able to get to. She wasn't the problem. We let them get too many chances."

"Isn't she Bill Howard's daughter? I forgot he died a few months ago. What happened to him?"

"Don't know for sure. The news said they just found him dead at home. Sam doesn't talk about it. They were having a lot of money trouble, with Sam's mother being so sick. People say he killed himself."

"Hmmm. Pretty tragic." He sounded sincere. "What's wrong with her mother?"

"Don't know that for sure either. Sam's really pulled into herself. She leaves right after practice to either go to work or to take care of her mom and doesn't come to anything. I think it's some kind of leukemia that has really expensive treatments. It's pretty well ruined the family."

Dad thought about that for a few minutes, then decided he hadn't said enough about the game. "Well, like you said, she didn't lose the game for you. None of you played well. And I've never seen you get pulled because you were winded."

"Mom said you came up once while I was having memory trouble. And that you seemed worried. Now, all of a sudden, when it's over, you expect me to be playing like nothing happened."

His tone softened. "You're right. I'm sorry. I don't know what caused your episode, but you look like your old self. I expected you to play like you always do."

"I'm not my old self. Something really weird happened, and it hasn't even been three weeks. I'm getting my strength back. I'll be alright when we get to regionals."

He *hmmmed* again, which I took to mean "You're not there yet."

"We'll make it," I assured him. "If we don't, we won't get that England trip they're setting up for February. Everybody's working their butts off to get that."

"The one that's going to cost you a thousand bucks."

"That's actually pretty cheap. We'll be staying with families of English players most places, and the money will pretty much cover our flights, the bus we'll use to get around, and some meals."

"Better play better than this evening." He was also returning to his old self.

I'd heard enough about my lousy game and changed the subject. "What are we going to do this weekend?"

"A & M has a game tomorrow. I thought we'd go."

"Can we go by your lab? I'd like to see what you're working on." What I really wanted was to check on something I'd seen in the Xhosa village—or at least *believed* I'd seen.

"There's nothing too exciting about it. I'm still looking at how confinement hygiene affects mortality in livestock. We're finding that domestic animals aren't nearly as disease resistant as we once thought—and definitely not as resistant as range-raised animals. Just like humans, nothing affects general health as much as good sanitation and a clean living environment."

"I thought you'd found that cattle were pretty resistant to pathogens in water, no matter where they're kept."

"Yeah. Cattle are," he said, distracted as I knew he'd be by things that really interested him. "But not so much with other livestock. Chickens, for example. And hogs. Hogs are susceptible to a lot of the same diseases we are."

"Well, I'd be interested in going by. And maybe we could ride a little."

"So you're back in a mood for horses." He looked over with a wry smile. "When I came up while you were sick, your mother said you didn't want to be close to them." He always called Mom "your mother." Never Mom or Jennifer. I guess he thought that sounded too familiar. Like he might still care for her a little.

"Like I told you, I'm back."

"Well, that's good. Your mother was finding the other you pretty hard to deal with—driving you everywhere like you'd never seen a car. She has enough trouble keeping her life together without the extra confusion."

I wanted to say that mom was keeping her life together pretty well, now that he wasn't part of it. For a brief moment, I found myself longing for the understanding company of Robert Caywood. Maybe Dr. Westover was on to something.

Emme

"I have learned new pieces for the piano," I told Mother when she asked if I would like to join her for one of the Bach choral preludes we often played as a duet.

"How could you?" she asked skeptically. "You have not touched the piano in nearly a month. You claimed you could not play."

"In this place I have been, they have quite wonderful music, Mother," I said, knowing that this would just be another opportunity for her to tell me I had been here all along and had said I had no memory of who I was. "As I have tried to tell you and Papa, some part of me has been in a most extraordinary world of objects beyond imagination that washed our clothing and dishes and carried us from one place to another without the use of horses. There is also new music that I like very much."

Mother had seated herself beside me at the piano and placed a hand on my own. "Emme, Doctor Begley is quite certain you have suffered from some display of hysteria and that all of this delusion has been imagined. Perhaps now that you are approaching womanhood . . ."

"And has this come from my imagination?" I interrupted, my fingers flying into the overture to *Oklahoma* by the composer Mr. Richard Rogers. As I played, I realized that I would now miss "A Night on Broadway." As delighted as I was to be home, I dearly missed my chorale class and evenings with Julian and Lena. I forced the thought aside. "And there is an arrangement of this that is a piano duet, Mother. How I wish I could have brought it with me!"

I felt her edge away on the bench. "Oh, Emme. Surely this is some form of possession. I have never heard such music!"

"I wish you could hear what they listen to on their tiny music boxes," I said. "Some that I found very enjoyable, and other that was not musical at all. It was unlike anything you have heard, Mother."

An hour later, despite the protests of Father, I was seated in the vicarage before Reverend Sutherland.

"I have most serious concerns about possible possession," Mother told the old minister, speaking again as if I were not present. The Vicar, who had retired from his appointment to our parish church in Ipswich, was a man whose gentle manner and uninspiring sermons had kept him in our small parish during his entire ministry. I loved the old man like a kind grandfather and believed him too genuinely humble to have aspired to higher office. His passion for justice, I suspected, had drawn him into the movement that had forced Father to flee the country, but his coming kept a bit of home with us in Bathurst. He had christened Mother, married my parents, and never shrank from telling Mother that she was becoming overly concerned about matters that were not as serious as she imagined. He smiled in the kind, quiet way he always responded to a parishioner's crisis, folding his hands with index fingers steepled and propped beneath his chin.

"Tell me, dear Rebecca, what leads you to believe our Emmeline is possessed?"

"The demon may have left her now," Mother said defiantly. "She has been much more herself. But, as I am certain you heard whispered about the village, for weeks she claimed she could remember nothing. Now that her memory has returned, she can suddenly play some of the most ungodly music. It can only come from some inner demon."

Reverend Sutherland turned to me. "Where do you believe you learned this music, Emme?"

"I truly do not know," I told him. "During these weeks while Mother claims me to have been in a state of complete forgetfulness, I believe I was somewhere quite different—at a time far in the future. I was part of a choral ensemble, and what I played for Mother were several of the pieces we learned."

"There is a piano in the sitting room. Will you play one for me?" He led us into the parlor and sat me at an ancient piano. The Reverend's wife, Hannah, who has a way of listening to all that goes on in the house, but usually more discreetly, appeared in the doorway, wiping her hands on her apron. I decided to play my favorite, the accompaniment to a piece titled "The Music of the Night" that I think is quite beautiful. When I finished, there was silence. Then the vicar said quietly, "That was lovely—and, my dear Rebecca, did not sound at all demonic."

"That is *not* what she played for me," Mother said indignantly. "Play the Reverend the first piece you played this morning."

I sighed, positioned myself more firmly on the Sutherland's small piano stool, and brought the *Oklahoma* overture back to memory. Then, as Mr. Lee liked to instruct, I "played it like I meant it."

Again, there was silence. Then, "Oh, my!" from Mrs. Sutherland in the doorway. I turned to look at the vicar. He sat solemnly in a large, rolled-arm chair by the window, hands clasped against his chest, chin tilted upward, and eyes staring at the ceiling. "I admit," he said finally, "that that was more demonic. But I quite liked it! A lively tune, and one I could listen to again, Miss Emme. And where did you say you learned this music?"

"I was given the music to learn in this dream place I have been this past month."

"And what do *you* think took you there?"

I hesitated, then confessed, "Noluvo believed I was cursed by the Xhosa elders for doing that which is forbidden."

"As I said," Mother insisted, "she has been possessed by an evil spirit."

"At the command of Xhosa elders?" Reverend Sutherland regarded Mother with an indulgent smile. "I think not. And I do not believe that any goodness can come from an evil spirit. The first piece Miss Emme played was quite lovely, don't you agree?"

"And the second?"

"Different, but hardly devilish. And I must tell you, my dear Rebecca, that the Church no longer practices exorcisms and has not for two hundred years. We leave that to the Papists. We do not entirely reject the idea of demonology but believe that it ended at the time of our Lord."

"Then what, pray tell, has happened to Emmeline?"

"A most intriguing question," the vicar mused. "But tell me, Rebecca. Have you ever, in a dream, found yourself composing a poem or singing a piece of music that, upon awaking, you are certain you did not know?"

"Not to the degree that I could then play it," Mother insisted.

"But perhaps Emmeline can. She is a most talented musician, as we have seen from her abilities to play at services. You have often said that she quite outshines your own talents."

"And all of her imagining of horseless carriages, machines that wash and dry clothing, and pictures of people moving about and speaking?"

"A most fertile imagination. And very little else for a young woman to think about in this village, a thousand miles from civilization."

Mother stood indignantly. "You are no help at all. And should she have another bout of hysteria, I shall bring her to you. You can see how imaginative she is then!"

"Please do. But pray, Miss Emme. Did you learn other pieces while in this dream state?"

"Yes. Several."

"Then I would very much like to hear them," the vicar said, and Hannah moved from the doorway to take a seat beside the window.

"You were kinder to me during your cursing," Noluvo said as she helped me with my hair the following morning.

"Oh? In what manner?"

"You did not treat me as your servant. You asked about my village and people, and sought my advice about some matters."

"But you *are* my servant."

She returned the brush to my dresser and selected a tortoise shell comb. "I do not have to be reminded of that. But the Emme who was here treated me as a friend. She wanted to visit my village and asked to learn some words in Xhosa."

"You forget your place," I said sharply, but thought immediately of Julian and Lena. Ally would be very comfortable with people who were unlike herself. I gave Noluvo a moment to consider her impudence, then asked out of curiosity, "During this last month, did I ever say that perhaps I had another name? That I might have come from another place?"

The girl was silent, still smarting from my rebuke. Then she said, "You did not mention another name. But you did speak of other places. A land called Texas. And of objects I had not heard you speak of before. I-phones and androids. You were not at all yourself."

"Then I knew of these things, even though I could remember nothing of my life before coming here?" I was speaking mainly to myself. *Was it possible . . .?* I had not been willing to fully embrace the thought before. *Could there, in truth, be an Ally who had come in spirit to Bathurst while I was in her place?"*

I turned from the dresser and took Noluvo's hand, something I had never done before. "I would like you to remember something. And you must never tell anyone that I have asked this of you. It will be our secret. Can you promise me that?"

Noluvo looked quietly down at our clenched hands. I chose not to release her. "Yes. I will promise," she said after a moment.

"Should this ever happen to me again, and should I appear to be this person who does not remember who she is? Ask if I am Ally Wallis. Can you remember that name?"

"Yes. Ally Wallis."

"I am going to write it on a paper and leave it in my center dresser drawer. I know you read very little, but should you forget, show me the paper and ask if I know the name. I will write several other names with it. Ask if I know who these people are. Will you do that for me, Noluvo?"

"I will. But I should hope that you are not again cursed."

"I will do all I can to avoid it. But should it happen, please. Ask about Ally Wallis."

"Do you believe another spirit was here? As part of you?" Her voice wavered at the thought and I felt her hand tremble.

"I know only that I believed myself to be some other place. And that the person you tell me was here knew of that place."

"If it was another spirit, I liked her," she said, looking again at our hands. "That person was kind to me."

Ally

While Dad sorted through observation notes that his lab assistants had left, I sat at the work table in his office thumbing through a folder of photos of microscopic organisms he'd handed me when I asked about parasitic diseases.

"What are these?" I asked when he stopped reading long enough to grab a gulp of coffee.

"Common waterborne pathogens. Some affecting humans. Some animals. It says on the back of the photos."

I flipped them over. "Oh, my God! Cholera. Typhoid. Were these pictures taken from live bacteria?"

"Some." He'd turned back to his reading.

"Did you take them here?"

He looked up, thought about what I'd asked, then answered, "Some. Not most."

The photos that interested me the most were side-by-side images of a dark-skinned ankle with a round sore. Next to it was a similar looking lesion with a white worm, wrapped around a match stick, being pulled from its center. I'd seen sores like that before— in the village where the hunters took me. I held the pictures up.

"And what are these?"

He dropped a page back onto the pile of reports, doing little to hide his irritation. "That's a Guinea worm."

I laid the picture down. "Sorry. But we're spending half my Saturday with you here in your office while you read these reports. I thought maybe you'd at least have time for a question."

"I came up yesterday to be there for your match," he said, the irritation slipping away. "That meant leaving here about noon. Otherwise, these would have been out of the way. And I remember you saying you wanted to come to the lab to look at some of this information."

"I did. But partly to ask you about it."

"Just give me a minute." He quickly finished skimming the top paper. "Now, what do you want to know? Still about the worms? They're almost extinct as a human disease. Just a few cases this last year in Sub-Saharan Africa. They used to be endemic throughout Africa and much of Asia."

"How'd they get rid of them?"

"Like most waterborne pathogens. Keep people with active cases out of the water supply. Boil or purify drinking water. Separate toilet sites from water sources. The larvae are carried by a water flea and, though both are tiny, they can be filtered out pretty easily with a fine cloth."

I looked behind him at the rows of books that lined his office shelves. "Do you have a pretty basic book about this? I'm good with you doing stuff for another couple of hours before we go riding if I have something worth reading."

He quickly looked his shelves over, then pulled down a thick three-ring binder. "This would be better. It's a collection of articles on Third World techniques for water and waste treatment by UNICEF, the World Health Organization, and universities from around the world. This is what we have our students read before we get them thinking about simple and affordable systems we can apply to livestock operations. Why the sudden interest?"

"Something that came up in class," I said, and started to read.

We decided to skip the game and rode during most of the afternoon. Dad lives on 20 acres east of College Station along the Navasota River and keeps three horses, one just for me. Tonto's an appaloosa, named after the Lone Ranger's sidekick. There are great riding trails east of the river in Grimes County on ranches owned by some of Dad's friends. We can take off after lunch and not cover the same ground during a four-hour ride.

It's when we're riding that I can understand why Mom married

Dad. He quits being Dr. Christopher Wallis and becomes a fun guy who's interested in what I'm doing and thinks it's all pretty okay. He's a good-looking guy and must have been, like, really something in his twenties. So I can see Mom's attraction to him. But most of the time, he's so wrapped up in his job and in the latest international agriculture project he's working on that he forgets the people who are closest to him. When he started being away for months and was only checking in about every two weeks, Mom decided there wasn't really much reason to be married. Except for me. And that was a time when I didn't seem to matter too much to him either. He still takes off for months at a time, but now that I'm old enough to do stuff with him and ask interesting questions, we're starting to get along. Especially when we ride.

"Are you still thinking about vet school after college?

"Even more," I said as we splashed up out of the place we always forded the river and turned the horses up a dirt road that followed the bank.

"Keeping your grades up?"

"They've been really good until this past month. And then I only slipped in Trig. But Mr. Cooper's been good about catching me up."

"So—tell me about this sudden interest in waterborne diseases."

I thought he'd probably be curious, so had been thinking about what I'd say.

"I've got sort of this new web pal. One of my teachers wanted us to find someone who lives in a completely different country and get to know them—find out how they live and what they like. I linked up with this girl in South Africa. She's been telling me about some of the problems the native people still have down there."

"A native girl?"

"No. But she lives outside of the big cities. In a smaller place called Bathurst, down in the Eastern Cape."

"I've never been to that part of the continent," he said. "Up north. Morocco. Algeria. Parts of Egypt. What got you to talking about diseases?"

"I'd seen on the news about an Ebola outbreak and asked if they had trouble with it where she lives." I have to admit, I was kind of impressed with how well I was improvising. I hadn't really planned the story this far out.

"Pretty much in the tropics around the equator," Dad said, reining his horse more closely beside me. "They still aren't positive what causes an outbreak, but it seems to be transmitted by monkeys. When it shows up, it's usually around the Congo and Rwanda, and they immediately jump on any reported cases as soon as they learn about them. What did your friend say?"

"Pretty much the same thing. She said most of the problems around them are still related to water and sanitation."

"I'm not surprised. That's been a problem with native peoples all across the continent. Symptomatic of poverty and little education."

"Yeah. Well, that's what got me interested."

"What's your friend's name?"

"Emmeline. But she goes by Emme."

"Not a name you hear much anymore. What does her family do?"

"I think her dad raises sheep." I knew as soon as I said it that it was a mistake. Dad's passion is raising any kind of animals. "But I'm not sure," I added quickly. "Some kind of farming."

"Interesting! Sounds like a great project by your teacher."

"Yeah, it is." Time to shift gears before I got in too deep. "Did you breed Shania this fall?"

The best way to shift Dad's attention away from work was to ask about horses. He rode a pretty seven-year-old quarter horse mare named Shania who he insisted, more adamantly than was convincing, wasn't named after Shania Twain. He liked to get a good foal out of her every year.

"Yes. I bred her in July using AI this time. A stud from New

Mexico."

Ah. I was back on safe ground. "That Armstrong farm we visited?"

"Yes. A stud named Winter Warrior. Great pedigree."

For the next three hours, we talked horse breeding. It was a good afternoon with Dad. On Sunday, we spent six hours driving back to Texarkana and didn't say a hundred words during the whole trip.

Emme

When Mother brought in the letter, I was in the parlor reading the Scott novel she said I had been enjoying, but could not recall in the least.

"Delivered by the Bradshaw's servant girl," Mother said with a knowing smile. "And I believe she is awaiting a reply." The *Miss Emmeline Caywood* on the face was in a neat, feminine hand, the flap sealed with a daub of red wax.

My heart jumped in my breast, not in anticipation, but from a premonition that this was not an invitation I would welcome. But with the girl waiting, I had no choice but to read it immediately. I slipped a finger beneath the seal, broke it, and unfolded the sheet of parchment with Mother hovering over me. It was as I expected.

My dear Emmeline.

I would be most honored if you would allow the pleasure of a visit at your home this Thursday afternoon at the hour of three o'clock. I have wished to become better acquainted since we arrived from England. Regrettably, our occasional passing in the village and brief exchanges while at services have given me scant opportunity to speak. I am aware that you choose not to ride but with your agreement, perhaps we could walk for an hour and learn more of each other's desires. There are few young people of our age here in Bathurst. To better make your acquaintance would add great pleasure to my days. If Thursday is convenient to you and your family, or if another time would be more suitable, please entrust Lumka with your reply. I eagerly await your letter.

Most respectfully,

Edward Bradshaw

"Well, what is it?" Mother asked as soon as my eyes ceased moving across the page.

I made no effort to disguise my displeasure. "As I am certain you guessed, it is a request from Edward to visit me here."

Mother reached for the letter as if anything Edward Bradshaw had to say to me was intended for her as well. "And why does that displease you?"

"Edward is a selfish, arrogant brute. And look at this hand. This was most certainly written by his mother. He lacks even the talent to write his own letter. I have no desire whatsoever to spend an hour with Edward Bradshaw."

"Emme, there are few eligible men here. Edward is by far the best of the lot."

"I do not wish to settle for just the 'best of the lot,' Mother. And beyond the few eligible English men in Bathurst, there is a good supply of Boer farmers."

"I will *not* have you marrying a Dutchman."

"I am not at all interested in marrying a Dutchman—or anyone at all at the moment. Yet I fear Edward is. He is nearing twenty. He should be courting Mary Lindstrom. She is past eighteen and quite taken with him."

"And as fetching as a dog's breakfast."

"*Mother.* I have never heard you say such a cruel thing. The girl is not at all pretty, but she cannot really help herself, can she."

"I am simply being honest, Emme. Edward finds you attractive. You are approaching marrying age. And there is no harm at all in getting to better know the young man. His girl is waiting. You must send a reply."

"Father thinks I should return to Suffolk to marry in a few

years—to Cambridge where there are many more eligible men and our family can provide introductions."

Mother's countenance fell. "We have discussed that. I am certain we can never safely leave this place. And I dread the thought of my only grandchildren being half a world away."

"If I were to go to Cambridge as Emmeline Caywood, no one would suspect me to be anyone else. And do you dread the thought more than that of your daughter marrying a selfish and ignorant bore? Where do *I* enter into those thoughts, Mother?"

Her crestfallen face colored visibly and she returned Edward Bradshaw's letter. "There is no harm to be done in being neighborly and receiving the young gentleman. Please. Return a note that tells him you will be most pleased to have him come by."

The alternative was a week clouded by one of Mother's moods. I moved to the writing desk and scribbled a brief reply, folded it, and applied my own seal.

"There. I said I would be pleased to receive him on Thursday at three o'clock." Mother hastened back into the hallway with the note.

Now—what to do with Edward Bradshaw for several hours on Thursday? If my instincts were correct, I need only ask him to tell me about himself, and he would fill the rest of the time.

Edward arrived in his best bib and tucker, his cream trousers tucked into smartly polished knee-high boots, his navy long-tailed waistcoat covering a white, high-collared shirt with ruffled front. A black top hat gave the appearance of having just stepped out of one of London's most fashionable shops. I thought how out of place he looked in our modest colonial village. A peacock in a henhouse. Like his letter, he was a complete creation of his mother with very slight traces of Edward about the edges.

For the first ten minutes, we sat awkwardly in the parlor while Mother nervously served tea and Edward struggled to make conversation.

"That is a lovely frock, Emmeline. Did you fashion it yourself?"

"I did. But it is hardly new. I believe I have worn it to services on several occasions."

Silence. Then, "Are you quite yourself again? You gave us all a terrible fright when you . . . well, seemed to have lost all memory of who you are."

"Yes. I am quite myself again. Thank you."

He fumbled at the brim of his ridiculous hat. "It is a most pleasant day. If you rode, we could take a canter along the river to where the smaller Kowie joins the main stream."

"Yes. If I rode, we could. I feel much safer with both feet on the ground, thank you."

More silence while Mother delivered tea. He sipped nervously.

"Will you be attending the soiree in Port Frances on Saturday?" he asked finally. "I shall be taking Father's carriage and would be most honored if you would accompany me."

I had guessed that the upcoming party, which Edward chose to call a soiree, might account for the timing of his visit and had prepared in advance. "I will be playing several pieces. Mother and I will be going early to become familiar with the Le Roux's piano. But thank you for the invitation."

"Perhaps I could bring you home."

"Perhaps." I had anticipated this as well but had not yet thought of a good reason to refuse.

"I would enjoy your company." More silence. After a few moments, "Shall we walk then? Perhaps to the river and back?"

"Yes. That would be lovely." I reserved my question until we left the road south of the village. A side lane wound between new hedgerows that could as easily have been in Suffolk. Father had planted them to separate our pastures from fields of maize, rye, and barley that were the staples of other Bathurst farmers.

"Are we going to where your father is building his mill?"

"I thought we might. Yes."

"Tell me about it," I asked casually, then prepared for a good listen.

Edward had come with a walking stick that he now swung forward with each step like a city dandy. He stopped and raised it in a broad sweep, indicating the fields on the south side of the lane beyond the hedgerow.

"You know, of course, that these are Father's fields. He has as much in maize as any man in Bathurst, and more in rye and barley. We are now delivering it by wagon to Port Kowie where it is shipped to Port Elizabeth to be milled." He again gave the cane a jaunty forward swing and continued our walk. "When the mill is complete, we will be able to mill all of our flour here—for Bathurst and for the other villages about."

"And when do you anticipate it being completed?"

"Early next year. The mill stones should be arriving at the port within the month. Father has the wheel in place now, and you should be able to see it much as it will look when it is in operation, but without the stones."

"And what will your role be?" Edward had a reputation in the Bathurst community for lording over the Bradshaw's house servants and farmhands, but for doing very little himself. "He is as lazy as a hedgehog in winter," Father liked to say, which made little sense in Bathurst where we had neither hedgehogs nor anything like a Suffolk winter. Mother defended Edward, pointing out that he had little need to work, with the family as well situated as it was. "That's no excuse for being such a bludger," Father argued, not caring for Edward much at all. "He's as useless as any man on the Cape." But Edward's laziness did not hamper his ability to praise himself.

"Father plans to leave the running of the mill to me. He says there could not be a better man for the job. It should leave me, next to Father, the best situated man in Bathurst." He awaited my reply, but I spared him the embarrassment.

The mill stood on the bank below one of the few cascades on the river. Its millwheel did not extend into the water, but had a wooden sluice running to its top to carry water onto its stepped buckets. Father and I had passed it in the carriage the week before. He had explained that, whenever possible, new mills now relied on top-fed water rather than wheels placed directly in the stream. "If in the flow of the river," he explained, "the wheel cannot turn any faster than the river's current. A free-standing wheel is able to gain momentum as water pours onto it."

For the sake of conversation, as we approached I asked, "Why isn't the wheel placed directly into the flow of the river, like the mills I remember in Stowmarket?" Edward shrugged slightly, then caught himself. "It better preserves the wood," he said and left it at that.

His tour was brief and unenlightening. I asked enough about the exposed shafts and gears to realize how little he knew, sensing his relief when we were finally making our way back toward the village.

"I am looking forward to beginning my own family here in Bathurst," he said as we again entered the hedge-lined lane. "I hope to marry within the year." Another anticipated conversation.

"I hope that I may be able to return to Suffolk within the year," I said. His step hesitated, his cane in mid-air. He looked at me dumbly, then resumed his step in silence.

"I pray you will reconsider," he said after a most awkward pause. "You are clearly the finest young woman along the river."

"I am one of only two eligible young women in the surrounding villages," I said without looking at him. "Unless, of course, you consider the Xhosa girls."

"Though there are only two, you are a very lovely woman, Emmeline. I could not hope for a better choice."

"Perhaps if you also returned to England, you would find many who are better. With your new mill and fields of grain, you should be able to attract many women of better standing than I."

"I am not looking for a woman of better standing," he said without thinking at all about what that might imply.

"Perhaps you should be. My thinking now is that I will be hoping for someone away from farms and native villages and ships that arrive no more than monthly."

He walked with head down, his walking stick flipping forward with each step to jab irritably at the path ahead. As we turned back onto the port road, he finally spoke. "Perhaps we can visit again at the soiree, after you have had time to consider and to talk with your Mother."

"Perhaps we can," I said, and little more was spoken until we reached the house.

My performance at the party came early in the evening. The festivities were held at the home of one of the few French Huguenots to remain in Port Frances, Mr. Etienne Le Roux, who continued to manage trade along the Cape for the Dutch East India Company. His mansion, for that is what it was, sat on a low hill on the east side of the river, overlooking the bay. All of the white residents of Port Frances, Port Kowie, and Bathurst fit comfortably into his spacious drawing room where he had what was reputed to be the finest piano along the coast. It was indeed a lovely instrument, but I knew as soon as I touched the keys that it was a mere shadow of the one in Mr. Lee's classroom. Mother and I arrived two hours early to allow me to practice the three pieces I had selected. The sound was still rich and full compared to our own piano. I could have played for hours had not what Edward called the soiree interfered.

Though there were several other women in the Cape villages who played, I had become the most accomplished. These performances were now an expectation at village parties when the host had a piano. I began with a brief prelude by Bach, followed by a Haydn sonata. I then announced that at Reverend Sutherland's request, I would play a new piece that he particularly enjoyed. It was entitled *The Music of the Night*.

When I completed the number, the room was first silent, then burst into applause. Madame Le Roux asked, "Who composed this lovely piece?"

"A composer named Webber," I said. "I have just become familiar with . . . ," and suddenly I was suspended in mid-air, looking sideways at a ball that flew directly toward my face. Before another thought could enter my head, it careened off my forehead, knocking me backward onto the grass.

Ally

We were sitting in the Icehouse having a coke and chips with queso, trying to make sense of everything that had happened. Julian still wasn't ready to buy the "you really went somewhere else and another person's soul came here" explanation.

He licked queso laced with jalapeño from his fingers, wagging his head at the same time. "I don't think it could happen. The past doesn't exist anymore, and the future hasn't happened yet. There's just now. And a second from now, this moment won't exist."

"Except like you said before," Ryan said in his usual snarky way, pointing at a camera in the corner. "Want to know what happened a second ago? They can show you."

"Yeah. But you can't interact with it," Julian argued. "It's like a photo."

I swiped a chip through Julian's dip. "All I know is that there were two things going on at once. This Emme was here. You were all talking to her and listening to her play the piano. And I was in this little village in South Africa trying to explain to Emme's dad why I liked horses, because she never had."

"Maybe it was all going on in your head at once,' Julian suggested. "That's your doctor's theory. They say you're only using a small part of your brain. Who knows what's going on in the rest of it? Maybe this other life was running in a different part like two tracks on a CD. Both seemed real."

"And the part that was telling you she was Emmeline—the part I don't remember—could all of a sudden play the piano? Mr. Lee called Mom and told her how good I was and talked her into buying a better keyboard. So we've got this Roland thing sitting in the sunroom, and I don't have any idea what to do with it."

Julian held up a chip like it was some kind of special memory stick. "I think we remember everything that happens around us. It

116

all gets filed away back in there somewhere. You've seen people play and watched where their fingers go. When something triggers that part of your brain, you can copy it."

"But pretty well the first time? I'd think my body would need some training." I remembered Coach Gillion's constant lecturing about the importance of developing muscle memory.

Julian's mouth bowed downward. "Good point. But wouldn't that be the same if, all of a sudden, someone else's mind showed up in your body? Could she play really well right away, using your fingers?"

"You'd have to ask her." I remembered trying to vault onto Maisy's back and not having the leg strength. Maybe he was right and this was all a brain thing. "I just know how real everything felt. If it was all in my head, it sure was like I was living two complete lives. Smell. Taste. Touching stuff. I rode this horse right up to the minute I came back. Though my mind knew just what to do, I can assure you that when I first started to ride him, that butt hadn't spent any time in the saddle."

Lena sat back straight against the cushion of the booth. "I think it all happened," she said firmly. "We looked up Emmeline Caywood and there she was, getting married. How could Ally have known that? It's not like she was in any history book or something. And if you were going to flip out and imagine you were someone else in some other place, who'd pick some little pitstop in South Africa? I think Ally went there. And Emme came here."

"Like how?" Ryan snickered. "Through some stargate or something? And for what reason?"

Lena wasn't backing down. "Just because we can't explain it, doesn't mean it didn't happen. It makes as much sense as Al suddenly knowing how to play the piano. And not knowing a freaking thing about soccer. And, like, having all these facts about this Bathurst place because she heard about it somewhere and it got stuck in her brain. Anyway, I've got an idea. Let's see what happened to Emmeline after she married this Pearce guy. Like

Ryan said, at least that much of the past is probably still in some file. My lita can help us track her kids and their kids, and right on up to now. What if we can find some great-great-great granddaughter who's still living in England? I mean, that would be a real person *now* who's linked to this girl whose mind either came here or who you think just exists in Ally's head."

A thought occurred to me for the first time and the second it hit, it scared the bejeebers out of me. I felt the fine hairs bristle on my arms and an icy finger run along my spine. "I don't think I want to know," I said. "What if . . ." I stopped and thought about it another minute, wondering if I should even say it out loud. All I could think of was *I need their help with this.* So I decided to let it out. "What if . . . it leads to me? I think Wallis is a British name. And what if Emme was some kind of past life? Like reincarnation, or something? I don't think I want to know."

"*Oh my God*," Lena said, loud enough that people at other tables looked in our direction. "I'll bet that's it. I mean, I'll bet this is your great great-grandmother or something and you've come back as her. We've *got* to look this up."

Ryan scoffed. "This is nothing but bullshit."

"I like the reincarnation idea," Julian said, again holding up a chip. "I've read about people who can remember past lives. Maybe this was all genetically imprinted on your brain or in your DNA somewhere."

"I don't like any of these ideas," I said. "I think I'll just let this rest for a while."

Lena leaned toward me over the table to keep people around us from becoming too curious. "How can you *stand* not knowing? I mean, suppose you're descended from this person. Maybe there's something you're supposed to know or do."

But it was all starting to scare me as much as the switching did. "I want to let it rest," I insisted.

It rested for just over two weeks. Our soccer team made the

regionals. I'd managed to get back into pretty good shape and Gillion was keeping me on the field for the full match. We were playing in Marshall, and Dad had driven up for the game. Lena had a corner kick and I was elbowing my way into position in front of the goal. Her kick was perfect. I pushed in front of a girl from Mt. Pleasant and jumped, knowing there was a good chance I could drive a header into the net. The next instant, I was seated at a piano surrounded by applause, all directed at me.

Emme

I had been basking in the most appreciative applause I can ever recall from a Cape Colony audience when, without a moment's forewarning, I was surrounded by wild cheering and a ball bounced against my forehead, knocking me backward onto the grass. I knew instantly that it had happened again. I had become Alyssa Wallis and was engaged in one of her infernal soccer matches. I gazed wildly about but was immediately fallen upon by Lena and all of the other girls on the team. Beyond the pile of perspiring bodies, I could hear a much more riotous applause. I tried to cry out from beneath the smothering pile. "Help me! I am being crushed!"

The girls rolled off, leaving only Lena kneeling beside me. "*Perfecto*" she gushed, shaking me by the shoulders. "That goal should cinch it." Then she looked at me more earnestly and her forehead wrinkled. She crouched further over me.

"Al—you okay?"

I sat and leaned forward, elbows on Ally Wallis's bare knees. "It has happened again," I whispered into my hands. "I am Emme. I have come back."

Lena grasped my arm and dragged me to my feet, shouting toward the man they called Coach Gillion. "We need a sub here!" He waved a hand. One of the other girls, one I recall from Chorale named Madison, hurried to the side of the pitch until recognized by a woman in a black shirt, then ran out to take my place.

"Just sit until the match is over," Lena whispered, walking me to the bench. "Tell Coach that header really rattled your brain. I'll get you out of here as soon as I can."

I sat at the end of the bench, wishing that I could cover my legs or, I should say, Ally's legs. I was not at all comfortable with bare legs in front of all of these people, particularly the men in the crowd. But they were caught up in the match and did not seem at all concerned. Coach Gillion kept looking down the bench at me.

"We need you back in there, Wallis," he shouted. "As soon as you feel better."

"I rattled my brain," I called down to him, repeating Lena's expression. He looked away with disgust.

We won the match by one goal—the one that had bounced off my head. During a very noisy ceremony, the team received a placard stating that we were regional champions for 2020, which seemed to please the other girls and Coach Gillion very much.

"What happened to you in there?" he grumbled as we walked back toward the building where the girls showered and changed into their other clothing.

"I banged my head," I told him again.

"Better get that checked." With the first note of concern, he added, "We need you ready for state." Before they showered, he followed the team into the changing room and had everyone gather about him.

"I promised you that England trip in February if you got this far. Guess I should have said, 'if you win state.' He laughed as if he had said something humorous. "But I'll stick to my promise and finish getting that set up. The way this works is that a regional association there arranges matches in four cities, not too far apart, with a day between. You stay with the families of English players to keep the costs down. Any of you going to have trouble coming up with the grand this will cost?"

Lena leaned toward me. "He shouldn't be asking this in front of everyone. But that's Coach."

Two girls hesitantly raised their hands. I remembered them from school as Samantha and Maria.

The coach frowned at the two. "We'll see if we can do some fundraising. We really need you, Sam." He did not mention Maria.

"That's Coach," Lena whispered more acidly.

"It will also depend on how my mother's doing," Samantha said. "I can't leave if she's not doing well."

"It's just a week," Coach muttered. Lena sniffed sharply.

Coach glared over at her, then swept the circle with his eyes. "Okay, then. Great game. Three super goals and aggressive defense. Get yourselves cleaned up and have a great weekend. I'll see you on the field Monday." He hunched out of the room and the girls scattered. Lena led me to a long cupboard that held Ally's clothing.

"Hurry and shower and let's get out of here," she said. I chose not to follow the others who had removed all of their clothing but a white towel. When they were out of sight, I changed quickly into what Ally had hung in the cupboard, feeling again the discomfort of the very small underthings with the tight pullover top that took the place of a bodice. I waited by the door until Lena was dressed and came to find me. She took my arm and led me around a corner to a place between two rows of the metal cupboards.

"Is that really you in there, Emme?"

"Yes. It is."

"*Mierda*," Lena murmured, staring into my eyes as if she might see who was truly inside. "What were you doing when you left to come here?"

"I was at the piano, performing at a party."

Lena stepped back and clasped a hand over her mouth. "*Oh, my God*," she whispered, her expression a mixture of shock and amusement. "Ally's going to be *so* screwed."

I asked what I had been fearing since my conversation with Noluvo. "Do you believe Ally has gone to take my place?"

Lena nodded slowly. "I'm sure of it. We checked. And there really is a you . . . I mean, there's a real Emmeline Caywood."

"I am quite certain of that," I said indignantly. "I was simply not certain if there is an Alyssa Wallis."

Lena nodded even more slowly. "Oh, yes! There's definitely an Ally. It's how all this switching back and forth works—and *why*—

that we haven't been able to figure out."

"I am just as certain I cannot help with that."

Lena started toward the door of the changing room, then stopped abruptly. "Your dad's outside. Have you met him?"

My heart leaped into my throat. I had seen the picture in Ally's bedchamber but had not met the man. "Should I again say I cannot remember the past because of the ball striking me?" I suggested.

Lena shook her head. "I don't think I'd go with that again. Better play it by ear."

"Play it by ear?"

"You know. Wing it."

"I am afraid I do not understand."

Lena tilted her head and studied my face. "This is totally amazing. I mean, make things up as you go. Do you understand that?"

I nodded, but was not at all certain how I could be expected to do that.

Ally's mother and Julian stood at the end of what I had learned from my last exchange were called bleachers. A man paced nervously nearby who I knew must be Ally's father. It was clear from some distance that her parents were not comfortable being together. The man was just close enough that I knew he was with them, but far enough to avoid conversation. When he saw me, he smiled as much with relief as pleasure, and started toward us.

"Great match, Al," he said, extending his arms. As uncomfortable as it made me, I knew he expected an embrace and I dared not resist. He wrapped his arms about me and kissed my forehead, then released me quickly and stepped back when my own arms remained at my sides. Lena had walked past us to Jennifer and Julian and was whispering to both. I smiled awkwardly at the man, knowing that if I spoke, my accent would cause him concern. Jennifer stepped up and took my arm.

"Ally's still a bit dazed from the header. I think we'd better skip pizza tonight and get her home."

"You mean I drove all the way up here, and we don't get any time together?"

Jennifer turned me toward her and asked, "Are you feeling like going out this evening, Ally?"

I shook my head and looked as apologetic as I was able.

The man put a hand against my hair. "Are you getting checked for these head injuries? I think you'd better lay out until you get cleared by a doctor."

I nodded.

"Well, I guess I'll head on back then. Great game. I'm glad I was here for it." He gave me another brief embrace. I returned it more willingly, knowing it would help him leave without delay. He eased me away, looked into my face for a long moment, again kissed my forehead, and walked toward the row of automobiles.

"Ally," Jennifer said quietly, "Lena says you've had a relapse. That you're thinking again that you're Emmeline?"

I nodded slightly. "I *am* Emmeline."

She glanced after Ally's father who was now driving his automobile out of the parking area. "I think we'd better go directly to the hospital. We need to find an answer to this."

Lena moved close beside me. "The hospital won't have the answer, Mrs. Wallis. I think Ally and Emme really trade places. We *do* need to find an answer, but it won't be from Dr. Westover."

Jennifer slumped back onto the edge of the bleachers, her face showing the same worry I had seen when here before. "Lena, that's the craziest thing I've ever heard. It's just not possible. Some event—the fall in chemistry class, the ball hitting her head tonight—triggers this change." They were talking again as if I weren't there. Jennifer turned to Julian. "You've been with her right along, Julian. What do you think?"

He shrugged. "I can think of a couple of explanations, but none of them make a lot of sense. I can understand how the personality change could happen, but not the changes in what each can do. And she knows a lot about this Bathurst place that I've really had to dig to find."

"And we found Emmeline with Lita's family search program," Lena added. "She really existed, and got married in England."

My breast tightened suddenly and I was short of breath. I reached nervously for Lena's arm. "What is this about finding me? And that I married?"

Lena's smile showed embarrassment. "This was while Ally was here. We looked you up." She paused, then added when she saw my confusion, "There are records that go back for centuries that can tell you when people lived, who they married, what kids they had—all that kind of stuff."

Jennifer stood again from the bleachers. "And you found Emmeline?"

"Yup. If you don't want to take Ally to the hospital, let's go to your place. I have Lita's log-in. I'll show you what we found."

Jennifer looked at me with a resigned sigh. "Do you have a headache? Are you at all dizzy?"

I shook my head. "No. Just confused and frightened. I had wished that this would not happen again."

"*Ohhh*," Jennifer murmured. "So had I. So had I."

At Jennifer's home, things looked much as they had when I was here before. My sketchbook was on the table beside the bed in Ally's bedchamber, open to the drawing I had done of myself. Lena picked it up and studied it while Julian started the computer on the writing desk.

"Where did you learn to draw like this?"

"I have always enjoyed sketching and painting. When we lived in Ipswich, I studied with Mr. Constable when he was in the city."

Julian looked up from the computer. "What Constable was that?"

"Mr. John Constable. He is from East Bergholt, which is nearby. Father arranged for me to study with him. But before we left England, he was spending many of his days in London."

Jennifer had seated herself on the foot of the bed and shook her head as she listened. Lena had determined, and I was becoming convinced, that the very soul of Ally Wallis was changing places with my own, a mystery that Jennifer was not prepared to accept. She looked over at the portrait Lena held. "I've heard of this Constable," she said. "But I thought he was a landscape painter."

"He is best known for his paintings of the Suffolk and Essex countryside," I agreed. "And he himself did not find being a portraitist to his liking. But he relied on it to make a living. That is how Father came to know him." I blushed at my own boldness, but added, "He thought me more talented in that area than he was himself."

Jennifer lowered her head into her hands. "Oh, Ally. What am I to think of all this? You've never been at all artistic in that way. I—I don't think I'm up to any more of this tonight." She stood, gave me a smothering embrace, and left the room, closing the door behind her.

Julian spoke from the writing table. "That's just what it says here. Constable painted the area around Dedham Vale in Essex and found portrait work dull. Who did he marry, Ally?"

It took a moment to realize he was speaking to me. "Oh." I had to think for a moment. "He married Maria Bicknell, perhaps four years since."

"Amazing," Julian muttered.

I moved behind him and gazed over his shoulder at a representation of Mr. Constable's painting of Flatford Mill on the River Stour. "Why, that is his father's mill. How can his painting be in this computer?"

Julian pointed at a printed message below the painting. "It still hangs in a museum in London." Though I had learned to expect such miracles during the first change, they still filled me with wonder and dread.

"Could you draw me?" Lena asked, stepping up beside us with the sketchpad still in hand.

I studied her from head to toe, considering how I might pose her. "I should think so. Do you have a lovely dress? Perhaps if Jennifer could purchase some paints. . .."

"Oh no. I'd rather have a drawing. And maybe one of me running after a ball in my uniform."

"With your body in motion? I have no training sketching bodies in motion."

"Then it will be a new experience for you." Lena pointed at the painting in the computer. "This one of the village shows children walking around. I think you'll be good at it. But let's get to what we came here for." She took Julian's place at the writing desk, her fingers flying over the computer letters. After only a few moments, a copy of a page from a church registry appeared.

Lena pointed at the second entry. "See. There you are. Emmeline Caywood marries Charles Pearce, schoolmaster. This is from Cambridge in 1823. You married October First."

I leaned closer to the computer. Could this be me? But there was my father's name. Robert Caywood of Bathurst. "How. . . how can it know what is yet to happen?" I stammered.

Lena looked up at me, her creased forehead showing her puzzlement. "Because it's happened—a long time ago. Remember? It's 2020 now, not eighteen-something."

I slumped into a second chair beside the desk. "I cannot fathom this. How, if I am here now, and at my present age . . . and Ally is in my place, and at her present age. . .. How can either of us be married?"

"Yeah. Blows my mind too," Lena said. "But this is a record of what happened between now and whatever time you came from. What? 1820? This happened three years later—and just under two hundred years ago."

Julian spoke from beside the window where he held the small tablet I remembered when here last. "I've noticed something that might help." He grinned across at me. "And it might let us know if you or Ally married Charles Pearce." We both looked at him curiously.

"This may just be coincidence," he said, "but Emme was here the first time for twenty-eight days. I haven't figured the hours, but it was twenty-eight days. Then Ally was back for exactly twenty-eight days. I know that's not a lot to go on, but if this happens every twenty-eight days, we can figure out who was there on October first of 1823."

Lena looked back at me. "Do you want to know?"

I shook my head. "Surely this will not continue for three more years. And surely I will find my way home again. It cannot be Ally whose name appears in this registry."

Lena clasped her hands in front of her chin. Her face had become even more animated, and her eyes gleamed. "Maybe it's all planned, and there's a switch just before the wedding. Or maybe this is what Al was thinking. That you're really the same person and reincarnated—or one descended from the other." She appeared almost giddy. "This just blows me away!"

Julian tapped away at his tablet. "I'll run it. It's going to take a few minutes."

"What I can't understand," Lena continued in the same excited voice, "is why we couldn't find a record of your birth?" She turned back to the computer. "We figured you were born in about 1804 in Suffolk to Robert and Rebecca Caywood. Ally remembered hearing your family say you'd lived in Ipswich before moving to some little village. But we couldn't find you."

I began to answer, then realized with a shudder that I had come near to breaking a sacred pledge made to Father. *"You must never speak of your former life in Suffolk to anyone,"* he had warned. "I . . . cannot imagine why there was no record." I could hear the waver in my voice. Lena looked at me suspiciously.

"When was your birthday?"

I saw no reason to lie about that. "April twenty-third."

"In 1804?"

"Yes."

She tapped at the computer, waited, then leaned toward it, hiding the image from my sight, as a copy of another registry record appeared. After a moment, she turned back to me. "The only record it shows for an Emmeline, being born to Robert and Rebecca in Ipswich on April 23rd of 1804, is for St. Lawrence Parish. Could this be you?"

"I truly could not say," I sputtered, amazed and fearful that this magical device could know such things.

"Was your birth recorded at the St. Lawrence church?"

"Yes. . . yes, I believe it was." I dared not lie about such a thing.

Lena's mouth curved into a puzzled frown. "But the name that's given for this Emmeline isn't Caywood. It's Grenfell."

My voice caught in my throat and I looked away, daring not to speak.

Julian spoke from beside the window. "Should I look up the Grenfells in Ipswich in 1820, the year you say you went to South Africa, and see what it says?"

I felt my entire body begin to shake. "Do these cursed tablets know everything?" I stammered, looking at Julian.

His face showed new concern. "Not everything. But there's usually something about important people and events. What are you afraid of here, Emme?"

"If you look and there is something there, who will know?"

"Only us. But anyone else could look it up."

"And the people in Bathurst? Will they know?"

"Ally doesn't know. So she can't tell them. And if you switch again, you can tell people only what you want them to know."

Lena's voice was subdued, but curious. "Are you a Grenfell, Emmeline?"

"I promised my father that I would say nothing . . . .."

Lena spoke more firmly. "You're not telling anyone in Bathurst—or in 1820. And maybe this has something to do with why you're here."

"I cannot possibly imagine what."

"So you don't have to break your promise, let me see what's here in Wikipedia." Julian fingered his small tablet, then said to it, "Grenfell, Ipswich, England, 1820."

The moment the woman's voice began to reply, I knew I would have no need to break my pledge to Father.

Ally

The first thought that came into my head was Lena's "*Mierda!*" It had happened again! And this time I wasn't stretched out on that lumpy bed in a dark room. I was decked out in Emme's nicest dress, seated at a piano in a fancy room, surrounded by people who seemed to believe I'd just played something pretty fantastic. An older man with a heavy thatch of salty gray hair and the long sideburns the men all wore seemed especially pleased.

"Bravo!" he shouted, clapping enthusiastically. "Please, Emme. Play one of the more vigorous tunes."

Mierda! I thought again. How was I going to get out of this mess? Emme must have just finished playing something before the switch. Thank God she wasn't in the middle of a piece. I looked desperately around the room for Rebecca and Robert. Rebecca was seated at one end of the group beside a young man with curly brown hair. Both looked as excited as the old man and not about to cut the performance short. Where was Robert?

I found him standing near the back of the room, watching me carefully enough that I wondered if he'd noticed the change. *Please*, I pleaded with my eyes. *Get me out of here!*

He moved forward as if he'd heard me speak the words, pushing through the seated group to the piano. "I think Emme has taken what time she should," he said brightly. "We need to save some of the surprises for our next party. I know we are all most anxious to hear Mrs. Acton sing." He offered his hand and I took it gratefully, following him through the still-adoring crowd to where he had been standing at the back. A tall, angular woman took my seat at the piano while a shorter, rounder woman with a pile of blonde curls stood smiling beside her. As the accompaniment began, Robert leaned toward me.

"Are you not feeling well, Emme?"

"It's happened again," I said. "I'm Ally, and I'm back in this dream or whatever it is."

He looked at me seriously for a long moment, then led me to where Rebecca sat beside the young man, bending close to her ear.

"Emme is not feeling well," he whispered. "I feel that I must take her home. If you wish to stay, perhaps you could extend our apologies to all and ride back with Reverend Sutherland."

Rebecca stood and led us to the side of the room beside a high window draped in rich green velvet. She looked at me suspiciously, then glanced back at the young man who had followed us with his eyes.

"Edward has expressed a desire to take Emmeline home," she said quietly. "If she must go now, perhaps he will be willing to take her." Beside the piano, Mrs. Acton's shrill voice trilled "Young man, I think you're dyin'" from a song that seemed vaguely familiar.

Robert smiled a tight smile. "Emme is having some forgetfulness again. I fear she would be poor company. And I would not be entirely distressed to leave a bit early myself."

"How convenient," Rebecca muttered. "But I do wish to remain until the party is over. Perhaps Edward will allow *me* to accompany him."

"I should think he would be most grateful to have the time to press his suit," Robert whispered as Mrs. Acton began the sixth or seventh verse of what I now recognized as an old folk song, "Barbara Allen." Rebecca glared at us both, but said nothing.

"Please offer our regrets to the Le Rouxs," Robert said, and led me from the room as Mrs. Acton sang "And slowly, slowly raise she up. And slowly, slowly left him . . .."

Once beyond the scattered lamps of the harbor village, the night was lighted only by a faint dusting of stars and a sliver of moon. Robert had lighted a lamp that swung from a post and iron hook attached to the side of the wagon box. It swung loosely as Maisy trotted into the dancing yellow circle it threw in front of her. The motion cast ghostly shadows across the trees that bordered the track as it climbed away from the coast.

"Kind of eerie, the way the light moves," I said after ten minutes of silence.

Robert nodded. "Maisy knows the road and could travel it in the dark. But the lamp keeps the leopards away." Neither of us spoke for another moment, then he said "Tell me what happens to you, Emme, when you have these losses of memory."

I still had the image in my head of the corner kick bending toward me and wondered if this was all the result of another blow to the head. But Lena's computer search had convinced me Emmeline Caywood was real, or had been, and I knew there was no way I could have come across that little bit of trivia. I wasn't exactly the kind of student who poked around on historical websites or read books about early British colonies in Africa. My extra reading had been limited pretty much to what Bayless required in class and to books about horses and veterinary medicine. This was more than a dream or a hallucination. I was sure of it. And I needed someone here other than Noluvo who believed that.

"It's not exactly that I forget," I explained, "but that all the memories I have are from another time and place. I mean, it's almost too weird for me to begin to tell you about. I feel like I'm another person, who's had this other life. Then, all of a sudden, I'm here in Emme's body." I hesitated, then added, "And from what my friends told me when I was back home, I think Emme's mind, or whatever you want to call it, goes to be in my body."

Robert glanced over, forehead furrowed.

"You most certainly appear to become a different person. Your manner of speech changes. You walk and sit differently. You suddenly find enjoyment in pursuits that have not been of any interest. And you become quite skilled at them." He paused, then,

"Tell me about this place you believe you have lived before."

I shuffled nervously on the seat, feeling more intensely the discomfort of being in Emme's stiff, unforgiving clothes. "Well," I said, thinking like I was introducing myself to some stranger for the first time, "I've always lived in Texas. Born and grew up in College Station until my mom and dad divorced and Mom moved to be closer to her sister in Texarkana." I paused, looking over to see how much of this new stuff Robert was going to be able to take in at a time. I could tell I may already have passed the limit.

"Texas. I am not familiar with Texas."

"Texas is a state in the USA."

"USA?"

"Yeah. You know. Like, America."

"America, as with the former colonies?"

I couldn't restrain a quick laugh and remembered what Rebecca had said about this being 1820. "Yeah. Like the colonies. Except there are now fifty states that cover the whole continent—and more. Texas is just one of them." I fished back into memory for what I could remember from my Texas history class. "You probably think of it as being part of Mexico, or New Spain."

Robert's brow furrowed more deeply. "When do you believe you have been living? What year?"

"Twenty twenty. Two hundred years from now."

"That is not at all possible."

"Just what I've thought. But here I am. And my friends there think Emme shows up there while I'm here." The wagon jolted through a rut in the road, throwing our shoulders together. The bump was very real. Not a dream bump or a hallucination. For some reason I can't explain, it convinced me more than anything that had happened before that I had switched bodies with Emmeline Caywood.

Robert straightened on the wagon seat, rolled his shoulders to work out the cramping we were both beginning to feel, and asked, "Your parents in this later time. What does your father do?"

"He's a college professor and veterinarian. An animal doctor. And Mom runs a small print shop that makes things like banners, posters, brochures. That kind of stuff. And she gives riding lessons on weekends."

"Your mother works?"

"Oh, yeah. Most moms work."

"And what other things do you find different about this time you believe you came from?"

"*Ohhhh*," I said with a long sigh. "I don't have any idea where to begin. I'd really never realized how much the world has changed in two hundred years."

"In what ways?"

"*Everything*! The way we get around. The things we have in our houses. The way we get information. I mean, there's practically nothing that's happening anywhere in the world that you can't learn about in just seconds. In fact, we can even look back and see what happened to people in the past. We found Emme in one of our searches."

Robert's head jerked around in astonishment. "You say that while you were away, you were able to look back and see yourself? That cannot be possible."

"Not *myself*. Emmeline Caywood. And your name was listed. Robert Caywood of Bathurst, Cape Colonies. We looked for a record of her birth but couldn't find one."

"For her birth as Emmeline Caywood? Where did you search?"

"Records of churches in Ipswich, England, for around 1804."

"You traveled to Ipswich?"

This was getting to be far too complicated. "No." I tried to hide the exasperation. "We have ways of looking up information in what's called a database that can go back and search written records from all over the world."

"But you know, of course, that you were not born Emmeline Caywood."

It was my turn to be confused. "No. I didn't know that—but I heard Rebecca say something about it to Dr. Begley when I visited him last time." He looked ahead across Maisy's back beyond the circle from the lamp, considering what he should say.

"Yet you said that you *did* find something about Emmeline Caywood."

I knew this was going to confuse things even more but said, "Well, yes, and this was about something that hasn't happened yet—in this time. Emme's marriage. She marries someone from Cambridge, England. A schoolteacher named Charles Pearce."

Robert jerked back on the reins so sharply that Maisy's abrupt halt almost threw me forward off the seat. The lamp swung within a hair of jumping off the hook. "Charles Pearce? Of Cambridge? You say this as if you have no inkling who Charles is."

"I've no idea. But Emme marries him. Three years from now."

"You don't recall that my sister's husband is a Pearce? From Cambridge? And that his brother has a son, Charles? Surely you must remember this?"

The night was starting to get cold and I shivered a shrug, wrapping my arms about me in Emme's slick blue dress. Robert reached behind the seat and pulled a blanket from the bed, wrapping it around my shoulders. "Like I've said," I continued. "The only things I know about Bathurst and you and Emme's life are what I learned when I was here before."

"This is *beyond* impossible," Robert muttered, flicking Maisy back into motion.

I had to agree. It was far enough beyond impossible that somehow it had happened, and I needed to find some way to convince him. If only I'd been able to bring something back with me other than what was in my memory. The wagon bounced again into a rut and the oil lamp again jumped high in the looped hook. *Something like a flashlight*, I thought. And then it came to me.

"Did you keep my riding clothes?" I asked.

Robert glanced over with a smile. "Your mother wanted to rid the place of them. But I hoped the Emmeline who enjoys riding might reappear. I have them put away."

"I need to ride back into Port Kowie in the morning. There's something I want to show you." It was time to bring some of the future to Bathurst.

When I reached the paddock the next morning, the gelding was in distress. Before the last switch, I'd started to break him, but the jump back had cut that short. As I started to fit Prince out for the ride into the port, I could see that the gelding had become grass fat, a condition that comes from feeding too long on a spring-grass pasture. And he was rocking back to keep weight off his front feet. Robert was leaving early for the upper sheep pastures. I called him over to the corral.

"Don't turn the horses out today," I suggested, pointing to the gelding. "I think the bay's starting to founder."

Robert looked closely at the gelding, then back at me. "I see nothing amiss with the horse."

"See the swelling in his belly? And how he rocks back to keep weight off his forehooves? Those are signs of founder. If you turn him out today, he may be bad enough by evening that we can't save him."

Robert studied me with amused confusion. "I assume you know this because you are not Emme."

I gave him a "what can I say?" shrug.

"What do you suggest we do?"

"Keep him off new grass—and limit Prince and Maisy to fifteen minutes in the pasture for a few weeks. I'll take the gelding with me this morning and have Mr. Pickering re-shoe his fronts. He can adjust the angle of the hoof and give him some pain relief. And it will improve blood circulation to the laminae. It's going to take a few weeks to get over it, if we caught it in time."

"The laminae?"

"The blood-rich tissue around what we'd think of as the horse's toes." I knew I was sounding like Dad, but for once, it felt pretty good.

Robert shook his head in wonder. "Take him with you, and tell me what Jacob has to say." He placed a hand on my shoulder, looked again at the uncomfortable gelding, and left the paddock, mumbling something I didn't quite hear.

I doubt Prince had been ridden since I took him to the Xhosa village. He was as anxious as I was to get on the road to the coast. As I saddled him with the sun still glowing below the trees along the river, he pawed nervously and sniffed at me as if making sure the right Emme was inside, then nudged my shoulder to say, "Good to have you back." As soon as we were at the end of the lane, he wanted to break into a gallop. I reined him back, keeping the gelding at a gentle trot.

"I'll turn you loose on the way back," I promised. He seemed to understand.

A line of shadow was still climbing the steeple of the Port Frances church across the river when we crested the hill and cantered down toward Pickering's forge on the Port Kowie side. The burly blacksmith had started work early, beating out the blade of a long, curved scythe before the day began to simmer. When I swung down from Prince in my trousers and man's shirt, he lowered the glowing blade into a water bath, tossed his hammer onto a scarred wooden work table beside his anvil, and stood with fists planted against his hips. He looked me up and down like I was as naked as one of the Xhosa women. A broad smile broke across his bearded face.

"I heared a fortnight past that ya was ridin' about in men's clobber, Emme." His heavy accent, Rebecca had told me, identified the man as having come "from up north." Yorkshire, she thought. "But I never imagined ya ta be such a ballsy young'un!" He laughed a deep, throaty laugh and walked closer, still running an amused eye over my outfit.

"It would be hard to stay on Prince at a full gallop with one of those women's saddles and a dress," I said, tying the horses to a post beside the open forge.

His shaggy brows arched and his laugh quieted to a chuckle. "And you do have a strange way of talkin', like they said! What's up with ya, Emme?"

"When I dress like this, I try to speak English like the Boers," I said, returning his smile. "How am I doing?"

He grunted. "Don't know why ya would want to be talkin' English like a Dutchman. And I'd say yer not doin' it too well. What brings ya into the port so early?"

"First, I need some new shoes on the bay. He was left out on new grass too long and is starting to founder."

"Founder?"

"Yeah. Is that a word you use?"

He laughed. "I'm a founder, Missy. A bloke who works with metals."

"No. I mean founder like with a horse illness. The front hooves turn and die back."

"Ah, yes. From eatin' too much barley."

"Yeah. Or too much new grass. Do you know how to re-shoe him to shift his weight back while he recovers?"

"Aye. I've done it a few times. I hope ya caught him in time. You'll need to be leavin' him overnight."

"I can do that. And there's one other thing." I pulled the small enameled clock from Emme's dresser out of a leather bag I'd thrown across Prince's saddle. "I have a huge favor—and one that will be hard to explain. But I need ten small disks of zinc about the size of one of your pennies. Maybe a little thicker. And eight lengths of the copper wire you have in boxes on the counter in the shop. I don't have any way to pay for them but will bring them back without damage. Well, the wires will be bent up," I corrected. "I'll leave this clock with you as a trade until I bring the stuff back."

The smithy folded his arms across the front of his leather apron, cocking his head to one side. "Now, what kind of a barmy thing is that? Ten coins beat out of zinc and some wire."

"It's a surprise for Rob . . . for Father."

"One ya want to share with me?"

"Not now. I don't have everything here I need to make this work. But I might later, if Father says I can."

The big man stalked over and took the clock from me. "This is worth a good bit more than ten bits of zinc and some wire, Emme."

"That's so you know I'll bring the stuff back."

"The stuff?" He pronounced it *stoof*. "Well, I'll not be keepin' your clock so you can get a bit of *stoof* from me that you're pledgin' ta bring back." He walked to a crude wooden box in a corner of the forge and scooped out a handful of small silver chunks, then drew a flat metal template from a hook on one of the corner posts. He held up the plate, showing me the row of progressively larger holes.

"This one be about the right size?" He stuck a calloused finger through one near the center. "I should be able to beat out some zinc pennies while you go in and get yer wire from Alice. She's been doin' some bakin', so you may have to eat a scone before she'll free ya to come back. I'll make up yer coins, and you can return the *stoof* when you come back to get yer horse."

"I may need them longer than that."

"When ya feel ready, then."

I nodded at the hole choice. Just the size of what Robert called his cartwheel pennies. "I left before breakfast," I said. "I'd love one of Alice's scones—and, thank you."

"Anything for a barmy lass," he said with the same deep laugh.

Alice was upstairs when I rang the bell over the shop door. She hurried halfway down the steps before seeing it was me. My outfit stopped her dead still and she seemed to want to say something, but changed her mind. Instead she said," I just cooked up a nice batch of scones. Would you like one with some butter, tea, and a bit 'o jam?" She pronounced butter about the same way the big smithy said "stoof." *Booter*.

"Yes. Thank you. I'd love some."

She paused again, puzzling over my accent. Then asked, "Would you like to come upstairs? Or I could bring them down."

"I need to pick out some wire. If it's not too much trouble?"

"Oh, not at all." She lifted her skirt and hurried back up to her kitchen.

There were four boxes of wire on the counter, each with a different stiffness. I took eight lengths of the one that was most pliable and poked around through the shop's mix of kitchenware and farm supplies until Alice again appeared with a plate of scones and a tea set. She set them on the counter and came around to pour the tea.

"Help yerself to a scone. And what is it y'er needin' with a bit o' wire so early of a mornin'?

"It's a demonstration I'm making for Father. Mr. Pickering said I could just borrow these if I brought them back."

"It's a demonstration, is it?" Alice said, clearly not certain what that meant.

"Something I think he'll find interesting." I daubed butter and jam on a scone and took a big enough bite that it startled Alice. Proper English girls, I could tell, were a bit more dainty with their scones.

"I see you brought your appetite. And I so enjoyed your playing at the party last evening. Such a lovely talent. I was sorry you and y'er father had to leave so early."

"I was suddenly taken ill," I said, saying it the way I thought Emme might. "I haven't eaten since. And these scones are great! Thanks." I could tell from Alice's expression that at least that last part hadn't been what Emmeline would say.

I gulped half a cup of tea and gathered up the wire. "Well, I'd better be getting back outside. Mr. Pickering's making some things for me and might have questions. Thanks for breakfast. Loved the scones!"

Alice followed me outside and around the side of the shop to the forge where the blacksmith was smoothing the edges of ten round, silver disks. He held one out in his giant paw as I came up. "Is this what you were thinkin', Miss Emme?"

"Perfect." I glanced around at the boxes scattered about the floor until I saw one with pieces of scrap iron he had sheared or pounded off tools he was making. "Can I take a couple of small pieces of that iron?"

He shrugged and let me pick out two fingernail-sized scraps. "Anythin' else you'll be needin?"

"A very small horseshoe? Do you have anything for a pony? I'll bring it back too."

He grinned at me quizzically, then fished into another box and pulled out one about half the size of those he put on Prince.

"Yup. That will work just great." I put the shoe, metal, and wire into the pouch on Prince's saddle and held out a hand to the burly blacksmith. "I'd better be getting back. Rebecca wasn't that excited about me coming this early—and dressed like this."

He looked at my hand with the same amused grin, then gave it a firm shake with his massive paw. "I want to be seein' this thing yer makin', Emme. Can ya be showin' it to me?"

I untied Prince and hopped up into the stirrup, swinging across the saddle. "I'll see what Father thinks. If he doesn't mind, I'll show you. Thanks again for the scone, Mrs. Pickering." I nudged the horse forward with my knees and waved back at the couple.

"Some'ut strange gotten into that girl," I heard Alice mutter. "But she's a good sight more likable."

I had only done this once—in Isenberg's physics class last year and with Julian's help. But he had let me do most of the assembly while he wrote out and diagramed the experiment. Before I reached the house, while the road still followed the river, I stopped at a place the Xhosa gathered clay for their pots, scooped a handful of gray mud into a jar I'd taken from Rebecca's kitchen, and found half a dozen straight reeds about the size of a pencil. Now I just needed a little cooperation from Rebecca.

She was waiting on the porch when I rode up, fists planted on her hips.

"Well, were you able to get what you went for?" she said before I was even off the horse. I swung down and tied Prince to the porch rail.

"Yes. Everything. The Pickerings were really helpful."

"So, Alice saw you dressed as you are?"

"Yes. She didn't seem to mind."

"Too polite to say what was on her mind, I would guess. And Noluvo prepared breakfast for you before we realized you had gone."

"Sorry. I left a note—and wanted to get to the port and back as early as I could. Did Robert say he'd be back for lunch?"

"Yes. *Your father* promised he would be back. What are you making?"

"I want you both to see something. It's a surprise, but I need a couple of things. You know that old felt hat Robert brought from England? The stiff one that was smashed and you both said needs to be thrown away? Can I have that, and cut it up into pieces? And I need some of the silk you had left after you made your party dress. You said it wasn't enough to make anything, but I think you kept it. I might not ruin it—but I might. So only let me have it if you don't care."

Rebecca didn't move. "Emme, I need to know what this is all about."

"Trust me, please . . . Mother." The word had the desired effect. She relaxed, dropped her hands to her sides, and gave her head a worried shake.

"I suppose we really do not need either of those things. I will fetch them for you."

"And some scissors. I'm going to put this together in the tack room. But first I need some of Rob . . . Father's pennies." As long as this Mother-Father thing was working, I may as well stick with it.

"He may not want you getting into his bowl of pennies."

"I won't damage them and will put them back."

I fished ten of his coppers out of the bowl he kept on the kitchen counter, filled a cup with water, and added two large spoonsful of salt. Rebecca brought the old hat, silk, and scissors and again took up her post on the porch, following me with suspicious eyes until I closed myself in the small tack shed.

The first piece of business was to make a disk from the river clay about four inches in diameter and an inch thick. Isenberg had us use modeling clay that wouldn't set up, but river clay would do. I looped the ends of two pieces of wire tightly together and wrapped one of the loose ends around a small flat piece of the iron from the Pickering forge. I then imbedded the metal piece in the top of the clay base, centered and flush with the surface. With one of the zinc disks positioned over the bit of iron, I cut four of the reeds to ten-inch lengths and stuck them into the clay around the silver coin at the four compass points. Sunshine had reached the shed's only window. I placed the clay base on the sill to dry and turned my attention to the hat.

Using one of the pennies as a template, I cut a dozen felt disks from the tattered brim, thinking as I did how much scissors had stayed the same over two hundred years. Rebecca's pair were all steel and a lot like some Mom had in a kitchen drawer. Isenberg had used cardboard circles to hold the electrolyte in our experiment, but said porous wood would work. I figured rigid felt should do the job as well and dropped the newly cut disks from the hat into the saltwater. While they soaked, I went in search of the solution to a problem I'd puzzled over most of the way back to Bathurst from the coast.

The solution had come to me when Prince brushed me under one of the pines that grew in groves on the west slope above the river, leaving a sticky smear on my arm. Two similar pines stood at the end of the cart path that linked the house to the road. It took only a minute to find a ball of the same, sharp-scented sap.

Back in the tack room, I fished the felt disks out of the brine, patted them with a cloth until damp, but not dripping wet, and moved the clay base back to the work table.

Now, if I remembered this right, it was zinc disk on the bottom against the iron contact. A felt pad on top of that, then copper penny topped by zinc, and another damp felt cushion. I repeated the sequence until the ten metal pairs were all in a stack, separated by soaked felt and held in place by the reed sticks. Twisting two of the remaining wires together, I attached a loose end to the top copper disk with a dab of the pine gum, then wrapped Rebecca's scrap of silk around all but the ends of the small horseshoe. With the remaining four wires twisted end-to-end, I wound them tightly around the full length of the cloth-covered shoe, beginning an inch from one end and finishing the same distance from the other.

My palms sweated with anticipation. I wiped them on my pantlegs and ran a critical eye over my contraption. Everything looked just like it had in physics class. With the wrapped horseshoe lying on top of the workbench where Robert kept his collection of spare bridle rings, bits, and buckles, I connected the bottom wire from the stack to one end of the shoe's coil. Pulling on a leather riding glove, I trapped a breath and touched the wire from the top of the stack to the other end of the coiled wire.

Nothing.

My heart dropped into my stomach like one of Pickering's iron ingots. In the distance, I heard Robert call to one of his sheep dogs. He would be at the house within minutes. Panic caromed through my head like the ball of an arcade game, bouncing against one negative thought after another. *Why did I think I could do this anyway? Would they now think I'm a complete nut case? Will Robert believe anything I told him last night?* I hunched over the stack, trying to see what might be different about how I'd put it together.

The more I looked at it, the more I realized that almost

everything was different. I'd used river clay instead of modeling clay. Could it have metal in it that was screwing things up somehow? Maybe felt *wasn't* the same as cardboard for the electrolyte. Had Isenberg added vinegar to his soaking solution? And there was that wad of pine gum on the top instead of the solder we'd used in the lab.

I bent low to look sideways at the ball of sap. Was that wire even touching the top penny? I stripped off the glove and pulled it loose, wiped it on my pantleg, and touched it back to the top coin. The jolt ripped along my arm like a kick to the funny bone and *Zap*! The fittings flew across the table to the ends of the shoe.

It happened so suddenly I stumbled backward, releasing the wire and ending up on my butt on the plank floor.

For a moment I just sat, startled by the unexpected stroke of luck. Then I began to laugh. It was a laugh of pure relief—and of excitement. But more than anything, it was a laugh of just plain satisfaction that something I'd once told Julian could never have any practical value in my life might be about to change it.

Outside the tack shed, I heard Robert reach the porch. I scrambled back to my feet. The tabletop needed to be rearranged, and I needed to get my heartrate back to normal before the big reveal.

"She's been in that tack room since she returned from the port," I heard Rebecca call from inside the house. "She asked that we both join her there when you returned." I stepped to the door, swung it dramatically open, and invited them in.

A crude wooden bench stretched along one side of the shed where Robert pulled on his riding boots. "This might take a few minutes," I said, indicating that they should sit. Though I'd been over it a hundred times in my mind, my practiced speech just didn't seem right, now that they were there looking at me with that troubled curiosity that seemed to have become their constant state. I decided to ad lib and just jumped in.

"Both times this change in personality has happened, I've told you that, for some reason I can't explain, whatever it is inside us that makes us who we are—our soul, or consciousness, or whatever—is switching between me and Emmeline. I come here. She goes to where I live in Texas. I've also tried to explain—and from what you've said, Emme tells you the same thing when she comes back—that I live way in the future. Two hundred years." Robert's jaw tightened visibly. Rebecca looked like she was about to burst into tears. Neither said anything.

"Every time this comes up, I know you think I'm crazy. That something's happened to me, or to Emme when she's here, that makes us have these delusions." I glanced over at the stack of disks on the workbench. "Since I came back this time, I've been trying to think of something I could show you that might convince you I've come from the future." Robert and Rebecca were also staring suspiciously at the stack.

"The problem," I said, "is that I can't bring anything with me. Otherwise I could show you a cellphone that takes photos or bring an electric lantern you could use in the house. But I'm stuck with what's here." I tapped at the side of my head. "That makes it really hard. I remembered, though, an experiment we did in one of my school classes. It's pretty basic but does some things I think you'll find pretty amazing." I paused, waiting for one of them to say something. *Anything.* No such luck.

"Okay. Have you ever heard of electricity?" I felt like old Mr. Isenberg asking if we'd ever heard of ergs or joules. I expected that, like we did, the Caywoods would give me blank stares. Instead, Robert said, "I have seen a demonstration of what is called a Leyden Jar and was told how it can store and then discharge what the scientist called electricity. It produced a jolt that knocked one of the men present—one foolish enough to volunteer, I might say—quite off his feet." He smiled nervously. "I hope you are not planning a similar demonstration."

Thank God, I thought, blowing out a quick breath as I remembered how close I'd come to deciding a Leyden Jar would

147

be a perfect demonstration. But then, I couldn't remember when it had first been created. Must have been before 1820.

"No. No Leyden Jar, which can store a charge of electricity and release it through a conductor. But once it's discharged, the electricity is gone. What I've made is something that can generate a continuous flow." The Caywoods looked puzzled, but I knew Isenberg would have been *really* proud. "What about batteries? Do you know anything about batteries?"

They looked at each other. "Such as in 'batteries of cannons?" Robert asked.

"No. Like in batteries that can make the electricity you saw demonstrated. This thing I've made here . . ." I pointed over at my creation, ". . . is what's called a Voltaic Stack after a man named Volta who invented it. It was the first real battery ever made. And to be honest, I don't remember when that was. But I don't think it's happened yet."

"This Volta," Robert asked. "Was he Italian?"

Oh, no! Was this after the time of Volta? I would have bet my horse Tonto that Isenberg said Volta invented this thing in the nineteenth century. Could it have been *really early* in the nineteenth century?

"Yes. He was. Have you heard of him?"

"I did read some years back that he made an impressive presentation to the Royal Academy, though I do not recall the nature of the demonstration."

Good. Then you should figure I wouldn't know about it either. Plus, I was about to take this a step beyond the Voltaic Stack to something Isenberg had said came along years later— electromagnetism.

"I think this may be what he demonstrated," I said, looking as confident as I could and praying I could get it to work again. "But I've also added an element that came along much later." I stepped over beside the workbench. "If you will kindly join me here at the table . . .."

Robert stood. Rebecca stayed solidly glued to the bench.

I beckoned to her. "This won't hurt you. I promise . . . as long as you don't touch anything."

He helped her to her feet and edged her toward me, but a safe distance from the pile. I slipped back into Isenberg mode. "What I've done here is stack sets of two different metals, copper and zinc, on top of each other in sets, separated by a felt disk that's been soaked in what we call an electrolyte. I can't exactly explain how it works, but the combination creates a current—the kind of electricity you saw released from that Leyden Jar. But in this case, it flows continuously. You might think of it as being like water that runs through these wires." I looked up at them for some indication they were following, but saw only curiosity from Robert and discomfort on the face of Rebecca. I put Robert's leather gloves back on and picked up the loose end of the wire that had been on the top of the stack. The gloves prompted Rebecca to retreat another step.

"Now, this wire goes from the bottom of this stack and around the horseshoe." I traced the line with my free hand. "When I connect this wire end to the top of the stack, the electricity made by the pile of metals runs through these loops of wire and magnetizes the horseshoe. I've seen you use small magnets in the house, Rebecca, to pick up the pins you scatter when you sew."

She nodded suspiciously and pressed in beside her husband, clutching his arm. I touched the wire to the top penny and, with a scraping snap, the pieces of bridle I'd lined up a few feet from the magnet shot across the bench to cluster at the ends of the shoe. Rebecca fell back with a gasping squeal. I separated the wires, and the rings and buckles relaxed back onto the table.

Robert stood for a long moment, looking first at the Voltaic Stack, then at the coiled horseshoe, then at me. He stepped closer and bent over the battery, studying one side, then the other.

"May I touch the buckles?"

"Yes. Nothing has happened to them."

He scooped them into one hand and deposited them in a pile near where they had first been. "Do that again," he said.

Rebecca had retreated to the bench and stood watching wide-eyed from across the room. I touched the wire to the copper. The metal fittings flew back to the magnet.

"Remarkable," Robert murmured. "Will this work with other metals?"

I remembered Isenberg's lecture. "Not all. It will with iron and steel. But copper and zinc won't be attracted."

Robert peered again at all sides of the stack. "How strong is it?"

I shook my head a little, amazed that all these questions were coming, with no, *How do you know all this stuff?*"

He understood the shake to mean, "I really don't know" and I went with it. He had his own small anvil and hammer on a stump beside the workbench. I lifted the hammer and set it at the edge of the table. "I haven't tested the strength yet. It depends on how many metal pairs we have in the stack. The more pairs, the stronger the force. I'm not sure ten pairs will pull this weight."

"May I try?"

I pulled off the gloves and handed them to him.

"Robert—please be careful," Rebecca whispered from beside the bench.

"Hold the horseshoe in one hand and touch the wire to the top of the stack with the other," I instructed. "Then move the magnet toward the hammer. See if there's some point at which the hammer starts to move."

Robert donned the gloves like an excited child, carefully lifted the horseshoe in his left hand, and completed the circuit with his right. At about a foot, the hammer began to slide. He released the connection, then touched it again to pull the metal head forward.

"Rebecca, what an incredible device!" She stood with arms folded protectively across her chest, gazing not at Volta's magical stack, but at her bewitched daughter.

"Oh, this is more than I can bear!" she exclaimed, and rushed from the shed.

Robert slowly removed the gloves and turned his attention to me. For the first time, his gaze seemed to be piercing my eyes, searching what was beyond. He took my hand and led me across to the bench.

"Please sit," he said. "I have not listened to you before as honestly as you deserved. Tell me what you want me to know." He glanced back at the stack on the table. "And when we have visited, please sketch a drawing of this thing for me in great detail. With your permission, I should like to send it to my cousin, William Sturgeon. It was he who wrote me about Volta. He envisions himself to be quite the man of science."

Emme

We were at a public house where my friends like to gather on Friday evenings. There were no longer Friday night football matches, and meeting at Hopkin's Icehouse seemed to have taken their place. Around us, the walls were covered with placards of every variety, large preserved fish, and television sets that displayed sporting events and people talking about sport. I was seated at a large corner booth with Julian, Lena, and Lena's friend, Ryan. The nights had turned cold and Samantha Howard, who worked as a server after school, had just delivered mugs of coffee and a hot chocolate drink I liked very much.

"Sam, you've got to come with us to England," Lena said as Samantha slid in beside me, saying that it was her time for a work break. "We don't have anyone who comes close to you tending goal."

Sam twisted nervously at a paper napkin and seemed to fight back tears. "Yeah. I'd love to. Mom seems to be holding her own. But even if I could find someone to watch after her, this job doesn't even pay for her medicine. I'd never be able to come up with the money for the trip."

Lena placed a hand on hers and gave it a squeeze. "There's always a way. We've just got to figure out what it is."

Sam returned the squeeze, then stood and wiped at the corner of her eyes. "Well, better get back to the old grind," she said, which didn't make sense at all to me, but the others appeared to understand.

Lena leaned forward heavily on her elbows. "We gotta do something to help her. And the rest of us, too. If we don't have her, we may as well stay home. We'll get creamed," which I understood to mean "badly beaten."

Ryan threw an arm over the back of the booth, arched his chest like one of the bantam roosters the sailors bring to the Cape from the East, and sneered across at me. "What if Ally's having one of her 'I can't play soccer' times? You're gonna get creamed anyway. And you gotta quit thinking you're responsible for solving everyone's problems, Lena. You don't want Sam gone if her mom dies. And she's pretty sick."

Lena glared daggers at him. "Her mom's doing better. And Sam's either at school, working her tail off here, or taking care of her. She needs a break. And we're only gone a week. If Ally's not playing, Maddy can fill in. She's not as good, but we'd get by. But we don't have another good goalie. And what difference does it make to you if I try to help Sam? You could use a little more compassion yourself."

He shrugged, but kept his arm on the seat back and his chest puffed out. Julian pulled out his phone, laid it on the table, and started rubbing his finger across the screen as he did when he was looking for something.

"I want to hear more from Emme about what her dad was mixed up in," he said. "We found online that Robert Grenfell appeared to have left England in 1820 to escape being arrested for sedition. And that it was related to something called the Peterloo massacre. Ally . . . or Emme? You said you didn't want to talk about this after the soccer game, but maybe tonight. What do you say?"

Ryan scoffed. "You're starting to call her Emme now? You guys are so full of shit."

Julian ignored him. "You feeling like telling us about this tonight, Emme?"

I had considered it every day since the switch, wondering if Lena was right—that perhaps our family's misfortune had something to do with why I was changing places with Alyssa Wallis. No reason made sense to me, but I saw nothing to be lost by sharing what had happened to the family with these friends two centuries removed from Bathurst. They had ways of learning so much and, as Lena had made clear to Ryan, she enjoyed helping when she could. The three of them sat and looked at me expectantly. I drew a deep breath and began.

"I do not know how much you wish to know. But yes. We are Grenfells and have a fine estate, Grenfell Hall, in Suffolk near Ipswich. Before his death, King George—that is King George the Third—was deemed unfit to rule, and had been for a good ten years. His son, now George the Fourth, has ruled in his stead as Regent."

Ryan interrupted from his perch opposite me in the booth. "This George the Third. Would that be nutty King George of the Revolution?"

"The Revolution?"

"You know. The colonies rising up against you Brits, *Emme*."

Julian glared across at him. "Let her tell her story. Go ahead, Emme. Sorry about smartass there."

The way they spoke to each other was an embarrassment, but I chose to ignore it and continued. "Yes. That would be the same King George, but before my birth. He ruled for nearly sixty years. Wars with France, that ended just five years before we left home, have drained the nation of its wealth. People have been unable to find work and have been living in great poverty and squalor. Yet the new king, even during his regency, has lived an extravagant and disdainful life, showing little concern for others, especially the common people. It finally led this year past to riots in parts of the country."

"Such as the Peterloo riots in Manchester," Julian offered.

I nodded. "Tens of thousands gathered on St. Peter's Field in Manchester in protest. To scatter the crowd, mounted cavalry charged into the masses, sabers drawn. Hundreds were injured and more than a dozen killed. Because the charge reminded the people of the recent battle at Waterloo, and the site of the gathering was St. Peter's field, the tragedy has been named the Peterloo Massacre."

Lena leaned again over the table. "I don't know a lot of English geography, but I've been checking out the map for our soccer trip. Isn't Manchester a long way from Ipswich? How did your father get involved in all this?"

"Father has long been a critic of the Regent's extravagance and disregard for the people. But his brother, Stephen, who lives in Preston near Manchester, is a much more outspoken voice of opposition. He was one of the men who openly encouraged the riot."

I could see from Lena's expression that she was still awaiting an answer to her question. I explained.

"Stephen is a hot tempered and outspoken man, but not one who is skilled with the written word. Father agreed to write and have printed pamphlets that stated the case against the Crown's excesses. These were distributed widely by Stephen among the poor and played no small part in bringing sixty thousand people to the field. In response to the riots, parliament quickly passed what are known as the Six Acts. One is the Blasphemous and Seditious Libels Act. Under this law, Stephen was arrested and sentenced to fourteen years in prison. Father received warning from some of the dissenters that he was next to be charged."

Julian finished the story. "So you took off. Left the country."

"A party from Ipswich had already been organized to go to the Cape. Sir Donkin, who led the party, is not a friend of the Crown. He arranged for Father and two of his sympathetic friends, our vicar and the family doctor, to accompany him. They changed the ship's manifest to include a family of Caywoods, and we assumed the name."

"What happened to your house? To Grenfell Hall?" Lena looked from me to Julian, as if he might better be able to answer her question.

I told her what little I knew. "We have been told it was taken by the Crown as punishment for Father's sedition." I also found myself looking to Julian to confirm my words. He fingered his phone for a moment, then nodded soberly.

"Still owned by the Royal Family." He extended his cell toward me. The screen displayed a list of British royal properties. Near the bottom was Grenfell Hall. "It shows it's being leased to some antique dealer," he said.

My heart lifted for a brief instant, then sank with crushing force. "It has lasted all this time. But the family has not been able to regain it."

The others, even Ryan, slumped back gloomily against the red cushions of the booth, none speaking for several minutes. Then Julian said, "I'd think a case could be made that the hall should be restored to the family. I can't see how anyone could argue now that the charge against your father was just. If you had proof that it was your ancestral estate, maybe a case could be made to get it returned to the family."

I took his arm and held it until he looked up at me. "Who do you see when you look at me, Julian?"

He shrugged. "What do you mean?"

"You now call me Emme, but you see Alyssa Wallis. Not Emmeline Grenfell. And so do others. Even if I had proof the hall belonged to the Grenfells, I would have no case as a Wallis."

He grunted his agreement and again fell silent.

Ryan slipped down into a normal sitting position. "I've been working on this theory about what's happening with Ally and Emme," he announced. For the first time, everyone at the table gave him their undivided attention.

"It's the whole *Matrix* thing being played out—like in the old movie. We're all part of a virtual game, but none of us knows it, cuz we're all in it. The master architect is the one who selects what attributes go with each character, so he can switch them around any time he wants. For some reason, he's decided to mess with Ally and Emme's characters."

Julian scoffed. "Great theory. But why did he decide to start messing with two characters all of a sudden? And how does that explain the time warp?"

"There *is* no time in the game," Ryan said, throwing Julian a look that said *This should all be obvious to you.* "You know when you're playing, all levels of the game are operating at the same time. You can go back to an earlier level any time you want. When you get there, it's running just like the one you were in. For some reason, the big guy's decided to swap characteristics for these two."

"So you think we're all game characters," Lena scoffed.

Ryan shrugged. "Could be. No way of knowing."

"Well, just to go with your stupid theory for a minute, what's the reason for the switch?"

"Doesn't need to be a reason. Maybe it's just to add interest to the game."

"Sorry. But I think I'm more than some little Latina character your master architect dreamed up."

Ryan leaned back again against the cushions of the booth. "That's cuz you got *two* attributes. You think every good idea's gotta come from you, and you think you gotta save everyone."

Lena turned away, shaking her head. "I got one other attribute. I know dumb when I hear it. But your great theory reminds me that there *is* something I think we need to do. We can't do it here, though. But before we leave, I want to see what Ally brought."

I had forgotten the primary reason we had decided to meet at the Icehouse. My sketch of Lena. I had the sketchbook tucked behind me on the bench and pulled it out, spread it on the table, and flipped the pages to the charcoal drawing I had done of Lena playing soccer. The gasp from the three in the booth turned every head in the pub.

"Oh, *my God*!" Lena spouted. "This is incredible!" Ryan pushed forward on the bench and leaned over the drawing, then looked up at me with the first sign of respect I had seen from him.

"You did this? It's almost like a photograph. It's like you caught her right in the middle of a kick. How'd you get her face so good without looking at her while you were doing it?"

"Ally has a picture of the team in her room. I was able to look at that."

Julian tilted his head to the side and studied the drawing. "How long did this take you?"

I shrugged. "Three or four hours."

Lena held up the sketchbook and admired the drawing at arm's length. "Wow!" She murmured. "Everyone on the team is going to want one of these." She closed the pad and sat back, looking absently at nothing in particular like she did when her mind was busy. We all recognized it and waited expectantly for what we knew would come.

"That gives me another idea," she said after a moment, not disappointing. "First of all, we don't let people know you did this. Sign it 'Emmeline Caywood.' Then we put it up in the trophy case that's just outside our locker room. I'm thinking maybe three hundred dollars for an original drawing of a player. The money goes into a 'Send Sam to Suffolk' fund. Didn't you say Ipswich is in Suffolk, Al? A couple of the towns we play in are near Cambridge, and I like the sound of that—Sam to Suffolk."

Julian looked at her skeptically. "Three hundred dollars? I mean, the drawing's great! Professional. But do you think players will pay three hundred bucks?"

"Not players. Their parents." She held up the sketch. "Mine will pay that for this in a heartbeat, and they aren't rich. You end up paying that much for senior pictures. And where else could you get something like this? That's why we put Emme's name on it instead of Ally's. So it looks like it's by some professional artist." She grinned slyly at Julian. "I've got an assignment for you. I'm going to make up a sign with a web address where people can order. We'll put it in the case by this picture. Your job is to develop the website." She flipped the pad back to one of the drawings I had completed of Bathurst during the earlier switch. "We've got four or five great drawings here we can show, including that portrait of Emmeline and this one of me. She'll look like a regular commercial artist."

Ryan still had to play the skeptic. "What if other people find the site and want to order pictures?"

Lena shrugged him off. "We ignore them. Just don't respond. Emme can just do the team pictures we get orders for. We raise the money we need for Sam and close down the site. Five drawings should do it. If we get more, we can put the money into a fund for her mom's meds."

Julian turned to me. "Great idea, but maybe we should check with the artist. And probably with Sam. She might be embarrassed at being singled out for this kind of help."

"She will be," Lena agreed. "But anything we do to help will embarrass her. So we'll just have to let her be a little embarrassed. And I think we can set it up so no one knows where these are coming from. What do you say, Ally?" Lena changed what she called me as frequently as she hatched new schemes.

I had been considering the idea as Lena spoke and knew that if I wished to, I could complete a drawing each evening. Like the piano, the skill came to me easily, and my studies with Mr. Constable had helped me become most proficient. "I can do this," I said. "And I like Samantha very much. I would be delighted to help her. But we need to include Maria as well. She also could not afford to go."

Lena's face reddened. "Oh, yeah. That's right. My bad. We'll have to think of something else to call the fund. That would help Sam feel better anyway." She looked pointedly at Julian. "Can you create the site over the weekend? My concern is that if Ally and Emme switch again before we get these drawings finished, we're out of business. Ally can't even make a stick figure that looks convincing. So we may only have a few weeks. If we can put this up Monday, I'll say orders have to be in by Friday."

Julian gave an amused shrug. "Let me take the pad. I think I can get something up tomorrow. How will people pay?"

Lena's ideas were still flowing. "I'll talk to Hannah's mom who works in the principal's office. She can collect for us and doesn't need to know who the artist is." She turned to Ryan. "And *you* need to keep quiet about this—about who's doing the drawings. Do you think you can manage that?"

"Hell, yes," he said. "This'll be fun to watch. At that price, I'll bet you won't get two other players to order pictures."

"How much?" Lena challenged.

"What do you mean, how much?"

"How much will you bet? A hundred bucks?"

Ryan smirked. "Yeah. I'll bet you a hundred bucks."

"It goes in the pot if I win. Now, Ally . . . Emme? Can you come over Sunday afternoon if I pick you up? We need to follow up on this other idea I have."

I nodded.

"Then what are we going to call this now," Julian wanted to know.

Lena sat back, again gazed fixedly at the ceiling, then snapped her fingers. "There are sixteen of us if Sam and Maria go. We'll call it "Send Sixteen to Suffolk."

Ally

Robert listened for nearly an hour, often shaking his head in wonder, occasionally asking a question, and becoming more and more troubled. I described my world as best I could, knowing there were a thousand things I wasn't remembering to tell him that would blow his mind. When I could see we were getting close to overload, I stopped and let him decide where he wanted to go next. He stared at me again for a long moment with that penetrating gaze, trying to decide who I really was. Then the *real* questions began to spill out.

"I still cannot begin to fathom how what you describe is possible," he began. "But I am astounded at the changes I see in you. Your new abilities and knowledge. Your loss of some of the old ones. But if this has indeed happened, what is the reason? Surely, there must be one."

I raised both hands in surrender. "I have no idea. I think about it all the time and still can't come up with anything."

"And you truly believe Emme's . . . *soul* is somewhere else. In another time, and in your natural body?"

"Yes. I do believe that."

"And that while you are with me now, she is with your family, talking as we are, and aware that she is still Emmeline."

"I believe that. Yes."

"Do you believe these *switches*, as you call them, will continue?"

"I really don't know. I thought when I went back that it was a one-time deal. Then it happened again—and after exactly the same number of days. I guess we'll know in a few weeks."

"And what if this switching should stop with her there, and you here? Have you considered that?"

"Yeah. Almost every day. You're really good to me, but I'd like to be home."

"And I would like to look at my daughter and know that she is who I believe her to be," he said, his eyes misting. "Tell me. What can I do to . . . to try to end this? Or, at least to make it better?"

While I'd been working on the experiment, I was hoping it would come to this and had decided what I'd say. "Please," I said. "Accept me as me. Don't try to make me Emme. I'll try not to embarrass you, but the things that might do that will come from putting me in situations I can't handle—like playing at that party."

He nodded thoughtfully. "I'll do what I can to keep your mother from placing you in those difficult spots. Are there other ways I can help?"

"If there's anything that's made me wonder if I have a purpose here, it's seeing some of the diseases the Xhosa have. Just from looking at their villages, I can think of half a dozen things that would really make a big difference. I'd like you to let me go with Noluvo to the villages to see if I can help. And there are some of the same things I can recommend for you—things that will keep you and Rebecca from getting some kinds of illnesses."

He was stooped forward on the bench and I saw his brow furrow. "You know how distraught your mother remains over the loss of your brother. She sees the disease among the Xhosa and is terrified that you will become ill."

"I understand. But I think I'll be all right. Most of the illnesses there have a pretty specific cause. One that I can avoid. Will you let me?"

He nodded as he stood. "I will do my best. I cannot fully say that I accept this as more than a very puzzling condition of the mind, but I am willing to treat it as what you describe. Just be understanding if your mother does not."

During the first switch, I'd wondered how the Xhosa could have so much sickness and the English so little. After the first week, I knew at least part of the reason. All the English drank was tea. The kettle went on as soon as the first person in the house was out of bed in the morning and remained near a boil until bedtime. By the time the first cup was poured, most kettles had boiled for half an hour, killing whatever went into them with the water. Rebecca was also something of a clean nut, helping Noluvo scrub floors and counters every day with a strong lye soap. The result was that their hands were getting cleaned at the same time. But both were the result of dumb luck. I started my new health campaign at home with a set of basic fifth grade hygiene rules:

Don't drink any water that hasn't been filtered and boiled for at least three minutes.

Filter and boil another large kettle over the fire every morning to use to wash hands and dishes.

Don't wash anything in the big kettle. Pour the water into another pan.

Wash your hands with Rebecca's lye soap before and after fixing any food.

Peel or thoroughly wash any fruit or vegetables that aren't going to be cooked.

Don't eat meat that isn't well cooked.

Clean teeth every evening with salt water.

For this last item, I made floss out of wool and boiled and balled up wool fiber to make a simple brush. "Clean teeth make a bigger difference than you'd think," I explained, then tried to give a simple explanation of the whole idea of germs. "They're so tiny you can't see them. But they cause all sickness. Things I'm telling you about will kill most of them." Robert listened with curious interest. Rebecca rolled her eyes and muttered to herself but yielded to Robert's insistence that they do as I asked.

I found that one of the things I enjoyed about being in Bathurst was watching Robert and Rebecca. She fussed. He was tolerant and patient. He cursed the hyenas and wild dogs that pestered his lambs. She wrapped him from behind and teased the anger out of him. One never left the house without the other sending them off with a kiss and a look that said, "You are the center of my life." *Someday . . .*, I thought as I watched them, *I want that*.

Both seemed to have noticed, without my saying anything about it, that I smelled better than they did. They began to wash every morning and Robert again after a long day in the fields. Water for the village came from a common well. I was able to convince him to tell the other families in Bathurst that *nothing* should ever be dumped into it.

"It would be a good idea," I suggested, "to have Mr. Pickering make a lightweight metal grate to put over the top so some animal doesn't fall down in there. But still, I'd always filter the water through a piece of linen before it goes into a kettle."

I learned from a Scotsman named Kinkade, who had dug the village well, that it was eleven meters deep. He admitted that it should have been deeper and didn't have enough flow during the dry season to supply the town if everyone drew on it within the same few hours. "We've all agreed to a schedule during the winter months," he informed me in his rolling Scottish brogue. "Each family has an assigned time. That way, the well has time to re-charge between draws."

"When the well's low in the winter, why don't you take it deeper?" I suggested.

The little man shrugged. "Schedule does the job—and saves me going down in that pit."

I had learned enough from Noluvo to know that nothing happened in the Xhosa villages without approval and support from the headman. In the case of her village, that was her grandfather, the one she thought had cursed me. I figured his superstition and that cursing just might be the mojo I needed to get him to listen to some of my suggestions. I started with Noluvo.

I'd taken the Voltaic Pile apart, scraped oxidation from the zinc disks so it would work well again if I showed it to the Pickerings, and practiced with my pine gum until I could keep the top lead tight against the penny. With a new set of saltwater-soaked felt circles, I put it back together and took Noluvo to the tack shed. This time, I didn't mess with harness buckles. We went straight to moving the iron hammer.

"I learned about this in the place I visit during the cursing," I told her. "The place of magical things." She stared fearfully at the hammerhead as I drew it slowly across the benchtop with the wrapped horseshoe.

"I was told in this place how I can help your village with some of the sickness. The chief of the magic place told me to show your grandfather, and tell him I can help your people. Will you take me to him?"

Noluvo shook her head, her eyes glued on the sliding hammer. "This is dark magic. He will not wish to see it. He will say you cannot come to the village and may place another curse on you."

"If we tell him first that I have been given a message for him? That I was told to show him magic to let him know I can help heal the people?"

She cocked her head to the side, thinking. "You were told this?"

"I learned in the place I go how to help people with some of the sicknesses you have. I learned this magic there so I could show your village that there is power in what I say."

She still wasn't convinced. "I must go to him first. I will tell him what I have seen and ask if he will see your magic."

"Does your grandfather have anything that is made of metal? Like this hammer—or the buckles and rings from the bridle?"

Her forehead furrowed and she stared thoughtfully at the hammer head. "He has beads. And a knife that was given to him by the Boers."

"Does he always have the knife with him?"

"Yes. It shows that he is chief."

"Good. See if we can visit him at the village."

She arrived the next morning before sun-up with word that her grandfather would see me.

"When?" I asked.

"When? When we go."

"He did not say what time?"

Noluvo laughed. "Time is for the English. We will go when we can. If he is not there, we will wait."

At breakfast, I announced my plan to visit Noluvo's village, then sat silently while the Caywoods argued about whether it should be allowed. Robert finally insisted. Rebecca stood from the table in a huff and busied herself clearing dishes.

"And I'd like to take that big wooden platter you use when making bread," I said. "I'll bring it back, of course."

Rebecca spun from the counter and glared at me with such a dark look that for the first time, I think she began to believe this wasn't her daughter looking back at her. But she said nothing. Robert thought for a moment, then nodded.

As I left with Noluvo, Rebecca again stood on the porch, arms folded tightly. "Your father insists that I allow this," she called after us. "You know I do not approve. Please, be careful—and do not eat *anything*."

The village was a twenty-minute walk along the road that led to the coast. The rough circle of huts was open at one end, with the headman's lodge facing the opening. It was larger than the others and more oval, mud-plastered and whitewashed, with a low door covered by an animal skin. As we entered the open circle between huts, a young girl joined us, looking up at me with wide, curious eyes.

"My sister, Zodwa," Noluvo said. "You wanted someone to help."

I smiled and Zodwa turned shyly away, pressing tightly against her sister's side.

"Does she speak English?"

Noluvo shook her head. "I have told her what will happen. I hope she will not be frightened."

A wiry young man leaned against a long spear beside the chieftain's door, wearing the short skin skirt I'd seen on the hunters along the river. He looked me over with unveiled amusement, then pulled the door flap aside. I followed Noluvo into the dimly lit lodge.

Her grandfather sat on a high wooden seat at the far end of the hut, his sandaled feet on an ornately carved stool that looked like a snub-nosed crocodile with its tail curled around its side. The dark, withered man was wrapped to mid-chest in a dun-colored robe of homespun cloth. A leopard skin hung loosely about his shoulders, with two clawed paws nestled in his lap. One bone-thin hand gripped a dark wooden staff capped in hammered brass. His short gray curls were crowned with feathers stuck into a twisted cloth rope that circled his head. Around the edge of the room, the elders of the village sat in a silent ring, all holding long curved pipes and puffing blue smoke into the close air.

As Noluvo led me forward, I glanced quickly about the inside of the lodge. The mud plastering was pressed into a weave of interlaced sticks that formed the walls, woven together with no signs of being tied or fastened. There were few furnishings. Two low tables that held shallow wooden bowls. A collection of raw clay pots behind two of the seated men. No fireplace or mud oven.

Noluvo shuffled reverently up to her grandfather with arms pressed tight against her sides and eyes down. She spoke rapidly for several minutes while the old man studied me with inquisitive ebony eyes, tilting his head slightly to better see the bread tray and contraption I held in my hands. Around us, the elders sat in complete silence.

Noluvo took a step backward and whispered, "I have explained to grandfather that you have come to show him your good magic. What do you wish to say to him?"

"Tell him that in the place I learned this magic, I also learned how I can help with sickness in the village. If he can trust me, I would like to help make your people healthier."

Noluvo conveyed the message. The old man's eyes narrowed slightly, but otherwise his face remained expressionless. Then he nodded ever-so-slightly.

"Ask if we may borrow his knife," I whispered.

Noluvo passed along the request. The old man's face further creased into an uncertain frown, then the hand hidden beneath the robe groped for the knife and held it out to his granddaughter. Noluvo handed it to me. The foot-long blade was keenly sharpened steel with a steel guard and carved bone handle. It would be perfect.

When I learned we would be able to meet with the headman, I'd decided to try to get by without calling what I was doing magic. The superstition would take care of itself. I didn't need to feed it. It wouldn't make sense to try to explain electricity or electromagnetism, but that didn't mean I should present it as something other than what it was.

I said through Noluvo, "I would like to show you something I learned how to make in a place I have visited. It is called science. When we use science, we can do things that may help with the sickness in the Xhosa villages." As Noluvo translated, she said the word science just as I had hoped she would—as if it were a natural thing and not some mysterious power to be feared. Her grandfather again nodded.

I held up the Voltaic Pile, allowing him to inspect it. "This is made of clay and wood and metal that I gathered from places near the village. You could make one of these yourself. But see what it can do when put together in the right way?" I knelt and placed the stack on the floor, then had Noluvo and Zodwa kneel on either side, holding the tray between them. Behind me, I heard the tribesmen rise and move forward to form a half-circle, peering over our shoulders. I placed the chief's knife on the tray, connected the wire leads on the stack, and had the girls bring the tray down over the top of the magnet. With a leather-gloved hand, I lifted the horseshoe and moved it up under the edge of the tray closest to the chief. Instantly, the knife whirled with blade forward and scooted toward the headman. The old man didn't flinch, but behind me, the circle of men stumbled backward with an audible gasp. I moved the magnet slowly around beneath the tray, guiding the blade as I went. Zodwa's eyes had doubled in size and her hands trembled, but she maintained her grip on the tray. I lowered the horseshoe to the dirt floor.

"This is not magic," I said, rising with Noluvo and Zodwa. I took the knife from the tray and handed it back to the chief. "If I can show you. . . ." While he held the knife, I lifted the crude battery and slowly moved the shoe toward the knife until he began to feel the pull. His dark eyes fixed on the blade, then on the silk-wrapped horseshoe. I eased the magnet closer, struggling to keep it from snapping forward against the knife. The chief tightened his grip, unwilling to yield to the mysterious force. I pulled the magnet away, breaking the attraction, and again placed the stack on the floor.

"This is not magic," I repeated with Noluvo interpreting in her click-click language. "There are forces all about us in the world. If we learn to use them, they can do many good things for us."

The old man pointed with his knife at the magnet. "This can stop the sickness?"

I shook my head. "This just shows that there are many forces we do not understand. And nothing can stop all of the sickness. But I can help with some."

"I have seen white man's magic before," he said through his granddaughter. "It is not always good."

I nodded. "I would only do what I believe will be helpful."

The chief pointed with his knife at my left hand. While working with the gelding two mornings before, the horse had bolted suddenly and stripped a coarse hemp rope though my palm, leaving a wide, angry burn that Rebecca had wrapped with a wool strip.

"What has happened to your hand?" the chief asked.

I held it out, surprised at the question.

"I injured it training a horse."

"Remove the wrap," he instructed. I glanced over at Noluvo who had translated. She told me with her eyes that I'd better do as I was asked. I untied the knot across the back and unwrapped the bandage. The chief inspected the burn, his face wrinkling with amusement. "You could not heal this sickness?" he asked.

I felt my face flush. "It will heal with time," I murmured.

The headman spoke to Zodwa who hurried from the hut. I stood awkwardly facing the chief in silence until she returned. With her was an older woman with a clay bowl of gray paste. She took my hand, turned the burn upward, and smeared it with the salve. She knelt, left the bowl beside the crocodile stool, and hurried from the hut.

"This will heal your sickness," the old man said, his dark eyes smiling through his creases. "Our people have survived here since the beginning of time without the white man's magic."

I looked meekly down at my treated hand, which had already lost some of the burning, then at the chieftain's feet.

"I have also seen good magic from the white man," he continued through his granddaughter. "Noluvo believes you to be a wise woman. What wisdom do you bring us that can help the people?"

I looked up again into the headman's inquiring eyes, then gratefully over at Noluvo. "There is power in one thing that can help with much of the sickness that remains," I said contritely.

The ancient chief carefully inspected the blade of his knife, then tucked it back beneath his robe. "And what is that?"

I had learned the Xhosa word from Noluvo as we walked to the village. "*Amanzi*," I said. "Water."

Emme

Before meeting with Lena on Sunday I completed another sketch, this one of Samantha diving to keep a ball from entering the goal. Jennifer had shown me how to insert a small object she called a "drive" into the side of the computer. In it were pictures of all of the students who attended the school. A section was dedicated to sport and displayed members of the soccer team—one picture of the team as a whole, and many of the girls playing at their positions. I was especially taken with one of Samantha stretched out in midair, her arms straining for the ball. My sketch, I thought, added even greater energy to her movement.

At Lena's home, I was relieved to find that none of the other friends were there. I was not feeling in a mood to tolerate Ryan's cynicism and, though Julian tried so hard to support me when I was in Ally's body, I could feel that he missed her. Lena appeared to like us both equally and took great joy in her new conviction that she now had two quite different friends.

Lena's *lita* had baked what she called *polvorosas*, a small biscuit with a cross cut into its rounded top. It tasted like Mother's shortbread. She insisted that we each eat at least three before she was willing to release us from her hovering watch. They were delicious. I ate twice that many which pleased her. She put what were left in a small sack of brown paper and pushed the rolled top into my hand. "You take these to your mother," she insisted and waved us away to do whatever Lena had planned for our afternoon.

"Before we begin . . . ," I said, spreading my sketchbook open on Lena's dining table to the new drawing.

"Oh, Emme," she murmured, now willing to call me by my true name when we were alone. "This is so *amazing*! Can I put this up in the case with the one of me?"

171

"Of course. But I would like it to go to Samantha when we have completed our effort to support her. And she should not pay."

"For sure! And this one took you about the same amount of time?"

"Less, I should think. I was able to look at the picture on the school's drive."

"I think *everyone's* going to want one. And their families can all afford it—except maybe Maria's. She lives with her mom, and I don't think they have a lot of money. But she said her grandparents were helping her with money for the trip."

"I'll do one of her anyway, if she wishes. And she should not pay. Since I cannot play as Ally does, this is the least I can do. I *do* pray she is back when you travel to England. It will make everything so much simpler."

"You don't want to see the England of 2020?"

I shuddered involuntarily. "I am not at all certain my mind could withstand it."

Lena continued to study the sketch. "We haven't figured out what causes this yet and maybe never will. But if Julian's right—that this is going to happen every twenty-eight days—Ally will get back about a week before the trip." She looked up with a broad grin. "Maybe that's why you switch. So you can do these pictures, and she can be here to play."

"A very unlikely reason for all this changing about."

Lena pushed the sketchpad aside and opened her computer. "If there's a better reason, maybe we can begin to find it today. We're going to forget for now that you were a Grenfell and go back and look at when you married Charles Pearce. I want to trace your ancestry up to as close to now as we can. Maybe there's someone out there right now who needs to know about Grenfell Hall."

I pulled a chair up beside her. "This all makes me most uneasy. Looking back on the part of my life that has not yet happened. What if we find great tragedy?"

She stopped her striking at the keys and stared thoughtfully at the screen. "Yeah. I can understand that. Well, I'll do the checking and won't tell you what I find unless I need your help. And we'll only look at what follows your family line." She turned the screen so that only she could see it and poked away for a few moments.

"Okay," she said finally. "Here we have a chart that shows the children of Emmeline Caywood and Charles Pearce. Do you want to know anything about your kids?"

This was all becoming too frightening. "Must we do this?" I pleaded.

She seemed to collapse over the computer. "No. We don't have to do it. And I guess if I were you, there's some stuff I might not want to know. But I think this could help us figure out why you're here."

"Then proceed. Just tell me only what you must."

She peered at the screen, her face darkening to the point that I felt I must ask. "Do you see great unhappiness? Do I live without children?"

She shook her head and brightened. "You have a daughter you name Melissa." She looked over and smiled. "Remember that, or you'll mess this all up. Now—let me follow this Melissa." She typed for another moment, then stretched back, brows arched and mouth upturned into a satisfied bow. "And here's a chart someone did that shows Melissa married a Franklin Burton of Lime House in London. And—let me see—it has five generations of descendants from Melissa Pearce and Franklin Burton. *Wow.* This is so cool!" She opened a notepad beside the computer and spoke as she wrote on the pad.

"Son Edward Burton married Ruth Harmon. Their daughter, Lydia Burton, married James Yates. This was in 1911, so we're into the last century. Daughter Margaret Yates married John Bailey in Boston, Massachusetts. So you have ancestors who came over here. Am I telling you too much?"

I shook my head numbly, struggling to follow the chain of marriages and name changes.

"Okay. Son Nathaniel Bailey married Katherine Nettleton—still in Boston. Their daughter Hannah married Tyler Howard in Kansas City, Missouri, in 1978. That's the end of this chart." She looked over at me questioningly. "What do you think?"

"I'm sure I do not know what to think. This all seems so . . . so impossible! To know who comes after me for five or six generations. Who could know such information?"

Lena shrugged dismissively. "Oh, there are people who spend all their time going though old records and putting this all together. Someone who's one of your descendants through Melissa looked this all up. In fact, it tells us on this page who put it together. Want to know?"

"The name will mean nothing to me."

"It could. There's also an email contact."

This suddenly became far too threatening. "Oh, I couldn't possibly."

"I'll bet people contact her all the time. This couple that married in '78 would be—let's see—probably in their sixties. So she might be one of their kids. Different name, so I'd guess she's married."

"What is the name?"

"Sarah Olsen."

"Does it have a city address for her?"

"No. Just the email."

"What would we ask of her?"

"Maybe what children this Hannah and Tyler had. Where they live. We don't need to say why we want to know. But we know some of your descendants ended up in the US—and in the Midwest. Maybe that has something to do with why you're here."

If I knew why I was here, could I stop the changes, I wondered? Nothing we had thought of earlier had given us an explanation. As Ryan liked to say, "What do you gotta lose?"

I agreed. "Write down the address. We will send her a message."

Lena glanced back at the screen. "This has an active link. I just need to click on it. What do you want to say?"

I could not think of a thing. "You decide. You have completed the search."

Lena moved the mouse to the link and clicked. "How about this?" She typed as she spoke.

"Hi, Sarah. My name is Ally. I found the chart you submitted on MyTree and wondered if you could tell me more about Hannah and Tyler Howard? Did they have children? If they did and you know who they are and where they live, are you willing to share the information? I'm working on a family tree that might connect. Thanks!"

She looked up and said again, "What do you think?"

I shrugged. "This seems quite harmless."

Lena read it again silently, arched her brows, and decisively clicked her mouse. "Well, let's see what we learn from this."

When we met at the Icehouse the next Friday, Lena had not heard back from Sarah Olsen. The response to my drawings had been what she had expected. We already had eight orders. I had completed five during the week, using the pictures on Ally's school drive.

"These are *terrific*," Julian said, looking over at me as if having Emmeline instead of Ally wasn't so bad after all. "You've been talking about going to vet school. Maybe you should think about art . . .. " He suddenly realized who he was talking to and stopped abruptly. "Anyway," he mumbled, "these are great."

Lena smirked at Ryan. "That's a hundred bucks you owe the fund. I'll trim these and take them to Hannah's mom on Monday. And I'll get the word to these girls that they can pay and pick them up. Fifteen hundred dollars, right here, Al. Eighteen with mine. You've got three still to do. I'll bet by the end of the day Monday when these get shown around, we'll have another five. Want to bet me again, smartass?"

Ryan sniffed from his stretched position across one corner of the booth.

"I'll expect to see your money in the fund Monday afternoon," she said.

I slid the sketchbook over toward Lena. "Jennifer bought another pad for me. I can work on the others while you get these displayed."

Julian intercepted the book and opened it to one of the sketches. "What does your mom think of all this? Your sudden ability to draw like a pro?"

"She remains confused but tries to be very understanding. I believe my loss of interest in riding troubles her more than my new-found talents. She seems to have accepted Dr. Westover's explanation."

Julian chuckled. "And what has that been?"

"He believes that whatever led to this change in the first place has caused me to become what he calls a savant. I take that to mean someone with a particular gift in a special area."

Julian's chuckle spread into a cynical laugh. "And at regular intervals, you lose your savantness and go back to normal?"

"He does say that he has not seen or read about anything similar."

"I'll bet he's writing a paper about you," Ryan sneered. "For some psycho journal."

Julian's comment had prompted him to poke again at his cell. "You know, if this cycle thing is right—if you and Ally switch every twenty-eight days—you're due for another change on the twenty-fifth." He grinned slyly. "You need to get your pictures done before you're no longer a savant. And . . . ," he swiped his thumb upward, ". . . you're going to change again a couple of days before Christmas. You'll be here and Ally there. Bummer for both of you."

Lena's phone buzzed that she had a new email. She tapped in her code. I was fretting over Julian's announcement, hoping he was correct about a switch on the twenty-fifth, but praying it would be the last, when she uttered a loud *"Whoa!"* Her eyes gleamed as if she had just learned she was winner of some prestigious prize.

"This might tell us a lot," she said cryptically, then paused for effect, her eyes darting to each of us. "Sarah Olsen's finally getting back to us. She said the request came to an email connected to her MyTree account she doesn't check that often. But she's glad to help. Hannah and Tyler had two children. A son and a daughter. She's the daughter and still lives in Kansas City." She paused again dramatically. "The son was an older brother named Bill who she says passed away a few months ago. And get this! He lived in Texarkana."

Ryan's arms slid off the back of the booth and he hunched forward. "Bill?" he repeated. "Bill who?"

Julian glanced over his shoulder toward the pub's kitchen. "Bill Howard," he said quietly. "Sam's dad."

Ally

I took the wagon to the Xhosa village with a large kettle strapped in the bed and Robert's magnifying glass in my pants pocket. Noluvo's father Cebo had been assigned by the headman to help me. Both were waiting in the center of the village when I reined Maisy up in front of Cebo's hut. He helped me hoist the iron kettle, so big I couldn't reach around it, down to the ground.

"The first thing we need to do," I told them, "is clean up the water you drink until we can dig a well here in the village. Did you get some water from the river?"

Noluvo nodded, holding up a jug she'd filled from the pool where the villagers washed, drew drinking water, and watered their animals. She'd moved a crude wooden table from her hut into the sun-brightened circle. We poured about a pint from the jug into a shallow bowl and I bent over it with the magnifying glass. As I'd guessed, the water teemed with wriggling creatures that looked like tiny translucent birds with a huge dark eye and two feelers where the beak should be. I beckoned for them to have a look.

Noluvo had seen the hand lens at the house. Robert liked to use it to light twists of dry grass into flame when burning piles of cleared brush. He had also shown the maid that when she held it over an object, it made it look many times its normal size. But when Cebo peered through it at the magnified bugs, he jumped back, crouching to stare sideways at the round lens. Noluvo placed a reassuring hand on her father's arm, explaining in Xhosa that the curved glass was nothing to be afraid of. It just made things look bigger.

"These bugs you see are water fleas," I explained. "They live in the water you drink and carry tiny eggs. When you drink the water, it leaves these eggs inside your body. They grow there and turn into the worms you get in your legs—the ones you pull out by twisting them about a small stick." Half the village had gathered about the table, craning to see what we were doing with the clay bowl and strange object Cebo now turned suspiciously in his hand. I pointed to a woman with the round, festering sores on her ankles.

"We must do three things to stop the worms. When you bring water to drink or to wash food that is not going to be cooked, you must pour the water first into this kettle through your best woven cloth." I emptied the bowl on the ground, spread a square of cotton cloth over the container, and again filled it from the jug.

"Tell your father to look at the water with the lens," I instructed. "Then look at the cloth." Noluvo explained and the man bent over the bowl, peered first through the lens, then around it, then back through the lens. Noluvo spoke again and he shifted his examination to the cloth. He nodded, muttered something in Xhosa, and pointed at the stains on the filter.

"He sees that the water fleas are on the cloth," his daughter said. "We can do this to keep the worms out of the water."

"Yes. But that will not be enough. There are other tiny bugs in the water, too small to see with the glass and too small to be stopped by the cloth. They must also be killed. The only way to do that is to boil all the water you drink. Pour the water through the cloth into this big kettle. Then put it over a fire until it bubbles and rolls. You must let it boil for . . . for as long as it will take to walk around the outside of the village. Do you understand?"

Noluvo nodded and repeated the instructions to Cebo, gesturing as she showed him how to make the filter and set the kettle over a fire. Her fingers rolled in circles as she described the boil. She then swept an arm in a full arc, telling him how long the water needed to bubble. When through with her pantomime, she turned and looked at me expectantly.

"Everything you eat that is not cooked must be washed with this water," I insisted. "Not in the kettle. Scoop water from the kettle into another bowl and wash the food in that water. Then throw the water away. Never put it back into the kettle." Noluvo translated and Cebo looked dubious, but agreed.

"If we put the river water through the cloth and boil it over the fire, why do we need a well?" Noluvo asked.

"Because drinking and washing food is only part of what you do with water. You wash your clothes and yourselves. When you use the river water, the tiny bugs get on your skin and clothes and can make you sick."

"The bugs will not be in the water from a well?"

"Not if you keep it clean. The well should be here—in the center of the village. Then when you . . . ." I struggled for a word she would understand. "When you do what the Caywoods do in the little hut behind the house . . ." I watched her face to see if she understood and saw recognition in her eyes.

"*Thabatha i-shit*," she said.

I couldn't hide a smile. Ah—a little English influence on the Xhosa language! Some of the villagers around us laughed.

"Yes. When you do that, it must be far from the well. If it gets in the well, it adds to the sickness. Nothing must ever be put into the well."

The villagers practiced what some of the books I'd read called "open defecation." I'd toyed with the idea of trying to get them to build outhouses. But it was more than I wanted to take on at one time. And the village was on a low hill to keep rains from flooding the huts. If the well was in the center of the village and far enough from their poop zones, they wouldn't get runoff into the well water.

"That is two things," Noluvo said. "What is three?"

I held up a bar of the Caywood's soap. "Rebecca has shown you how to make this. When you wash yourselves and your clothes, you must use soap. If there are other tiny bugs in the water, the soap will kill many of them."

"The people wash now in the river."

"Yes. And as long as they do, there will be sickness. We must dig a well and use the water from the well to wash. People and clothes."

"Who will dig this well?"

I looked around at the villagers. "You will. I will get one of the English to show you how."

"The English do not come to the village."

"I'll have to change that," I said, and left Noluvo and Cebo to filter and boil water while I went to convince Angus Kinkade to show the Xhosa how to dig a well.

Angus lived on the river a mile above the new mill. As other immigrants like the Pickerings had abandoned farming and returned to their former trades, the enterprising Scot had bought up their farms and now rivaled the Bradshaws in landholdings. He employed most of two Xhosa villages as farm workers, cultivating hundreds of acres of wheat and barley. Angus was the one man in the Bathurst colony who appreciated my riding outfit, and his farm had become a favorite place to take Prince George for a good gallop.

Angus had married a Boer woman named Gisela who was as tall and sturdy as her husband was small and wiry. She was known around Bathurst as a moody, private woman who rarely came into the village and never attended church, which automatically made her suspect. She sniffed at the fancy dresses the English women strutted about in on Sundays and whenever they could find other excuses to pretend they were back in the mother country. That may be why I liked the woman.

She came to the door of their cottage when she heard me ride up, wiping bread dough from her hands onto a blue and white checked apron.

"It's good to see ya ridin' again," she called out in her Scottish Boer English. "We've been missin' ya this past month."

I swung down and let the big woman give me a warm hug. "I haven't had much chance to ride. Mother objects, and it takes

Father a few weeks to get her to allow it again."

"It does me good to see a woman ride like she isn't sittin' on a park bench," she said with a laugh. "Come in and have a cup'a. I could use a little company."

"I don't have a lot of time. Maybe I can ride out again tomorrow when things aren't quite so busy. I came to see Angus. Is he here?"

"Clearing a new field with the blacks," she said, nodding toward a wagon track that led away from the river. "I keep tellin' him we have as much as we can manage, but there's never too much for the man."

I couldn't resist a glance beyond her at the simple adobe cottage with its rough thatched roof. She seemed to read my mind.

"Oh, it's not that he dreams of bein' a rich man like Bradshaw. We have all we need to live a comfortable life. He thinks he needs to give work to every native in the territory. We have 'em comin' now from three villages."

"That's good of him," I said. "It's what Father thinks all the farmers should be doing."

"Aye. Yer father and Angus is about the only two don't see them still as heathen slaves."

"Well, I'll go see if I can find Angus and come back to see you tomorrow."

She laughed, leaned back, and stared at me with hands on her hips as I swung back up onto Prince. "Sometimes, Emmeline, you do na' seem at all like the same girl."

Angus had his pair of bay Shire draft horses chained to a stubborn stump when I rode up. He left the pair in the hands of two young tribesmen and came over to greet me.

"Come to give me a hand, have ya, lassie?" he joked as I swung down from Prince.

"Come to see if you can give *me* one."

"Ah. And what could I be doin' fer ya?"

"Do you remember our house girl, Noluvo?"

"Ah, yes. A bright young thing, as I recall."

"I would like you to help the men in her village dig a well."

Angus chuckled, scooping the flat cap from his head and mopping his forehead with the back of a sleeve. "They won't hear of it, lassie. I've been trying with these up here ta get them to dig one for goin' on a year now. They see no reason for it."

"I've convinced Noluvo's people to dig one."

"Well, have ya now? And how did ya do that?"

I grinned. "Used a little magic. And showed them the water fleas in the river water they drink. I told them I could help cut down on the sickness in the village."

He nodded, impressed. "Two of these villages have a spring. Don't have nearly the sickness of the one I just started givin' work to. Perhaps you can be showing this new one some of your magic."

"If this works with Noluvo's village, they can tell the others. But I need a well."

Angus shrugged. "You know I do what I can to help the native people. I'll show them how. But it's the wrong time o' year. We need to be diggin' during the dry."

"When I talked to you before, you said the Bathurst well couldn't keep up with a heavy draw. Once we get down to water, can't we drain it fast enough to take it down another yard until the dry season comes? Then we could go deeper."

Angus cocked his head with an amused smile. "You do think about the daftest things for a lass. But aye, we could get it deep enough to give them water 'til the dry begins if we have a week without rain. I do na' like to be diggin' when it's rainin' every day."

"If we have good days, when can you start?"

"Ah, you are a sassy one! I need this week to get this field cleared. If next Monday's dry, meet me at the village as soon as it's light."

I couldn't resist giving the little man an enthusiastic hug. He smelled of dirt and sweat.

"And I *do* like a sassy lass," he said as I released him.

On the river road as I neared the edge of the Kinkade farmland, a rider approached at a loping gallop, slowing to a trot as he saw me. He was dressed in fancy English riding gear with high leather boots, a tailed riding jacket, and a ridiculous Abe Lincoln top hat. He reined a beautiful sorrel mare up beside me and looked me over critically.

"Your mother said I might find you up here," he said without introduction. "And she gave me warning that I would find you in this outfit."

Someone Emme knew, I realized. I better handle this carefully.

"A much more comfortable way to ride than in a dress," I said.

"You appear to have changed your mind about the safety of having both feet on the ground."

I had kept Prince moving forward at a relaxed trot and the rider had fallen in beside me. "When coming this distance, I much prefer to come by horseback," I said, trying to speak as Emme might.

That seemed to puzzle him, and I realized he knew only the non-riding Emmeline. After a moment he said, "I trust you have had time to consider my desire to keep you here—to persuade you not to return to Suffolk, but to make a permanent home in the colonies."

Whoa! This was suddenly much more serious than I was ready for—and a conversation Emme needed to be having with this guy. Not Ally Wallis. Then I remembered Lena's search on MyTree and her finding Emme married to a Charles Pearce of Cambridge. There was a chance that *this* was Charles, but my gut said *No way!* Maybe one of my reasons for being here was to have the *huevos* to tell this guy to take a hike.

"Have you discussed this with your mother?" he pressed, riding slightly ahead so he could look back at my face.

"And my father," I said, guessing Robert wouldn't favor Mr.

Top Hat. "I'm still planning to go back to England before I settle down. Probably to Cambridge."

He dropped back to again ride beside me. "You will not do better for yourself than becoming a Bradshaw," he insisted. "And could certainly do much worse."

Ah! This was a Bradshaw. The mill people. "I'm much more interested in making sure I find the right partner," I said. "And settling in Bathurst isn't my idea of a good time." I glanced over and saw anger, confusion, and frustration.

"What has become of your speech? And why do you feel compelled to ride in these most unbecoming clothes? Are you suffering from another episode, Emme?"

"I'm suffering only from this slow pace," I said. "Come on. I'll race you back to the house." I nudged Prince into a full gallop and leaned forward over his neck, letting him know I wanted to run. I heard the Bradshaw man spur his mare after me. Glancing back, I could see him gripping his top hat and leaning over his mount, his face grim and resolved. But his mare was no match for the stallion.

Emme

We had all been so stunned by the Bill Howard revelation that we left the booth at the Icehouse without further conversation. I had ridden with Lena and we stopped as we left to allow her to ask Samantha if she had an aunt in Kansas City.

"Yeah. Aunt Sarah. My dad's sister. She's great. Been trying to help Mom a lot. How do you know about Sarah?"

"I remember your mother mentioning her once," Lena lied. "We thought she might be interested in helping with this drive we've got going to get everyone to England."

Sam reddened. "She's already sending everything she can to help with treatments. If I *can* go, she'll probably be coming down to spend the week with Mom. I wouldn't want to ask her for anything more."

"Right," Lena said. "I get that. Just thought I'd ask."

I found that I could not take my eyes from Samantha's face. When I had sketched her, stretched in midair with such an intense look, I had thought fleetingly that there was something familiar about her. The eyes, mouth, and chin in particular. As I studied her before leaving the pub, I could see the resemblance. She had Father's strong jaw and intense blue eyes—features I had also drawn into the portrait I had done of myself.

Samantha looked at me quizzically. "You feeling okay, Al?"

"Yes," I said. "I was just thinking how good that drawing in the case is of you."

"I love it," she said, the flush deepening on her cheeks.

By the time we met again Tuesday, Julian had a new theory. "We've been trying to figure out why this switching's been going on and suddenly discover a connection to Samantha. I think that has to be part of it. Maybe the main reason. We've got to get Sam to England to do something connected to Grenfell Hall."

"Make a claim on it," Lena suggested. She had, it appeared, been having the same thoughts.

Julian nodded. "Maybe. But there are a couple of major hurdles. First, she'd have to show that the Caywoods and the Grenfells were the same people. That she's descended from the family that left Grenfell Hall just before it was confiscated by the king."

"Man!," Ryan snickered, stretching out in his classic Icehouse pose. "Confiscated! We're moving into some pretty heavy vocab here!"

"Give it a rest," Lena muttered. "If you can't follow the conversation, don't say anything."

"Just saying," Ryan grumbled.

"How about 'seized' then?" Julian said. "We'd have to find something that showed the Caywoods of Bathurst were the Grenfells of Ipswich. Then, that Sam is heir to the estate, if she is. It seems pretty unlikely that after six or seven generations, however many there've been, Sam's the rightful heir."

Lena disagreed. "Given a little time, I think we can run that through. And I'm willing to bet she is. That would explain why Emme's here and why we discovered the link."

Ryan couldn't stay out of the conversation. "So, suppose you're right. That Sam's the whatever great-granddaughter of Emmeline Grenfell. Why didn't Emme switch with Samantha instead of Ally?"

The question made enough sense that we all sat for a moment, turning it over in our heads. Julian tried his answer first. "Sam's got a lot going on in her life. Maybe she wouldn't be able to handle all this switching back and forth. And Sam's not exactly the kind of girl to want to get herself involved in something like this. Plus, can you see Emme showing up here and having Sam's mom to take care of right off the bat?"

"And maybe Emme's being here isn't all there is to it," Lena offered. "Ally's by far the most assertive of us. I can see that she might have some role in this too."

I had come up with a possibility of my own. "It is also possible," I suggested, "that I needed this group of friends. You have been the ones who have made these discoveries. Had I been here as Samantha, and she in Bathurst in my stead, would you have been this helpful to me?"

The guilt showed in Lena's eyes. "Probably not. We've all known Sam was having a pretty tough time and haven't really done a lot to help her. It's pretty much been her and her mom."

"Which raises the question," Ryan interjected, deciding to be more helpful now that I was suggesting these friends might be the reason Ally was chosen. "When do we bring Sam into this?"

Julian wanted to be cautious. "I say we keep her out until Lena can trace the ancestry. You were an only child," he said to me, "so maybe that's the way the line goes, all the way down. Sam's dad was the oldest. What we know looks good."

I saw no reason to tell them I had lost a brother and that, had he lived, he would have been heir, even though younger. The entire conjecture, that I had somehow switched with Ally Wallis to let a girl who was not even a close friend know that she may be heir to Grenfell Hall, was almost more than I could contemplate. I shook my head, bewildered. "Even if you are correct, I cannot fathom what *my* purpose is for being here. Let Sam know, and be done with it? What more am I to do?"

Julian's mind was still spinning. "Where do you think your father is with all this switching? Does he accept it in any way?"

"He and my mother are so confused. They fear I have lost my mind. But Father is much more willing to listen than Mother. She worries that I am an embarrassment to the family. And she is very anxious that I marry properly."

Julian chuckled. "Sounds like one of the novels we're reading. The ones you know so much better than we do. But maybe the job you have now, the one that's going to be critical to this for Sam, is to talk to your father about how you could prove you were owners of Grenfell Hall. Does he still have a title somewhere? Papers that showed ownership? And if they exist, how do we know where to get to them two centuries later?"

"And," Ryan said, starting to see new possibilities in his Master Architect theory, "how can we prove, this far in the future, that the Caywoods of Bathurst were the Grenfells of Ipswich?"

"May be tougher," Julian admitted. "Ownership of the estate might be filed in records that still exist, unless the Crown purged them. But proving the Caywoods were the Grenfells when the family was trying to stay off the radar? That might be tough."

"Unless," Ryan mused, sliding off the back of the booth seat and leaning over the table, "Emme's dad knew he needed to write something about that whole escape thing and put it somewhere where it could be found two hundred years later. Like knowing that there was a key that could be used about five stages farther into the game—to uncover a hidden power or secret." He looked at me with a satisfied smile. "Next time you switch, you've got some convincing to do."

Lena spent the next afternoon at her computer with me seated beside her, marveling at how it allowed her to explore a past that was yet to happen in my family.

"There's a Suffolk Record Office," she mumbled, tapping away at the keys as the screen moved from one picture to another. "And under that, a 'County Archives.'" A moment later she pointed at an entry. "Look here under 'Property History.' There's a link to 'Owners and Occupiers' records, but it says they start in 1844. Too late for you."

She clicked on a heading that stated, "Sources of information prior to 1844," leaned into the screen, and read aloud. "Ownership information prior to 1844 can be very difficult to find. In the cases of some estates, manor records were kept in book form that recorded ownership, transfers, and conveyances." She turned to me. "Would you say Grenfell Hall was a manor?"

"I should think so."

"Do you remember a manor record?"

"No. But I would not have known of such a thing. Father kept those records very much to himself."

"You don't remember anything like that being taken with you to Africa?"

"No. But again, I would not have known."

"Then you have *three* jobs when you switch again. Talk to your father about writing a letter that shows the Caywoods were the Grenfells, figure out where to put that letter so we can find it, and ask if there's a manor record for Grenfell Hall. You've been wondering what your role is in all of this. Get those three things done and get back here with the answers. I can't think of anything that's more important."

"Convince Father to write a letter that does not yet exist, to permit you to discover it now," I repeated.

Lena smiled broadly. "Yup. "If you can get that done, it's already around here somewhere. We just need to know where to look."

Ally

To say Rebecca was mad as a Texas diamondback was an understatement. My grandpa, Mom's dad, would have described her as "spittin' flames and starin' daggers.' I remember reading in a book Mrs. Bayless had us read about a woman who was "seething" and thought what a great word that was. *Seething*! It describes someone who's beyond shouting mad and is just plain squint-eyed, red-faced boiling over. That was Rebecca.

"I don't know how I can possibly show my face in public again after what you have done to Edward," she hissed, cornering me in the hallway when I returned from Noluvo's village the day after my ride to Kinkade's. "It is one thing to reject his proposal, which will most certainly be the best you shall ever receive. But to humiliate him as a gentleman and horseman was unconscionable."

Unconscionable. Another great word. I thought momentarily of telling her that I had never seen this Edward before he rode up to me yesterday. But I could see the "don't mess with me" sign flashing in her eyes and decided to be contrite and do what I could to further Emme's future.

"I don't think he proposed, directly," I said. "And I didn't do anything to embarrass the man. I told him I thought he could do better and that I planned to return to England before I get married. Then I rode home."

"You were *seen*, Emmeline! Esther Robbins was in the pasture with her husband and you . . . ." She stammered for the right words. ". . . you passed them in your father's clothing, riding at a full gallop, with Edward trying desperately to stay with you. He finally gave up and turned aside."

I had to stifle a laugh, thinking of one of the village women watching in awe as Mr. Top Hat tried to chase me down. "I invited him to follow. He just couldn't keep up. That mare is no match for Prince."

"*Couldn't!*" she sputtered. "*Couldn't*! What manner of speech is that? You are speaking like a common sailor. And Edward is the only serious match for you in the colonies."

"Yes. In the colonies. Robert thinks I should go back to England anyway."

"And *please* stop referring to your father as Robert. *He*, at least, deserves your respect. I fear we have no choice now but to send you off. Your father and I are unable to return because of his questionable judgment. And now you must, because you exhibit the same."

It was the first time I'd heard her criticize her husband. I suddenly felt very out of place and very ashamed. "I'm sorry," I said more gently. "But I am not meant to marry Edward Bradshaw." She seemed to collapse into herself and hurried from the room, leaving me standing alone in the hallway, dressed in Robert's muddy clothes, and wondering what the hell I was doing in Africa as Emmeline Caywood.

I spent most of the next week in Noluvo's village, helping with the well, conditioning the Xhosa to drink only filtered and boiled water, and trying to think of ways to add to my cures. I'd read in one of Dad's books on natural remedies for parasitic diseases that cannabis kills internal worms in both people and animals. Some of the earliest uses were in India and came to Europe with Dutch sailors. If the Dutch had shipped zinc into Port Kowie, I wondered if they might have slipped some Indian weed on board too. Angus turned out to be the right man to ask.

He had helped the villagers dig the first few feet of well, given them careful instruction about how to avoid cave-ins and about testing the sides after a rain, then stopped by twice a day to check on progress. The second afternoon, I caught him just as he was climbing onto one of his Shires to start back to his farm.

"Angus, do you know what Indian hemp is?"

He had grasped a handful of the horse's thick mane and was about to take a jump swing up onto its broad back. The question caused him to slip backward, staying upright only because of his grip on the mane. He looked over his shoulder at me with a mischievous grin.

"Well, lassie! You've changed yerself even more than I'd been thinkin'! And what are you wantin' to do with Indian hemp? Make a rope for well diggin', I suppose?"

"I've read . . .," I began, then corrected myself. "I've been told that the smoke and juice from Indian hemp can help kill the worms people get inside."

He stepped back from the horse. "You don't say!" His look was now more curious than teasing.

"With all the pipe smoking these people do, I thought it would be worth a try. And if I can find some, I can make tea from the plants to give to the children."

"T'would make them happier, even if it doesn'a kill the worms," Angus chuckled. "And yes. I know where there is some. There's some patches planted by the sailors on both sides of the river above the port. You've got yer horse there. If ya want to take the time, I'll ride with ya and show ya one."

"Are the patches the same?"

"Nay. The first one was planted years ago and is now pretty well left alone. Doesn'a do what the sailors like from it. The newer patch? Now, that one can turn a leopard into a lap cat, if you get my meanin'"

From what I'd read, the most important healing ingredient in hemp was called CBD. There was more of it in varieties that produced less THC, the chemical that makes you high. Some of both was good. But the less of the mind-blowing stuff, the better the medicinal value. I turned to my own horse. "Yes. I'd love to have you show me. Let's go to the old patch."

We rode almost to Port Kowie before he turned from the wagon road up into the trees along a small stream. Two hundred yards from the road, a large natural clearing had been planted with what I recognized as a gray-leafed variety of hemp, some as tall as my shoulder on horseback. The towering stalks were in heavy leaf and covered with buds.

"Whoa!" I muttered. "Does anyone own this?"

"Nay," he laughed. "I come myself sometimes when I'm feelin' the need for a remedy—though I'm inclined toward the other patch. The sailors all know it's here when they make port, but prefer the other one too. Most people have forgot about this one. Take what you want. I'm anxious myself to see if this thing yer tryin' works. But only come in the daylight, mind ya. This is leopard country."

I filled the pouch on the saddle with buds, then stripped off Robert's shirt and tied the arms at the cuffs, making two long sacks. Angus looked me over in my white chemise and laughed until I thought he would fall from the horse.

"You *are* a right one, lass," he sputtered. "Where were you when I was a courtin'?

"I'm completely covered," I defended. "And I want to take enough back to make a difference."

"You're makin' a much greater difference here than ya could possibly know," he said, and began to strip buds from the plants to help fill my shirt.

I used the top of Robert's tack room as a drying rack, covering the roof with leaves and buds. Rebecca sometimes watched from the kitchen window but had decided I was beyond salvation and should best be left alone until I could be shipped back to England. The weather remained dry and hot through the week. I decided after five days that my first crop was ready.

Just before sun-up on a Saturday morning, I saddled Prince and rode again into Port Kowie, taking the disassembled Voltaic Pile with me. I'd talked a few shillings out of Robert who seemed to be more sympathetic to my story every day and was visibly pleased that I had stood my ground with Edward Bradshaw. I wanted to buy a dozen small leather pouches that I could fill with pot for the Xhosa men. And I'd seen a blank journal in the dry goods shop. It was time to start keeping a daily record of what was going on—the only way I could think of to help Emme keep up with all the changes. If we switched again, and I was pretty certain we would, I had friends in Texarkana who could fill me in on the past month. Emmeline had no one who truly believed. I needed to leave her detailed notes.

As I expected, the rugged metalsmith was already at his forge when I reached the coast. He pounded away at an orange-hot piece of iron he was fitting to the front of a plow share, dipping it sizzling into a cooling barrel as I dismounted.

"How's the gelding doin'?" he called over the low roar of his furnace.

"Much better," I shouted back.

"Did me disks do the job for ya?"

"Perfect. If you have a minute, I'll show you why I wanted them."

"Got whatever time ya need, Emme. I been waitin' for you to come show me."

I cleared a space on his work table, leaving a pair of steel tongs near one end of the scarred wooden top. A set of felt disks were wrapped in saltwater-soaked cloth in my saddlebag and I laid them out with the zinc and copper coins. The massive man, bare-chested except for a seared leather apron, bent over me like a curious child while I assembled the battery.

"These metals bein' touchin' each other has some'ut to do with this, don'it now, Emme," he guessed.

"I'm impressed. Why do you say that?"

He leaned closer to the stack as I added disks. "I been workin' with metals me whole life and I've seen how they can do strange and wondrous things. Some will mix well with others, while others just don't wish to have a thing to do with each other. Or I'll be buffin' a piece of iron with some'ut and it will suddenly start drawin' itself to other iron about it. There's some'ut in the metals I don't understand."

This is a man, I thought, *who given the right education and a little opportunity, could have discovered what I'm about to show him*. I finished assembling the stack and wired one lead to the small, silk-wrapped horseshoe. He cocked his head and ducked sideways to examine the shoe.

"Why ya have the cloth between the wire and the shoe?" I had the sense that he had a suspicion but wasn't sure how to express it.

"Have you heard of electricity?"

"I've hear'd of it. Been told it's what our Alice feels when I walk across the rug to her in my fresh wool socks and peck her on the cheek. Makes her jump like a scared rabbit! And me at the same time."

"Yes. That's the stuff. It's a kind of energy . . . like sunlight. And there are other ways to make it. One is to put these two metals together with felt disks between them." I knew I was inviting the question, and he didn't disappoint me.

"What do the disks do?"

I shook my head. "It's more than I can explain. And a lot of it, I don't understand. The felt needs to be soaked in saltwater. It's called an electrolyte. Let's just say it helps move the electricity though the pile. The more of these pairs we put in the stack, the more electricity this thing makes. It then moves through the wires from one end to the other, just like water through a pipe." I traced the route with my finger. "When it goes around these loops, it makes the horseshoe become like that piece of iron you polish. It turns it into a magnet. But only while the wires are connected all the way around." Jacob Pickering's eyes followed my finger around the circuit.

"Now watch." I touched the second lead to the coil. The tongs jumped forward to snap against the horseshoe.

Rather than starting backward, Pickering slapped both of his huge hands on the tabletop and roared with joy.

"If I touch me tongs, will I feel the electricity?"

"I don't think so," I guessed, separating the lead. "But my guess is that if you hold the bare end of the shoe and touch this wire, you will."

His eyes glowed and he licked at his lower lip, then reached for both, quickly releasing the lead wire and shouting again in delight.

"So, this was your magic, Emme." His smile divided his beard like a swath from the plow he was making. "How did you know to make such a thing?"

"I can't begin to explain that either. But I promised to show you and return your zinc and wire. Here they are."

"Nay," he protested. "This is yours to keep. I'll make one meself, if you can give me some help."

"I think you know what you need to know. It's pretty much what you see here."

He leaned over the stack again, muttering to himself as he reviewed the order in the pile. "I'll make one up. If it doesn'a work, you can tell me when you come ta town again where I went wrong. Does the wrappin' need to be silk?"

"Other cloth might work. But I know silk does."

"I think Alice has a bit."

"Let me know if she doesn't. I'll bring you some."

I held out my hand, he took it this time in his calloused paw without hesitation, and said, "Deal!" and he roared again with laughter.

I bought what I needed and spent the afternoon back in my room leaving detailed notes for Emmeline. What was happening in Noluvo's village. How water had to be treated and protected. What the well should do for the village and how important it was that the people keep from polluting it. I described my cannabis treatment plan, gave her directions to the pot field, and explained what parts of the plant I thought would be the most useful and how I was drying it. Then I emphasized the need to keep the place secret.

"If you control this, you'll have a lot of influence," I wrote. "Don't give it up."

My final notes of the evening told her about my run-in with Edward Bradshaw, my announcement to him that I, or she, planned to return to England before getting married, and how upset her mother was with the whole affair—or lack of one.

"I've made things harder for you by riding around the countryside in your dad's clothes," I wrote. "And I've been using a little of the science we're learning in school to amaze people into following all this advice I'm handing out. I'm afraid I'm embarrassing your family by not being the proper English girl they think you should be. Maybe you can get some of that straightened out when you come back. But PLEASE. Stick with the water plan for the Xhosa and keep them using the Indian hemp. I think maybe this is my contribution to being here."

Noluvo took me again into her grandfather's lodge where the same circle of old warriors sat cross-legged against the mud-plastered wicker walls, drawing on their long clay pipes with serious faces. The chief had taken to the idea that his village would be the first with its own well. In less than two weeks, some of his subjects with the most serious intestinal problems were showing signs of relief. Guinea worm sores were gradually disappearing. He had positioned two stools in front of his wooden throne and gestured for us to sit.

"Is your hand well?" he asked.

I showed him my palm. The burn had virtually disappeared. He nodded his satisfaction.

Noluvo explained that there was new medicine that could help with the sickness and the headman turned immediately to me. I held up one of my pouches of crushed cannabis flower.

"The Xhosa like to smoke," I began, stating the obvious. "If you mix these leaves with your tobacco, it will also help with sickness of the stomach." I spilled some of the crushed hemp blossom into my palm, stood, and poured it into the outstretched hand of the chief. He sniffed at it, mixed it with tobacco from a small sack he wore about his waist, and waved to an attendant who crouched beside the chair holding his pipe. The old man tamped the mixture into the bowl, turned toward the attendant who lit the pipe as the chief took a long pull, then sat back, chin tilted upward. The taste met with his approval. He nodded and continued to draw on the pipe as I made my second request.

"There are many in the village who do not smoke. Children and some of the women. They can take the medicine by boiling it in water to make a drink. Put the leaves in a bowl, pour water over them that has just boiled, then drink it while still hot." I really had no idea if this was the best way to make a tea, but remembered reading that heat released the active ingredients in cannabis. This ought to do it. I held up about a teaspoon of the leaves and one of the clay bowls from which the Xhosa drink, placed the leaves in the bowl, and imitated pouring the water over the leaves.

The chief spoke to Noluvo who immediately rose and left the lodge, returning moments later with a steaming jug of water from the kettle that now constantly boiled in the center of the village. Her grandfather signaled for me to hold up the bowl while she covered the leaves with scalding water. He spoke again to Noluvo.

"Grandfather wishes you to drink," she whispered.

I'd spent half the night worrying that the old chief might ask me to smoke the stuff. I'm not a smoker, had never tried pot, and had made a commitment as an athlete to leave the stuff alone. But by the time we left for the village, I'd convinced myself I might need to take a puff or two if I was going to make a convincing pitch. I also knew I'd cough and hack all over the place. It hadn't crossed my mind that smoking something new wouldn't bother the Xhosa. Drinking something new? That was different. But I figured I could at least drink a bowl of hemp tea without gagging.

I nodded and let it cool, blowing across the top of the bowl until I could take a sip. It reminded me of green tea, which I'd always thought tasted like grass, and almost laughed out loud. Grass that tastes like grass. I took a longer sip and smiled, seeing in the chief's eyes the first signs that his smoke was taking effect on more than his worms. The hemp in the old patch must still have enough THC to be relaxing. He smiled back, the first time I'd seen the old man's toothless grin, and spoke again to Noluvo. She gathered the pouches we'd placed on the dirt floor in front of the stools and started around the circle of men, letting each take a pinch of weed to add to their pipes.

I took a deeper drink from the bowl, swallowing some of the leaves. This really wasn't too bad! I could feel my own smile slipping into a grin and held the bowl up to the chief like an offering. Before he could take it from my hand, I was leaning across a table in Hopkin's Icehouse hearing Julian whisper ". . . should be switching today."

Emme

Our vicar, Reverend Sutherland, has a hound named Homer that is known about Bathurst as the best tracking dog in the colonies. Three months after we settled in Bathurst, the Moore's four-year-old boy wandered away from the village. We all searched frantically throughout the afternoon to no avail, fearing a leopard, lion, or hyena had stolen the boy. As evening approached, the vicar returned to the parsonage for Homer. Mrs. Moore produced a shirt the boy had worn the previous day for the hound to sniff and Reverend Sutherland turned the dog loose. With shoulders hunched and nose to the ground, Homer trotted around the family home in widening circles, picked a general direction he decided the boy had taken, then swept back and forth across a steadily narrowing path until he guided the search party into a rocky cleft where the boy had crawled beneath a thorny acacia bush.

Lena Morales is the human incarnation of old Homer. When she determined that it was her task to trace the rightful heir to Grenfell Hall, she sniffed at the marriage record of Emmeline Caywood and Charles Pearce, made several sweeping circuits through what she called "the broader world of genealogical data," then selected several paths her sensitive nose told her would be the most promising. While I sat opposite her at her family's dining table working on the last few sketches I had yet to complete, Lena tracked along a narrower and narrower trail. Finally, she pushed back from the computer, placed her hands flat on the table on either side of the machine, and nodded with satisfaction.

"Just as we guessed. Although there may be legal stuff I'm not thinking about here, the line of inheritance looks to me like it runs straight to Sam's dad, Bill Howard. Since she's his only kid, I think it must come to her. I've been making copies of registry entries and certificates as I've gone and have a pretty convincing file."

"Remember," I reminded, "that property went to sons in my time, even if a daughter was older."

"I considered all that. One of the things I hadn't realized is how many children never lived to be adults. In one of these families—I think the Yates—there were six kids. Only Margaret lived to get married. Even if you consider male cousins, this line is pretty straight forward. It leads directly to Sam."

I laid down the charcoal stick I was using to give texture to Abby Strohl's uniform. "Then I had no sons?"

Lena reddened and gave a slight nod.

"Is it time to tell Samantha?"

Lena nodded more firmly. "I think it is."

"How much should she know?"

Lena had to consider this for a moment. "I'm not sure. So far, only the four of us know about the switching between you and Ally. And I think the fewer, the better. But at the same time, I'm starting to believe this might all be about her and her mom. Why it's happening, I have no idea. I can't really buy into Ryan's master architect theory. Maybe it's God or The Force or something. But whatever it is, I think this is happening partly for her. If that's right, she needs to know about the whole thing."

"Will she believe it?"

"I think she's ready to believe about anything if it will help her mom. And she's pretty tight-lipped about stuff. I'd trust her more than anyone else I can think of."

"What if nothing comes of this, though? She seems to be carrying such a burden already. I would not wish to add in any way to her distress."

"Don't you think she should be able to decide that? If you were in her shoes, wouldn't you want to know?"

"I most certainly would," I agreed. "I will ask Jennifer if I can remain out late this evening. Perhaps we can meet with Sam when she completes her work at Hopkins."

"Without Julian and Ryan," Lena suggested. "Just the three of us."

I used my wonderful little phone to call Jennifer.

Sam completed her work at ten. Lena and I had asked her to join us in our favorite corner booth.

"How are things going with your mom?" Lena asked, wishing to be thoughtful and sensitive before we changed Samantha's world.

"She has her good days and bad. This morning was pretty good. And I'd really love to stay and spend some time with you, but I need to be getting home to her. Was there something you wanted to talk to me about?"

We had agreed that Lena would do most of the talking, afraid that if I spoke, it may appear that I was delusional and having one of my strange changes in language and behavior. I could see, though, that she was struggling to know where to begin. She finally folded her hands in front of her against the edge of the table and said, "You know how sometimes Ally's been acting kind of different the past couple of months?"

I was hoping for a somewhat kinder beginning. Samantha looked embarrassed on my behalf, then her expression turned to worry.

"You haven't got something wrong, have you, Al? I mean, that's messing with your brain?"

I shook my head. Lena plunged ahead.

"No. It's not like that. And this is going to sound *really* incredible. But you've seen how, all of a sudden, Ally can play the piano really well—and can't kick a soccer ball without falling on her butt? And talks with a British accent?"

"Well—yeah. And I've worried that something might be messed up in her head."

Lena glanced cautiously around the pub. "We've, like, figured out that Ally and this girl named Emmeline, who lived two hundred years ago, are switching places. Not completely. But, like, their minds or souls or whatever you want to call it are switching."

Sam stared at her, then at me, then back at Lena. "You're joking here. Right?"

Lena shook her head slowly to emphasize just how little she was joking. "Emme—that's Emmeline—has been telling us this all along. And Ally, when she's here. But it took a long time for us to believe it. Now I'm convinced it's true, and partly because of you."

Sam leaned back, hands fidgeting in her lap and mouth rolled into a tight, downward bow. "Because of me." It wasn't a question, but a clear declaration of disbelief.

"Let me explain," Lena begged, and walked Samantha through learning about Emmeline and Bathurst, finding me in her lita's genealogy files as marrying Charles Pearce, then discovering that the Caywoods were actually Grenfells.

"These Grenfells owned a big manor house in England that was stolen by the king just after Revolutionary times," Lena explained. "When we were trying to figure out why Emme and Ally might be switching, we traced the Grenfell line forward to see if there were still any around who might help us with an answer. Guess what we found?"

Sam's eyes darted about, searching for some reason she might be expected to know the answer to this didn't-make-any-sense question. "No idea," she said.

Lena unclasped her hands and pointed a finger across the booth. "You. We found you. The last of the Grenfell line we could trace led us to a Hannah and Tyler Howard of Kansas City."

Sam paled.

"And the record that showed us a lot of this history was filed by a Sarah Olsen."

"Aunt Sarah," Sam whispered. "That's why you asked about her."

"Yeah. We sent an email to Sarah Olsen and asked if there were children of Hannah and Tyler. You know the rest. You're the last of the Howards—and really, the last in the Grenfell line."

Samantha's eyes narrowed. "And this search began on information that came from *where*?"

"Emmeline," Lena repeated, nodding at me. Sam turned her skeptical gaze on me and sat silently, looking me up and down. "And you're saying you are now this Emmeline?"

I nodded. "I know this is most difficult to believe, but I am here, and Ally's mind or spirit or soul or whatever you wish to call it is in my body in Bathurst."

"In Africa—two hundred years ago," Sam scoffed, turning her head scornfully aside.

"Emme's been doing the drawings," Lena blurted, hoping to add proof to her story. "You think that's Ally?"

Sam turned back toward me, still oozing skepticism. "Weird things can happen when something goes wrong in your brain."

"Including knowing stuff that Ally would have had no way of knowing? It's not even written down anywhere."

"Then how did you check it?" Sam challenged.

"By her telling us what we wouldn't find. Any record of what happened to Emmeline Grenfell who was born in Ipswich and disappeared with her family in 1820. Then a marriage record for Emmeline Caywood—daughter of Robert and Rebecca Caywood of Bathurst in the Cape Colonies. *No one* knew about that connection."

"How do you know it's right, then?"

"Somewhere, we're going to find it all written out."

"Where would that be?"

"We don't know. That's why we need your help."

"How can *I* help? I still think you're both nuts."

"I'm convinced the proof of that connection is kept by your family somewhere." Lena hadn't mentioned this before. I gave her a questioning look that matched Samantha's.

"What is this proof?" Sam asked.

"A letter, I think."

"Who from? When was it written?"

Lena smiled, knowing she was about to add to the weirdness. "It's from Emmeline's father. And it hasn't been written yet."

Sam collapsed back against the booth cushions. "What kind of bad joke is this? I've gotta get home to mom, and this is more than I can take in right now. You both look dead serious, and that really worries me."

"Think about it," Lena said. "And maybe call your Aunt Sarah. You going to be working Friday?"

Sam barely nodded.

"Please," Lena begged. "Don't say anything to anyone about this."

Sam gave us an "Are you kidding?" look. "Not likely. They'd lock me up with you two." She turned to me. "So, you think you're my ancestor—somewhere way back."

"I do. But before I came, I had no knowledge of this."

"And why do you think you're here?"

I had finally come to understand the answer as I listened to Lena. "To reclaim the right to Grenfell Hall for the family. And in doing that, to save your mother."

Lena had shared the documents she found with Sam and by the time we met again on Friday, Samantha was at least willing to confess she was a Caywood. She sat for the first few moments, staring at me as if I might suddenly transform before her eyes into someone else, a feeling I wanted to assure her I had every morning before I looked in the glass in Ally's bathroom. She finally shook her head and said, "I still can't really believe this. But I can't explain it either."

Lena leaned over the table, speaking in a whisper. "Somewhere—and we need you to help us figure out where—there's got to be proof that the Caywoods were the Grenfells of Grenfell Hall. Julian's trying to find out how you can make some kind of legal claim if we can establish the connection. But that proof, and some evidence that the Grenfell's owned the house outright, are going to be pretty important."

Samantha leaned in with me to hear what Lena was saying but remained skeptical. "You think we can really convince anyone that matters that the house belongs to me? And what would I do with it anyway? I'm not about to move with Mom to England and couldn't take care of it if I did. I looked up a picture of it. It's a really big place."

"A lovely home," I said, drawing another curious stare from Sam.

"Not live in it. *Sell* it," Lena whispered. "Right now it's rented by an antique dealer. I think from the royal family. They may just buy it from you to avoid bad publicity."

I had been with Julian and Lena when he agreed to see what he could learn about claiming ownership. "My first idea," he had suggested, "is that we put together all this documentation, see if we can find proof that the Grenfells owned the place and that it was taken from them by the king, and contact a couple of British papers about the story. They have a bunch of tabloids that are really popular. They love stories like this."

Lena had reminded him that the link between the Caywoods and Grenfells was still based only on the account by a girl who claimed to be possessed by the mind of a two hundred-year-old Caywood.

Julian thought that to be even better. "The tabloids would love that. They're sort of like *The Inquirer*. But it won't have much legal value. We need written proof."

"And that's where you come in," Lena said to me as we sat with Samantha. "Like we said before, when you get back to Bathurst, you need to tell your dad to write out a letter stating he's Robert Grenfell, owner of Grenfell Hall, in wherever that was you lived."

"Ipswich in Suffolk," I reminded her.

"Right. Ipswich. And that he left the country for the colonies with his family when the king was after him for writing whatever he wrote. The letter needs to list his family, especially you, as his surviving daughter. And if there's some record of ownership of the hall, he needs to tell you where it is. We've gotta find it."

"What reason will I give him for needing this letter?"

"You're going to be going back to England before you get married. Tell him you want to have proof, in case you can ever make claim to the old family house." As she was speaking, Julian entered the Icehouse, looked about until he saw us, and hurried over to the booth. I was starting to answer Lena, but he interrupted.

"I just got an alert on my calendar," he said, glancing about to be certain he was not overheard. "I should have been paying better attention, but today's your day. If the switch comes at the same time, you . . .."

I did not hear the rest of his warning. I was sitting on a stool, feeling very relaxed, and gazing up at the grinning face of Noluvo's grandfather.

Ally

For some reason, instead of feeling relief that I was home again, the whole thing struck me as hilarious. I sat back in the booth, looked up at Julian, then around at Lena and Samantha, and began to laugh until tears streamed down my face. All I could think about was that I'd just escaped that trip on pot I'd promised never to take. When I could talk, I said hi to Sam, pulled Julian down beside me, and winked at Lena. "You were saying . . . ?" I said to Julian and wrapped him in a bear hug.

He wriggled loose and kissed me on the cheek, watching to see if I'd shy away. Instead, I pulled him back and kissed him like I'd been wanting to for nearly a month.

"I think our girl's back," he laughed, slipping an arm about my waist and drawing me closer. "Am I right?"

I looked questioningly over at Samantha.

"She's okay," Lena said. "Tell us what's been happening, and I'll fill you in.

While Samantha Howard gawked in disbelief, I told them about making the Voltaic Stack, getting a lesson from the Xhosa chief about cultural sensitivity, and trying my health plan out on the village.

"There's this little man from Scotland who showed me where there's a big field of what they call Indian hemp. Before I went back this time, I found an article that said cannabis can help with parasites. When I switched, I was just showing them how to use it. Emme's going to find she's in a *really* strange situation right now. I hope Noluvo can get her out of there before she messes up everything I've done."

I could tell as I spoke that Lena was trying to be patient but was chomping at the bit to tell me something. When I finally sat back and looked around to see what people would say, she waited long enough to see that I'd stunned the others into silence, then jumped in. "Well, we've been pretty busy here, too."

During the next half hour, I learned about their tracing the Caywoods to Sam and finding out from Emme that the family had been Grenfells and had skipped the country after Robert stirred up trouble with his pamphlets.

"And get this!" Lena gushed. "The family had a lot of money and owned a big country house."

I nodded against Julian's shoulder. "I knew from some of the things people said that there was a family secret. In fact, from about the first day I was there, Rebecca's been telling people who must know about it, like the doctor, that she's worried I'm going to spill the beans."

"But they didn't ever tell you what the secret was?" Lena asked.

"Rebecca told me some of it and made me promise never to talk about it. I didn't know about this big house they'd left behind."

"So . . ." Sam said hesitantly, ". . . you really *do* go to this place in the past? I mean, your spirit does, or whatever?"

"Yeah. Blows your mind, doesn't it. But it happens."

"*Amazing*," she murmured. "But when they told me you'd done all those drawings, I couldn't figure out how."

"Drawings?" I looked questioningly at Lena, who laughed. "Yeah. Emme's been doing charcoal sketches of the team to raise money to get us all to England. They're *really* good!"

"I hope she got them done. You know how bad I am."

"Finished just in time," Lena said. "And we sent her back with an assignment." She explained about the need to get something in writing about the Grenfells taking the Caywood name. "Do you think her dad will do it?"

I nodded uncertainly. "I think so. When I first built the Voltaic battery I showed it to him and Rebecca. She just shrugged it off as part of my craziness. But Robert got curious. We've had some pretty good talks."

Julian was shaking his head and giving me his "Sometimes you amaze me" look.

"*What?*" I said.

"I can't believe you remembered how to make that thing—and got it to work. We did that, like, once in physics. And where did you get the zinc?"

"India. Or at least that's where it came from. This tinsmith guy in Port Kowie got it from Dutch sailors."

Now they were all giving me the look.

"It worked!" I repeated. "It gave me a chance to talk to Robert—Emme's dad—about how I knew how to make it and all that was happening. I think he's starting to come around. If Emme approaches this right, I believe he'll do it. But . . .," I figured they'd thought about this but had to ask, ". . . how does that do us any good? She can't bring it back with her."

"She'll have to put it somewhere where we can find it," Lena answered. "And tell us where that is when you switch again."

"You think this is going to keep happening?" Sam asked. "What if she doesn't come back?"

Lena leaned again with elbows on the table. "If this is all happening for a reason, and if you and this house in England are tied up in it somehow, there's got to be a few more switches." She looked over at Julian. "We've been looking up all this stuff, and one of the matches we're playing in England is in a place called Bury Saint Edmunds. That's about thirty miles from Ipswich. Can't be coincidence. I think by the time we go, we'll know where to find what we need. That probably means at least one or two more switches."

Julian nodded. "Another match is in Chelmsford. That's about the same distance in the other direction. Like Lena says, can't be coincidence."

Sam looked at me again with the same questioning expression. "So, this Emmeline is coming here to help us figure out how to get her family estate back. Why are you going there? I mean, it must be adding something."

I grinned. "Well, one of the native villages is getting to be a lot healthier. The blacksmith who lives out on the coast is learning a lot of physics. And . . ." it came to me as I was talking, ". . . I'm making sure Emme's getting to England to get married. Otherwise, you might be a Bradshaw and still be living in Africa."

I was finding it much more difficult to get back into the routines of regular life after this switch. Emme had been going to a resource room during most of my classes, and I had some real catching up to do—everything but Lit and Chorale where she was doing even better than I'd done. When I walked through the halls at school, kids looked at me like I had the plague or something. They hugged the walls as I passed, far enough away that they wouldn't catch whatever I had, and whispered what I knew must be "there's that girl who's been acting crazy." In class, they said the right things. "Glad to see you're feeling better. Nice to have you back." But I had the feeling they were all expecting me to fall off my chair at any moment.

I woke up in the mornings relieved that I was in a comfortable bed and glad I'd be able to have a bowl of Cheerios and a glass of OJ. But I just as quickly felt the slump that came with knowing I wouldn't be able to saddle up Prince and ride toward the coast to check on progress on the Xhosa well. I realized that in Bathurst, for the first time in my life—or, I guess, in Emmeline's life—I felt really useful. Like I was making a difference. I knew that in the eyes of the villagers I was an important person, and I liked it.

At the same time, I could see that my regular life was benefiting from my time in Bathurst. In chemistry I started paying closer attention, studying harder every night to really understand what Mr. Payne was talking about. Maybe human medicine was what I ought to be thinking about rather than vet school. I'd never been quite as excited as when one of the village women came up to show me that all her sores were healing and there were no new ones. Being Emme wasn't so bad. And being me could be a whole lot better.

Coach Gillion had asked if some of us could check with parents to see if some could come along on the England trip as chaperones. It seemed like a good time to let Mom know that maybe I'd been a pain in the ass in her life and would like to do better.

"You're asking if I'd like to go with you to England?" she asked with enough surprise that I realized I really must have been being a jerk. "I thought the last thing you'd want was your mother with you."

"It would be kind of fun having you along. And you haven't had a vacation in—well, I can't remember when."

"Are you feeling that you're Emmeline again?" she asked, looking at me suspiciously.

"No. It's me. I'd just really like you to go."

"We've only saved enough for you. I don't think we can come up with another thousand dollars."

"Don't tell Dad we have it," I suggested. "I think I can get him to spring for mine."

She was on me like a mother bear, hugging me like she hadn't since I was little. "I'd love to go," she whispered. "And I promise, I'll give you some space."

"It'll be good," I said, and hugged her back.

Sam's Aunt Sarah agreed to come take care of her mom while the team went to England. She drove down from Kansas City on a weekend to learn what she'd need to do. Lena insisted we meet with her at Sam's house and the minute we walked in the door, I got to know more about Samantha than I'd learned in sixteen years. The place was almost bare, with one of those hospital-type beds in the living room where her mom spent her days watching TV. The whole place smelled of sickness and antiseptic, like a hospital hallway. Sam brought old yellow, vinyl-covered metal chairs from the kitchen for us to sit on, flushing with embarrassment as she arranged them around a low laminated coffee table.

"Sorry I don't have better chairs—or a couch. We've pretty well had to sell everything." Need for the sale sat on an end table beside her mother's bed in five pharmacy-orange bottles.

"We're good with this," I said and went over to sit with her mom while Lena spread the charts and documents from her search out in front of Sarah Olsen. The woman looked about Mom's age with fair hair and light eyes. I could see Emme in some of her features.

"You know how doctors like to look at your family history to see if there've been patterns of illness?" Lena started. "We've been helping Sam trace your family back and found something interesting we thought you might be able to help us with."

Sarah looked over the pages on the table, then up at Lena. "Did you send me an email?"

Lena grinned. "Yup. But at the time, we didn't know you were Sam's aunt. In fact, it sort of came up by accident when she told us you were coming down to stay with her mom while she's away."

"Hmmm," she mused, studying the sheets. "I'm not sure what more I can tell you. You've got more family information here than I even knew existed. And I've been tracking this for about ten years."

"It's not the genealogy we're wondering about," Lena admitted. "We traced your line back to this Emmeline Caywood in Cambridge, England, and it stopped there." She pointed at Emme's name on one of the registry photocopies. "But there's no records of birth or anything for her that we could find. This marriage record shows that her father was a farmer in the British Cape Colonies in South Africa. We know that a bunch of people left Suffolk in 1820 to go down there. So we ran a search for a birth record of an Emmeline to a father and mother named Robert and Rebecca in Suffolk for the year Emmeline would have been born. We found one in Ipswich." She slid another page to the top of her pile. "But the last name's Grenfell. As it turns out, this Robert Grenfell got in trouble with the king for publishing some stuff that said the man was a heartless leech. The family disappeared." She paused and looked up at Sarah Olsen. "You haven't ever come across anything that would tie these together, have you? The Caywoods and the Grenfells? Some family record or some object you were told came from an old English estate?"

Sarah's brow furrowed. "I don't have anything in the way of heirlooms. Mom and Dad were farm people in eastern Kansas and barely had two dimes to rub together. There was an old clock that had been my grandfather's, but that was on the other side of the family. And I think my parents sold that when I went to college. Maybe there are ships' records of who went to the colonies in 1820 that would show a Grenfell."

"We found ships' records," I said from the bedside, "but they show Robert *Caywood* leaving with his wife Rebecca and daughter Emmeline. We're wondering if they took a new name before they left to cover their tracks."

Sarah glanced over at me, deep in thought. "That would make sense. But that far back, why does that matter to you so much?"

"Because," Lena said, uncovering a photograph of Grenfell Hall, "they left behind this house. If we can show they were the same people, we think this genealogy shows that Sam would be the legal heir."

Sarah glanced about the bare living room, then at Samantha. "That would be wonderful, but seems pretty unlikely. What do you think of all this, Samantha?"

Sam shrugged and looked over at her mother, then at me. "They've pretty well got me convinced. But we can't find that any record was left showing the family connection."

Sarah shuffled through the papers in front of her. "Can I get copies of these? When I get home, I'll go through everything I have, just in case I've forgotten something. But right now, I don't know what it would be."

Emme

Sunlight streamed through the door behind me coloring smoke a light, hazy blue that curled from a dozen pipes. The entire room seemed to glow, and my body—and it truly was *my* body—was as light as I could ever recall. I turned to Noluvo who sat beside me, seeming to be waiting for me to speak.

"What a wonderful place," I murmured. "We should have come here before."

Noluvo leaned forward and studied my face as if wishing to be certain who she was sitting beside.

"Emme?" she asked. "Have you returned to yourself?"

"I am very much myself. I must confess I have not ever felt so completely myself." I gazed happily up at the chief who also appeared very pleased with being himself. Noluvo took my arm and helped me to my feet.

"I believe we must go," she said respectfully to her grandfather who seemed not to care. "We will return tomorrow and help the village make the tea." She guided me past a row of old Xhosa men who smiled up at us contentedly. We pushed through a skin that hung over the door and out into the village circle where Maisy stood beside our wagon. Villagers crowded about us, but Noluvo shooed them away and helped me up onto the wagon seat. For the first time I could remember, she chose to drive the mare. I was pleased to allow it. She urged Maisy into a lazy trot.

"You have returned from the place you go?" she asked as we turned onto the Bathurst road.

"Yes. I have returned." I noticed that I was again dressed in some of Father's clothes, but it did not matter at all. In truth, I found them most comfortable.

"Missus will be very pleased. She has not been happy with you while you have been the other Emmeline."

"The other Emmeline?"

"Yes. The one who chooses to ride and will not play at the piano. The one who was not kind to Mr. Edward."

"Not kind to Edward?" I found the thought humorous to the point of laughter and rocked back and forth on the seat, unable to control myself.

"Perhaps we should stop and walk beside the wagon," Noluvo suggested. "Missus will not wish to see you like this." I did not object and we walked the remaining distance to the house. By the time we reached the garden, I was feeling much more my unsettled self.

Mother looked up when we entered but turned sternly away. I went directly to my bedchamber and changed my clothing into a dress and slippers. When I returned to the parlor, I went directly to the piano and began to play an etude that was one of Mother's favorites. I heard her come to the door. When I finished the piece, I turned and found tears streaming down her cheeks.

"I am back to my old self," I said quietly. "Please forgive me for causing you such distress." She came to sit beside me on the bench, drawing me close in a long embrace.

"I have been so worried about you," she whispered. She eased me away, holding me by the shoulders at arms-length. "I am delighted to see you dressed again as a woman. Perhaps this afternoon we can visit the Bradshaws. You can offer an apology to Edward for your behavior."

My head had cleared as I walked, and I realized that more tasks awaited me than Lena's three. In addition to finding a way to talk to Father about a manor record and the letter proving we were Grenfells, I must make peace with Mother, while continuing to resist a match with Edward Bradshaw. I had hoped the latter would not become an issue so quickly. But I had developed a new boldness while being Ally Wallis.

"Mother," I said directly, "I know how badly you wish for me to marry well. I assure you that I wish the same for myself. But in all of this . . . this *strangeness* that has been going on, I have come to be certain of one thing. I must return to England to marry, and I will marry well. I need you to trust me about this."

The dark mask again fell across her face, but almost instantly began to lift. "Your father assures me of the same. And I should just take pleasure in having the daughter back who is not set on riding across the countryside like some highwayman. Perhaps Jama can take us into the Port this afternoon to see if Martha has received a shipment of new fabric. You could use another dress."

The drive into Port Kowie and our return were uneventful and served mainly as an opportunity for Mother to sermonize on the benefits of feminine behavior. Martha had no new fabric, but was pleased to sit over tea for an hour and support Mother's position. As we passed the Pickering's shop on our way out of the village, the old smithy waved at me knowingly, leaving me wondering what else Ally had been up to while leaving Mother in such a state.

Back at the house, I took to my room to paint until Father returned, discovering a diary beside the bed that answered some of my questions. There was little wonder that Mother was upset. Ally had been making daily visits to Xhosa villages, dabbling in well-digging and medicine, and running about with the likes of Angus Kinkade. She seemed quite anxious that I continue her work in Noluvo's village, but I had no desire whatsoever to become involved in worming the natives.

Father had gone north with two other sheep farmers to hunt a pack of wild dogs that had been attacking his herds and sheepdogs. I heard him return before he reached the paddock and met him as he was unsaddling Prince. I took his arm as he carried the saddle into the tack room.

"I am *so* pleased to have you home, Father. There is something I wish to ask you to do for me."

He stopped just inside the door, saddle in hand, and cocked his head to the side. "You speak again like an English girl. And you have decided you can call me Father."

I led him toward the saddle rack. "That is what I wish to speak to you about. I need you to understand something that will be most difficult." I paused beside the work table where a stack of small metal plates was wired to a cloth-wrapped horseshoe. More of Ally's puzzling work.

He threw the saddle onto the stand and returned to the table, leaning over the apparatus. "What is this object, Emme?" he asked. "And what does it do?"

I walked slowly around the table, studying it from all sides. "I am quite certain I haven't the slightest idea. Do you wish to tell me?"

He pushed several bridle buckles together in the center of the table. "This is something you designed. You don't recall?"

". . . No. And that is part of what I must speak to you about."

"Is it true, as far as you can discern, that you and this Alyssa Wallis change places? At least, in the spirit?

I swallowed deeply and tears welled in the corners of my eyes. "You know, Father? And you believe?"

He touched two wires together and the buckles flew to the ends of the horseshoe. "You made this. Or your Alyssa did. To convince me she came from some future place and that you were there in her stead."

"I have so tried to tell you, Father."

He pulled me to him and nestled my face against his neck. "Yes. You have. It was so unimaginable. But she showed me the unimaginable."

I sobbed against his whiskered chin, pulling myself in even closer. "There are so many unimaginable things. I cannot begin to tell you."

"Have you permanently returned?" He eased me away and led me to the wooden bench, sitting with his arm about my shoulders.

"My friends there—two of whom you would like very much— believe we will trade places until a problem is solved. That is what

I wish to speak to you about."

"Well, we had best do it here. Your mother is not quite ready for all of this."

"It all began," I told him, "when these friends decided they must learn why Ally and I were switching. That is how they refer to it. They have miraculous ways of looking back in time and finding those who have lived before. They found me and learned that one of the girls there, another friend, is descended from our family."

I sat wrapped in the accepting embrace of my father as I hadn't since I was a young child and told him about Samantha Howard and her mother. I confessed that I had admitted to them that we were Grenfells, and that I had learned Grenfell Hall still stood, but was let by the Crown to a seller of antiques.

"They have uncovered records that prove Samantha to be my lawful heir," I explained. "But only as a woman married in Cambridge to your cousin's nephew, Charles Pearce. They find nothing that proves Emmeline Caywood to have been a Grenfell."

Father chuckled. "To Albert's son, Charles? A good lad. I see now why this other Emme was so set on keeping Edward Bradshaw at bay." His tone sobered. "But as for proof of the connection, we have worked so hard to leave no sign of it."

"Could you write a letter, perhaps witnessed by Doctor Begley and the vicar—and ideally by Sir Donkin—stating that you are Robert Grenfell, owner of Grenfell Hall? That you changed your name to Caywood upon leaving England to escape unjust punishment by the Crown?"

Father thought for a moment, then said, "It could be a most dangerous letter, Emmeline. Should it fall into the wrong hands, I could be returned to England and imprisoned."

"We would keep it safely here until I return to Suffolk. When I do return, I will safeguard it with my life and insist that my own children do the same. It must be kept in a place where Samantha and her friends can find it. Perhaps King George will not live too long, and you can return to live with us."

Father nodded slightly against my cheek. "We can only pray he does not ruin the nation while he lives. But where would you secret such a letter? To be certain it is safe, but likely to be found?"

"I may not know until the day comes. If I return to Texas, I shall tell them to ask in the family for that one possession they were cautioned never to lose or discard. That is where the letter will be."

"I shall think on this," Father said, urging us both to our feet. "And please, say nothing to your mother." He chuckled again to himself. "Charles Pearce. He *is* a very canny lad."

He kept his arm about my shoulders as we walked to the house and stopped me just before entering. "This Ally has done some very helpful work with the Xhosa while here. If Noluvo can help you understand it, our relationship with the people will be greatly assisted if it continues."

"She left notes for me in my bedchamber," I confessed. "Some of it is work that I would not find at all to my liking." Despite myself, I felt a twinge of jealousy for this double whose efforts appealed so much to my father. He seemed to sense my envy.

"There is so much that you do that she cannot." He turned me into him again, snuggling me against his chest. "And I have so missed holding you like this, never being at all certain who I would be holding. But if you are able to continue some of the work with the villagers, wearing a dress, of course, it would be an aid to us all."

"I shall do my best," I said, then suddenly remembered the other part of my assignment from Lena. I pulled away, still holding Father's hand. "There is one other thing. Is there some record, some registry for Grenfell Hall, that proves you were its rightful owner?"

Father gazed down at me uncertainly. "Why do you ask?"

"My friends fear that, should they find a way to show that we are indeed Grenfells, there may be challenge as to whether the family truly owned the estate. In some cases, families lived in such places at the pleasure of the Crown."

"These friends are wise and thorough," Father said, smiling grimly. "And there is such a record. It clearly shows that the hall and the surrounding lands have been owned by the Grenfells from the time of Charles I and that the family holds full title to the estate. Some lands have been sold since, and those conveyances are recorded in the record. I feared to bring it with us when we came. Had I been detained and searched, it may well have been destroyed. So I secreted it in the manor."

"Will it still be there?" I realized as I spoke that I was losing my own sense of time and place. "I should say, will it survive in this hiding place for two hundred years?"

"If the manor survives, the record should be safe. And you say the hall still stands?"

"Yes. And looks much as it did." We were *both* speaking as if the time had passed.

He led me to a bench beneath the parlor window. "I shall tell you where it is. If you are able to get to the hall after you return to England, you might retrieve it and secret it with the letter. If not, pass along this instruction to your friends."

Mother called from the doorway that supper was waiting.

"A moment, please," Father called. "We shall be in shortly," and he told me where to find the manor record of Grenfell Hall.

Ally

"The one great thing about having you back," Lena said, "is that you're a lot more assertive when you're Ally. When we've worked on this stuff, Emme mainly sits and listens."

"That's it? The only reason you like having me back?"

"Well, and you're a lot better soccer player. That's good too. And Julian likes you better. Emme gets pretty nervous when he forgets who he's with and gets physical. She doesn't like to be touched much."

"I can understand that," I chuckled. "This guy who's interested in her wouldn't even think of holding her hand while they walk together. And the race thing is really big there. I can see Emme being uneasy."

"If only you could play the piano and draw like she does. The perfect Ally!"

"Well, you'll have to settle for assertive soccer player while I'm here. If Julian's right, and these switches keep up and stay on schedule, I should be here for the England trip. I think then you'll be looking for good soccer."

"Except you won't know your way around England."

"Eighteen-twenties England," I reminded her. "And I doubt Emme saw much more than Ipswich and the area round it."

We were at the Icehouse waiting for Sam to finish her shift. Just me and Lena. Julian said he wanted to spend the evening on his computer seeing if English lawyers did *pro bono* work. Ryan was probably with him, blasting his way through some level of *Panzer Attack*. Sam's aunt Sarah had texted since getting back to Kansas City that she hadn't found anything that might hide a letter from Robert Caywood. Her parents hadn't owned much, and what they had handed down was old, handmade oak furniture she was certain didn't have any hidden compartments. "Simple people. Simple furniture," her text said.

A few minutes after ten, Sam slid into the booth with a burger and fries. "No time tonight for a dinner break," she muttered, picking up the burger and pushing the fries to the middle of the table where we could all reach them. "So, Sarah couldn't help. Maybe if Emme can convince her dad to write the letter, she can tell us where to look for it when you switch next."

I shook my head and pulled a long, crisp fry off the top of the pile. "I think Robert will write it. But we know Emme goes back to England to get married. I doubt she'd leave it in Bathurst. If she takes it with her, and that will probably be a year from now—well, from then—I'd guess she won't decide where to hide it until she gets there. Maybe after she's married."

Lena agreed. "I'm thinking she'll put it somewhere she thinks will safely be handed down from one generation to the next, without some temptation to give it away. And probably with whoever gets it in each generation being told to make sure it stays in the family."

Sam wiped catsup off her cheek with a napkin, chewed for a moment, then said, "but Sarah got most everything from my grandparents. Dad didn't want anything but this old World War II rifle his dad had. And that wouldn't have been around for Emme to hide anything in."

"Your dad didn't get anything else?" I asked. "Something he told you would be yours and to always keep in the family?"

"Nah. He wasn't much into things. In fact, the only thing he ever said anything to me about was. . . ." She stopped with the burger raised halfway to her mouth, eyes narrowing. ". . . was an old Bible. That's been so long ago, I hardly remembered. I was maybe eight or nine."

Lena was squirting catsup on a corner of Sam's plate and shot a stream onto the table. "A *Bible*? Is it that old? That would be a perfect place!"

"It was pretty old. We're not church people and I don't have any idea where it is. When Dad died, the minister asked if he had a Bible so he could see if Dad had marked favorite verses." Her face flushed at the memory. "Mom said she didn't know where it was, but we really didn't look."

I had lost interest in the fries. "Do you think it's still around? Where would he have kept stuff like that?"

"I know we wouldn't have given it away. He was pretty clear about that. All his old military things are in a trunk in our attic. He was in Iraq after the first Gulf war when he was only eighteen. That's about the only thing he held onto. His war stuff."

"Have you looked through it since he died?" I asked.

She shook her head. "It's kind of hard to get to. There's this square board in the ceiling in the garage and you have to get on a ladder and lift it out of the way. Most of the stuff is right close to the door, I think. That's the only place they put any flooring."

"You working tomorrow?" Lena asked. Sam shook her head.

"How about your house after school. Julian and Ryan can help. Will your mom care?"

"Mom heard us talking to Aunt Sarah about all this. She doesn't think it'll amount to anything, but she was really touched that you're all working so hard on it. She won't care if we look."

I dropped my fry back onto her plate. "Your place at five-thirty. I'll pick up a bucket of chicken."

Sam had backed their Corolla onto the drive, leaving open floor below the attic door. The square board that served as access probably hadn't been moved in ten years. Ryan brought a ladder in the back of his pickup. When he pushed the door upward, flakes of insulation showered down like gray snow. He slid the wooden square to the side, turned on an LED headlamp he kept in the glove box of his old F-150, and stuck his head up into the opening.

"A bunch of cardboard boxes," he called down. "No chest that I can see."

"It'll be behind them," Sam said. "You might need to climb all the way up."

Ryan mounted the ladder until chest-high in the attic, pushed himself on up into the space, and twisted to sit with feet dangling out of the opening. He scooted back and drew his legs up, disappearing until all we could see was the headlamp playing on the roof trusses.

"Do you see it?" Sam called.

There was no answer, then the sound of boxes being pushed across the makeshift floor and something being dragged to the door.

"Julian, you'll need to climb up and get this," Ryan shouted, his headlamp flashing about overhead. "I'll get it over to where you can grab a handle. It's not heavy. Just awkward."

Julian scrambled up the ladder as the end of a small leather trunk appeared in the dark square. He grasped the handle and slid it until he could lower it onto the ladder's top step, then eased it down into Sam's arms. Lena and I each grabbed a handle and lowered it to the floor. We all stood around it uncertainly while Julian helped Ryan find the top steps of the ladder and get low enough to slide the door back into place.

When we were all circling the trunk, Sam took a deep breath, looked around at her support group, and said, "Well, here goes! Let's hope!"

The trunk was fastened with a single figure-eight lock with a key slot in the center. Sam tentatively pushed the button upward, and the clasp snapped out. There wasn't the sound of a breath as she lifted the lid.

Nothing on top gave us any hope. The first few layers were old GI desert fatigues. Below that, her father had neatly folded a woven rug about the size of a bath towel, beautifully patterned in geometric red and black. Sam carefully lifted it out and held it up to let it drape open.

"Prayer rug," Julian pronounced. "Probably a souvenir your dad picked up in Iraq or Kuwait."

Beneath it, a box of letters filled most of the bottom, tucked tightly beside a cloth-wrapped rectangle. Sam drew out a handful of yellowed envelopes, saw from the return address that they were written by her mother, and unconsciously clutched them to her chest. I saw her eyes brim and her chin begin to quiver and knelt beside her, arm around her shoulders.

"This wrapped thing may be what we're looking for," I said, drawing her thoughts from the letters. Without her objecting, I lifted the wrapped block from the chest. The cloth covering was an old pillowcase. As I felt at it, I knew it held a book.

"*Eureka*," I said, remembering another of Isenberg's physics lessons. "I think we've found it." When I touched the cover inside the case, I knew I was right. The aged, cracked leather had tiny ridges that acted like braille beneath my fingertips. They said "old Bible." The back of the spine was torn away on one side. I slid the book gently out onto the woven rug.

"*Madre de Dios*," Lena whispered. "I think we'd better get some gloves or something to even open this up. How old do you think it is?"

Sam rose from beside the small carpet. "We've got some cotton gloves I keep for Mom to wear when her hands get cold." She hurried into the house, returning with two pair of white gloves while we remained crouched anxiously over the ancient leather book. She handed a pair to me. "You open it. You're the closest thing to Emme we've got."

"It's your family Bible," I protested weakly, hoping she would insist.

She did. "I want you to open it."

I gingerly lifted the thick cover and an initial blank page to expose the title page. Opposite it was a picture of Jesus sitting in the clouds, looking down on a bunch of adoring people. The title page read "The Christian's New and Complete British Family Bible," followed by a long description of all that was included. The New and Old Testaments. Something called the "Apocrypha at

Large, with notes and annotations. Practical Reflections and useful admonitions at the end of each chapter." The book had been published in Halifax, England, by Holden and Dowson in 1804.

Julian pointed at the top of the pages. "There's a little ribbon sticking out here. Maybe that's where we should look."

I carefully slipped a gloved fingernail between the marked pages and opened to the ribbon. Between the Old and New Testament sections, six lined pages had been included to record family history. The first entry, written in a flowing hand and still clear after two centuries, recorded the marriage of Charles Pearce of Cambridge to Emmeline Caywood of Bathurst, Cape Colonies, South Africa.

Lena leaned over the book, tracing a finger down the lines of entries of marriages, births, and deaths to the fourth page. "These are just like the records I found. Although all births are recorded, the marriages follow the hereditary line. And look here. The last entry. Samantha Evelyn Howard, born August 3rd, 2003. From Emmeline right to you."

Sam rocked back on her heels and stared at the entries. "That's Dad's writing. He put me in here. That may be the last time this book was out of the trunk."

"The pedigree's all here," Julian said. "But there's no letter. We could probably show that these entries are genuine, but that doesn't link Emmeline to Grenfell Hall. That's what we needed."

I gingerly turned to the back cover, looking for anything that might have been stuck between the pages. Nothing. But something was different. I propped the book on its back, looking down at the two covers. I pointed at the front.

"Look how much thicker this one is. It's like . . . ." With the book flat and the front laid back, it became more obvious. A paper book plate, missed when I had initially hurried past the blank front page, had been glued to the inside of the front cover. The owners of the Bible had gone to the trouble and expense of having it formally printed. It said, "The Family Bible of Charles and

Emmeline Pearce, to be cherished and preserved as a record of their descendants until the hall is restored." The plate was raised just enough to suggest something had been hidden behind it.

"Until the hall is restored," Samantha whispered. "It's like Emme is talking to us from the past."

"And I think we've found our letter," I guessed, tapping on the raised printed plate. "Have you got a razor blade or something we can use to slit along this edge?"

Sam pushed again to her feet and went to a metal cabinet along the back wall of the garage, returning with a thin, blue-handled knife. "How about a box cutter?"

I nodded. "But this one's your job. If it gets messed up, I want it to be you." She looked like she was about to argue, then dropped back to her knees, face scrunched in concentration. Holding the cover up with one hand, she slipped the thin blade under the outer edge of the printed paper and slowly worked it along the seam. Whatever had been used as glue had fused the paper. In some places, she left a thin slice of plate attached to the cover. When she reached the bottom, she slid the blade midway back up the sheet and lifted it gently. I leaned until I could see into the slit.

"I think I see something. But we need tweezers or . . .."

"Something like this." Ryan held out what looked like a pocket knife with all kinds of gadgets tucked into its side. A tiny pair of needle-nosed pliers extended from one end. "It's called a Leatherman. Comes in pretty handy."

I was just able to reach the folded pages without tearing the book plate. Three folded sheets of parchment slid out onto the carpet.

"Genius," Julian murmured. "This is really a stroke of genius."

Lena shook her head dismissively. "We almost missed it. If Sam hadn't remembered . . .."

"Yeah. But she did. And can you think of anything else a family's likely to keep and update over two hundred years? Emme would have expected Sam to know more about it than she did."

"Like I said," Sam said apologetically, "Dad wasn't very religious. But he kept it."

I laid a hand on her arm. "And we found it like we were supposed to. So it worked out. Let's see what we have here."

When we opened the pages, the top sheet removed all doubt. I read it aloud.

May 30, 1825

My dear Ally, Sam, Lena , Julian, and Ryan:

I cannot begin to tell you how much I have missed you all since my last stay in Texarkana. You remain among my dearest friends and memories. I write this knowing that you will find it with father's letter, and pray that you are able to use them to regain title to the Hall for Samantha's family. My dear husband Charles knows me to be a Grenfell, but nothing of my adventure with you. I do, nonetheless, amuse myself from time to time by imagining that our switching had continued and you, Ally, were faced with sharing a husband with me. I can assure you, you would have been quite delighted. You, Julian, perhaps not so much.

I told you before leaving where to find the manor record. I will not repeat it here, should this letter fall into the wrong hands before you discover it. I pray that you were able to find it and that it served as proof of Grenfell ownership. Father remains in exile, and I fear we shall both leave this world before a Grenfell can declare his true identity and reclaim the family estate. That I leave to you.

I have no way of knowing if we shall meet again, in this world or the next. Nor have I ever been able to fathom how and why our switching happened in the first place, other than to bless a future member of my family. With that conviction, I must believe that this was all for a purpose. My love to you all.

Your long past friend,

Emmeline

We sat on the floor around the prayer rug for a long moment without speaking. Lena finally broke the silence. "Well, we learned a couple of important things." She grinned across at me. "For one thing, you and Emme stop switching before we get a chance to find the manor record. But not before she comes here again, tells us where it is, and learns that she needs to hide these letters in the family Bible. So it looks like you'll be spending Christmas in Bathurst."

"The switching might last longer than that," Julian suggested. "This was written four and a half years after the time you've been spending in Africa." He shook his head in amazement. "This whole thing blows me away. Emme wrote this five years in *her* future. But she knows where to hide it because we will be able to tell her when she's here next." He pressed his fingertips against his temples, then burst them outward in a mock explosion and a loud "*Poooff*".

"But the switching stops before Emme gets married," Sam said.

"Yeah," Lena interrupted with a chuckle. "Now we'll never know if Charles loved her for her mind, or just for her body."

"Not funny," I said. "And you're right that this soccer trip can't just be coincidental. Especially since it takes us so close to Ipswich and Grenfell Hall. We've got to figure out how to get there when we're nearby. If we find the record somehow, that means we don't switch again after that. Emme didn't know if we found it when she wrote this."

Ryan had been fidgeting as if he were being blocked from

moving to the next level of an addictive game. "How about we read the other letter," he suggested. "Maybe we'll know more then." I opened the other two sheets and began to read.

"I, Robert Grenfell, do solemnly swear before God and these witnesses that what I write herein is God's truth."

For the next two pages, Robert described his involvement in the rebellion against the injustices of King George IV and the warrant for his arrest that had caused him to flee to the Cape Colonies. He claimed that his family estate, owned by the family since the mid-seventeenth century, had been wrongfully taken from him by the Crown and should be returned to his family as fair and just reparation for these injustices. He stated that his only daughter and rightful heir, Emmeline, would be returning to England as Emmeline Caywood. She would make what effort she could to reclaim ownership, should a safe opportunity arise. If not, when free men were again able to seek redress for injustices, descendants of the Grenfells would again petition the Crown to return the estate to its rightful owners. The letter was witnessed and signed by the Right Reverend Bernard Sutherland, Doctor Edward Begley, both of Ipswich, Suffolk, and Bathurst, South Africa, and by Sir Rufane Donkin, Governor of the Cape Colony of South Africa, Port Elizabeth.

Julian could hardly contain himself until I had finished reading. "*Perfect*," he exclaimed. "This is exactly what we've needed. Now, we just need to get someone important to pay attention to us."

Thursday afternoon was my session with Dr. Westover. We were meeting only monthly now. He had Mom come in for the first half hour to talk about how we were getting along and how she was adjusting to the changes in my personality. She told him she was doing fine, that in some ways, the other me was easier to deal with. I guess Emme liked to stay home, do her drawings, and play with the keyboard. Mom said Emme was especially excited about all the different sounds she could get out of the thing: Organ, grand piano, choir, percussion, and all those other settings. I guess her favorite is Strings. It was kind of depressing to hear your mom talk about how much easier you are to deal with when you're someone else. But at least she didn't say I was impossible when it was really me, and she admitted we had been closer since the last change.

After she left, Dr. Westover seemed to want to talk about what I could remember about my homelife at times when I was my other self.

"You mean, here?" I asked.

"Yes. Here."

When I said, "I only know what people tell me when I get back," he gave me his thoughtful, chin-rubbing *hmmm* and scratched some notes on his pad.

"And the talents you possess when this other personality manifests itself? You don't retain any of those abilities?"

"Nope. I'm just as talent-deprived as I've always been."

"Blessed with different talents," he corrected. "You are a very talented young woman under both circumstances."

"Okay. Short on talents people like to gush about," I conceded.

"Any residual desire to acquire these other talents?"

"No. Not really. I mean, it would be great to be able to play the piano really well. Everybody thinks that's pretty cool. But I haven't had any real interest in learning."

"How about the art? This amazing ability to draw?"

"No."

"That one's a bit more curious," he said. "One would think it's a talent that isn't quite as dependent on instruction and practice. More innate, if you will."

"Yeah. One would think."

He was quiet for a moment, and I could tell he was unsure about what he was about to say. But he said it anyway.

"This is such a unique case. I haven't come across anything quite like it in the literature. With your permission, I would like to write it up as a case study and submit it to several of the journals."

I didn't have to think about it. "No way," I said.

"What if I were to use pseudonyms? Disguise the subjects?

I shook my head. "Nope. No way. With all the searches people can do, there are no secrets. If you publish it, all anyone has to do is come to Texarkana and ask 'Who around here is having trouble with multiple personality disorder' or whatever you like to call it? Half the people in town would say, 'That Wallis girl.' I don't want to have people coming around talking to me about this. Or bothering Mom and my friends. No case study."

Westover frowned, but nodded. "Well, think about it. It's a most fascinating case. And we are depriving the scientific world of some valuable information."

"They'll have to do without. And maybe it's not that at all."

"By which you mean . . .?"

"Have you considered, even for a minute, that two minds or spirits or whatever could actually be changing places?"

"I'm a man of science," he said dismissively. "I don't believe that I know everything, by any means. But I do feel compelled to limit my diagnoses to the realm of the possible."

I chuckled. "When I'm this other person, I'm learning that what people believed to be impossible only two hundred years ago is all around me when I'm here. Maybe we're just in a similar position compared to what people will know two hundred years from now."

He smiled like you might to a little kid who has just said, "I wonder if I jumped out of an airplane, could I bounce around on the clouds?"

"I guess there is always that possibility," he said. "Tell me. Do you believe we are making any progress?"

"I don't know. What would progress be?"

"Are we getting any closer to you feeling that you might know what leads to these episodes? Anything you would wish to talk about?"

"I think it will stop soon."

"Oh? And why do you believe that?"

I wanted to say, "Because we've found the letters, and Emme should be able to tell us where the manor record is when she comes next." But instead I said, "Just a feeling I have."

Dr. Westover closed his notebook with an indulgent smile and ended the session.

Emme

Though I still had no desire whatsoever to reach some sort of truce with Prince George, I was beginning to find great satisfaction in the work Ally had begun in the Xhosa villages. Prince needed only to sniff at me to realize that the girl who loved to gallop across the veldt was somewhere else. Horses, it would appear, have a better sense for the true nature of one's soul than people do. Maisy and the wagon suited me very nicely. Noluvo now sat beside me as we rode the mile each morning to check on progress on the well and judge the effectiveness of Ally's medical treatments.

Angus Kinkade had assisted with building a waist-high wall of sunbaked brick around the well. Jacob Pickering fashioned an iron grate that covered its top when not in use, keeping small children, curious baboons, and Xhosa elders who had enjoyed too much worm treatment from tumbling into the new water source. Both men spoke to me as if I were an old friend, and I found each to be much more likable than I had before imagined.

To the headman's delight, the village was visibly healthier. The ailment that Ally had called Guinea worms in her written message had disappeared. Children who had languished beside their huts with swollen bellies now ran through the village with their once-healthier playmates. Even the rangy village dogs appeared to have gained weight.

In a hut opposite the headman's lodge, I helped Noluvo start a soap-making enterprise. Mother objected to her own supply diminishing with each village visit. I saw no reason why the Xhosa could not make their own. Ashes from burned leadwood and mahogany branches were soaked for three days in tall earthen jars above layers of straw and river rock. The water was then drained through a small drip hole into a kettle, then boiled until concentrated enough that the resulting lye solution dissolved a chicken feather. It was then strong enough to mix with animal fat to cure and shape into soap. The soap was my own addition to improved village sanitation, one I was certain Ally, maker of magic, would not have been able to provide. I may not know the science of her magnet, but I did understand many of the old folk ways. The villagers now used the soap when they washed both themselves and their clothing.

Noluvo had taken me twice to the place where the Indian hemp grows. I now dried it, as Ally had done, on the roof of the tack room. The chief insisted that all of the medicine be given to him. He passed it out to his people with great ceremony.

"It has given grandfather great power," Noluvo confided as we left the village one afternoon. "The people like the medicine, and chiefs from other villages have learned about it. He would like to know where the medicine grows."

I objected strongly enough that I believe it frightened her. "That must remain our secret. It is the best way for us to get your people to follow the rules about water. If other villages wish to have the medicine, they can do the same. We can give your grandfather enough for other chiefs. That will make him even more powerful." She understood and kept the secret between us.

One evening after supper, Father asked that I join him and Mother in the parlor. My first fear was that Noluvo's grandfather had come to him to complain that he was not being told where the medicine grew. Instead, Father spoke mainly to Mother.

"I believe it is time for us to send Emmeline back to England," he announced. "Mary will be delighted to have her live with her in Cambridge. With luck, she may be able to continue her studies with Mr. Constable. And we most certainly want her back where there are more eligible men."

"Now that she has so deeply insulted the Bradshaw family," Mother muttered.

Father bristled as I rarely saw him react. "If Edward Bradshaw is unable to deal with a strong-willed woman, he is not the right partner for our daughter."

Mother would not be silenced. "But if Emmeline is staying with your sister, those who wished to arrest you will know she is a Grenfell. She may be in danger."

"Few people know Mary to be a Grenfell," Father replied. "And officers of the Crown will not be interested in anyone but me. The order of law remains intact under this king, even if he flouts it. They have no case against our daughter."

"But they may force her to reveal where and who we are."

"Their interest, if it remains, is only in me. And after a year, I am of no importance to them if I stay out of the country and out of politics. And there is another reason we need Emmeline near the old estate. Should the monarchy change, we need a family member close to reclaim our property."

"Emmeline? You would leave that responsibility to your daughter?"

I inserted myself into the argument. "I am quite capable, Mother. Much more than you are willing to admit."

"But who is to know when you will have another of your fits of humor? You may not even remember who you are. Then what use will you be in reclaiming the hall?"

"My suspicion," Father said, "is that you do not wish to be so far from grandchildren when they arrive. Should the Monarchy change, we can all return. But until then, Emme needs to be in England."

"And when do you plan to send her?"

"As soon as I can arrange passage. Perhaps within a fortnight."

"Please, Father," I insisted. "Allow me to remain through the Christmas season and until mid-January. We are digging wells in two villages across the river. I should very much like to be here to see them completed."

Mother scowled. "You and your new obsession with the well-being of the Xhosa!"

I could see Father calculating in his head. "Yes. I think we should wait until then," he agreed, then added with a knowing smile, "we want you to be feeling fully yourself when you return home."

Ally

Julian called just after eight on a Thursday evening.

"I just got to my email and have one I think you'll want to see. Can I come over?"

I was curled up in a corner of the living room with notes Emme had taken on *Tess of the d'Urbervilles* for lit class. Big test tomorrow, and I hadn't been there for the Thomas Hardy discussion.

"I'm really not ready for Bayless's test. I'm pretty well up on the book we just finished, but I don't know anything about Hardy. I'm looking over Emme's notes."

"I don't need much time. Maybe half an hour. And I think you'll want to know about this when you see Lena and Sam tomorrow."

"Okay. Head on over. These notes are good, and I should be able to read through them again at noon."

"I'll be there in twenty."

I jotted down a couple of things Emme had written about whether Hardy was too free with his use of coincidence or was weaving in elements of destiny. That was the kind of thing Bayless liked to ask as essay questions. I walked out onto the porch to wait for Julian.

He swung into the drive about ten minutes later and had barely killed the engine before he was out of the car. He pulled his tablet out of a shoulder bag, plopped down beside me on the cedar bench, and kissed me fast enough that I knew he was thinking about something else. He proved it by asking, "Do you know what a solicitor is?"

"Some kind of call girl?"

"Not close. There are two kinds of lawyers in England. Solicitors and barristers. The way I understand it, the solicitors do the grunt work and the barristers get the credit and the big bucks. Sort of like the senior partners here. Well, I contacted this solicitor in London about Sam's family claim on Grenfell Hall. I attached all the genealogy stuff you looked up and a photo of the letter we found. His name's Trevor Emory and he sent a message back today saying they might be interested."

I *humphed.* "Well, that was easier than you thought. You said we might need to go public in the papers to get some attention."

Julian gave me his pretty-pleased-with-himself grin. "I sort of started that way. Have you heard of *The Sun*?"

"What? Is this *Jeopardy* or something? And what kind of question is that? You mean 'the sun' as in the big ball of flaming gas? Or Jesus?"

"No. The newspaper. *The Sun.* It's the most popular daily newspaper in England. Sort of a cross between *The Enquirer* and a regular paper, except for the skin shot they always have of some girl on page three."

"You're kidding."

"No. Look it up. *The Sun Page 3 Girls.* You'll see what I mean."

"So, what does this have to do with solicitors?"

"I started watching for articles in *The Sun* that talked about legal disputes and wrote down the names of law firms mentioned in the paper. I figured the ones that liked publicity and were interested in cases the media might jump on would show up in *The Sun.* This firm of Stacer and Mayfield represented plaintiffs in three cases over about a six-month period. So I found one of their solicitors online and sent him our stuff with an explanation of what we were interested in doing."

"Which is?"

"Reclaim the Grenfell estate for Sam and her family—the *rightful* heirs." Julian was getting a little testy.

"Did you say we wanted the hall given back?"

"No. Just that the estate should be restored to the family because it was confiscated by ancestors of the same royal family that's there now. And for unjust reasons. If they take the case, we can let them figure out what the best solution is. In fact, I'm thinking Sam and her mom would be better off if they just got compensated for its value."

"So, what did the guy say?"

"He said they were intrigued. That he'd take it up with others at the firm and let us know what they thought. But . . . .."

"I knew there'd be a 'but.'"

"But," he said, the irritation reappearing, "the guy wants to know what my interest is in all this. He asked for just what we thought they would. Proof the hall was the legal property of the Grenfell family and not some place they were allowed to live by the king."

"And what did you tell him?"

Julian leaned back and scowled. "I just *got* this today! That's why I called. I haven't said anything yet. We need to talk to Sam tomorrow and see what she wants to do."

"And we need that manor record," I reminded him. "When Emme comes back and lets you know where it is, maybe this Stacer and Mayfield guy can go get it for us."

"You mean '*If* Emme comes back.'"

"She'll be back. At least once. There's no real reason for all this to have happened if we can't get the record for Sam."

Julian looked doubtful.

"You don't think she's coming back?"

"Oh, I think she will. But I don't like the idea of having someone get the record for us. We need to get it ourselves and keep it with us every second. It's too valuable."

"You don't trust this Stacer and Mayfield?"

"A firm that shows up in *The Sun* every month? Well, no. I'd say I don't completely trust them. Plus, I think that's why you're going to England. This all fits together in some way."

I pulled out my phone. "I'll call Sam and Lena. We can meet before first hour."

"What about Ryan?"

I was never too sure about Ryan.

"We'd better include him," Julian said. "If he feels like he's being cut out, he'll be more likely to talk. And he's had some good ideas lately."

"Call him," I said. "We'll meet in the arch under the star at 7:30."

Mention of lawyers, suits, and national publicity made Sam skittish. "You mean we're, like, going to sue the Queen of England?" she asked Julian after he showed her the email from Stacer and Mayfield.

He gave her shoulder a reassuring squeeze. "I think if this works right, we won't have to. What we want is for them to agree the property was taken without just cause and either return it to you or compensate you for it. If it works the way we want, they'll figure the value and just pay your family what it's worth."

"So why look for some lawyer that loves to go public?" Lena argued on her behalf. "Why not just go to some really classy law firm and ask them for help?"

Julian shrugged. "We could. But I think this is likely to work best if the royals worry about bad publicity and know they're hearing from a bunch that isn't above taking the story to a rag like *The Sun*."

"I think he's right," Ryan chipped in. "From everything I see on my news feeds, they really hate bad publicity. I think we should see if this Trevor Emory, or Emory Trevor, or whatever his name is will put the squeeze on them."

Samantha wasn't convinced. "I don't want Mom dragged into this. She couldn't go over there if she needed to. And we can't afford to pay a lawyer."

"We ask them to take it *pro bono* to get the publicity, if they do that in England," Julian suggested. He turned to Ryan. "That means 'for free.'"

"I know that, smartass," Ryan muttered.

Julian went on as if nothing had been said. "And if not that, maybe they'll do it on a contingency basis. They get a percentage of whatever settlement there is. I've been reading up on that, and as of 2013, British lawyers can take civil cases on a contingency basis."

"What would a house like Grenfell Hall be worth?" I asked. "And what percentage goes to the lawyers?"

"Been reading up on that too. I found listings for a pot full of English manor houses. People must be wanting to get rid of them. But still, they run from about six hundred thousand to three million pounds. Looking at the pictures we've found of Grenfell Hall and based on where it is, I'd guess it will fall about in the middle. Maybe around one and a half million."

Samantha's ears pricked up. "How much is a pound worth—in US dollars?"

"Yesterday the pound was listed at a dollar thirty. So a sale of a million and a half pounds would bring just under two million dollars."

"And half of that goes to the lawyers," Ryan figured.

Julian shrugged. "We don't offer them fifty percent. We offer thirty. Another thing I read said special fees, such as the cost of experts and forensic examinations, can be extra. I say we offer thirty percent and tell them they need to take special costs out of their cut." He looked up from his tablet at Sam. "There would probably need to be some expert witnesses. They'll want someone to look at the letter to make sure it's the real thing. And if we find the manor record, that will have to be checked out. If we could settle for two million, that still could give this Stacer and Mayfield six hundred grand to work with."

"One point four million," Sam murmured. "This probably

sounds crazy, but that's not a whole lot more than we think Mom's treatments are going to cost—if she can get a transplant."

Lena had been swiping through something on her phone. "We leave here for our trip on Friday morning, January 31st. Fly from Atlanta overnight to London. Saturday's a recovery day. Our first match is Sunday in Maidstone and we play in Chelmsford on Tuesday. That's one of the places that's close to Ipswich. Wednesday's an off day. If we need to get to Grenfell Hall, that's when it's going to have to happen. Matches on Thursday and Saturday, then back to London and home Sunday. If Sam's going to meet with some lawyer, it will need to be after we find the manor record. So Friday's the only day that will work."

Sam again looked skeptical. "Will Coach Gillion let us go to Ipswich on our own? Or meet with some lawyer in London?"

"If we can get Trevor Emory and his firm to buy in, you'll need to explain all this to Gillion. If your moms agree that you can go, I think he'll let you if he knows what's going on and if one of the parents goes with you." Everyone glued their eyes on me. "Al, your mom's planning to go, right?"

"Yeah. And I think she'd go along with this," I said, and started thinking through what I could tell her that wouldn't send her and Dr. Westover off into Psycho Land.

Emme

The switch occurred as I was passing out weekly doses of the medicinal tea in the Xhosa village across the river where Ally had left me sitting astride Prince George. She would be delighted. I was much less pleased to find my lips firmly pressed against those of Julian and his hand gripping the left half of my bottom. I squealed involuntarily and pushed away, flustered by the ripple of pleasure that passed through my entire body. I had never fully been kissed by a man. Pecks on the forehead by my father and light brushes on the hand by gentlemen who wished to appear courtly. But not fully on the lips. It was much more pleasurable than I had imagined. But this was Ally's suitor. I had no business enjoying his kisses, and he had no business sharing them with me.

He withdrew at the same instant, seemingly gifted with a sense like Prince that the wrong person had suddenly reappeared. He held me away, his hand now against my back and a slight grin twisting his disappointed lips. My hands were on his shoulders.

"Hi, Emme," he said. "I expected you back today, but your timing wasn't great."

I stepped back and released him, looking quickly about. We were standing just outside a circle of light on the porch of Ally's home, Julian's automobile sitting nearby with its engine running.

"I expected it later as well," I stammered, then regained some composure. "Since I knew I would be away for Christmas, I had at least hoped to say goodbye to Father. Mother will think my hysteria-crazed self has returned, so there was no reason to trouble her early."

"We told Ally's mom there would probably be a change today, so she'll be ready for your personality to show up." He chuckled softly. "I hope you like the gifts she has for you. I think you're getting that horse blanket you liked from North Forty and a warmer jacket to take to England."

"I fear I will get more use from the jacket than Ally will from the music and books Mother believes she has kept secret." I did allow myself to take his hand, leading him back toward the door. "What is the time? I have so much to tell you but wish Lena and Samantha to be with us. They are the ones who must remember the details."

"Just after eleven. If you'd been an hour earlier, you could have caught us all at the Icehouse."

"Is the day Thursday? Perhaps I can send a message. We can meet early at school."

"No school tomorrow. It's Christmas Eve. Ask Lena if we can meet at her place. It's the most private, and her lita will have all kinds of Christmas stuff baked."

"Come in while I text."

"I'd rather you do it here. Your mom's peeked out a couple of times already."

We sat on the porch bench with Julian closer than he had chosen to be with me before. I let Sam and Lena know that I was back and would like to meet as soon as we could arrange it. "Your home, Lena?"

She answered instantly, suggesting nine o'clock. "People coming over later," she said.

Sam answered five minutes later. "Sorry. Was in bed. Long day. I'll be there at 9."

Julian leaned over and again kissed me lightly on the cheek. I did nothing to resist. "So, that's set. I'll come by for you— assuming you haven't learned to drive while you've been away."

I squeezed the hand I had chosen not to release. "I will be right here," I said, and went in to tell Jennifer I was going directly to bed. She could deal with the change tomorrow.

We chose not to call Ryan. If there was something that absolutely must remain secret, even Lena agreed Ryan should be left in the dark. And this must remain secret.

As anxious as I was to share what I had learned about the manor record, I spent the first fifteen minutes in Lena's living room marveling at a Christmas tree that was like none I had ever seen. Tiny lights of every color blinked and sparkled from top to bottom. At the ends of the heavier branches, small flower-shaped cups held pointed tubes with colored liquid bubbling inside. Brightly colored glass balls hung like ripe glazed fruit from every limb, and packages wrapped in shiny paper of silver, red, and green were piled beneath the tree like a shop's Christmas window on Princes Street. One corner of the room held a table with a scene of the Christ child's birth carved in rich golden wood; the Holy Family surrounded by shepherds, sheep, wisemen and their camels. A silver star hung high above with another tiny twinkling light shining down upon a thatched manger.

"This is so lovely," I whispered to Lena who stood patiently beside me.

She smiled and nodded toward her grandmother who dozed in an overstuffed chair that cradled her like the babe in the manger. "It's my lita. This is her favorite time of year. She has a stack of tamales on the table in the kitchen and a bag for you to take home with you."

I cast a wishful glance back at the tree. "Jennifer has a very simple tree. And I saw very few gifts beneath it."

"I hope Ally remembered to put them out. Look when you get back to see if there are some from her to her mom. If they aren't under the tree, they'll be in one of her closets. Her mom will put most of your stuff out tonight."

I made a mental note to check the closets when I returned home. "I must remember to be excited," I said.

In the kitchen, we gathered about the plate of tamales, a cornmeal dough filled with spicy meat, cheese, and peppers that she had cooked in brown banana leaves. Julian pushed the plate around to each of us. Sam and Lena took two. I, only one. Julian placed two on a plate beside his computer, poured green sauce from a small pitcher beside them, and handed the pitcher around to the rest of us. I could smell the sharpness of peppers. I watched as they peeled away the banana wrap. Julian and Lena spooned sauce onto the golden-brown shell.

Sam stood and walked to the cupboards, looking in one after another without invitation.

"The one left of the microwave," Lena said. Sam removed a drinking glass, filling it from the tap at the sink.

"I know I'm going to need water," she said sheepishly. "I remember Lita's tamales from last year."

I covered mine with sauce as the others had done and took a small bite from one end. The flour wrap and meaty filling were delicious and I dipped again for a larger bite. What had been a sharp, aromatic complement to the spiced beef gradually began to warm against my tongue and throat as if a small fire had been kindled in my mouth. I looked up wide-eyed at Sam who just grinned and pushed the water across in front of me.

"I'll get another," she said as the fire worked its way up into my nose and spread in a bright flush across my face. Tears on my cheeks did nothing to cool the spreading heat. Lena was up and at the refrigerator. "Sorry. I forgot you weren't you. Milk and bread will work better. Just leave the sauce off and you'll be okay."

I gulped the milk, soaked a slice of bread and held it in my mouth until finally able to choke out an exclamation. "*Oh, my!*" was all I could say, laying the tamale back on my plate and blinking back tears as the others made no attempt to smother their laughter.

"How do you eat such things?" I was finally able to ask. "The flavor is wonderful. But I have never encountered a food so hot."

"That's only about ten proof," Sam said. "You should taste the stuff Lena's brothers like to eat. It's like sucking on a road flare."

Julian returned us to the task at hand. "Okay, Emme. What do we need to know?"

I opened my sketchpad on the tabletop. "Find the picture of Grenfell Hall. I am going to sketch the floorplan."

Julian found a picture of our home on his laptop. We clustered our chairs to allow all to see the screen while I quickly sketched the layout of rooms on the lower and upper floors, showing where doors entered each. To add drama, I placed my drawings one above the other, added a directional arrow indicating that the right-hand side of the manor faced north, and asked, "Do you notice anything unusual about these?"

Julian answered immediately. "What's this long, narrow space at the right end of both floors? No doors."

"Ah! Very good. That is what you must find." I ran a finger along what appeared to be an enclosed hallway on both levels of my sketch. "The manor was built by William Grenfell, a member of Parliament and devout Puritan, in 1640. It was a time when both Parliament and the Puritans were in opposition to King Charles over both his leadership of the church and his disregard for Parliament's authority over taxes. Like my father, Sir William did not find favor with the Crown. When the house was built, a secret staircase was added to the north wing. It allowed William and his family, if the King's men visited unexpectedly, to leave the house from the upper floor through a hidden door in the master bedchamber."

Julian leaned over the drawing. "Is this secret enough no one will have found it by now?"

"Father believes so. He was the only person who knew of it when we lived in the hall. He thought it unlikely that one would stumble across it accidentally."

"And the manor record is in there?" Lena asked.

I pointed to the front corner of the enclosure on my sketch of the upper floor, then at the right-front of the picture on Julian's screen. "The entrance is in this corner. Just inside the hidden doorway is a landing, and on the landing, a small corner table. Father placed the record book, wrapped in leather, in the drawer of this table before the family left the house."

Julian's eyes narrowed. "So someone needs to get into the hall, find a way into this staircase, get the book, and get out again. Not exactly a simple job."

I tapped again on the drawing. "As I said, the entrance is in what was my parent's bedchamber. The walls are paneled in a dark mahogany. There is wainscoting around the entire room decorated with carved rosettes, spaced at a distance of about a yard. The door is released by twisting the rosette closest to this wall." I indicated the corner where the north wall met the front of the manor.

"After two hundred years?" Samantha wondered. "Would whatever's holding it still turn?"

I nodded. "I asked Father that very question. He thought it should not be a challenge. It is a wooden latch and should not rust. The fastener at the bottom of the stairs, the one that holds the outer door at the rear of the house, may be more difficult. It is held by an iron bolt."

Julian traced the route with a finger. "So you get into the stairwell from the bedroom here—and go down the stairs to a door here that opens onto the back of the house. Why won't the outer door have been discovered?"

I turned Julian's computer to better see the picture of the hall. "We are unable to see the rear in this picture. But the outer wall on the lower level is supported at regular intervals by heavy wooden beams. The wall between the beams is of plaster. The door is one section of plaster, fashioned so well as to appear just like the others."

"And you don't think it will have been re-plastered since you left?" Samantha wondered.

"That, I cannot say. It may have to be forced open."

We sat silently around the drawings, each expression revealing the impossibility of the task just outlined. Finally, Julian spoke.

"This may be information we give to the London lawyers. Let them get a subpoena or whatever and go in after it."

Lena objected immediately. ""No way. I think you were right before. We need to get this ourselves and not trust it to anyone. It's too important."

Samantha was dubious. "So we go to whatever town this is, break into the place, and hope the knob thing works."

"I've found everything I can on the antique dealership that leases the hall," Julian said. "It looks to me like they use it to display their high-end stuff, setting up rooms with period furniture. You walk around and see what the pieces would look like as they were used in the eighteen hundreds. If that's right, you might be able to get into that upper bedroom."

Lena shook her head doubtfully. "Without anyone being with us? They'll be watching everyone like hawks in a place like that. Probably cameras."

"You'll have to hope there are no cameras, then create a diversion."

"Yeah? Like what? Set off a fire alarm?"

"Maybe. If the rosette thing works, one of you should be able to get into the stairwell and out of sight in a few seconds."

"And what if the bottom door's stuck shut?"

"You'll have to come back out the way you went in."

"Carrying a two hundred-year-old book? Out of an antique shop. *That* should work."

Julian pushed back in his chair. "Look, I can get as much information as I can for you, but I can't go do the job. When you're in Chelmsford you're going to be what? Thirty miles away? You have an open day. You know where the book is. You're just going to have to figure it out once you get into the house."

Lena looked first at me, then at Samantha who still exuded uncertainty. "I don't know . . ." she muttered.

"You *must* do it," I insisted, knowing full well that I would not be part of the adventure. "And you, Samantha, must be bold. Your mother and the family depend on you."

Lena nodded. "She'll do what she needs to." She turned back to Julian. "But you aren't done. You need to get your Mr. Trevor Emory to accept the case. Tell him we'll bring the original letter and the manor book. If the lawyer guys aren't in, we can't get this done."

Julian agreed. "I'm going to tell him we have the book but want to hand deliver it. If you can't get to it, you can let them know where it is. I say we tell them we want to be compensated for the house or sell it, and offer thirty percent of what comes from a settlement or sale of the place. Are you okay with that, Sam?"

Her nod didn't show conviction. "We'd be okay with *anything*. Two months ago, we didn't even know about this possibility."

"I had hoped we could recover the hall for the family," I objected, knowing how much Father wished to retain the property.

"I don't think that's the reason for all this," Julian said. "But as a condition, we can ask that the estate continue to be called Grenfell Hall. Maybe someone can write a history of the place."

"That would be very nice," I agreed, realizing the truth of what he said.

Julian closed his tablet. "Okay, then. I send a note back to solicitor Emory as soon as we're through here, we see what the firm says, and you three start thinking about how to get the record book." He picked up one of his tamales and dipped it in sauce.

I knew what my responsibility was to be until Ally returned. Jennifer must be told just enough to be helpful, but not enough to make Dr. Westover aware of our plan.

We did not hear from Stacer and Mayfield until Christmas was two weeks past. I had been appropriately delighted with the saddle blanket and jacket, which was a lovely blue and had a hood that could be drawn tightly about my face. Of the many things I would miss from Ally's world, clothing was near the top. People here dressed for comfort, and I had become quite fond of Ally's jeans, loose shirts, and shoes that did not squeeze and pinch.

Jennifer was thrilled with the "Guidebook to East Anglia" Ally had secreted away in her closet and with a framed sketch of her daughter leaping to place the header that had won the regional championship. It was the only image I could think of that came close to representing both of us.

Ally's father came on Christmas day just after noon. We spent an awkward afternoon with my lack of interest in riding, and his uncertainty with what he called my "suddenly reserved personality and apparent need to feel British." Jennifer was watching the television when he returned me from an early dinner, a show in which performers competed to see who would be chosen as America's most talented. Most, it seemed, believed singing to be the greatest talent. I saw it as the perfect time to ask for her help while in England. I sat near her on the sofa.

"Have I mentioned to you that there appears to be evidence that Samantha Howard may be heir to an estate in England?"

She glanced briefly away from her program, then back at the television. One of the inventions I will not miss when permanently back in Bathurst is television. It has taken the place of civil conversation and of most other productive activity.

"Yes. You mentioned it. But it seems very unlikely to me."

"It now appears more certain. And the hall lies between two of the towns where our matches will be held. Chelmsford and Bury Saint Edmunds."

"Oh?" she murmured, intent on learning what one particular judge, a man with an accent much like my own, would say about the most recent performer.

"She and Lena and I would like to go to the estate on our free day following the Chelmsford match. Our hope is that you will go with us—so that Coach Gillion will allow it."

She sat silently, her brow slowly knitting as she allowed what I had said to force its way between performances. She shifted her position on the sofa to face me.

"You want to do *what*?"

"We wish to visit Grenfell Hall. The manor that was once the home of Samantha's ancestors."

"I don't think the school will allow it."

"They may if you agree to go with us. It is only thirty miles, and Lena tells me it is a very short journey by train."

"Has Coach Gillion agreed to this?"

"Lena is asking. It would be most helpful if you agreed to accompany us."

"I've never been on a train—here or anywhere else."

"Then it will add to the adventure. Lena has read about it and believes it to be very simple." I opened her new guide to East Anglia to a picture I had discovered while thumbing though the book the evening before. "This is the manor we would like to visit. Grenfell Hall."

She studied me for a long moment, her attention now fully on our conversation, then read the two paragraphs about what the caption beneath the picture referred to as "one of Suffolk's most picturesque manors." Finally she said, "If Coach Gillion agrees, I'll take you girls to see this house."

"Wonderful!" I slid closer beside her to give her our first embrace. She held me for a long time.

"Do you feel that these changes are shortening, Ally? Will I have you fully back sometime?"

"Soon," I assured her. "I believe it will be soon."

Lena waited to speak to Coach Gillion until Julian heard back from the solicitor. Mr. Trevor Emory informed him that the firm had completed its own research and found that our account of the hall's seizure was true. They had also traced Emmeline Pearce's descendants and had been led to the late William Howard of Texarkana, Texas, USA. With documentation from Samantha that she was William's daughter and sole heir, and with the letter attesting that Robert Caywood was indeed Robert Grenfell, they would agree to represent her in a civil action to reclaim the property on a contingency basis. The hall, their message estimated, had a market value of approximately one and a half million pounds. They were willing to accept thirty percent as their fee, but affirmed that expert witnesses would be necessary to confirm the authenticity of both the Grenfell letter and the manor record. For this, they insisted, another five percent would be required.

We gathered again at the Icehouse on Thursday evening at the end of Samantha's shift. She agreed to the terms.

"We need to send them an official copy of your birth certificate, of your father's death certificate, and a notarized statement that you are his sole living heir," Julian said. "Once they have that, they plan to contact legal representatives of the royal family, inform them of the claim, and request a response by the time you're in England. They'll threaten to go to *The Sun* with a story about a critically ill American woman who's being bankrupted by our healthcare system but could be saved if the English royals would return property stolen from her family. Trevor thinks the story would be a headliner. But our best option is that the Queen won't want the publicity." He spoke more directly to Samantha. "If Stacer and Mayfield don't get something that shows a willingness to at least investigate the claim, you need to get ready for some media attention. I think the papers here and shows like *24 Hours* will be all over this."

Samantha drew a deep breath and smiled nervously. "This all worries me so much I can't even sleep. I haven't said much to Mom because I don't want to get her hopes up. But if this becomes public, I guess we'll both have to be ready."

"I'm going to tell Coach enough about this to convince him we have to get to Grenfell Hall the Wednesday we're in England," Lena said. "Emme, I wish both you and Ally could be with us. We need her if we're going to win any matches. But it would sure be nice to go into that house with someone who's been there before."

"I will guide you through it several more times while I am

here," I assured her. "And on the day that I know you are there, I will be the one with a sleepless night."

Ally

Whatever or whoever it was, this great omniscient thing that was messing with our lives, it didn't care a lick about timing. Or maybe it did and got a kick out of seeing what Emme would do if dropped into the middle of chemistry class—or me poised primly on a piano bench at some posh Cape party. This time I was holding a small cup of crumpled leaves in mid-air, looking into the grateful face of a Xhosa woman who expectantly held out a bowl.

"Is something wrong?" I heard Noluvo say beside me. I looked over to see her holding a much larger bowl of dried hemp.

"No. No," I stuttered. "I forgot for a minute what I was doing."

She laughed. "You have changed again! Do you know where you are? Come. Give a cup to these women, and we will go outside."

I finished dispensing to three waiting women and followed Noluvo out into the center of the village. It wasn't her village, but I recognized it as the one where I'd switched when I was about to swing down from Prince's back—another of the Great One's little timing experiments. Nearby, villagers drew water from a well surrounded by new brick.

"You've expanded business since I was here last."

"Three villages have wells. And all use the medicine. We fetch and dry it for Grandfather. He sends us to the villages to give it to the other chiefs."

"I'm surprised no one's tried to follow you. Those women looked pretty anxious to get their dose."

"We leave as if we are going to Fort Kowie. There are places where we can see for a long distance in every direction. If we see anyone, we continue on to the port. If no one is following, we take the path to the medicine field."

"And no one has tried to stop you on the road after you get it?"

"Grandfather is the headman for all the villages here. If someone took it from us, he would find them. They would be punished and their village would lose its medicine. The people all know to leave us alone."

"You and Emme seem to be getting along better."

"She is a very kind and caring person, now that she allows herself to be."

"Are we through here for today?" I was feeling unusually comfortable for a switch and looked down to see that I was in my riding clothes. "What's with the outfit? No dress for Miss Emme?"

"When you last became Emmeline, sitting with Grandfather and the elders in his house, you decided that you liked these clothes when gathering medicine and visiting the villages. But you still do not ride Prince."

"Well, that's progress. Let's get home. I need to let Robert know we found his letter."

Noluvo didn't seem to care what letter I was talking about. "Robert is in the field trimming hedges," she said.

"Then I'll take Prince out to find him."

"That would be good. Then he will know you have changed again."

I found him on the north boundary of the farm with a line of Xhosa workmen, trimming and shaping the bramble hedges that served as natural barriers to the sheep. He saw me approaching from a distance and stopped his work, watching with an amused smile as I reined in the stallion.

"I see my other daughter has returned."

"One of life's little surprises. Do you have time that we can ride together?"

He quickly inspected the condition of the hedge they were shaping, gave brief instructions to the Xhosa men, and walked the short distance to where the gelding grazed beside a pole gate. I swung down and opened the gate, led Prince through, and waited until Robert followed before latching it closed again.

"I see the gelding's taken to you."

Robert ran a hand along the horse's side. "You did a good job with him. And I learned to treat him like a friend rather than some dumb beast."

"There's no better partner when they trust you," I said, stroking Prince's neck.

We rode toward an open stretch of veldt that bordered the river, increasing our pace until both horses ran stretched into a full gallop. The gelding strained to stay with Prince, with Robert leaning hard over his neck, laughing with a delight I'd never seen in the man. We reined the horses up at the top of a low rise that overlooked one of the wide, calm stretches of river where animals came to drink. Below, the grassland was dotted by herds of kudu and impalas. Zebras lined the bank, drinking, raising their heads alertly to test the air, then returning to the water. Downstream, a family of elephants, a matriarch and five younger cows with calves, splashed and hosed themselves, wary of two cape buffalo that snorted and shook their massive heads from across the watering hole.

The air smelled of wild things. I drew in a long, deep breath and stretched forward over the stallion's neck. "This is such an amazing place. I'm really going to miss it when this all ends."

Robert studied me curiously. "You believe the changes will end soon?"

"We found your letter about becoming Caywoods when you were chased out of England."

His expression turned to confusion. "Emmeline asked for a letter, but I have yet to write it."

"You will. And thank you. We really needed it."

"And what did I write in this letter?"

"Whatever you felt you needed to say. It will be what the letter included."

"And how did you know from my letter that you may not be changing again?"

"Emme left a note with it that showed she didn't know if we ever found the manor record. I'm assuming you told her where it is and that my friends now know. But if *she* didn't know if we were able to get it, that means we don't switch again."

He sat in silence, watching the cautious dance between the mother elephants and the buffalo. When he spoke again, his voice had become melancholy. "I shall miss you, Alyssa Wallis. Had I been blessed with another daughter, I should have been very happy if it were you."

I wasn't much the type to tear up, but felt my eyes fill anyway and said aloud what I'd thought every day I'd been in Bathurst. "If I could have two fathers," I said, "I'd pick you."

He reached across and held my arm, his smile showing less sadness. "The fates have given us to each other for a time, and I thank them for that. But there is something I would like to ask of you, if you believe this to be your final time with us. Teach me what you know—about how my flocks might be improved, about caring for the horses . . ." his smile broadened, ". . . and about what makes the horseshoe into a magnet."

I laughed and sniffed away the tears. "I can tell you what I know. But I really don't understand a lot of the science myself. And we don't have the medicine here to take really good care of the animals. One of these days, there will be these things called antibiotics. Now, that's where you can *really* start making a difference."

"Do you know how to make them? These antibiotics?"

I thought fleetingly about seeing what would happen if we let some bread mold and fed it to sick sheep. Would there be any penicillin in there? I decided it had to be way more complicated than that and let it pass. "No," I admitted. "I don't know how to do it."

"Do you know why you and Emme change places?"

The question caught me off-guard. But I guess it made sense that if we knew so much in my time—how to make machines fly, how to create photos and send them instantly around the world as bits of information to be reassembled at some far-off computer— we might very well know how to exchange consciousness. Why couldn't those little sparks of energy that create thought and awareness be hacked into and re-routed to some equally distant brain? A puzzle for Julian and Ryan to work on.

"No one in my time knows why this has happened," I confessed. "A doctor there wants to write about it and send it out to all the scientists in the world to get them working on it. But even he doesn't think it's really happening. He's more in line with Dr. Begley. Thinks there's some chemical imbalance in me that's creating this new personality."

Below us, the elephant matriarch bellowed and charged one of the buffalo that had ventured too close, sending it splashing back into the river.

"The greater mystery," Robert mused, "is why it happened to Emmeline. And to you. To return Grenfell Hall to the family after all these years?"

"And save my friend's mother, if this all works out."

"So you believe this may all be for the sake of changing one person's life?"

My thoughts jumped from Samantha and her mother to Lena, then to Julian and Emmeline and Robert and Noluvo and to her people. They settled finally on Alyssa Wallis.

"Many, many more than one," I murmured.

Beginning the following afternoon, Robert returned from the fields at 3:00 and we spent the rest of the days working with the horses or discussing what basic science I remembered from physics, biology, and chemistry. We started with breeding sheep.

"What is this breed?" I asked as we rode north through his

pastures toward Angus Kinkade's farm. "I come from cattle country and don't know squat about sheep."

"In Britain, we call them Leicester Longwool. We brought them with us."

"What do you want from them?"

"What do I want from them?"

"Yes. Good wool? Lots of meat? Better weight gain? Better survival rates for lambs?"

"Ideally, all of those qualities."

I wracked my brain for a date from biology class but couldn't come up with it. "Has Darwin shown up yet?" I asked. I figured he'd have heard of the man if his work had been published.

"Darwin? That is not a name I recognize."

"Hmmm. Soon, I'd guess. I know some selective breeding was done before he came along, but I don't know how much or where. Anyway, I see all kinds of sheep when I ride around. Angus has a breed that looks more like goats. Fat tails. Hair instead of wool. Floppy ears. What's good about them?"

"They were here even before the Dutch arrived. They're a hardy lot, eat anything, and endure the rain and heat well."

"And what don't you like about them?"

"Ill-tempered. Large boned. And no wool, of course."

"So why does Angus raise them?"

"They survive here well and thrive on the plants that flourish in the dry season. He sells the meat to passing ships, so isn't worried about wool."

"The Boer farmers beyond the river have another variety. They look more like yours, but with shorter faces. Very good-looking wool."

"They call them Merinos. I believe the Dutch initially were given them by the Spanish."

"And what do you like about them?"

"Mild temperament. And as you said, very fine wool. But they do not carry the weight of my Leicester sheep. And are not as well-suited to this climate."

"What I'd do, if I were going to be around for a while, is begin two experiments. I'd find rams in those two herds that have the qualities you would most like to see in your own. Separate out a few good ewes from your flock and breed them to those rams. Pick the male lambs you get from those ewes that show the best traits, and breed them back into a couple of other good Leicester ewes. Take that through about five or six generations and see if you're getting sheep that display the traits you like best in each breed. You need to keep the three flocks apart and keep careful records. That's how you'll get better stock."

"Our effort now is to keep our breeds apart—to keep them pure," he objected.

I shrugged. "You asked. And that's what I'd do. Create a breed of your own. Call it Bathurst or Caywood Crossbred or something. Your wool and meat buyers aren't going to care how pure your stock is."

He slouched over the saddle, brow furrowed deeply, and stared into his horse's mane. After a moment he straightened and his face relaxed. "Tomorrow we will go talk Angus and one of the Boer farmers out of their best rams. You must help me select."

Each afternoon the topic changed. We talked through every horse ailment I could think of affecting skin, hooves, legs, eyes, bellies, and brains. As I described them, I realized how much we had come to rely on vaccinations and antibiotics but told him what I knew about how feed management, proper shoeing, immediate treatment of cuts with alcohol, and keeping the horses out of the sun and off new grass could reduce health problems.

"What we need," I admitted, "is to be up north where there are some Arabs around. They've been raising and treating horses for centuries and would know all the good folk remedies. We've come to depend so much on medicines that I don't know a lot of the old ways."

"You appear to have educated yourself out of much of the old wisdom," Robert said with a chuckle. "That is a lesson you need to remember."

I used the Voltaic Pile to begin some basic lessons in atomic structure, dredging out every memory I had of what Mr. Payne had been covering all year and what I'd learned from Isenberg. Robert easily grasped the idea of tiny particles that made up everything and was fascinated by my rudimentary explanation of how they bonded to make different substances. He rubbed thoughtfully at his arm, then turned his hand slowly, examining the surface of his skin.

"And I am made of these same atoms?"

"Yes. Mainly carbon and water, with lots of other stuff mixed in." I had to do some quick mental switching between chemistry and biology.

"Then what makes me alive? Different than the stones in the wall there?"

"Ah. You've got me there. If I knew the answer to that, I might know why I switch with Emme. We haven't figured that one out yet."

"You are quite an amazing young woman, Miss Alyssa."

"Not nearly as amazing as I should be, with all the chances I've had to know this stuff," I confessed.

"You are still young."

"Yes," I said. "There is that."

On the twenty-eighth day since the last switch, I asked that we spend the afternoon at the house. If I guessed right, it would happen in the early evening. I talked mainly to Robert and Noluvo, with Rebecca thinking I was just babbling. I told them what a beautiful place this was, and how I loved to ride across the grasslands, watching for new animals I hadn't seen before. I had Noluvo explain in detail what the treatment programs were for the Xhosa villages. We agreed that the next step to making real improvement would be to convince the people not to *thabatha i-*

shit just anywhere, but to make something like a latrine. Rebecca looked up from her sewing with such anguish in her eyes that my last thought was that she was the one who would benefit most from the evening. Then I was gone.

Emme

Each afternoon I memory-walked Sam and Lena through Grenfell Hall. If time permitted, we gathered at the Icehouse at our favorite booth. I had become particularly fond of their burgers and fries. My friends chided me for my choice of hot chocolate rather than the Coke they believed should go with burgers.

"I love this drink and the cream on top. And it goes perfectly with my burger," I argued.

On this particular evening, I was assuring Sam and Lena that their decisions, once in the hall, should be quite simple. "We have no way of knowing who will accompany you through the house, if you gain entry at all. Most of the rooms have at least two exits. Once you have the record, if you must return into the house from the stairwell, move directly to the outer doors and stay out of rooms with only one exit." The two nodded their agreement.

"Lena, take us through the lower floor, explaining what should be avoided.

Lena leaned back against the stuffed back, closing her eyes. "We will probably enter from what you call the east portico. That will take us into a large reception hall with the dining room to the left and the drawing room to the right. Both have other exits into the central hallway that runs through the middle of the house" She peeked open her eyes long enough to receive an acknowledging nod from me and Sam, then continued with a detailed description of the remaining first-floor rooms and central stairway.

I clapped my hands in quiet applause. "Excellent! Now, Samantha. You take us through the upper floor."

Samantha chose to watch us both for our approval as she spoke. "At the top of the stairs is another open reception hall and sitting area. To the right—and now we're facing the front of the house because of the turn in the stairs—are some storage rooms and closets and four small bedchambers for the maids and gardener. Stay out of those rooms. No way out but back down the hall." We appeared to approve, so she plowed resolutely ahead.

"To the left are the four family bedrooms and dressing rooms. Each has doors into the hall and into the room beside it. The one we need to get to is the master bedroom at the end on the right. Once inside there, go to the left corner by the windows. Twist the rosette in the wainscoting closest to the window wall. That should open the panel into the hidden staircase. Once inside, get the book and try to get out the door at the bottom of the stairs. That releases by pulling back a bolt."

"And where is the book?"

"In a drawer in the corner table, just inside the top entry."

"Remember," I reminded her, "there is no apparent drawer. The front may appear to have a cross brace beneath the tabletop. Pull it from the bottom."

"Right," Samantha nodded. "Got it."

"And the most direct route out of the house if you must re-enter the bedroom?"

"Out the bedroom door into the hall. Left down the hall to the stairs. Down and out the back door to the rear portico."

"Very good. I believe we have reviewed this enough. Do you have other questions?"

"If we can't leave the property through the front gates for some reason," Lena asked, "what's behind the house in the back?"

"A large garden. A small patch of woods, and a high stone wall. But after this many years, I have no way of knowing what you will find."

Lena nodded. "I'll take a look on Google Earth when I get home. It would be good to know."

Samantha reached across the bench and took my hand. "If this is your last time here, what would you like to do before you leave?"

Her touch sent a spark into my heart as if it had come from

Ally's stack of metal disks. I had never had friends like the two who now sat with me. Not in Ipswich, and certainly not in the lonely world of the colonies. In that moment, I realized that I would miss them more desperately than any of the marvels that surrounded me. Without trying to resist, I began to weep.

Lena and Sam were beside me, each holding an arm and sniffling away their own tears.

"More than anything, I should like to spend time with you," I whispered. "I have never had such dear friends." Then I straightened myself and wiped at my eyes with a napkin. "And Ally's work with the Xhosa people has been truly remarkable. I should like to learn what I can about improving village health. And I should like to eat a burger every day—with hot chocolate."

Lena leaned her head against my shoulder and laughed. "Ally will love you for that. And we can spend all the time you want together. For one thing, you need to get out and run with me after school every day."

We were all laughing now. "I so hate to run. Though it *is* more enjoyable in this body."

"Al's not going to have much time after you switch to get ready for England. We need to keep her in shape."

"Then I shall run. And we will come here afterward for a burger."

Samantha found a book called *The National Geographic Complete Guide to Natural Home Remedies* and another titled *Low-Tech Methods for Clean Water and Sanitation.* I found the home remedies book most helpful, full of advice about herbal medicines, poultices, and improvements to diet. The book on purification of water recommended use of materials yet to be discovered in my time. Ceramic filters. Plastic soda bottles. Something called a UV light wand. It astounded me that so little was known just two hundred years before—and that so much would be discovered in such a short time.

Each afternoon I ran with Lena after practice, finding that Ally's long stride, loose limbs, and well-developed lungs made it much more enjoyable than I had imagined. Coach Gillion had learned that I did not play well "when having one of my episodes," so allowed me to work with weights while the others worked on skills. I now showered with the other girls with much less shame and little concern about what they were thinking.

"There is one other wish," I told Julian one Friday afternoon as I gazed upward at a thin streak of cloud I was told trailed a huge flying machine as it raced across the sky. "I should like to fly." He said nothing at the time. Just looked at me with his thoughtful smile.

He called the next morning to say he would come for me in half an hour. "I'd like to take you for a ride," was all he would say.

We drove into Arkansas beyond the edge of the city, stopping before a long building with a square tower beside it. He walked me to a smaller metal structure and into a cramped front office.

"I'm Julian," he told a solid, middle-aged man whose chest and belly showed that he had once been fit but was now enjoying more food and drink than exercise. His hair was cut very short on the sides and square across the top. A thick mustache drooped along both sides of a mouth I guessed was smiling behind the brush. He extended a hand.

"I'm Bart. You're the girl who wants to fly?"

My heart nearly stopped. Some dreams are more easily expressed than faced up to. "Oh," I stuttered. "I hadn't imagined that it might truly happen."

"It can truly happen if you want it to. Your friend here has paid for a half-hour. Are you up to it?"

"What would it require of me?"

"Come with me," Bart said. "Your friend can come along. No more for two than one, and this is a four-seater." He led us through the empty building and out onto a vast expanse of pavement. Sitting near the building was a red and white machine with long straight wings and an upright tail, standing on three wheeled feet. Bart opened a small door in the side and invited me to look in. The interior was much like an automobile, but with a yoke-shaped handle at the end of the driving column and many more dials and gauges below the front window.

"What do you think? Want to go up?" Julian had obviously warned this man that I might be hesitant.

"Is it safe? Have you done this many times?"

Bart laughed through the mustache. "Twenty-five hundred hours. And I'm still here to tell about it."

"Twenty-five hundred hours?"

"In the air." He pointed upward. "Always made it back down."

I could not imagine anything more terrifying and exciting. I turned to Julian. "And you. Have you done this before?"

He shook his head. "But I'm game. You convinced me it was time."

The thought flitted through my mind that it was quite careless of me to be taking this risk while living in Ally's body. But then, she was galloping recklessly across the veldt on that demon-possessed stallion.

"I would like to go," I declared and began to climb up into the machine.

Bart took my arm. "Let's put your friend in back. You can sit up front with me where you can see better."

I let Julian climb into the rear, then took a seat beside Bart with one of the yoke handles only a foot in front of me.

"I've already done the walk-around," Bart said, "so we're ready to go. Buckle up."

As we did in the automobiles, I cinched a strap across my chest and tightly about my hips. Bart clipped a sheet of instructions into a holder on his yoke and began to mumble to himself as he read the items, flipped switches, touched buttons, and pulled knobs. He grasped the yoke in both hands and turned it back and forth with no apparent result. But he appeared satisfied. Sliding the window beside him open, he leaned out and shouted *"Clear Prop"* at the top of his lungs. None of this, from having to read instructions, to mumbling as he touched buttons, to shouting at no one in particular, gave me a greater sense of security. I glanced back at Julian who read the tension on my face and tried to relieve it with a shrug and with what Lena would call a lame smile.

Bart pressed a button and suddenly a twisted arm that stood at the front of the machine began to move with a coughing rumble. The rumble smoothed into a sustained roar and the arm whirled until it disappeared into what was only a whistling blur. Bart grinned over at me.

"Ready?"

I gulped the fear deeper into my throat and grasped the door handle. "Yes. I am ready."

"Hands away from the door." Bart's warning further poked at the lump in my throat.

Suddenly the machine lurched forward. Bart twisted a small bulb on a curved rod down in front of his mouth and spoke to it. "Texarkana tower, this is Cessna November Three Seven Niner. Request permission to taxi Runway Two-Two."

Overhead, a voice replied, "Roger, November Three Seven Niner. Taxi runway Two-Two and hold short. Winds two-seven-zero at seven knots. Pressure two nine nine four. Call when ready for takeoff." The fear in my throat poured down into my stomach and pressed me like a lead weight into the seat.

Bart drove the machine across the field and halted again beside a striped stretch of road that disappeared into the distance. He spoke again briefly with the voice overhead, then guided us out onto the strip and pushed one of the knobs fully in. The machine increased its roar and jumped forward, moving at a rate that exceeded even the automobiles. Then suddenly the earth dropped out from beneath us. I gasped so loudly Bart turned and laughed aloud. "Relax," he said. "Look out, and enjoy the scenery."

We rose skyward until I could see the entire city stretched

below. "How is this possible?" I marveled aloud. "This machine is so heavy, and we are soaring like a bird."

High above the countryside we ceased to climb and Bart drew back the knob that appeared to give the machine its power. He gently rotated a wheel beside his hip. "Would you like to fly it for a few minutes?"

"Oh, I could never do such a thing. They will not even allow me to drive one of the cars."

"Much simpler. There's nothing to run into up here. Take the yoke there very gently." Before I had time to consider, my hands were clamped around the two handles.

"Easy!" he said with a chuckle. "You don't need to strangle the thing. The secret is a light touch and very small, gentle corrections. When trimmed up like this, the plane wants to fly itself." He watched until my hands relaxed a little, then lifted his own from the yoke. Mine tightened like vices.

"No. *Gently, Gently.*" I slowly relaxed my grip and the machine seemed to relax with me.

Bart leaned over against his window. "I think Julian said you live north of town off Seventy-one. Now, look out to make sure we're clear of other aircraft, then start a very smooth turn to the right." He mimicked with his hands the way mine should turn. I eased the yoke to the right, trapping my breath with exhilarating anticipation. The machine turned with me but began to descend. "A little back pressure, and a little pressure on the right rudder pedal," he instructed. "Down by your feet. Again, *very* gentle and smooth as you turn." I pulled back slightly, eased my foot onto the right pedal, and the machine rose smoothly in response.

"Excellent," he said. "You're a natural. Now, back the other way until this dial reads three-four-zero. Then straighten up and hold that course." I reversed the yoke, my breast swelling with a nervous joy I had never experienced. As a numbered ball in front of me spun toward 340, the machine began to rise. He placed his hands again on his yoke. "Back pressure off again. Now, can you see your place below?"

I followed the road until I saw the curved drive, the long, low house, and the stables at the rear. "There it is!" I exclaimed, leaning forward against the yoke. The machine plunged into a dive. With a panicked shriek, I released the handles and threw myself backward against the seat, squeezing my eyes tightly shut. I opened them to the sound of Father's voice, speaking to me from across the sitting room. He was saying something about the difficulties of getting the Xhosa to shit in a privy.

Ally

When the little bell dinged and the flight attendant announced we could use larger electronic devices, I began to feel like I could relax a little. I'd only flown commercially once before, a flight with Dad from Dallas to Las Cruces, New Mexico, to visit a quarter horse farm. It had been a summer scorcher that had bounced us around like galloping a three-legged mare along a rocky riverbed. I'd barfed up my breakfast in one of those paper bags they have in the seat pockets and pretty well grossed-out everyone around me. That had been my only, and very worst, flying moment until I found myself in a plane about one tenth that size, staring down at the ground while the pilot scrambled to pull us out of a screaming dive. Bart—that was the guy's name—said it wasn't really that bad. But if Julian hadn't insisted Emme go to the bathroom just before the flight, I swear I would have peed my pants.

It had almost been enough to keep me off this plane. But I'd paid, or I guess I should say "Dad had paid," the team was going, and I couldn't very well chicken out. As it turned out, the early morning was cool, the sky clear, and the takeoff smooth enough to encourage me to let go of Lena's arm and relax back into the seat. We were flying from Shreveport, Louisiana, the closest airport of any size, to London through Atlanta. Half the team had never flown, and the middle section of the plane buzzed with excitement.

Lena grinned over at me. "Are you relaxed enough to tell me what Julian told you at the airport? It looked like something we need to know." Samantha stretched across the aisle to listen.

I took a deep breath and rolled my shoulders to work the tension out of my back. "He heard overnight from those attorneys. Stacer and whatever. They told him the people who are checking things out for the royal family had traced the line of inheritance and admitted it ended up with you, Sam. They also got the copy of the letter from Robert—Emme's dad—authenticated as well as they could using the copy and are willing to admit the Grenfells and the Caywoods are probably the same people."

Sam looked at us both expectantly. "That should pretty well do it then, shouldn't it? Maybe we don't even need the book."

"They also told Julian that these other attorneys weren't willing to concede that the house belonged to the Grenfells. I guess the records they could find from that time show that the royal family took it over when Emme's family left, but not who had clear title to the place. It's still going to be real important that we find that record."

Lena looked back at where Coach Gillion sat beside Mom, three rows behind. "Coach is okay with us going on the train on Wednesday, as long as your mom comes along. Do we need to go over the floorplan with you again?"

I shook my head. "I see it in my sleep. That's all we've talked about since I got back."

"You still think it's best for Sam to go into the stairs?"

I glanced over at Samantha. "Yeah. If for some reason you get caught, you can claim there's evidence this is your family's property. For Lena and me, it would just be trespassing or vandalism or something."

Sam wasn't so sure. "This makes me so nervous I've been sick. I'm not like you two."

"You can do it," I assured her. "We'll be right there with you."

In the Atlanta airport we looked just like what we were: a bunch of country kids visiting the big city for the first time. We tried to pretend we knew what we were doing, but anybody watching could see us gawking at planes that were bigger than anything we'd ever seen and talking too loudly about going to London, like it was something we did every day.

The plane to England *was* bigger than any we'd ever been on. I don't know what kind it was, but in our part, the back where regular people sit, there were three seats on each side and four in the middle. The team was packed into three rows across the center and were so wound up Coach and Mom had to tell us to shut up and go to sleep when the lights all went out. Most of us watched movies and maybe slept for two hours before we landed at Heathrow.

By the time we got through all the customs hassle it was about 7:00 a.m. London time. A woman with Emme's accent who was our host lady from the East Anglia Women's Football Association met us as we left customs and loaded us onto a bus to tour the city. Her name was Mrs. Shockley.

"What you must try to do," she warned, "is remain awake as long as you possibly can today. This will help re-set your internal clocks and adjust to local time more quickly."

The only thing that kept me from completely crashing as soon as we got into the city was seeing things I'd always dreamed of seeing in London—the Parliament building, Big Ben, The Tower of London, Buckingham Palace. Even then, I was staring at them bleary-eyed through a mental fog. We switched to one of those big red double-decker busses like you see on posters. All eighteen of us went straight to the upper level where the breeze and exhaust helped keep us conscious. At Buckingham Palace we stumbled off to have our pictures taken with the guards in the big shaggy hats, walked in a stupor through Westminster Abbey whispering about it being the place Kate and William got married, then shuffled up through the tower to take a covetous look at the Crown Jewels. Just enough movement to keep us from collapsing. At every stop, Mrs. Shockley gave the same warning.

"Look *both* ways before you step onto a street. Remember—the closest cars are coming from your right, not your left. We don't want to be losing one of you before you get to play a match." We nodded numbly and shrugged it off until Madison just about got clipped by a black London taxi. From then on, it was sixteen girls with arms-out at every crossing mumbling "Look right. Look right!"

When we left the city on our regular bus to drive to Windsor, it was like someone stuck a needle in my arm and pumped me full of anesthetic. I had never felt so completely wiped out. In about two seconds, I was gone and everybody with me, including Mom and Coach. They woke us up for a groggy hike through a few rooms in Windsor Castle, then gave up on us, loaded us back on the bus, and let us sleep our way to the hotel.

Our first match was Sunday afternoon in a town called Maidstone, east of London. We traveled over in the morning by bus, what the English call a coach, for a 2:00 p.m. start. The afternoon was cloudy with light drizzle, and the field was on the soggy side. About fifteen minutes into the match we got our first lesson in why the association lady had told us to stay up as late as we could Saturday. Jet lag hit like a ton of bricks. Even though Emme had done a much better job of keeping my body fit during the last switch, I felt like I was running in thick mud at high altitude. As I looked around the field, the other girls were doing the same, slogging along like they were in a dream with sandbags tied to their ankles. The only thing that saved us was that the English girls weren't that great—a new team just beginning to get its act together. But even then, if we hadn't had Sam, we'd have had our butts kicked. She'd slept more than the rest of us on the plane, managed to stay awake longer during our day in London, and didn't feel as much of the afternoon crush that wiped out the rest of us. Her four saves gave us a 2-1 win.

"Learn anything?" Coach asked as we dragged ourselves off the field and into the school building where we were showering and changing. But he said it through a giant yawn that left us all laughing, including him.

"Don't worry," Mrs. Shockley said. "About 2:00 a.m. tonight, you will all be wide awake. Try to get back to sleep, or at least rest until six or seven. Gather here when you get cleaned up. I will introduce you to your host families."

The girl I stayed with was named Mora Pobgee, two names I hadn't ever heard before. Her family lived in a suburb on the outskirts of the city in what they called a semi-detached—a duplex to us. I had sort of expected that we'd find fifteen girls like Emme on the teams we played. But aside from having an Emme accent, Mora was a lot like me. She lived on her phone when her parents weren't insisting she leave it alone for a while, liked the music I liked, except country, and dressed pretty much like I did. The family drove me around Maidstone in a car that said it was a Ford but was smaller than any Ford I'd seen in Texas. The rain had picked up and we stayed in the car, passing an old castle and stone bridge that dated back to way before Emme's time, and talking a lot about where I was from. Do you all ride horses in Texas? Does everyone own a gun? Do you eat a lot of barbeque? My answers didn't seem to disappoint. When they saw I was politely fighting to stay awake, we headed back to the semi-detached.

The bed in their spare room had a thick quilt thing on it that made me feel like I was wrapped in a pile of Robert Caywood's best lambs' wool. I managed to sleep until four, dozed for a while, thinking of getting to Grenfell Hall, then got up about five-thirty and jogged through their little neighborhood of white-painted duplexes until seven. The morning had cleared and I could feel England all around me and Grenfell getting closer. I kept glancing down to make sure my boobs hadn't grown and my arms turned soft and pale. Mora's mother served the same full English breakfast I'd come to love in Bathurst. I began to feel that maybe I was getting close to knowing for sure why I had become Emmeline.

We toured Canterbury that day, then drove out to the coast to Dover. Monday had brightened and warmed into the sixties. For the first time, I saw the England that Emmeline and her family had loved so much. The fields were velvet green, even in winter. The hedgerows and sheep-dotted fields surrounded vine-covered cottages I knew must have been there when Emme lived in Grenfell Hall. Calendar perfect and peaceful in a way that made me wonder how this land could ever have chased a family away. I looked over at Sam who was also gazing out the window, chin on her fist, and a tear creeping down her cheek. She glanced back at me, gave me an embarrassed smile, and brushed it away.

We dominated our second match in Chelmsford. Lena and I could feel Wednesday creeping up on us and played like a couple of maniacs. Sam was a savage in goal, and the others picked up their own pace, just to stay with us. Between halves, Coach asked where all that energy had been all season. We didn't dare tell him that we just didn't want him to have any excuse to change his mind about giving us a free day on Wednesday. We won 7-0.

My host family in Chelmsford was named Ransford and knew about Grenfell Hall. "A lovely place," Mrs. Ransford said at dinner, relieved to have something familiar to talk about. "It's about forty miles up the A-12. These country homes are becoming so difficult to maintain that many are being converted to other purposes. Grenfell Hall now serves as offices and display space for a very upscale antique dealer. Everything is quite pricy, as I recall."

The Ransford's home was what was called a rowhouse, a two-story red brick, squashed between two houses exactly like it in a row of identical houses that lined both sides of a quiet city street. The front door stepped right out onto the sidewalk. There was a tiny yard in back with a gate into an alleyway that separated the Ransford's street from one just like it across the alley. As I looked around their sitting room, I didn't see much to indicate the Ransfords spent a lot of time at pricy antique places.

"Have you been there? To Grenfell Hall?" I asked.

Mrs. Ransford smiled self-consciously. "When it first opened, it was quite the sensation. The rooms are all decorated to look like the period of the early 1800s. It's a bit of a museum tour, really, with everything for sale."

"You said there were offices. Are they in the house?"

"One wing of the upper floor, I believe. It has been several years. I don't recall exactly which. Why, if I might ask?"

"One of my friends' families lived in the hall back about 1820. We plan to stop there tomorrow to see it."

"One of your friends on the team? How lovely! Oh, you will find it charming," she said, and the conversation turned to Texas.

Emme

There was something decidedly distressing about realizing that I should very likely never see my Texas friends again or enjoy a hamburger and hot chocolate at Hopkin's Icehouse. I was delighted, to be sure, to be home with my family. Mother showed the greatest relief, rising from her chair to come over to embrace me when, in the middle of a conversation about health in Xhosa villages, it became apparent that I had "returned to my senses."

But as days passed, my thoughts turned often to riding in automobiles, speaking to anyone I wished, no matter where they were, on my cell phone, and nights at the movies. I longed to be sitting in a school classroom with conversation going on around me about books that were yet to be written and science that was yet to be discovered. I dreamed of having those moments again when Julian, a boy I would not have allowed myself to talk to here in Bathurst, had forgotten that I was Emme and pulled me close, playing his fingers through my hair, and kissing my forehead with a tenderness that took my breath away. I understood why Ally cared so deeply for this man, and why she saw in him a bright, handsome, and tender companion.

I had experienced the terror and exhilaration of flight and often wondered how Ally had reacted to finding herself sitting in that flying machine, gazing down at the earth far below as Bart, the mustached driver, struggled to overcome my carelessness. Father appeared to share some of the same yearning. Though he assured me daily that he was delighted to have me home, I sensed that he missed the Emme who had ridden with him across the veldt and talked to him about making magnets of horseshoes. There is a depression that accompanies knowing you have lost something dear that can never be regained. Both of us shared a gloom on some days that made even Mother wish that Ally would return.

I began to ponder as well how much it is good to know about one's future. I knew that I must return to England. But would I be returning because I wished to? Because Mother and Father thought it best? Or would I be going because I now knew that destiny demanded it of me? Would I truly marry Charles Pearce? Would I find him attractive and truly love him? Or would I feel that I must entice the man to marry me because a descendent—no, a *friend*—in a future that now seemed more dream than reality, depended on me to become his wife? Father had begun to plan for my departure as if he also felt compelled to support this foreordained destiny. I now wondered daily if my life was truly my own.

The one part of my future-past that clearly was not a dream was what I had learned. I had wished so badly to be able to transport back to Bathurst some of the marvels that surrounded me. But I returned each time without pockets or luggage and only what I had packed into my imperfect memory. Though I continued with my piano and reading to pacify Mother and to nourish my own love of music and literature, I spent more of my time with Noluvo, working with the Xhosa on sanitation and learning from their tribal healers.

Perhaps the clearest message from the books I had read on folk remedies before leaving Texarkana, and one that had been stressed by Ally in her final notes, was that we should look first to the collective wisdom of those who have been struggling with diseases through the ages. They have survived because they discovered ways to treat the conditions that most threatened them—cuts and bone breaks, water-born illnesses, toothaches, and the bites of poisonous creatures. Their babies still often died young, and some illnesses were a death knell. There was much the Xhosa could learn from what Ally and I knew, but perhaps more that I could learn from sitting at the feet of the native healers, the people they called *amaxwele.*

I learned of their uses for aloe, the native plant I had seen sold in various forms in Texas stores, but used by the Xhosa to treat burns and rashes. The *amaxwele* taught me when to use buchu plant and devil's claw, the leaves of a dozen trees to make poultices and brew foul-tasting drinks that cured diarrhea and reduced the seriousness of colds and influenza. Together we experimented with the Indian hemp to see what other cures it might bring. The women assured me I might become an *amaxwele* if I stayed long enough in Bathurst and continued to study with them.

But a ship from Bombay, bound for London, was due in Port Elizabeth in a fortnight. Mother now agreed that I must go. I prepared boxes of roots, leaves, barks, and mineral powders, and wrote lengthy notes on mixtures and expected results. Dr. Begley presented me with a dog-eared copy of a book entitled *Pharmacopia Loninesis* that contained remedies from my own British past: the use of roots, barks, herbs, and minerals to treat most every malady. Perhaps I was meant for Charles Pearce because, as a schoolmaster, he might be amenable to my having a shop where I could dispense natural medicines. The book showed me that England was rich with a variety of medicinal plants of its own and dozens of ways to use them. I would seek out someone there who knew the ancient healing arts and could continue to school me. And I had a letter to deliver, secreted beneath the front plate of a Bible I had yet to acquire. And a daughter to bear. A daughter I would name Melissa.

Ally

The bus dropped us at the train station in Ipswich just before 9:00 a.m. Coach and Mrs. Shockley checked schedules to Bury Saint Edmunds on a board in the station. We agreed on a 3:14 p.m. departure that would get us there in time to meet our host families and share dinner with them.

"Please," Mrs. Shockley said. "Be on that train so we don't inconvenience our hosts. The rest of the team is going to Cambridge for the day to tour the university. We will be back to meet you when your train arrives." Coach just gave us a look that said, "I'm hanging it out for you here, Wallis. Don't mess up."

A cab from the station delivered us in front of a set of intricate wrought-iron gates just outside the village of Barham, about six miles from Ipswich. We had seen the pictures on Wiki and had mentally walked the floors of Emme's drawings. But neither prepared us for the scale of the place that rose beyond an eight-foot wall of chiseled gray stone or for the acres of manicured lawns and gardens that surrounded it.

"*Mierda*," Lena whispered. "This is a *mansion*! Emme didn't tell us she lived in a place like *this*! Is this what you were living in in South Africa?"

I shook my head while Mom studied us suspiciously. "Not even close," I murmured. "They gave up a lot."

Lena turned to Sam who stared dumbstruck through the massive iron gates. "And this might be yours. I think I'd hang onto the place, dump the job at the Icehouse, and move your mom over here."

I couldn't smother a chuckle. "Paying to keep it up with what? And maybe we'd better check to see if they've added indoor plumbing."

There was no one watching the gate. As we walked up the long, circling drive, two cars passed us heading for a graveled lot near what we recognized as Emme's "east portico."

Five wide steps climbed to a covered, half-circle porch. The white, eight-foot double doors stood open to the morning breeze. We paused on the top step and watched as a couple entered the front hallway. The hall had been divided in half by long tables, creating an entrance and exit lane. As the couple approached the narrow entry gap, an attendant relieved the woman of her handbag and placed it in one of twenty cubbies that stood on the middle table.

"Big trouble," Lena muttered, quietly enough to escape Mom's ears. Sam was carrying a shoulder bag that we'd planned to use to sneak the registry out of the house.

I grabbed Sam's arm and steered her back down the steps. "Mom, why don't you and Lena go in. Sam wants to look around the grounds a bit first. I'll stay with her." Before she could object, Lena grabbed Mom's elbow and guided her into the building. I walked Samantha along a gravel path that stretched toward each end of the manor.

"I'm going to stay outside with your bag," I told her. "You get into the stairwell, get the book, and bring it down the stairs to the back entrance. I'll watch for you there. You can hand me the ledger, go back into the house, and come out with Mom and Lena."

Sam stopped dead still on the path. I could feel a shiver pass down the arm I still held. "I can't do it, Ally. I know I'll get trapped in there and panic. I'll mess it up for everyone."

"It's your book. I just thought you'd like to get it."

"It's almost as much yours as mine. You're the one who's been switching with Emme. And, please. Would you go get it? You're *so* much better at this kind of thing."

I couldn't think of a time when we'd ever done "this kind of thing." But I knew what she meant. When it came to taking a few risks, Sam wasn't first in line.

"Alright. I'll try to get it. Do you think you know where the door's supposed to open?"

"I think so. But let's walk back there and have a look."

As we rounded the corner of what I figured to be the north end of the hall, Sam glanced over at the light jacket I wore.

"Do you think they'll check your pockets?"

I patted at my chest. "I put Ryan's headlamp in this inside pocket. I don't think they'll pat me down."

"That's another reason you need to go," she said. "You brought the light."

The wall in the rear looked just as Emme had described: light brown stucco separated into sections by heavy timbers. In the corner where she said the door opened onto the back, a waist-high privet hedge grew along the entire length of the house. Two feet separated it from the wall, room for the caretakers to get behind to prune and clear away leaves. Three other visitors strolled along a path near the back of the property, but were walking away from us. I tightened my grip on Sam's arm and dragged her behind the thick bushes, crouching out of sight. Even when looking at the wall from a few feet away, we couldn't see any sign of a door.

"If it's here, they did a pretty good job of hiding it," Sam muttered.

I looked at the tight seams along the timbers. "Or it's been resurfaced sometime. Maybe a couple of times."

"What if it won't open?"

"Then I'll try to figure out how to get the book out through the front. Or maybe I can open a window and drop it out. I'll figure out something."

"And what do you want me to do?"

"Stay where you can see this corner. Be ready to get back here and out of sight if you see the wall move at all."

Sam plopped onto the ground behind the hedge. "I think I might just sit right here."

When I entered the front hallway, the attendant looked me over with a quick smile and pushed a register in front of me, asking that I sign in and enter city, country, and entry time.

"Wow," I said. "You'd think this is Fort Knox or something." She didn't seem to know about Fort Knox, but got the idea.

"Our inventory is very valuable. We can't afford to have guests remaining in the hall overnight." She glanced at the address I'd entered. "You must be with the two women who just came in."

I nodded, relieved that she hadn't seen me turn with Sam on the steps and walk down the side of the building. She gave me another quick once-over and waved me through. No purse or bag, no problem. But I knew that when Mom and Lena came back out, I'd better be with them.

I found them in what had once been the dining room. It still looked like an overly furnished version of the same thing. There were two tables with full sets of china and polished silverware and what I would call buffets pressed against all but the window wall. The dealer had them labeled as "sideboards." Another attendant roamed the room, keeping a distant but watchful eye on the five people who browsed through the furnishings. She was a nicely dressed woman about Mom's age. As we neared her in our circuit of the room, she asked if there was anything special we wished to see. We'd prepped Mom to say that Sam's ancestors had once lived in the hall, and we wanted her to have a chance to see it. But with Sam outside, that was going to sound pretty lame.

"I'm kind of interested in finding an old authentic bedside table," I improvised. "We're just working our way upstairs." The woman smiled and nodded. "You will find a good selection there."

As we climbed to the second floor, Lena leaned toward me and whispered, "Is Sam coming in?"

I shook my head. Mom was ahead of us and I added, loud enough for her to hear, "She wanted to check out the grounds first." Then I mouthed to Lena, "I'm going in."

Lena frowned and mouthed back. "They're watching everyone in here. And there are cameras." She gave a nod toward a black eye that glared at us from the top of the staircase.

I nodded. "You need to create a diversion."

She rolled her eyes to say, "Yeah—and how do you suggest I do that?"

When we entered the bedroom Emme had described, I saw that we had at least one thing working in our favor. The single camera in the room was mounted high in the corner above where we'd been told the secret door would be. I was pretty certain it couldn't see that tightly into the corner. But we needed a lot more than a diversion. Like the dining room below, the walls that didn't have windows were lined with furniture—big, heavy dressers and those free-standing closet things. The rosewood wainscoting still ran around the room. Between pieces, I could see some of the carved rosettes. The dresser beneath the camera was maybe four inches from the wall and a yard from the corner. The important rosette was behind it.

We did a circle of the room under the friendly, watchful eye of a young man who was maybe twenty and got our second break. While I pretended to check out a fancy old four-poster bed, Lena bent to take a closer look at a porcelain washbowl and pitcher that looked a lot like the one Emme had beside her bed in Bathurst. Out of the corner of my eye, I could see the room guy giving her butt a long, admiring look. Now, Lena's cute enough to turn some heads anyway. Big, dark eyes with full lips and skin as smooth and polished as some of the walnut that surrounded us. It was one of the reasons I'd always hated to see her wasting her time on Ryan. Half the guys in school would walk barefoot across hot coals for a chance to go out with her. But she just couldn't see it.

I worked my way back over to her, suggested we go into the next room, and led her and Mom back into the hallway. Mom went on into a bedroom across the hall.

"Let's go back in," I said. "When I get close to the corner where the door is, ask the guy to tell you something about that washstand you were looking at and the stuff on it—and maybe that bedside table next to it. I'll see if I can reach back and twist that knob. If the door opens out, we're screwed. If it goes in, I'll slip inside and close it after me."

"He may stand so he can still see you."

"He thinks you're hot. I saw him checking out your butt. Keep him looking your way."

Lena grinned. "My butt's not going to keep him occupied very long. You better be quick."

"If I can get the bottom door open and the book to Sam, the problem's going to be getting back into the room without being seen. Since I signed in, I have to leave with you. If I can get in there at all, I don't know how long it's all going to take. You'd better keep an eye on the wall. If you see it crack back open a little, do *anything* to get his attention again. Pull up your T-shirt or something."

"Yeah. Right. He looks more like a butt guy."

"Well, just get his attention until I'm back in the room."

We strolled back into the master bedroom. I went left and Lena right. As I neared the corner, she called to the attendant. The name on his badge said "Nigel."

"Excuse me, Nigel. I wondered if you could tell me something about this stand here, and this flowered bowl?"

He had been standing beside the four-poster and immediately moved toward her. I moved just as quickly to the corner and looked up at the camera to make sure it couldn't see me. I eased in beside the dresser and stretched behind it until I could grab the carved knob. Which way to twist? If the latch was on the door rather than the wall, it would probably slide down into a slot. So, twist clock-wise.

By pressing my back against the wall and reaching until my shoulder was crammed against the dresser, I could get a pretty good grip on the carved flower. Nigel was telling Lena that the nightstand wasn't as old as some of the other furniture but was a well-crafted replica and worth the money. I twisted as hard as I could. Nothing moved. Nigel shifted his attention, looking down the opposite wall toward another stand. Lena lifted the wash basin and asked what it was made of. I tried to imagine what the inside of the latch might look like. Maybe the latch wasn't on the door, but on the wall beside it. If that was the case, it might drop toward me into a slot on the door and turn counter-clockwise. I gripped the rosette as firmly as I could, keeping my eyes on Nigel, and tried a hard, left twist.

The knob slipped a quarter-turn with a muffled squeak. I spun away from the wall, grabbing the handle of one of the dresser's drawers. Nigel turned to look across at me.

"Sorry," I mumbled. "Is it okay if I look in the drawers?"

"Yes," he said, sounding just a little irritated that I'd drawn his attention away from the captivating Lena. "But please pull on both handles at once. It will draw the drawer out more evenly."

"Yeah. Okay,"

"Don't mind her," Lena assured him. "She can be kind of a klutz." She took his arm and turned him gently back to the porcelain basin.

I watched to be sure he was sufficiently distracted, then slipped back against the wall and again grasped the carved flower. This time I pulled outward as I twisted as much as my grip allowed. The knob turned another quarter turn and I felt the wall give behind me. Lena had lifted the pitcher and was examining the pattern. *Oh dear God*, I thought, *Don't let this wall squeak*!

Gradually I pressed backward against the paneling, keeping my arm extended to maintain pressure near the opening. The wall moved with surprising smoothness and within seconds, there was a foot-wide gap. I pushed steadily until I could slip behind the dresser and into the opening, easing the panel closed behind me. The space around me collapsed into suffocating blackness.

I groped for the headlamp in my inside pocket, keeping a hand on the door to press it tightly into place. My thumb fumbled for the button on the light. I felt nothing but a moment of panic, then realized I had it upside-down. I pressed the bottom and a shaft of light shot down toward my feet. Sam would be freaking out by now if she were in here.

The latch had worked as I guessed, sliding against the back of the door. I pushed it again downward until just an edge held the panel in place, then pressed my ear against the wall. Lena's voice was no more than a muffled drone in the room beyond. There was no indication of excitement or alarm. I slipped the lamp's band over my head and looked around.

The stairwell was just as Emme had described it, but coated with a quarter-inch of fine dust and draped with feathery cobwebs. I started to suck in a deep breath to slow my pounding heart, but immediately felt a sneeze rippling up from the back of my nose. Trapping it shut with the fingers of both hands, I threw my head back and mouthed the word "purple." Someone told me once that tilting your chin up and saying "purple" stops a sneeze. Either that, or having my nose clamped shut, did the job. Instead, tears gushed onto my cheeks. I stood for a long moment, waiting until the sneeze passed before I dared release the pressure. The space smelled like moldy bread. Mouse and rat poop carpeted the floor and I couldn't step without adding more smell to the thick, musty air. The place was full of two centuries of stale. I pulled the neck of my T-shirt up over my nose, swept away cobwebs that hung just in front of my face, and turned slowly in the passage.

You need to get your ass in gear, I thought, sweeping the light around like a miner in a coal pit. *Nigel's going to notice I'm not in the room. Sam's waiting outside. Mom will be hunting for me. Get moving!*

The small table was wedge-shaped, pressed into the corner where the outer walls came together. I hadn't thought about mice and rats. No drawer would be safe from the gnawing little beasts. Over two hundred years, there wouldn't be anything left of a hidden book. Bracing one hand against the table's top, I pulled at the bottom of what looked like the cross brace Emme had described. The drawer screeched reluctantly outward. I froze, trapped my breath, and listened. Either the squeak had ended conversation in the next room, or I was too far from the wall for sound to penetrate. After a full minute with no voices near the hidden door, I slid the drawer far enough out that I could see what was inside.

Robert had been smart enough to anticipate mice and rats. Whatever was in the drawer was in a flat, square box made of tin, with rough, soldered seams joining the folded edges. Rust covered what I could see of the top and sides to the point that some of the top was beginning to flake through. As I lifted it up, the bottom fell away, leaving a package covered in cracked, chocolate-brown leather. Thin hide straps wrapped the block in both directions, tied on top with a neat, flat knot.

I laid the disintegrating tin lid on the tabletop and gently lifted the covered record from the drawer. The tanned skin felt brittle against my fingers and I was afraid that if I dropped the thing on the stairs, it would shatter like an old whisky bottle. Tucking it under one arm like a fullback, I swept the light down into the stairwell, brushed the web curtain from in front of my eyes, and felt my way gingerly down the creaking staircase.

The small landing at the bottom crunched with dry rodent droppings. Even with the shirt mask, the air tasted like musty poop. My eyes stung and lips begged to be licked, but I knew I needed to keep my mouth sealed tight.

The inside of the wall that blocked the lower stairwell was solid wood planks, held together by wooden cross-braces. Heavy iron hinges supported one side, and a slide bolt as thick as my thumb secured the other. I tried to move a knob on the bolt into the release position, but it was rusted tightly in place. Time seemed to be spinning forward, with every second drawing someone closer to starting a serious search for me in the house. Stepping back, I focused the light on the bolt and drove the toe of my sneaker up into the crusted handle. Instead of popping up into open position, the metal loops that held the bar disintegrated into a mass of rusty flakes, leaving the bolt hanging loose from the hoop that held it to the frame. I leaned my free shoulder into the door and pushed. It didn't budge. Drawing what breath I dared through the cotton mask, I drove my foot again into the brace beside the broken bolt.

Beyond the door, I heard the stucco siding crack and splinter. A thin bar of light opened on the bolt side of the door. I pushed it again until the opening was wide enough to pass the package through. Sam peered urgently into the stairwell.

"Here!" I eased the wrapped record through the breach in the wall. "Push the door back in place as well as you can and get out the front gate. We'll be there as quick as we can. If we don't meet you out at the road in twenty minutes, get a taxi and catch the train we're supposed to be on. You need to get that to London on Friday." Before she could answer, I turned and clambered back up the dust-coated steps.

At the top, I pulled my shirt back into place, dusted myself off as well as I could, and got one hand on the latch to the wall panel. With the other, I doused the headlamp, returned it to my pocket, and as smoothly as I could, eased the door inward a few inches. In the room beyond, I heard footsteps, a pause, more steps, then the sudden crash of what sounded like a dozen china plates hitting the floor.

"Oh, *mierda*!" I heard Lena cry. "I am *sooo* sorry! I just wanted to look at the mark on the bottom again." More footsteps rushed in her direction. I pulled the panel far enough inward to slip out beside the dresser, grabbed the wainscoting to pull the panel closed behind me, and twisted the rosette knob. Nigel crouched beside Lena on the far side of the room, picking up shattered pieces of the porcelain pitcher, his back to me. I quickly re-dusted my shirt and jeans and scraped the bottoms of my sneakers against my pantlegs. We didn't need a set of dusty footprints tracking across the floor from a blank wall. Nigel continued to bend over the broken pitcher and I nearly reached the open hallway door before Mom hurried through. I spun and fell in beside her as Lena looked up with complete horror on her face.

"I'm *so* sorry Mrs. W. I was thinking of buying this anyway. I'll pay for it. I brought some extra money with me and . . .."

Mom and I knelt beside her and helped gather up rose-colored shards. "Get us a price, please," Mom said to Nigel. "And if you can find a broom, we'll be happy to sweep this up."

"Go down and tell them what happened," Nigel said calmly. "They will have a price at the desk. I will find someone to sweep up."

We slunk from the room, Lena bent into a forlorn slouch. "It was eighty pounds," she mumbled as we headed for the stairs. "How much is that in dollars?"

"We'll get it taken care of," Mom said. "Let's find Sam. I think we'd better be heading back to the station."

As we entered the front hallway and Mother approached the desk, I looked out across the acre of lawn to the front gate. Samantha stood nervously beside the gray stone wall, her shoulder bag pressed tightly against her side.

Emme

I began to feel that God or some evil demon was playing a cruel hoax on me. To have been exposed to a life of unimaginable luxury and wonder, then be returned to a lifeless village in the African bush without promise of return, was almost more than I could bear. I began to long for sleep, praying that at least some blessed dream might take me back to the land of movies and pizza and into the warm embrace of a colored boy I could not even acknowledge if he were to pass me in Port Kowie. I felt some guilt at imagining myself in Julian's arms, but it is in our dreams that we experience guilty pleasures, and I was now left with nothing but my dreams.

To awake was to face another day of tedium, even if it included visiting a village with Noluvo. We now had tried everything we knew might improve Xhosa health and I yearned to learn new remedies. Father shared my discontent. Mother saw my distress as even more troubling than the changes in personality. Both now wished me on my way to England and return to a life that would at least offer greater opportunity.

There were days when I questioned if it had happened at all. Perhaps I had indeed been under some Xhosa spell and imagined a future of flying machines, pianos without strings, and cases that held all of the knowledge of the world within their thin interiors. But then I would chance upon Father tinkering with his Voltaic Pile or see the results of Ally's hemp tea on the health of a village. It had happened, but to what end? I had learned that I would marry Charles Pearce, that descendants would immigrate to America, and that a great-granddaughter, many times removed, would be faced with trying to save her ailing mother. But to not know the fate of our estate at Grenfell Hall and of my Texas friends was a greater burden than never to have known them at all. I counted the days until the ship would leave Port Elizabeth, imagining a stormy passage during which we were set upon by pirates, just to break the monotony of weeks at sea. I threw myself into Father's breeding experiments to give my mind something other than Bach and Austen to fill the days.

In a little-visited corner of the farm that had been carved out of the bush, I began to transplant Indian hemp from the patch in the forest, entrusting its care to Noluvo.

"This is your future," I told her. "The medicine gives you and your grandfather great power. Your control of this patch makes you even more powerful than he is. Study the folk ways and become an *amaxwele*. With the medicine, you will become a leader among all the villages."

One night in a dream I was again with my friends, but back in Grenfell Hall. I saw them as if I were a disembodied spirit, hovering above a corner of the house and able to see everything within. Ally had slipped undetected into the hidden stairs and had found the manor record, breaking her way through the lower door to deliver it to Samantha. As I watched, she returned to the secret door in the bedroom and cracked it open. A young man stood beside a large bed, watching Lena who appeared to be wandering aimlessly about the bedchamber, but with a watchful eye on the section of wall.

There! She saw it move! But if Ally pulled it farther inward, surely the man would see it. Lena moved away from the panel, searching the room frantically.

"The pitcher!" I shouted. "Break the pitcher!"

Lena turned toward the table that held the washbasin, glanced quickly back at the crack in the wall, and lifted the pitcher, turning it to look at its bottom.

"*Drop it*! *Drop it*!" I cried, and the pitcher slipped from her hands. As the crash jarred me from sleep, I saw the panel pull inward and Ally slip from behind the wall. Beside my open window, a sudden gust had thrown the curtain against my own pitcher and swept it to the floor. Father was at the door, peering into my darkened room.

"Are you alright?" he called.

"Yes," I said. "It was only a dream."

Ally

We sat in a conference room in the London offices of Stacer and Mayfield. Sam, Lena, Mom and I were on one side of a long table with two solicitors from the firm at the ends and three lawyers and a rare documents expert representing the Crown facing us. Our team had taken the train from Bishop's Stortford, where tomorrow we would play our final match, into London's King's Cross station. The other girls wanted the experience of riding the train, and our coach driver wasn't too excited about having to steer that huge thing around the city in Friday traffic. Coach Gillion and the other players had walked to the British Library to see the Magna Carta, a Gutenberg Bible, and original manuscripts by people like Chaucer and Dickens—cool stuff I was sorry I had to miss. But I wanted to see this Grenfell Hall deal to the end.

The room was pretty basic: the long table with six chairs to a side and a few more scattered along the walls. A woman brought in tea, which seemed to be a ritual part of any meeting in England, and asked if we wanted anything else. We weren't sure what "anything" might include, so we all declined.

Trevor Emory sat at one end of the table. The other lawyers looked at him like he was supposed to get things started. He wasn't at all like the solicitor of my imagination: tall, with wavy hair combed straight back, dark eyes with a glint of self-satisfaction, and a permanent half-smile on his well-formed lip. This Trevor was short and just a few pounds heavier than I am. A ring of sandy hair circled a shiny bald head like one of those Caesar crowns. His round, wire-rimmed glasses were the most distinguishing feature on an otherwise unimpressive face. Not my idea of a lawyer who would strike fear into the hearts of the Queen's best. But then, here they were, sitting across from us, looking toward him for direction.

"Right, then," he said when everyone had their tea. "We seem to be in agreement that Miss Samantha Howard of Texarkana, Texas, USA, who has provided appropriate identification, is indeed the direct descendent of Robert and Rebecca Caywood of Bathurst, South Africa. We are further agreed that the letter provided by Miss Howard from Robert Caywood, stating that he was, in fact, the Robert Grenfell who left the hall in 1820 to escape arrest by the Crown, is authentic and sufficient proof to establish that relationship." He looked at the documents guy who gave a curt nod.

Trevor continued. "We also have agreed that by British law, Samantha Howard would be the rightful heir to any heretofore undesignated property owned by the Grenfells. Am I correct in my statement of these stipulations?" The group across from us all mumbled their agreement.

"The unresolved question, then, is whether Robert and Rebecca Grenfell were, in fact, full and rightful owners of Grenfell Hall, or if the rightful owner was the Crown, which granted provisional occupancy to the Grenfells at the Crown's pleasure." Again, the opposing lawyers nodded.

"I might interject before we proceed further," Trevor said, "that even if proof of ownership is established for the Grenfells, the Crown might claim that ownership was forfeited by a violation of the Blasphemous and Seditious Libels Act of 1819. I hope it unnecessary to remind my colleagues that this act is now viewed as an unfortunate stain, both on our nation's history and on our system of justice. To now punish a descendent because an ancestor was charged under this act would not play well in the public eye."

My assessment of Mr. Emory was improving by the minute. The other lawyers glanced quickly at each other. A man who'd introduced himself as Sir Archibald Quinly-Denham and appeared to be the head guy for the three, spoke on their behalf.

"We have discussed this matter. Should ownership be

convincingly established, we will not contest right to the property based on a violation of the Six Acts."

Trevor nodded his satisfaction. "Very good then. Our purpose for being here today is to view that proof. Other than request her identification, I have not spoken with Miss Howard since we all came together in the room. But she assures me that she has proof of ownership with her. Is that correct, Miss Howard?"

Samantha opened her shoulder bag, drew out the bound leather package, and laid it carefully on the table. Everyone leaned intently forward, gazing at the tied bundle.

"This does not appear to have been opened for some time," the document man said. "And it looks rather fragile."

"We haven't opened it," Sam said, following the script we'd worked out the night before. "We just got ahold of it and were afraid we'd mess it up if we tried to take this cover off."

Sir Quinly-Denham arched a critical brow. "You expect us to make a decision based on a sealed record?"

"We expect your guy to be able to un-seal it."

"And you say you just acquired it?"

"It was being kept here until we picked it up Wednesday."

"May I inquire as to who was keeping it?"

"We'll tell you later. After your man here checks it out," Samantha said nervously.

The document guy squinted skeptically at the package. "I'm afraid I am unwilling to attempt to open such a fragile piece without being certain of its ownership. If this came from a museum, for example, we could very well be in violation of some antiquities law."

Sam gave me a look that said, "Okay, this is where you said you'd step in."

I did. "We got it Wednesday at Grenfell Hall."

Mother gasped audibly beside me. I gave her a quick "*Sorry, but be quiet*" look and plowed ahead. "Sam's family has passed down this story about where it was hidden. Until now, no one's been able to check it out. But when we learned that the letter from Robert Grenfell was authentic, we figured the story was also true. It was right where we were told it would be."

"You stole this from Grenfell Hall?" Quinly-Denham questioned, cocking his head to one side and speaking with that kind of highbrow English that sounds like your mouth is full of mush.

"No. We didn't steal it. We took it from the place Sam's ancestors said it would be. If the house is her family's, it can't be theft." I sneaked a sidelong peek at Solicitor Trevor who couldn't suppress a smile.

"And where, might I ask, was it hidden that it wasn't discovered over all these years?" asked Sir Q-D.

"In a sealed staircase. Along one of the outer walls."

"And you were able to get in by . . .?"

"Opening a secret door."

"This all sounds quite preposterous."

I knew right then why Sir Q-D had a double-barreled name. You needed a name like that to use words like "preposterous" and pronounce them like you're underwater.

"It will be very easy to check out. Call Grenfell Hall. I'll give instructions to whoever answers on how to find the stairs." *Or*, I thought, *we could just tell them to go look at the rear outside corner of the house.* Sam told us after we were headed for the train that she had pushed at the door as hard as she could, but wasn't sure it had sealed back tight.

Quinly-Denham pulled a cell from his inside jacket pocket "That should be simple enough." He tapped in his security code, found the app he wanted, and asked it for the phone number for Grenfell Hall, Suffolk. He listened with a smug smile until someone answered, then said, "Yes. This is Sir Quinly-Denham, a barrister with Quinly-Denham and Marshall. A plaintiff in a case we are handling has just informed me that she took an old record from a secret staircase in Grenfell Hall on Wednesday. She tells me that if I allow her to give you instructions, she can lead you to the place where it was hidden. Would you, or someone else there, be willing to follow this young lady's directions and tell me what you find?"

He listened with the same smirky smile, then said, "Very well. I am handing her the phone. She's American, so you may need to listen carefully." He reached across the table with the phone.

"Hello? My name's Alyssa. I'm one of the women who broke the pitcher upstairs on Wednesday." Q-D's smirk faded a little.

"I'm going to give you directions to a hidden door in that room. Do you have a flashlight?"

"A what?" the woman asked.

"A torch," Trevor translated.

"A torch," I said.

"Oh, yes. I have one here in the desk."

"Take it with you. I'll wait while you go upstairs. And I'm going to put you on speaker. Is that okay?" The voice said yes, I touched the phone to speaker, and laid it in front of me on the table. Q-D's mouth was now no more than a tight, puckered line. We listened as she climbed the stairs and walked down the hall to the front bedroom.

"I'm in the room," the voice said.

"Okay. Go to the corner on the left side by the windows. See that dresser there? You may need to pull it away from the wall a little."

We heard her muffled request for help from Nigel and the dresser scrape across the floor.

"Okay. Step into that space between the dresser and the wall."

"I'm there."

"On the wainscoting—see that first carved rose? Twist it to the left, counter-clockwise. It shouldn't be very hard. I just latched it a little."

There was a pause, then, "Oh, *my God!* . . . Nigel, run and fetch Cecilia. She must see this." Another long pause as footsteps hurried out, then back into the room. "Our manager is with me now," the woman's voice said breathlessly. Mr. Quinly-Denham's face was now a pasty white.

"Okay. Turn on your flashlight—your torch—and step in there. There are lots of cobwebs, so be ready. Look around and tell us what you see."

We could tell from the scraping and shuffling that both women had squeezed their way into the stairwell. The same voice said, "My! What a mess we have here!"

"In the corner there," I directed. "What do you see?"

"There is a small table. The drawer is open. It looks as if it contained a tin that has partially rusted away."

"And the top is on the table," I added.

"Yes. The top is on the table." Q-D shook his head grimly.

"Go on down the stairs and push on the right side of the wooden door when you get to the bottom. It may take a pretty good shove, but should open."

Two sets of footsteps hesitantly descended the stairs accompanied by "*Oh, it is absolutely filthy in here!*" and "*I am getting these cobwebs all over in my hair!*" Then, the soft grunt of a push, followed by two louder ones and another, "*Oh, my God! This opens on the rear of the hall. I think I can push through here . . .. Oh, thank God, I can breathe!* I'm outside now with our manager. How did you know about this? And didn't the three of you leave through the main door?"

"I passed the book out through that door to a friend and came back into the bedroom," I said. "That's why my other friend broke the pitcher. So I could get back in while Nigel helped her clean it up."

"Why didn't you simply tell us about this?" another woman's voice asked sharply.

I thought, *Oh, yeah. That would have helped us get it here!* But said, "For reasons Sir Quinly-Denham will tell you about. I'm giving the phone back to him."

Q-D took the cell, his voice much more subdued. "I will be getting back to you later today or tomorrow, ladies. I know this may appear to have been an act of theft and vandalism, but there is much more to it than I can tell you now. Please leave things as they are. I'll have a man come out to explain and take a look at the passage." He didn't wait for a reply and clicked the phone off.

"It appears you found the record as you said," he muttered. "But we still need to examine it to see if it provides proof of ownership. If it does not, you may all be charged with theft."

I avoided looking at Mom, but could feel her glare on my shoulder.

The expert man carefully lifted the bundle, turning it in his hands as he examined the tied leather straps and cracked covering. "I cannot examine the object here. This needs to be opened and examined under laboratory conditions."

"We need the information by tomorrow," I said. "Our group leaves Sunday morning very early."

"That may not be possible."

I reached for the bundle. "Then we'll open it here."

He shielded it with his arms. "I will get to it today. And have a report to all of you tomorrow."

Trevor spoke from the end of the table, his voice light with amusement. "With one of our people present. And I'm loving this story. It's going to be a blockbuster if it goes to *The Sun*."

"Nothing leaves this room until we know what the record says," Q-D insisted. "If you want a just resolution, we must insist on absolute confidentiality."

"You have just threatened these young ladies. That doesn't speak well for a just resolution. But it does add interest to a news story."

"Let us see what the record shows," Q-D said less smugly. "I am certain we can reach some agreement."

Trevor turned to the four of us. "Are you satisfied with information about this by tomorrow?"

We shared glances and all shrugged in agreement.

"I need a stated 'yes,' if you don't mind," Q-D said irritably.

We "yes-ed" down our side of the table.

Trevor rose. "I'll find someone to monitor the inspection of the record and will call you ladies as soon as I have word." He turned to the expert. "By noon?"

"By noon," the man said.

"Then I think our business is complete for today. "

"Not by a longshot," Mother murmured as we rose from the table. "You ladies have some major explaining to do."

The girls' team from Bishop's Stortford was good. Though we played with the passion of women who smelled victory, we drew at 2-2 and agreed against a shootout. Somehow, a draw seemed right for our final match. Solicitor Emory called Mother just as we returned to the field from the locker rooms.

"It's for you," she said, handing the phone to Samantha.

Sam took the phone, listened for several minutes in silence, then started to sob, dropping slowly to her knees on the grass.

Emme

There has not been a day in the five years since we last switched that I have not thought of Ally—or Lena, Julian, or Samantha. Some simple moment in my day will give me pause, and I find myself lost in a memory. I will be pouring dried chamomile into a jar in my London shop and find myself standing atop a footstool, gazing absently at nothing at all while in my mind's eye, I first discover Ally's harvest of hemp leaves spread across the roof of the tack shed. If at home, I will suddenly become aware of Charles' laughter and he will say, "You are off again in your fantasy world. Am I with you this time?" I wish that he could have been. My friends would so like him! If they had any fears that their prophecies had forced me into an unhappy marriage, I could assure them that they had simply been looking back on a match destined by heaven long before they found it in their computer.

I have often thought of hiring a carriage and returning to Grenfell Hall to see if I can rescue Father's record and insure its safety. But the safety of family has prevented it. George IV continues on the throne and is truly a lazy, extravagant, contemptible man. If Father were here, he would again be engaged in pamphleteering and our family would be fugitive. As it is, Charles insisted we move after our marriage from Cambridge to London to avoid my being identified by someone who might still wish to prosecute the Grenfells. The move has been good for us. Charles teaches at a boarding school for the sons of London's growing class of men of commerce. I care for the moods and ailments of their bored and temperamental wives from my shop in Fetter Lane.

On this autumn day, the moment that again swept me in memory to my former friends was the arrival at my door of a carriage drawn by a black mare that looked for all the world like Maisy. I could hear Father telling me, as he had when he finally came to believe that our switching was more than a reflection of my hysteria, why Ally would not ride the mare.

"Maisy is far too docile for her liking," he had said when I asked why Ally preferred Prince George. "She always hopes to meet your friend Edward on the veldt and teach him another lesson in horsemanship." The comment had injured my pride, but he had seen it and pulled me close to him. "But she is never able to fill our home with music as you do," he said, and I knew he cared for us both.

The carriage was driven by a young black man wearing the livery of one of the city's most prominent merchant families, ship owners known to still run an illicit trade in slaves between West Africa and the Americas. I judged the coachman to be about the age of my assistant, Benjamin, who helps me scour the markets, docks, and fields about London for medicinal plants and minerals and prepare them for patients. Behind the driver, the matron of the house sat stiffly in her seat, waiting for him to lower a step.

"Trouble," I called to Benjamin who was shelling the seeds of pumpkins at a counter at the back of the shop. "Why don't you take Melissa into the back."

He glanced up at the parked carriage, nodded grimly, and stepped around the counter to scoop up the toddler who played with a stack of painted wooden blocks. They disappeared through a curtain into the storeroom. Lady Bayard swept into the shop as if entering the kitchen of her Arlington Street mansion, jarring the bell over the door and looking about for someone to command.

"Good morning, Mrs. Pearce. I trust your day has been more pleasant than mine."

I stepped back to the floor and gave what she could interpret as a curtsy. "My day has been very pleasant, Lady Bayard, thank you. And it troubles me to learn that yours has been less." Normally I would engage my customers in small talk. Ask after their families and inquire about their engagements about the city. Lady Bayard wanted none of this and made it clear if I ventured in that direction. "My family matters are quite my own," she declared when, during her first visit to the shop, I made the mistake of asking. "And as for my involvements, your concern is to help me feel my best when I attend."

I waited for her to announce her most recent ailment. She glanced quickly about the shop, her face tilting upward to heighten the impression she was gazing down her nose.

"I don't see your boy. Is he about? I wish this to be a private matter."

"He is in the back with my daughter, Melissa. We can speak quietly at the front. I am certain it will be quite private."

Lady Bayard backed toward the door, waited until I was beside her, then turned to trap me between herself and the entrance. She glared through the window at her coachman who sat completely ignoring what was going on in the shop.

"I am beginning to have such flushes," she whispered urgently. "I know it comes with age. But they are so *intense*. . . and come at the most inopportune moments."

"An unavoidable inconvenience of our sex," I agreed. "But one that can be lessened. I will give you some nettle tea that you should drink each morning and evening. And I have just received a new remedy from America that I requested just for this condition." I pushed past her and drew a square bottle of dark powder from glass-fronted cabinets along one wall of the shop. "They call this snakeroot or black cohosh. I will give you a small spoon to measure a portion that I want you to take each morning with your breakfast. You may wish to take it with honey. It can be quite bitter."

She looked dubiously at the medicine as I scooped it from the jar into a folded paper packet.

"Snakeroot. I find the very word distasteful! And black cohosh is no more appealing."

"I have heard it called baneberry. Perhaps that would make it more palatable."

"From America, you say?"

"Yes. First used by the native people there."

"The savages? Oh, my!"

"Apparently, their women suffer from the same distress."

Lady Bayard again looked about furtively. "Speaking of savages," she said in a hushed voice, "what do you plan to do with your boy?"

"My boy?"

"Your black man. Benjamin."

"I plan to do nothing with him. He works for me."

She leaned closer. "The radicals are beginning to fuss about slaves still held in England. Many of us are shipping ours to the West Indies and leasing them to plantation owners. If you wish to do the same with your Benjamin, my husband can recommend a trustworthy owner in Jamaica who will pay you well."

"Benjamin is a free man. There have been no slaves in Britain since the Slave Trade Act was passed. That has been some fifteen years past."

Lady Bayard rolled her eyes dismissively. "Please! The act simply outlawed *trading* in slaves. Most families of rank in Britain still own many." She leaned closer. "Many have kept them here in London—like my man there. The authorities choose to look the other way."

"That is unfortunate," I said, knowing that I risked the ire, and probably the loss of business, of a patron whose business I could lose without a single regret. "Benjamin is a free man and works here as any man might."

"Is he associated with the anti-slavery society? Many of the free blacks are. And there is a new voice among them. A young black man who is helping our slaves flee the country and find refuge in the free states in America. Perhaps your Benjamin is that man." She sniffed at me down her up-tilted nose. "I have been told by another of your patrons that you once lived in Africa and are sympathetic to their cause."

"I did once live there. And I am quite supportive of the law as it now exists in Britain. I pray that it might be extended to all of the Empire and to all of America as well."

"*Humph!*" Lady Bayard huffed. "I shall take your remedies because I cannot live another day with such discomfort. But you shall not see me again." She drew sufficient coin from her handbag to cover five orders of the treatments, dropped them into my hand, and stalked from the shop. The step was still in place beside her carriage and she mounted it with three brusque steps. She lowered herself indignantly onto the seat and glared straight ahead until her enslaved coachman stowed the step and drove the mare out of sight along Fetter Lane.

Benjamin emerged through the curtain, holding Melissa in the crook of one arm.

"Thank you, Mrs. Pearce. That is an evil woman."

I nodded without comment and turned back toward the footstool where I had been pouring the chamomile. The bell over the door again drew my attention to the front. Another young black man stood there, this one in the work clothes of a common laborer. He gave Benjamin a familiar nod, then turned his attention to me.

"Mrs. Pearce?" he asked. "Emmeline Caywood Pearce?"

I nodded, surprised to hear my maiden name.

"Benjamin told me I'd find you here." He spoke with an accent and cadence that was at once familiar, but foreign to this part of London. He stepped closer, studied me up and down in a most uncomfortable way, then smiled and nodded with satisfaction. "Pretty much what I'd expected." He then straightened as if on official business. "I was asked to find you and deliver a message," he said cryptically, glancing again at Benjamin and pausing to give Melissa a long, appreciative look. "I believe you'll understand it without explanation." His smile broadened and his eyes appeared to mist. "They found the book just where you said it would be.

Everything worked out for Samantha and her mother. They all send you their love." He turned and moved toward the door.

I *did* understand but was stunned into silence. As the man had delivered his message, I knew why his accent and cadence were familiar.

"Julian!" I shouted after him. But he was gone.

OTHER BOOKS BY ALLEN KENT

Unit 1 International Thrillers

The Shield of Darius
The Weavers of Meanchey
The Wager
The Marburg Mutation
Straits of the Between
Ring of Thorns

The Whitlock Trilogy (historical fiction)

River of Light and Shadow
Wild Whistling Blackbirds
Suzanna's Song

The Colby Tate Mysteries

Murder One
Eye for an Eye

Mystery/Thrillers

Backwater
Guardians of the Second Son

www.ingramcontent.com/pod-product-compliance
Lightning Source LLC
Chambersburg PA
CBHW022136170626
46807CB00005B/1965